THE BOXWOOD TORSO

A SEBASTIEN GREY NOVEL

RYBURN DOBBS

ISBN: 978-1-7352506-2-5 (Paperback Edition)

ISBN: 978-1-7352506-3-2 (eBook Edition)

Cover Design:

Danna Mathias, www.dearlycreative.com

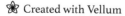 Created with Vellum

PROLOGUE

A thin layer of ice began to accumulate on the yellow police caution tape as it whipped and twisted in the freezing rain. Despite the temperature, a crowd began to gather on the opposite side of the street, necks craned and toes tipped to get a better view past the emergency vehicles and first responders. A chatter of speculation competed with the hum of the idling fire trucks. It was clear that something serious was afoot. A small fire was surely not sufficient cause to send half of the Cheyenne, Wyoming police department to this half-built, half-occupied neighborhood on the north side of town.

"What is it?" one woman asked.

"A fire," replied a younger woman, holding an infant wrapped in a snowsuit. "In the lot over there."

"Well, I know that! But what's on fire?"

"It's a bunch of clothing or something," offered a middle-aged man.

"I heard it was a dog," a youth straddling a bike said.

"That's awful!" howled the older woman. "Who reported it?"

"See that guy over there talking to the officer?" said a second man, who pointed. "He saw the smoke and called the fire department. I don't know why the cops are here."

"Probably just trying to get overtime on our dime," spat a voice from the back.

One of the individuals in the crowd—a tall, skinny man in his late forties, who had yet to speak and was perhaps a little less confident in neighborhood gossip—decided to get more of a first-hand account of things. He pulled his orange knit cap over his large ears, crushed his discarded cigarette under a Vibram boot heel, and made his way across the street toward the caution tape.

"Excuse me, officer," he called to the nearest uniform, after bending down as if to tie his boot lace.

A young police officer turned and approached the questioner. The cold had turned his irritated face apple red.

"I'm sorry, sir. You'll have to get back over to the other side of the street."

"I was just wondering what's going on. Is something on fire?" asked the man.

The officer shook his head at the stupidity of the question.

"It's just a small fire, sir. Nothing to be concerned about."

"Oh, that's good. What's with all the cops?"

"Just routine. Probably some kids playing with matches," replied the officer, not really answering the man.

"Okay, thanks." The man turned around but suddenly stopped mid-pivot. "Hey, come to think of it, I did hear something last night."

"Oh yeah? What's that, Mr. . . . ? I'm sorry, what was your name?"

"Jones. Bob Jones."

The officer pulled the glove off his right hand and retrieved a small notebook and pen from his back pocket.

"What did you hear last night, Mr. Jones?"

"It was kids, a group of kids. Teenagers, I think. Yelling, screwing around. So, like you say, it was probably just kids playing with matches, something like that."

"And about what time was that?" the officer asked as he shook the pen to force the ink to the tip.

"Oh, I would say around midnight."

"Thank you, Mr. Jones. Now, if you don't mind, I really need you to get back with the others over there. We'll get an official statement from you a little later. You live near here, I take it?"

"Yes, sir. I'm just down the street. Four doors down from the empty lot on the left. Can you, uh, can you tell me what's on fire?"

"No, I cannot. We won't know until the fire department is done. I'm sure it's nothing though. Now, why don't you head on back over with the others, Mr. Jones?"

"Sure, sure. Smells pretty bad though, doesn't it?"

This last statement was made to no one in particular, as the officer had already turned and rejoined the semi-circle of official personnel who were attentively watching the firefighters pour water onto something the size of a campfire.

This man was a curious sort who ignored the officer's injunction that he rejoin the crowd on the opposite side of the street. From where he stood—belly up to the yellow tape—he could just make out some of the officers' conversation a few yards away. Though it was difficult to be sure, he thought he caught some of the important bits.

"So, you think it's . . ." asked one officer.

"Looks like it," replied another.

"Are those legs? I can't tell."

"We'll know soon enough."

"Maybe it's a side of beef?"

"Barbecue gone wrong, you mean?"

"Sure."

"Does your barbecue smell like that?"

"Well . . . no . . ."

"I bet it doesn't wear a jacket either. Hey! No more water on that thing. You're washing away evidence."

That was quite enough for the man in the orange cap. He backed away as calmly as he could—and slowly, without signaling any alarm, made his way back to the gallery of spectators. His eyes never left the ground.

"What did they say?" someone asked, as he pushed his way through.

"Just some sticks and trash on fire," he replied without looking up.

This news seemed to take some of the excitement out of the crowd, although he could not be sure, nor did he stop to find out. Continuing through the patch of onlookers, he made his way to the sidewalk then turned left, heading toward the newly completed homes on the south end of the street.

Once outside of his pickup truck, he paused to light another cigarette and looked back. The group of onlookers was thinning out, as was the black smoke. Ominously, a river of water from the fire hoses had worked its way down the street. Boxwood Avenue would soon become an ice rink. It was time to go. With any luck, they would be home before it got dark.

"Well, did you find it?" a man much younger than himself asked from the passenger seat.

The driver reached over and dropped a silver Zippo lighter into his passenger's hand. "I don't recommend you pursue a career in arson," he muttered through clenched lips before making a U-turn away from the curb.

The rear of the truck fishtailed as "Bob Jones" gunned a left turn onto Highway 85, heading north. The passenger stared into his sideview mirror, nervously looking for flashing lights. It wasn't until they drove over Horse Creek, about ten miles up the road, that the passenger felt relaxed enough to flip open the newly recovered monogrammed lighter—a gift from his father —and hold the flame against the white tube between his own lips.

1

Detective Tiffany Reese ran a finger down the list of names on the sergeants' test results, her pale-pink nail polish barely reflecting the fluorescent lights of the investigations bullpen. She swept a lock of medium-length hair from in front of her eyes, but still she failed to spot her name in the top quarter of the list, or the second quarter. Finally, somewhere between the halfway point and the bottom, her slim finger stopped and her heart sank. Reese, 14th.

"How'd you do, Reese?" a voice called out from just behind her.

Damn it, she thought as she walked away without answering.

While it was true that this was her first time taking the sergeant's test, and most deputies of the Custer County South Dakota Sheriff's Office tend to score poorly on their first try, Tiffany felt confident she would buck that trend. She had studied relentlessly and felt more confident than her results would suggest. She also felt ready for the interview phase of the test. Clearly, that preparation was now in vain. Custer County was a small department and there were only four open sergeant spots this round. It was highly unlikely the process would mine as deep as number fourteen.

Damn it.

Another voice called out her name as she hurriedly made her way down the hall toward the stairs that led to the locker rooms. It was a voice she couldn't ignore. She turned and poked her head into her sergeant's office.

"Hey, Hank. What's up?" Tiffany spoke with a forced pleasantness.

"What do you mean, 'what's up'? How'd you do? Did you see the results?"

Tiffany stood at her sergeant's door without answering. She was too upset, feeling like she might cry and certainly not wanting to contribute to a stereotype.

"That bad, huh? Come on in. Close the door."

Sgt. Hank LeGris got up from his chair and walked toward her. As he got closer, Tiffany felt herself nearly crumble. She was going to lose it. Hank must have sensed this, as he appeared for a moment like he would wrap his strong arms around her in a hug of consolation. Of course, he didn't. Ever the professional, Hank just sat on the corner of his desk and placed a large, meaty hand on her left shoulder.

"I'm sorry, boss. I don't know why I'm so emotional about this. It's stupid."

"It's understandable, Tiff. You studied your butt off for that test. But if it makes you feel any better, it took me three times to get a decent score. And it's just a test, really. It says nothing about how good of an investigator you are. You know you're my best detective, and a damn good friend."

"I know. You're right. I guess I just figured I would do better. I got myself all worked up."

"Where'd you land?" Hank asked.

"Fourteenth."

"Well, you beat my first try. Plus, I gotta be honest with ya. I'm glad."

Tiffany put her hands on her narrow hips and shot Hank a look of indignation.

"Settle down, Tiff. I just mean this is good for me. I need you on the team. If I can avoid losing you to the jail or to patrol, then I win. That's all."

"I don't want to leave investigations either, but at some point, I have to."

"I agree. I'm just glad it's not right now. Which reminds me, there's something I was going to talk to you about anyway, but I wanted to see how the sergeants' test played out."

Tiffany knitted her brows in curiosity.

"Have a seat," said Hank, pointing to the chair in front of his desk. "But open the door first. We don't want anyone thinking there's anything inappropriate going on in here."

"Ha, ha. Very funny," laughed Tiffany as she pulled the door open, then sat down. "So, what's on your mind?"

Hank leaned over to open one of the lower drawers on his desk, then took out a file folder and placed it in front of Tiffany before sitting down himself.

"Were you aware the lieutenant applied for a cold case grant?"

"No, not at all," replied Tiffany, taking up the folder and opening it.

Hank continued, "All of this news about familial DNA solving old cases has got everyone spun up. The Department of Justice has freed up a bunch of money for local law enforcement to try and clear unsolved homicides. Our grant application was successful."

"How many cold cases do we have?" asked Tiffany, as she skimmed the papers in the folder.

"More than you might think for such a small department. I counted thirty-nine going back to the seventies."

"Wow. That *is* more than I would have thought. So, you want me to work some of them? Is that what you're getting at?"

"I want you to work all of them."

"What do you mean, 'all of them'? That would be a full-time job."

Tiffany waited for a reply from her sergeant, but he just sat there with a knowing demi-grin on his face, his blue eyes bright and his grayish-brown goatee bent upward. She felt her chest and guts tighten.

"Are you taking me off of active case work? Is that what this is about?"

"Don't be stupid, Reese. This isn't a punishment. I think that test has made you paranoid . . . or insecure."

"Don't make me come over there, boss. I'm relatively sure I can take you." Tiffany replied with a smile, realizing she over-reacted.

"You're still on the team, and you will still assist with other cases. But think about it. Every one of these old cases is a head-line waiting to happen. It's all gold."

Tiffany turned to gaze out the window and into the granite hills, blowing her brown bangs out of her walnut-colored eyes.

Hank continued, "The grant stipulates we dedicate personnel to work old cases full-time. The feds want to make sure the money is used as intended and not squirreled away for AR-15s or something. We need to set up a cold case unit."

After a few moments, she began to sync with Hank. She saw his offer for what it was. Hank had always treated her like a big brother would; he always looked out for her best interests. And he was now doing it again.

"So, you want me to be part of that unit?" she asked, still staring out the window in contemplation.

"Well, here's the thing. Based on the size of our agency, we didn't get a whole lot of funding. Just enough for a full-time detective and maybe a part-timer. I was thinking about bringing in a retired detective—maybe Anderson. I hear his wife is driving him nuts."

Tiffany laughed out loud.

"Seriously, have you met his wife? Anyway, *you* are the unit —or, at least, I'd like you to be." Hank let that sink in for moment, then continued after getting no response. "Look, I can't make you do it. Well, actually, I can, but I don't want to do it that way. These kinds of cases are hard. I can't have some ass-dragger sleepwalk through this. I need the best. This has to succeed. That grant wasn't easy to get, and from what I'm hearing, there are some command staff who weren't enthusiastic about going down this road. This will be an opportunity for us to show what we've got. *You* give us the best chance of success, but only if you are willing."

Tiffany shifted her eyes to her sergeant. "Hank, you know I'm willing to do whatever you need. I always have been."

"Exactly."

"So, has Anderson agreed to come back? When do we start?"

Hank lifted a hand and pressed it into the air. "Wait a minute. Just hang on. Anderson was only a thought, an option. Now, hear me out on this. What if we brought in an expert to work with you? A consultant, so to speak."

Tiffany grinned and raised her eyebrows at her boss.

"Okay, stop it. I know what you're thinking. You think . . ."

Tiffany interrupted with a snort of laughter. "You're trying to do the matchmaker thing with me and your brother, aren't you?"

"No, that's not it at all. I'm . . ."

"I will have you know, Sergeant LeGris, that your brother and I have been in close contact ever since he helped us out this summer."

"Really?"

Hank looked surprised. Tiffany realized this was the first

time in several weeks that she talked to him about his brother or even mentioned they had been in contact.

"Like I said, that ship has already sailed."

"So, you two are an . . . uh . . . an item?"

"What are you, eighty years old?" she said. But Hank did not amend his question. "I guess we are. I mean, I'm not really sure."

Hank widened his smile.

"So, there's no need to scheme here. Like I said, whatever you need, I'll do." Tiffany started to stand.

"You are not dismissed, detective."

Tiffany quickly sat back down. Hank was way more serious than she realized.

"Now, let me continue. Regardless of your relationship with my brother, the fact is he is one of the best forensic anthropologists in the country, not to mention a better detective than you."

"Hey!"

Hank put his hands up in a conciliatory gesture.

"I'm kidding, I'm kidding. But you do agree that he would be perfect for this?"

"Absolutely. He's amazing. I would love to work with him again. And, of course, he's moving here anyway."

"And he's moving here anyway," echoed Hank. "You see how smart I am? You underestimate me, Miss Fancy Pants."

Tiffany tilted her head and raised an eyebrow.

"Do you have permission to bring on a consultant?"

"That's my business, Reese. But yes. Yes I do. The grant covers it. And after the events of this summer, Lt. Breed was only too happy to consent."

"And does your brother know you are roping him into this? What makes you think he'll do it?"

"You're kidding, right? If you walked over a cliff, he would be right behind."

Tiffany tried not to smile but failed.

"So, you already talked to him about it?" she asked.

"Not yet. He's in Germany. He's on some archaeology vacation or something—although I'm sure you already knew that."

"Yes I did, actually. And it's not an archaeology vacation. He's speaking at a conference."

"Well, good for him. Since you and the little brainiac are in contact, I'll let you tell him about it. He'll be glad to know he has a job when he gets here. And take that folder with you. There's a list of case numbers in there. I've already taken an inventory; they're all in the storage room. What are you laughing at? What's so funny?"

"I was just remembering a conversation your brother and I had when he was here. It was the night before he left. I asked him if he would consider moving up here . . . you know, to be closer to family. He asked what he would do for work, and I said that maybe the Sheriff's Office could bring him on as a consultant. We both agreed that was not likely."

"That's interesting. I recall having a similar conversation with him, just before I put the little geek in his fancy car and sent him home."

Tiffany got up and headed for the door. A sudden surge of gratitude came over her. She turned back toward her sergeant.

"Thanks, Hank. I know what you're doing. I really appreciate it."

"Are you talking about the cold cases or my brother?"

Tiffany smiled, flipped Hank the bird, and resumed her trip to the locker room.

By the time she reached the bottom of the stairs, Tiffany's mood was remarkably improved, and like her boss, she was not sure which of these recent developments accounted for it.

2

Tiffany hit send on the email and closed her laptop, wondering what Sebastien would think of all this. Hank had said that his brother would do anything for her, but there was really no evidence of that, was there? It was true that Sebastien was clearly smitten with her, and maybe they had become something of an "item," as Hank had called it, but it was also true that Sebastien was anything but a risk taker. There were a thousand good reasons why he shouldn't get involved professionally with her or his brother, but above everything, Tiffany was pretty sure that Sebastien's love of solving a difficult case, or thirty-nine, would tip him over the edge.

"What are you doing in here, Reese?"

"Oh, Paul. Hank asked me to look at some old cases, so I moved my desk down here. I hope that's okay. I shouldn't get in the way of patrol, I don't think."

Sgt. Paul Casey's large frame almost filled the entire doorway. He looked around the cramped storage room with its moveable shelving units against one wall and stacks of boxes against the other. "I got no beef with it. In fact, it'll be nice having you down here. But you better close the door. We got roll call in a few minutes and you don't want those yahoos bothering you."

"Great idea, Sarge. You wouldn't mind pulling it closed on your way out, would you?"

The sergeant nodded faintly and started to exit. The door almost made it to the fully shut position when Casey cracked it open and poked his smooth head back in.

"Hey, I . . . uh, heard you didn't do so . . . I mean, on the sergeants' test, I heard . . ."

"Yeah, Paul. I tanked it. Thanks for bringing it up though."

"Oh, no. I didn't mean anything . . . you know. I was just thinking, maybe I could help you study for next time. I aced it my first try. We could get together and I could give you some pointers or something. Maybe over a drink?"

"That's very generous of you," replied Tiffany, trying to look appreciative rather than annoyed. "I will definitely keep that in mind. Good luck with those yahoos in roll call."

The door was just about clicked shut when Tiffany called out, "Oh, hey! Paul!"

The sergeant leaned his head in a second time and Tiffany continued.

"I didn't know they found Amber Harrison's remains."

"Who?" Sgt. Casey looked confused.

"Amber Harrison. She went missing in 2013. I was away at college at the time. I didn't know they found her."

Tiffany raised a large blue binder as she spoke. On its spine was a handwritten label: *Amber Harrison Homicide. 13-042.*

"Oh, yeah. Sorry. It took me a second. Actually, they never did find her."

"But it says right here . . . homicide."

Tiffany tapped the spine of the binder.

"Well . . . technically they didn't find her body. But they

found her car, which had her blood in it. I wasn't a part of that though. I was working helicopter patrol."

"Like I said, I was away at college. I knew her from middle school. But we lost touch in high school. I always just figured she ran off to the big city or something."

"So does everyone else."

"Does?"

"We never told the public about finding the blood. The sheriff thought it was too risky to assume she was dead. But they treated it like a homicide until it just went cold. Truth is, I think most of the investigators think she did just run off."

"Where did they find her car?"

"It was parked in front of her house, as I recall. Now, the public *was* told that. You were probably just too busy breaking hearts in college to pay attention to hometown news."

Sgt. Casey gave a lewd wink as he pulled the door shut.

Tiffany shook her head and exhaled loudly. This was the problem with being one of the few females in the sworn ranks of the department. Hardly a day went by when some testosterone-laden lug didn't try to hit on her or make some sort of comment. It was bad enough with the guys her own age, the single ones. But the married ones, like Sergeant Casey . . .

Tiffany thought back to a conversation she'd had with Hank shortly after she joined the Investigations Bureau. Hank happened to witness one of the other detectives make a comment about how she looked "nicely wrapped" one particular day. The poor jerk was put on call every weekend for a month and Hank pulled Tiffany into his office for a little talk.

"Look, Reese, as long as you work for me, I'm going to do my best to make sure you get treated like everybody else and not as a woman. Okay, okay . . . you know what I mean. But you gotta know that cops, male cops especially, aren't used to being told no, and they're not used to caring if they offend anyone. All day long, people comply and do what we tell them to. For the most part, anyway. These jackasses somehow forget that when it comes to work and home relationships. So, I want you to promise me something. Stick up for yourself, okay? Yeah, yeah, I know you know how to report sexual harassment. Do that too. But don't be afraid to kick someone in the proverbials either. You feel me?"

The memory made Tiffany giggle audibly. Little did Hank know at the time that she'd already put many a man in his place. She could take care of herself, thank you very much. Both her father and her brother were law enforcement. She was more than familiar with the macho drill. But still, in the handful of years since that conversation, she had ample opportunity to recall those words of warning. The thought occurred to her that with Sebastien around the station, maybe she wouldn't get hit on so much. On the other hand, maybe she needed to draw a line with Sebastien. After all, they would be working together, she thought. That was, if he agreed.

These thoughts generated a vaguely unsettled feeling, which Tiffany tried to push away by getting back to work. She set the Amber Harrison binder to the side, consulted the list of cold case homicides Hank gave her, and began to search the shelves for the next one.

A TALL WOMAN with platinum hair walked through the international terminal with an earnest stride, quick and purposeful like most airport travelers, while pulling a maroon hard-shelled suitcase behind her. She paused momentarily to check her phone for the appropriate gate number, then resumed her mission. Approaching the gate, she stretched to her full height to scan the crowded waiting area for an open seat and saw only one, next to a prim-looking man with shortish dark hair. He appeared pleasant enough, well dressed and reading what looked to be a thick and serious book. She hurried ahead to claim the small square and rest her long, weary legs.

"My, that looks like heavy reading," she said to the man next to her after several minutes.

The man looked up from the page, smiled meekly, and said, "Yes, it is," before returning to his book.

In their brief exchange, she got a better look at him. He was certainly youngish, even younger than herself and probably in his early-to-mid thirties, although his wool trousers, cashmere V-neck, and suede vest gave the impression of someone much older. His eyebrows were as dark as his hair, though not too thick. Groomed, maybe? His face was average, though pleasant, his lips thinnish, and his nose maybe a little large in contrast. His cheeks bore the signs of frequent and careful shaving, and his cognac eyes were a tad melancholy or concerned, she thought. She wondered inwardly if the man's travel was due to some unfortunate expediency. Death of a family member?

"Are you going to Atlanta?" she ventured.

"California," he said, then went back to his reading.

"Do you live there? Or here?"

"There," replied the man without looking up.

This man clearly did not want to talk. Maybe he really was on a grim errand. Oh well, she thought. She pulled a fashion magazine out of her large leather handbag and flipped to where she last left off.

"I'm sorry. I didn't mean to be rude. I was just finishing that chapter. It's quite a technical book and I have a hard time keeping up. Plus, it's in German and I'm a slow German reader."

The man spoke suddenly, timorously, after several minutes, as he put a mark in the book and closed it.

The woman was a bit startled by the interjection but

pleased, nonetheless. She leaned over toward his space to read the title of the book: *Alte Menschliche Bayerns.*

"Sounds very technical indeed. *Ancient Humans of Bavaria.* Are you some sort of archaeologist?"

"Anthropologist," he responded.

"Oh, I see," she replied, not seeing. "What does that mean, actually?"

"These days, it mostly means I look at the remains of dead people for a living."

"For goodness' sake, why?"

"To figure out who they are and how they died," replied the young man in a dry tone.

"Oh! And there were dead people here in Germany who needed your help . . . I mean, needed to be identified?"

"No. Well, I mean, kind of. But I mainly just came to give a presentation at a conference. What about you? Is Atlanta your final destination?"

"No, I'm heading to Dallas. Finally going home, thank heavens. This is my second trip over here this year. I'm director of procurement for a hospital chain and I've been trying to close a deal on a significant purchase of medical imaging devices."

"That sounds interesting."

The woman crinkled her nose. "Does it?" she asked.

"No. I guess it doesn't."

"It's not. Believe me. What did you mean, 'kind of'?"

"Sorry, what?"

"When I asked if there were any dead people here in Germany, you said, 'kind of.'"

"Ah, yes. A former colleague of mine asked me to look at some remains from an archaeological site. That's what this book is about, actually." The man patted the book in his lap for emphasis.

"But you're not an archaeologist?"

"No. My specialty is modern humans."

"I'm sorry. You have me a little confused."

"So were the Germans," he replied.

The woman laughed out loud, prompting a stern look from an older man sitting opposite her. The man with the book turned slightly red, she noticed.

"Tell you what, Mr. Anthropologist, why don't you tell me about your confused Germans, then I'll tell you about mine."

SEBASTIEN GREY CONSIDERED the woman carefully as she walked away to find something to eat. Replaying the interlude in his mind, he wondered if he had scared her off, scolding himself for being so open about his work. He should know better. Not everyone wanted to hear about death, decomposition, and murder. Nor should he have broached the subject of his presentation: "The Application of Modern Dismemberment Cases to Archaeological Contexts." *Oh geez, Sebastien, she's probably praying to God her seat isn't next to yours.*

Sebastien closed his eyes and took in a deep breath, counting to ten in his mind. Counteracting negative self-evaluation took deliberate effort, a mindful changing of mental direction, his therapist had told him. The glass could always be half full. It was up to him.

Upon further assessment, he considered that he had actually done quite well with this stranger—a lovely stranger, too, by the way. He engaged . . . eventually. He asked her questions about her job. It was all very genuine, he felt. Tina, his therapist, would have been proud of him. Was this another sign of his incipient improvement, his progression from awkward hermit to a normally functioning person?

This line of musing was interrupted by the soft *ding* of his phone receiving an email. He retrieved the device from his vest pocket quickly, hoping the email would be from Tiffany. It was.

Sebastien,

I hope you are having fun over there in Germany. But not too much fun! I know what a crazy party animal you can be. Wink. Bad news. I crapped the bed on the sergeants' test. I don't think I'll get an interview. Oh well. I'm sure it's for the best, but it still pisses me off. When you get here, you can buy me a drink to cheer me up.

I have a huge favor to ask you. Hank just assigned me to work cold cases full-time for a while. I guess we got some sort of DNA grant from the feds. Anyway, there are a lot of them and I get to pick which ones I want to work first. In fact, I think the whole thing is on me. Yikes! Is there anything you think I should look for in the cases? If you were doing this, what kind of things do you think would make a case more solvable (aside from DNA, duh)? Oh, and before you answer, you should know that YOU are doing this with me. Hank wants you to help as a paid consultant. So, you have a job here after all. Didn't that work out well? I hope you agree to help me on this. I really need you. I think we make a great team.

Either way, please give me any tips you have ASAP. I'm going to start sorting through the cases today.

Your new boss,

Tiff

Sebastien re-read the email a half dozen times, his mind spinning as he devoured its contents. *I really need you. I think we make a great team.* He took a screenshot of those words. He wanted to preserve them, to look at them whenever he wished. It was childish, but he didn't care.

As usual, excitement turned into trepidation as he overthought and overanalyzed. This could be just another chance for his true nature to be revealed. His insecure, inadequate nature. What if familiarity did, in fact, breed contempt? What if, through the course of the collaboration, Tiffany realized this last summer was a fluke? That he was not that smart and would not be that helpful?

For the second time that morning, Sebastien broke into a

mental count. As he did so, an interesting and wholly unprecedented thing happened. About halfway between ten and
fifteen, Tiffany's voice broke his numerations and filled his
mind with her own brand of smarmy wisdom:

*Or, Sebastien, you dope, maybe your considerable experience will
actually be helpful. Maybe you will be doing me and your brother a
great service. Maybe this is a sign. You are needed. It's going to be all
right. Calm down, Sebastien. This is good. This is right. Now get
your ass out here.*

The clock near his gate indicated he still had ten minutes
before boarding was to start. Just enough time to fire up his
laptop and reply to Tiffany. Sure, he could probably do it when
he got home. But he wanted her to know, as soon as possible,
that he was in.

Tiffany,

*Sorry about the sergeants' test. It's just a matter of time, though,
don't you think? You're a great cop.*

*Of course I will help you. I had originally planned to wait until
the building sold before coming out there. But I see no reason for that
if there is work to be done. I'm on my way back now, and as soon as I
get home, I will start making arrangements. I'm excited to help you,
but I'm not sure how useful I will be.*

*As you go through the cold cases, I would keep a few things in
mind:*

*-Never assume that every piece of physical/biological evidence
that could be tested was tested.*

*-Separate out cases in which evidence is still kept and can be re-
tested. I will want to examine any human remains.*

*-Never assume that everyone who should have been interviewed
was interviewed.*

*-Never assume that the all of the most basic and obvious inves-
tigative steps were done.*

*-Focus on cases in which witnesses or suspects are likely to still be
alive and can be recontacted.*

If I think of anything else, I'll email you. I'm really excited to team up with you.

Sebastien

Sebastien was placing his laptop back in its bag when the tall Texan re-emerged from a crowd of travelers, hurriedly walking toward the now open gate.

"Come on, anthropologist. Maybe we'll sit together, and you can tell me about more cases. I've never been one for in-flight movies, and reading on a plane makes me sick."

3

"About four million, give or take."

"Really? That much?"

"Well, I need to pull the comps, but based on what I'm seeing in the market, that should be in the ballpark."

Sebastien was escorting the appraiser around the rear of the building and toward the man's car. His Cardigan Welsh corgi followed behind them, unleashed and obsessively sniffing and marking anything vertical.

"Parsifal, come on now. Keep up."

"Cute dog. Interesting name."

Sebastien offered no reply. Experience had taught him that those who wondered would not appreciate, and those who appreciated would not wonder.

"Well, thank you for coming out. I guess you'll be crunching your numbers, or whatever."

"Yes, Mr. Grey. It might take a week or so to get everything worked out. Of course, we don't need anything too formal at this point. Your agent just needs to get a sense of a reasonable listing price."

The man drove off and Sebastien turned to gaze at his building from the sidewalk.

The Art Deco structure was known to the locals as the Block, mostly because it took up an entire block of downtown Vineyard in the easternmost edge of the Northern California's East Bay. It was bought and renovated by his grandfather in the eighties and passed on to him from his mother after she died a few years ago. His brother Henry, Sgt. Hank LeGris of the Custer County Sheriff's Office, inherited the liquid assets, which were significant. The income from the Block's residential and commercial tenants constituted the vast majority of Sebastien's living, with his occasional forensic case thrown in. The building was home to several businesses on the lower level, as well as four apartment units on the upper story. The largest apartment, on the southwest corner, was Sebastien's demesne.

"Dr. Grey! Dr. Grey!"

Sebastien turned eastward, visoring his eyes from the mid-morning sun. It was Mr. Shelby, waving to him from the door of his bookshop on the southeast corner of the building.

"Hello, Mr. Shelby."

"Come in, come in, doctor. I have a treat for *Sir Parzival*."

Sebastien carried Parsifal over the threshold of the Red Oak Antiquarian. The brightness of the day was immediately smothered by the dimness of the shop. The walls, lined with dark-cherry bookcases, were painted burgundy. A long table sat in the middle of the narrow space. Shelby had once told him that the table was made in the eighteenth century and imported from France. It was red oak, he had proudly told Sebastien, and provided the name for the establishment. On the table lay several old books, some opened, most not. Two banker's lamps were placed a few feet apart, ready to illuminate at the pull of their brass chains. The whole space had the unmistakable smell of oldness—a combination of mold, old chocolate, and coffee.

"Sit, sit," insisted Shelby, as he disappeared behind a curtain at the back of the store.

Sebastien took one of the dark-brown leather chairs between the table and the curtain. Parsifal began to lick his lips as he stared toward the jostling drapery from his perch on Sebastien's lap.

"Coffee? Brandy? Coffee with brandy?" called out Shelby, Oz-like.

Sebastien looked at his watch, which told him it was really time for neither.

"Uh. No thanks."

"You're no fun, Dr. Grey. Has anyone told you that?"

Shelby re-appeared carrying a tray. He must have a customer coming in, Sebastien reasoned, from a quick scan of his clothing. He was wearing a dark-green corduroy jacket and a white button-down shirt with brown windowpanes, neither of which appeared up to the task of containing the hexagenerian's largish belly. His green knit tie looked uncomfortably tight.

"Yes, they have. Often. Are you expecting someone?"

"My clothes, you mean? Yes I am, in fact. A big fish. A professor from the university. He's been saving up for a first English edition of *Don Quixote*. And I am going to make his dreams come true. For seventy-five thou, of course."

Shelby put the tray on the end of the table and tipped a ceramic carafe over two porcelain cups, then topped each off from an unlabeled bottle of brown liquid.

"Here you are. And here is yours, Parsifal. There you go. Such a good pup."

Parsifal took the biscuit from Mr. Shelby and jumped down under the table. His tail wagged violently as he gnawed on the proffered treat.

"Seventy-five? Wow, that is a lot. I had no idea there was so much money in old books."

"Antiquarian books, Dr. Grey. And there is. Unfortunately, deals like the one I'm doing today do not happen that often. I mostly trade in the low-to-middle end of things. Oh, no offense to you, doctor."

"None taken."

"That reminds me. Sorry about that little, um, mix-up in Munich. I had no idea that book was stolen."

"Oh, that's all right. No harm, no foul."

In all of the excitement about working with Tiffany again, Sebastien had forgotten about his little brush with the Munich demimonde, although it was just a few days ago. Shelby had made arrangements through some obscure intermediary for Sebastien to acquire a rare volume of Rossini's complete works while he was in Germany for the conference. Unfortunately, the seller of the book turned out to be a con man, forger, and art thief, whom the Bavarian State Police had under surveillance. Sebastien's erstwhile book purchase was inter-rupted by men with guns drawn, and ended with him prone on the cold hardwood floor of the bookshop, spread-eagle.

"They didn't drag you off to jail, did they? Bastards."

"It didn't quite come to that, although my hosts at the university had to vouch for me with the police."

"Excellent. Here, let me make it up to you."

Shelby stood up and walked to the far wall, pointing to a spot among the books.

"From here to . . . right about here. This is what I have in music. Baroque, classical, then opera, ordered from best to worst. Italian, French, then German on the bottom shelf. Lots of great Wagneralia, which I'm sure you can appreciate; I certainly can't understand it. Pick one. Whichever book you like."

One of the three canister lights, which were mounted in the

ceiling and pointed toward the bookcase, caused the bald crown of Shelby's large head to shine. A dewy sweat was beginning to form amongst the wrinkles that were once his hairline.

"Are you serious? You don't have to do that."

"Nonsense. I insist. German bastards."

Shelby returned to his chair while Sebastien carefully perused the books. For the next several minutes, the only sound was a soft crunching coming from under the table and the clinking of Shelby's cup against its saucer.

"What's this?" Sebastien asked finally, pulling a book from the shelf from about knee level and showing it to Shelby.

"Oh my, you don't know? And you call yourself an opera scholar."

"I don't recall ever calling myself that," replied Sebastien in a matter-of-fact tone.

"That is *Klein Zaches genannt Zinnober* by E. T. A. Hoffman, or *Little Zaches Called Cinnabar*. That was the inspiration for the aria '*Il était une fois à la cour d'Eisenach*,' from Offenbach's *The Tales of Hoffman*. You know, the scene in the prologue when Hoffman and his friends make fun of the dwarf?"

"I always thought that was cruel."

"Yes, well . . ."

"I'll take this one, if you don't mind."

Sebastien waved the small book in Shelby's direction.

"Of course, my friend. It's all yours."

Sebastien was intrigued. He always felt sorry for Mr. Kleinzach, whoever he was. He imagined a sort of kinship with the unfortunate dwarf without knowing why. He decided then and there to explore that feeling. This book would be a good place to start.

"So, Dr. Grey, who was that man you were with outside? The man with the tape measure and camera? Are we due for a new roof?"

"No, that was a real estate appraiser."

Shelby lowered his cup with a sudden clank against the saucer.

"An appraiser! Good grief, man! Please tell me you're refinancing."

"The building is paid off. No, I'm thinking of selling."

"Selling! Why on earth would you do that? The place must be a gold mine!"

"I'm considering a move, actually. To South Dakota."

Shelby abruptly and with great drama placed his cup and saucer on the table, then disappeared behind the curtain again, this time emerging with two shot glasses.

"Drink up, young man. You are clearly not of sound mind."

Sebastien took a filled glass from Shelby but did not drink.

"I have family there. I think I told you that."

"Ah, yes. You went there this last summer, didn't you?"

Sebastien nodded.

"Well, if you want my advice, you may want to visit in the winter before committing. My daughter lives in Minneapolis and, if it's anything like that, there are just two seasons: July and winter."

"I met someone."

Shelby threw back his brandy and wiped his mouth with his jacket sleeve.

"That, my dear boy, should make things considerably warmer. So, who is this lovely, er . . . girl?"

"Why does everyone always do that?"

"Hey, hey! I'm a man of the world, Dr. Grey. A man of the world never assumes."

"Sounds to me like you did."

"Then apologies, dear landlord. Now, tell me about this fair maiden."

"She's a cop."

"Ah! A sturdy woman, no doubt."

"She's beautiful," Sebastien replied softly, sounding as if in a dream.

"Goes without saying, I'm sure. Refill?"

Shelby held out the bottle with a histrionic tipping motion.

"No thanks."

"And how did you meet this woman?"

"You remember I told you I was there to help out my brother?"

"I do recall that, yes."

"He's in law enforcement. Did I tell you that?"

"No, but that is fascinating."

"He's been up there for several years. He went to Montana State, where he met his wife. Then he got a job with the Sheriff's Office in Custer. Now he's a sergeant in their Investigations Division."

"Lots of crime in that part of the sticks?" Shelby asked.

"I wouldn't have thought so. But based on my experience so far, I can say there is a fair amount of murder and mayhem."

Sebastien waited for a response, but Shelby only tapped a finger against his glass in silence.

"Well, anyway, he wanted my input on a case—a couple of cases actually. She was working on them too."

"Ah, yes. Work and pleasure. Did I ever tell you about the Russian girl I met while . . . never mind. Continue."

"There's not much more to tell. She's very bright and she seems really interested in my work."

"Is she single? That seems a rather critical piece of information."

"Yes, she's single. And I think she likes me. She kissed me. I mean, we kissed."

"Damn, son, when do you start packing?" Shelby said, his wide smile showing his yellow teeth.

Sebastien shifted uncomfortably in his chair causing the leather to squeak, which startled Parsifal. The dog exhaled loudly from under the table as he settled back into his slumber.

"I'm still not sure."

"About moving, you mean?"

"It's a big step. What if I get out there and things don't work out?"

"Sounds like a rather low-risk proposition, doesn't it, what with your family there for support? Aside, of course, from the frostbite and the fear of crashing your pretty Range Rover into someone's livestock."

Sebastien resisted the urge to reply. The fact that the cat was now out of the bag, so to speak, unnerved him somewhat. The news of his move was now public and Mr. Shelby would no doubt push the rumor through the community. Maybe this was Sebastien's own subconscious way of ensuring he actually went through with it. No going back. Fate was now pushing *him* inexorably into the cold unknown. His eyes began to lose focus against the wall of books.

"You know what your problem is, Dr. Grey?" Shelby pronounced, after a few minutes of silence.

Sebastien jerked from his malaise and looked at Shelby, who was staring at him intently.

"I have many problems."

"Too much introspection. It's a bad thing, Sebastien. A misuse of the imagination. Nothing good ever comes from over-analyzing. A fool thinks dreams were made to be dreamt. Nonsense. They were meant to be chased. And you deserve it. How long have I been in your building? Hell, since before you owned it! It's always you and that damn dog. No offense, Parsifal."

Parsifal rolled to his feet and readied for action upon hearing his name.

"Either you're taking your dog out for a piss or you're locked away in your apartment. Or talking to me. I'm an old man,

Sebastien. I was here when your grandfather owned the building. You could learn a lot from him, you know. Maybe you just weren't paying attention. Your grandfather was bold. He took chances. Now you're benefitting from that. You better channel the old man, Sebastien, before it all goes away."

"I know. You're probably right. I'm definitely going to go."

"What was that line from Henry the Fifth? Something about loving yourself."

"'Self-love is not so vile a sin . . .'"

"' . . . as self-neglecting.' Yep, that's the one. 'Self-love, my liege, is not so vile a sin as self-neglecting.' A beautiful line. Time to stop neglecting yourself."

"I need to sell the building though. Could take a while."

"Do you though?"

"What do you mean?"

Shelby made a fist and poked the outstretched thumb back toward himself.

"I can take care of things for you. Look after the tenants and all that. Hell, I might even buy it."

"Really?"

"Oh, hell no, son. I don't have that kind of money. But yes. I'd be happy to run the place."

"I would pay you, of course. Or maybe give you a break on the rent."

"Exactly what I had in mind, Dr. Grey. Exactly what I had in mind. Hear that Parsifal? You and your human are headed to the Great White North. This calls for a celebration. Hang on. I'll be right back with the good stuff."

Sebastien watched Shelby disappear behind the curtain for the third time and realized the road was now clear for him. There were no excuses, nor did there need to be any. An abrupt feeling of excitement came upon him. Positivity and happiness were beginning to clear away the trepidation.

4

Immediately after leaving Shelby's store, Sebastien set to work preparing for the move to South Dakota. It would probably be temporary, he realized. He would still need to come back for whatever business would be necessary to sell the Block. But he made the rounds to his tenants and assured them operations would continue without interruption and he was always a phone call away, although he didn't mention to anyone that Shelby would be watching over things. He hoped that would be short-lived and low-key. He also left a message for his therapist.

Early the next morning, he packed the Range Rover with as much of his clothing and other necessities as would fit and set off for the two-day drive. He would take largely the same route to South Dakota as he did just a few months prior, omitting any excursion through Lake Tahoe. Unlike his earlier trip, he was in a hurry this time. The uncertainty of seeing family for the first time in years, and the anxiety of wondering if he could actually help his brother, was notably absent this time around. Plus, now he knew that Tiffany was on the other end of the drive. This was a mission, not a meander.

And indeed, Sebastien made excellent time. He reached Casper late on Wednesday evening and decided to stay over and leave as early as possible in the morning. By 8:30 a.m. on Thursday, he was pulling onto the dirt road that led to Hank's circular driveway.

"So, what's the plan, little brother? You here for good now?"

"I guess I am."

The brothers were sitting on Hank's back patio, staring into the tree-covered landscape beyond the back fence. A brisk wind pushed fallen leaves against the concrete at their feet, making a scraping sound.

"I'm glad, bro. I really am."

"Um, thanks."

"And the Block? What about that? Are you going to keep it?"

"I'm putting it up for sale, but I have someone looking after it in the meantime. It may take a while."

"What are you asking for it? If you don't mind my asking."

Sebastien was afraid of this question, though he knew it would come up. When Sebastien inherited the building and Hank the cash, both were roughly equal in value. But the real estate values in the Bay Area had ballooned in the subsequent years.

"The appraiser thinks around four million."

Hank suddenly looked grave. He lowered the coffee mug, which had been poised at his bottom lip, and put it on the patio table.

"I was thinking on the drive up here that we should split it. You know, whatever is above and beyond the value when I got it —after they kill me with taxes, of course."

"You don't have to do that, Sebastien. I think it's great. I mean, sure, it pisses me off a little. But I'm glad for you, really. And don't feel bad for me, by the way. I made out just fine. We're doing great."

There was nothing in Hank's face that convinced Sebastien of the veracity of the statement.

"What if I want to do it? What if I want us to start again? You're all I have left."

"You don't have to do that. Grandad wanted you to have that building."

"I think, technically, he wanted it to stay in the family, and he knew you were already married and out of state. So, it was more of a practical thing."

"I hadn't thought of that."

"Good. Sounds like we agree. The proceeds from the LeGris family investments stay with the LeGris family." Sebastien emphasized that ultimate *family*.

"Well you're out, then, little brother. You changed your name to Grey, remember? Rookie mistake, doctor."

"I'm not the only one who wanted a name change, *Henry*."

The men turned their heads at the sound of the sliding glass door opening.

"Well, who do we have here? Hello, Sebastien."

Sebastien raised himself from his seat to return Melissa LeGris's embrace, which he did awkwardly. He was never comfortable with casual hugging, although in certain contexts . . .

"Hello. How's the uh . . ."—Sebastien gestured to Melissa's Montana State sweatshirt— "coming along?"

"Baby, Sebastien. We're calling that a baby," Hank smirked before draining his coffee.

"Oh, shut up, Hank. Be nice to your brother. He came a long way to help you . . . again! It's going great. Thank you, Sebastien. Everything looks good. In fact, I just came from the doctor."

"That's my boy," Hank declared as he stood up then leaned over to rub and kiss Melissa's belly.

"Oh, do you know it's a boy?" Sebastien asked.

"No, your brother is just hoping it is. He's tired of getting ganged up on by the better sex."

"Words you will never hear me say," replied Hank.

"You're a disgusting old man. Sebastien, when did you get here? Are you hungry? Oh, who's this?"

Parsifal was curled up on the chaise, snoozing and utterly unaware of the new arrival.

"Sebastien's calling that a dog."

"What's gotten into you today? Don't mind him, Sebastien. I think he's just in an extra good mood because you're here to bail him out again."

"That's okay. And this is Parsifal."

"Well, he's just adorable. Kirby is going to love him."

"He's really good with people and totally house-trained."

"I'm sure he is."

Parsifal looked up, eyes wide with concern as Melissa stroked his dark back.

"Can I make you some eggs or something, Sebastien?"

"Oh, no thanks. I ate earlier. Thanks for letting me stay here, by the way. It's just temporary, I promise."

"Well, of course. You're family. You and Parsifal can stay as long as you want."

"She doesn't mean that," winked Hank.

"Shouldn't you be on your way to work?" Melissa snapped back, slapping Hank on the shoulder.

"Yes, we should be. Sebastien has a lot of work to do, and I'm due to get yelled at by the lieutenant. I'm thinking of a nice dinner tonight. Would you mind making some reservations for us?"

"Oh, big spender. You're taking us to town tonight?"

"That's right. You wouldn't have heard. I'm a millionaire now."

"Wait . . . what . . .?" Melissa called out as the brothers retreated through the house to the garage.

36

"Tiffany will be there too," Hank called back.

AFTER THREE DAYS bunked down in the storage room, Tiffany could see the flaw in her plan. There was just not enough room in the tiny space for a proper organizational effort. Fully half of the binders, which had been collecting dust on the movable storage shelves, were now dispersed into separate piles surrounding Tiffany's newly installed desk on the vinyl tile floor. Each stack represented some category of cold case optimism: physical evidence yet to be analyzed using modern techniques, DNA yet to be tested, skeletal remains to be re-examined, and witnesses to be recontacted. In the center of the small space lay the largest pile, consisting of cases with multiple potential avenues for investigation/testing. The remaining binders on the shelves would have to wait. There was plenty to do now, plenty to get her started. Spoiled for choice, one might say. But where to begin?

Tiffany stood up from the floor and reached her clasped hands toward the ceiling, arching her stiffened back, which produced a soft popping sound. She was quite petite, though a little taller than average, and very fit. Extra duty as a PT instructor out at the academy was a great way to stay in shape, she found (not to mention the extra pay). But no level of fitness could overcome half a week of standing, reaching, sitting, bending, twisting, and otherwise contorting one's way through fifty years of investigative jetsam.

"I love what you've done with the place," declared Hank, holding the door open just wide enough for his head to breach through.

Tiffany turned around, startled.

"Hey, boss. It's a mess, isn't it? I'd invite you in, but . . ."

"No worries. I just came down to bring you something," Hank replied without moving or opening the door.

"Okay. Well? What is it?"

Hank opened the door wide with a flourish and stepped aside to make way for Sebastien.

"Sebastien! You're here! I didn't know you were coming this soon!" Tiffany's eyes widened and her ivory teeth beamed with delight.

"I was hoping to surprise you," he said, looking a little sheepish.

"I *am* surprised! And you came just in time. Did you drive up again?"

"Yes I did." Sebastien looked around the small space. "What's all this?"

"This is your life for the next, uh . . ." Tiffany looked at Hank for help, who merely shrugged. "Where are you staying, with Hank and Melissa?"

"Just until I find a place."

"You wouldn't believe how hard I had to twist his arm," added Hank. "He was planning on hiding away in a hotel. Not this time, bro."

"Well, I bet Kirby loves your dog. You *did* bring your dog, didn't you?"

"Of course. And she hasn't met him yet."

"She's at school," said Hank. "Well, hey, look. I'm going to let you two kids get caught up and get to work. It looks like you have a lot to do. I didn't bring the good doctor up here just for giggles, you know. Join us for dinner tonight?"

"Sure."

"Excellent. I'll have Melissa text the details. Now you two behave."

Once Hank was gone and it was just the two of them, Tiffany looked directly into Sebastien's eyes. He looked nervous. He quickly broke the mutual stare and looked down at the binder-littered floor.

"I can tell you've been busy. Where do you want to start?"

Tiffany shoved a binder out of her way with her foot to clear a path, then closed the distance between them.

"I thought we'd start where we left off," she declared while reaching out to pull Sebastien's face toward hers and lean in for a kiss. "I missed you, Sebastien. I thought a lot about you these last few months," she said softly afterwards, their noses almost touching.

"I've thought about you every day. Every single day," Sebastien replied, his voice shaking. "I'm so glad we kept in touch."

"I am too, Sebastien. And I think it's fantastic you came. I wasn't sure you would."

Sebastien returned her tight embrace; the familiar smell of his cologne brought her back to the first time they met, in the Custer County Coroner's Office amidst the rotting remains that brought them together.

After a moment, Tiffany broke away from Sebastien and made her way to the chair behind her desk.

"Now that we got that out of the way, we can focus on work," she said. "And, by the way, that's the last time I will ever kiss you in this building."

"Then to whom do I complain about my pay?"

"Ah, you brought your sense of humor with you. Good. I predict we'll need it. We also need to make room for a chair for you in here. I'm not giving you mine," Tiffany smiled. "Now, if you don't mind, open the door. We don't want to be the subject of office gossip."

After propping the door open, Sebastien stood in the center of the small space and resumed his scan of the room and the explosion of binders and reports.

"So?" he prompted.

Tiffany replied from her chair, using a pen as a pointer.

"I tried to separate things out per the advice you gave me. That pile over there, by the door, are cases that may have subjects or witnesses we can re-interview. Those binders there are cases that have physical evidence that can be re-tested or that wasn't ever tested in the first place. That big mess by your feet includes cases with multiple areas of approach. You know, I couldn't help but notice a lot of questionable police work as I went through these."

"That's to be expected, right?" replied Sebastien.

"Is that why you were so cynical in your email? I mean, you suggested I never assume this or that has been done or even done properly."

"I've seen a lot. People watch TV and they think every case gets the maximum effort and all investigative avenues are exhausted. That's just not the norm. But maybe I'm a cynic. What's with these here?"

Sebastien pointed to three towers of binders that ran along the bottom front of the desk and reached almost to its surface.

"Oh, those are the Sebastien stacks."

"Please, tell me. I'm dying to know."

"Those all represent cases that involve skeletal remains."

"Oh, yes. Those are the Sebastien stacks, are they? Do you know if the associated remains are still around? Or were they disposed of?"

"Some are still in evidence. I verified that with the coroner. I figured we can go over there tomorrow and see what's what."

Tiffany leaned back in her chair and smirked mischievously.

"You didn't smile nearly that big when I kissed you."

"I'm sorry, but we are not to talk about that while in this building," Sebastien replied, his own smile growing even larger.

"Okay, smart ass. You better watch yourself."

"I always do. I've recently been told that's a bad thing though. Anyway, I have a suggestion for how to make some room in here."

"Please tell me."

"I'd like to take these skeletal cases back to Hank's. I'll go through them tonight and over the next few days. Maybe I can help prioritize those."

"Fine with me."

"What's with the cases that are still on the shelves?" Sebastien asked.

"I haven't looked at those yet. And there's another shelf behind there too. It's one of those moving storage things. The button is between the edge of the shelf and the wall."

"Wow, there are a lot more than I expected."

"It looks worse than it is. Most cases have multiple binders."

"The federal grant involves DNA, right? Do we need to limit ourselves to DNA cases, or are all cases fair game?"

Sebastien was sitting on the corner of the desk now.

"That's a good question. I'll have to ask Hank about that. Remind me tonight. Why don't we get the skeletals to your car and make room for another chair? We can share the desk. You still got that beautiful Range Rover?"

SEBASTIEN LOOKED up from the case he'd been reading and began studying Tiffany's face as she flipped through her own thick binder. He had wondered, these last few months, if his mind had created a false picture of her. Had time and distance inflated her beauty—her graceful features; her small nose; her soft, pale skin; and her oval face that, when he first met her, seemed plain, but gradually revealed its golden ratio the more he saw it? Was it all still real? Was it ever real? Yes, he concluded, as he stared at her.

Desperately hoping his excitement hadn't been too obvious, Sebastien was trying his hardest to be professional, despite feeling like a kid in a candy store, like Wotan heading to Valhalla. He had fully expected a tepid reception from Tiffany. He didn't know why; it was just his nature to fret, he supposed. But that kiss! How glad he was that Tiffany confirmed it for him. She still had feelings for him. What was it she had said: "start where we left off"? What ridiculous luck. Not to mention, he was getting to do the very work he was made to do. What was the catch? When would the other shoe drop?

"What are you looking at, anthro boy?"

"I'm sorry," he said repentantly.

"Don't be. I can read your mind, Sebastien, and I was thinking the same thing."

"Oh yeah? What was I thinking?" he replied playfully.

"You were thinking how awesome I am. How I'm a great detective. And how great it's going to be to work with me."

Sebastien caught himself before his over-excited mouth spat out too much of the truth. *Be professional, Sebastien.*

"Sorry to break the bad news, but I was just wondering what case you were reading. You seem pretty absorbed by it."

"I am. I actually knew the victim, Amber Harrison."

"Really?"

"Well, kind of. She and I were in middle school together. I lost touch with her in high school."

"What kind of case is it?"

"That's the interesting part about it. It's technically not a homicide, even though we're treating that as a possibility. It's officially a missing persons case. The subject's car was found in the driveway of the home she shared with two of her friends. There was some blood in it, which the lab tested and confirmed it belonged to her. But there wasn't enough to say for sure she was killed or even seriously injured."

"So why is it a missing persons case, then?"

"Well, like I said, it may not be. But the public thinks it is. Apparently, we chose to leave the blood that was found in the car out of the press because we couldn't say for sure if it was related to a crime. Plus, there were so many people who felt she may have just run off that we couldn't ignore that possibility. Evidently, she had made some statements about meeting a guy and taking off to Los Angeles with him. That would explain her leaving the car, which was registered to her mother and not technically hers."

"Do you think we should start off with that case?"

"I don't know. Why don't you look at it after I'm done, then we'll talk about it?"

"Sounds good."

"Which case are you reading?"

Sebastien lifted the binder off of his lap and passed it over to Tiffany.

"Oh, yes. The Ruthanne Cleary homicide. That's one of the oldest cases in here. She was found in an empty field, stuffed into a metal barrel. Her skull was cracked open and her hands and feet were bound, if I recall."

"Are we missing another binder for this or are there additional notes somewhere?" Sebastien asked.

"Are you talking about the witness statement?"

Sebastien nodded.

"No, we're not."

"So, now you see why I'm so cynical. A witness saw a brown van pull into an empty field and roll out a metal barrel, the same field and the same barrel the victim was later found in. The witness gets the plate, but there is no record—zero—of the plate ever having been searched or anyone looking for the van."

Tiffany leaned back in her chair and knitted her hands behind her head.

"I agree. Total cluster. Any suggestions?"

"You have a crime analysis unit, right?"

"Sure. A very good one, in fact."

"Good. Let them research the plate, brown vans from the era, etc. This has no business clogging up your brain."

"Geez, I didn't think of that."

"And do the same with any others like it. Any case that needs records searched or people found, give it to them."

"That might be almost half of everything on the floor."

"Perfect. Let's go through them and put the crime analysis cases on one of the empty shelves. They can come grab them as they have time."

"Great idea. But let me take you upstairs and introduce you. The analysts should at least meet the person who's so happy to throw them under the bus."

"No thanks. I'll pass."

"Negative, doctor. You're an official part of the team now. The shy act will just have to take a back seat. Don't worry. I'll protect you."

5

Tiffany held the door open to the decomposition room while Sebastien rolled in the cart bearing three brown banker's boxes. The room they chose was a special autopsy suite meant to contain the smell of putrefaction and reduce the spread of possible infectious disease. Fortunately, the space was not being used, so it would make a good place to go through some of the skeletal cases.

"Are you sure these are all you want to look at?" asked Tiffany as she pushed the door closed.

"For now, yes. These three seemed to have the most potential to me so far."

Sebastien retrieved the top binder from the stack of three he had brought and laid it open on the metal table.

"Okay, 88-301. Let's start with the most promising one."

Tiffany thumbed through the first few pages of the binder as Sebastien began laying the bones out on the table.

"Oh, yeah. This one looked interesting. Hikers found a skull and some other bones out at Hell Canyon. What do you mean by 'most promising'?"

"Because we already have the answer, or half the answer."

"Oh really?"

"Yep. Hang on, I'll show you."

Sebastien arranged the few bones in anatomical order on the table: the skull, some vertebrae, and an upper leg bone.

"There we are. Now, if you look in the case binder, you'll see a report from the anthropologist who examined these bones back in '88. Go ahead and read that, would you?"

Tiffany flipped through the pages until she found the anthropology report.

"Male, likely Caucasian, aged thirty-five to forty-five, 5'9" tall. Small-caliber gunshot entry wound to the frontal bone 2.5 centimeters above the right eye orbit, exit wound through the right parietal 3mm lateral of lambda. Elements recovered include skull and mandible, left femur, atlas, axis, and C3." Tiffany looked up from the page. "Okay, I understood about a third of that. Lambda? Atlas? Axis?"

"The lambda is just a landmark on the back of the skull. Atlas and axis refer to the top two vertebrae in the spinal column. The atlas is so named because it figuratively holds up the head—like the Greek god Atlas holding up the world. The axis, second vertebra from the top, has a little knob sticking up that allows the atlas to rotate on top of it. See that?"

Sebastien held up the small bone in his gloved hand and tapped a finger against the protrusion.

"We call that the dens. It's like a tooth, but rounded on the top. Things move along the axis, hence the name. And then the C3, this vertebra here, connects to the bottom of the axis."

"That makes perfect sense," replied Tiffany, as she gathered all three vertebrae in her own gloved hand and attempted to fit them together.

"So, last night at Hank's, I looked through this entire report. Nowhere did I see any reference to how these three vertebrae might have gotten separated from the others."

"They might still be out there, I suppose?"

Tiffany had successfully refit the three bones and was holding them up to the light, examining them like precious jewels.

"You have superpowers when it comes to finding things," she continued. "We can always go take a look, although thirty-plus years is a long time for the rest to go undiscovered Quite a few hikers go through that area every year. Dog walkers too."

"Oh no, I've found them already. At least, I think I have."

"Great. Here we go again. Should I pull up a chair for this?"

The lights from the ceiling reflected off Tiffany's white teeth, framed by her thinly glossed lips.

"We never did discuss kissing in the Coroner's Office," Sebastien ventured.

"That's off limits too. I'm serious about that stuff, Sebastien."

Tiffany's smile quickly disappeared and she pointed a rose-painted fingernail at him as she spoke.

"I'm really sorry. I didn't mean . . ."

Sebastien's brain kicked into panic mode. He began to scold himself for screwing things up so quickly.

"It's fine . . . it's fine," she said. "Look, I feel the same way you do. I promise. I'm just under a lot of pressure right now. We both are. I really, really want this to work out. I want to work with you, Sebastien. We have a lot of cases and a lot to teach each other. We can't screw this up. No one can know about us— besides Hank and Melissa, I mean. Do you understand?"

"Of course I do. I know. You're right."

"Good. Now let's keep going. We don't want to have to work late and ruin our evening. Anyway, you were saying?"

A wave of relief worked its way down his own atlas, axis, C3, and beyond. Properly chastened, he resumed his disquisition.

"Let me see those vertebrae for a moment."

Sebastien pulled a magnifying glass out of his messenger bag and held it up to each small bone, in turn.

"Yep. Pretty much what I suspected. Here, take the magnifier lens and look at the edges of the C3 and axis."

"What am I looking for?"

"The bottom of the C3 looks like it's been shaved. See the flattened surface?"

"Oh, okay. Yeah. There it is."

"Now check out the other side of it, the top. See those cuts and nicks? Same with the bottom of the axis—cuts and nicks."

"Are you saying somebody did this?"

"I'm saying this is dismemberment. Somebody cut off this guy's head. It did not fall apart as a result of decomposition. Grab that femur, the leg bone there. Take a look at the ball on the end. See any cuts?"

Tiffany positioned the magnifying lens over the bone.

"Hey, look at that. There *are* some cuts. And a kind of hole in the top."

"That indentation is supposed to be there. It's the obturator foramen."

"What did you just call me?" giggled Tiffany.

"Oh, sorry. I mean, that's where a ligament attaches. But those cuts do not belong there. Again, dismemberment."

"I don't remember seeing anything about dismemberment in the report."

"Neither do I. It's not there. It was overlooked. Either that or the marks were mistaken for rodent gnawing."

"Lovely. What about the other half? You said you found it."

"To be precise, I do think the other leg and both arms are out there somewhere. But the axial skeleton—the trunk—I think I know where that is. Or perhaps *was*. How far is Cheyenne, Wyoming from here?"

"Hang on. I *am* going to need to sit for this."

Tiffany pulled the stool from under the counter along the wall and rolled it to the edge of the autopsy table.

"Okay. Now I'm ready for you to tell me that some bird carried it off, just like that skull from the RV park this summer."

"Very funny. Do you recall the supplemental report that was made about a year after these bones were found?" Sebastien nodded toward the open binder on the table. "It's buried toward the back."

"Hmm. Let me think. Um. Okay, I give up. No, I don't. But, in my defense, I went through a lot of cases."

"Yes, you did. Anyway, there is a report in there about a torso being found in Cheyenne, Wyoming back in '87. Evidently, it was left at a construction site and set on fire. There must have been a bulletin or something put out because one of the detectives on this case found out about it and looked into it as being a possible match."

"That would make perfect sense. Head and leg in one place, torso in another, although it's quite a ways away and the torso would have been found, what, almost a year earlier? Plus, it must not have been a match anyway."

"There is a note in there about it not being a match. But here's the problem. You cops are too damn literal and far too trusting of the so-called experts."

"So, you're saying I shouldn't trust you? And . . . literal? I don't even know what you're talking about."

"Somebody in Cheyenne, back in '87, measured the spinal column from the torso and came up with an estimated height for the individual as five foot seven. Our guy here was given an estimated stature of five-nine, based on measurements of the femur. Two different heights—therefore, no match."

Sebastien waited for Tiffany to respond, but she wasn't biting.

"Anytime I reconstruct stature—whenever *any* anthropologist worth their salt reconstructs stature—we always give a possible range of heights. The formulae always produce a range and, based on the bone you are measuring, that range could be anywhere from three to five inches."

"You're saying our guy could actually be between five-six and a half to five-eleven and a half? And torso guy . . . it was a guy, right?"

"Affirmative. The genitalia were intact."

"Torso guy would then be between five-five and a half to five-nine and a half—so the ranges overlap."

"Correct. And here's the most important fact: Any measurement based off of burned bones, or heated bone, would be massively out of whack. Bones shrink when they are heated. They lose moisture. Plus, the spinal column is not a great feature to use for stature reconstruction in the first place."

"And there was no mention of DNA testing in the file?"

"Not in '87. The technology was barely out of England at that time. And no, no mention of it anyway."

"So, the Cheyenne torso could very well be connected to these bones?" There was growing enthusiasm in Tiffany's voice.

"Oh, absolutely. And I think they are. The human skeleton has seven cervical vertebrae. We have three here. Guess how many were still connected to the torso from Cheyenne?"

"Four," answered Tiffany flatly.

"That's right. Four."

Tiffany suddenly stood up from the stool and excitedly declared, "We have our first case."

"We have our first case," Sebastien repeated with a smile.

TIFFANY STEPPED out of the room to put a call in to Cheyenne PD. The cell phone reception was not great in the depths of the Coroner's Office.

The gist of the conversation, once she got through to somebody who actually knew something, was that the torso case was still cold and the victim still unidentified. There were a few leads at the time, a few possible matches. But those turned out to be unproductive. The PD did not know if any of the remains were still being stored. Tiffany would have to contact the Laramie County Coroner to find out if that was the case or not. But Cheyenne PD would be happy to have her come down and take a look at the case files.

The Laramie County Coroner was easier to reach but less helpful. They would have to check their records, she was told . . . and their storage. It was a big county and they had so much material in their freezer that they tended to "dispose of" the older items to make space. *What exactly does that mean?* she wondered with concern, as the woman on the other end of the line went to search for the remains.

On her way back into the autopsy suite, Tiffany paused to take in Sebastien through the large glass window. He was eagerly on to the next set of remains, the next case. The part in his dark hair failed, allowing a sepia lock to hang diffidently over his forehead as he stared down at his work. His youthful profile betrayed an innocence, and even, for someone so intelligent, a gullibility. She suddenly felt a power she did not want. Did she have feelings for him? Yes, she decided. Undoubtedly, yes. But she would need to be careful and slow. There was no rush.

"Okay, cowboy. How do you feel about a road trip?"

"What did they say?" Sebastien looked up from the bones on the table.

"The torso case is still unsolved. They never identified the guy. No one is really working it, of course. But we are welcome to come look through the files and evidence."

"Evidence? That's great. They still have the remains, then?"

"Well, not so much. They kept the spinal column, but the soft tissue is now gone. I don't suppose we can get DNA from bone?"

"Generally, sure. But charred bone, maybe not. But we'll be able to see how closely our vertebrae fit onto theirs. We may even be able to match up the tool marks."

"You mean those cuts?"

"Exactly. This will be good. How far away is Cheyenne, by the way?"

"Four hours, give or take. And speaking of road trips, I thought we'd grab some lunch after this and run out to Hell Canyon to check out the scene where our remains were found —just for context. What?"

"I'm just realizing how much alike we are. Either that or I'm rubbing off on you."

"Don't flatter yourself, doctor. Hank didn't put me in charge of cold cases for nothing. What are you working on now?"

Sebastien retrieved one of the binders and handed it to Tiffany.

"Case number 2012-1023. It's a Jane Doe, according to the file."

"Don't tell me. You'll be the judge of that," Tiffany snickered.

"Actually, I quite agree, based on the diameter of the humeral head."

"Oh, well, of course! That's exactly what I was thinking."

"Whatever, detective. Anyway, there wasn't much recovered, as you can see. Just some vertebrae, a left scapula, left humerus, and a left clavicle. Basically, the shoulder girdle: left shoulder blade, left upper arm, and collar bone. All of which is still connected by desiccated tissue."

"So why is this a cold case, rather than just an unidentified deceased? What's the crime? I didn't read the whole binder. Once I saw that the remains were in storage, I just set it aside for you."

Sebastien held up the trio of shoulder bones and yanked

the pieces apart. The move reminded Tiffany of someone pulling cans of beer from a six pack.

"This is why. See the hole?" Sebastien held up the shoulder blade in front of Tiffany's face and poked his gloved pinkie through the oblong aperture in the middle portion of the blade, wiggling it for effect.

"Bullet wound," asked Tiffany as she carefully took the bone from Sebastien. "Pretty large one too."

"Yep. And kudos to the pathologist who recognized it. The blade portion of the scapula, the triangle that runs down the upper back, can be quite thin and punctures easily. I have rarely seen a shoulder blade that did not have some sort of defect in it—whether from rodents, weathering, or some other natural process. It's just so thin—like tissue paper, in some places. But the pathologist took the extra step to x-ray this one and found metal particles along the wound. That was a very heads-up move."

"Where was this found?"

"Let me see . . ." Sebastien consulted the report. "Says here, a mile and a half north of Fairburn, wherever that is. Next to some railroad tracks. A surveyor was waiting at the railroad crossing in his truck when he looked out the window and spotted some bones lying on the ground."

"Fairburn? Wow. That's way out there. East county. There doesn't seem to be much here to go on—except, of course, DNA. Which is the point of the grant. I guess we put this on the list for testing and comparison."

Sebastien took the shoulder blade back from Tiffany and placed it carefully on the table, as if he hadn't forcefully torn it from the rest of the shoulder girdle a moment ago. His face suddenly fell into a study of concentration, and he began to softly run his thumb along the large linear protrusion at the top edge of the shoulder blade. Finally, after a minute or so, he let out a soft "hmm."

"What?"

"Hmmmm."

"Sebastien, what is it?"

"Nothing. Just thinking. You're right. This will be a good one for DNA."

"What is this last case you brought?" asked Tiffany, picking up the final binder from the table and opening it to the first sheet as Sebastien began to stow the shoulder girdle back in its cardboard container.

"This is one I think we can clear up pretty quickly. Take a look in the box. It should be a skull and nothing more."

Tiffany moved the previous two case boxes back onto the cart and lifted the last one onto the table.

"It certainly smells awful. I'm afraid to open it," she said.

"That's freezer burn."

"Are you serious?"

"Sure. It's just like when you have boxes of stuff in your freezer at home for too long. They start to stink. Don't you recognize that smell? It's the cardboard box, not the skull."

"Excuse me. Nothing in my freezer smells like that. It's gross."

"Are you going to open it, or are you afraid?"

"Shut up, city boy."

Tiffany lifted the lid off of the box and leaned over to look inside.

"Oh. You're right. That doesn't smell so bad. What the heck is it though?"

"It's a trophy skull."

"That doesn't help me."

Sebastien lifted out the contents of the box and put it on the table. The skull looked very old, and even ordinary, except for the splotches of bright colors that appeared to be poured over the top of it.

"This is candle wax. The skull was used to hold up a candle, or candles. Going by the large amount, it looks like it was used for that purpose for quite a long time."

Tiffany gave a half-grimace and asked, "A candle holder? You mean like a devil-worshipping thing?"

Sebastien picked up the skull and turned it over in his hands, inspecting it closely and squinting as he did so.

"Maybe," he finally replied. "But I don't think so. I've seen quite a lot of this kind of thing actually. This skull is Asian."

"Asian as in, from Asia? Or as in, Native American or Hispanic?"

"Hey, I'm impressed! I wish I could have gotten my students to pay attention that closely."

Tiffany tapped her temple with her index finger and smiled. "I'm not just a pretty face. And no, that is not an invitation to comment."

"I wouldn't dare. Do you want me to show you a trick?"

"Sure."

"Okay, you hold the skull from the back so the face is looking upward to the ceiling and the upper teeth are pointed at me."

Tiffany took up the skull and held it out in front of her. "Like this?"

"Yep, that's it. Now watch. I'm going to lay this pencil across the nasal aperture, the hole where the nose would go."

Tiffany watched in fascination as Sebastien balanced a pencil over the nose of the skull, with the eraser pointing to her left and the tip of the pencil pointing to her right.

"What in the world are you up to?" she asked.

"Just watch. I'm going to put my finger between the pencil and the cheek bone. Watch what happens to the pencil."

As Sebastien's finger slid through the narrow space, his knuckle pushed the pencil off. The yellow cylinder hit the floor and rolled across the room, resting against the wall with a soft clank.

"See?" he asked.

"No offense, doctor, but big damn deal. You knocked the pencil off."

Sebastien looked a little disappointed, reminding Tiffany how sensitive he could be.

"Yes, I knocked the pencil off. That's because there is not enough room for my finger to pass between the cheek bone and the pencil. In other words, this person's cheek bones protrude, giving him a 'flat' face, a classic Asian-shaped face. If there was enough room for my finger to go through without knocking the pencil off, that would mean his cheeks recede, giving him a somewhat angled profile."

"So you're saying this pencil trick is how to tell Asians from other races?"

"It's one way. Of course, it's not always reliable given the amount of trait mixing that goes on. But yes, this skull is very strongly Asian, if I can put it that way. I would rule out Native American or Hispanic."

"Okay, that is a pretty cool trick. How does this help us though?"

"I believe this skull was brought back from either Korea or Vietnam as a wartime trophy. It was then used as a novelty or a decoration."

"Morbid," Tiffany muttered. "Where did it come from anyway?"

"Somebody died of natural causes, I think. This was taken out of their home when it was cleaned out by the family. They called law enforcement. Hence the binder in your cold case room."

"Then it's a homicide, but it's from the war? Is this crack what killed him?"

Tiffany pointed to a large break on the left side of the skull, just over where the ear would be.

"Not likely. That looks like it happened postmortem. Somebody probably dropped it or something, although it probably made the original investigators think it was a suspicious death."

"What do you suggest we do with it?"

"I'll write up a report and see if that's enough to get him a proper burial."

"Well, look at us, Sebastien! We've already solved a case! Wait till we tell your brother!"

6

Sebastien alighted from the passenger's seat of Tiffany's cruiser and surveyed the area around the small, oval trailhead. Just in front of him rose two large granite cliffs, the slopes of which were speckled with bare pine trees poking up like toothpicks. Between these, a dirt trail led deeper into the canyon.

"Is this where 301 was found?" asked Sebastien, referring to the dismemberment case from 1988.

Tiffany stood by the driver's door of the car, clenching a piece of paper between her teeth and pulling on a small backpack.

"Ith wit fend dun duh terl," she replied.

"What?"

Pulling the paper from her mouth, Tiffany tried again.

"It was found down that trail there. About two miles in, according to the original report."

"Is this a particularly popular trail?"

"Sure. I've hiked here several times myself, although I don't know how popular it was back in '88. Come to think of it, I don't know if it was even here then."

Sebastien hesitated a moment, looking at Tiffany across the hood of the car.

"Yes, I have my gun. See? Come on. I'm sure word has spread throughout the mountain lion community that you are not to be messed with," joked Tiffany, referring to Sebastien's run-in with a big male cougar just a few months prior.

"That's not exactly how that went down," he replied nervously as the two started down the trail.

"Actually, we have more of a chance of running into a bighorn sheep than a mountain lion, I think."

The addendum did not bring Sebastien any comfort. The reality of moving from his cozy suburban sanctuary to the place where he was nearly mauled to death was beginning to sink in. He had been too distracted to factor that into the calculus of his relocation.

Tiffany took the lead as they made their way, allowing Sebastien to drop a few paces and take her in. Her short ponytail bounced against the nape of her pale, graceful neck as she ambled down the trail. Her perfume, or lotion, or whatever, wafted past, surrounding him in an atmosphere of vanilla, dirt, and pine. Sebastien's eyes started to trace their way down between her shoulder blades, over her backpack, which was tucked neatly into the small of her back, and downward to . . .

"What's the holdup?"

Tiffany stopped suddenly and turned to face him.

"Oh, nothing. Nothing. I'm just keeping an eye out for mountain lions."

"I wouldn't bother, Sebastien. If we're being stalked, the lion would be behind us. You wouldn't know it until it jumped on your back and ripped your atlas, axis, and all of your C vertebrae out."

Tiffany started up the trail again and Sebastien hurriedly caught up, shifting his eyes upward to trace the rocky angles and brushy slopes as they passed by. In doing so, he paid particular attention to any potential hiding spots, but actually didn't see much. He started to relax, realizing for the first time what a lovely day it was. Sunny and bright but with a crisp breeze that signaled autumn, now in its adolescence, would someday die at the harsh hands of winter.

"What happened to the trees?" Sebastien called up.

"The Jasper Fire. About twenty years ago, I think. Some idiot dropped a match and started the biggest fire in South Dakota history."

"That sucks. Seriously."

"Yep. So why don't you tell me about your trip to Germany? How did your speech go? What was your presentation on?"

"That's actually a funny coincidence. They asked me to give a presentation on how modern dismemberment cases can be useful for understanding ancient ones."

"You're kidding?"

"No, it's true. Essentially, my thesis was that the same motives that drive modern dismemberment cases also apply to many of the ones found in archaeological sites."

"You mean like how in this case, we think the purpose of the dismemberment was to conceal the body, to dump the remains in different places?"

"Exactly. One of the problems in archaeology is that we tend to map our own romantic notions on to people of the past. As a result, if we see something like butchered remains, we think it's evidence of human sacrifice or some Earth-worshipping ritual. It rarely occurs to us that what we could be seeing is just evidence of a crime. Some dude got ticked off at someone else for stealing his spear, or necklace, or *something*, then stuck him and hid the body."

"I guess you see everything like that, don't you?"

"What do you mean?" Sebastien replied, feeling a bit challenged.

"You have to admit that your world is pretty dark. You see

this kind of thing all the time. Maybe it has, I don't know, jaded you a bit."

"I guess that's possible. But, on the other hand, the more of something someone sees, the more they understand it. I'm drawing conclusions from a larger dataset than most people. And besides, someone has to do what I do."

"Oh, I know. Believe me. The whole Sheriff's Office has been singing your praises nonstop since you found those bodies. Thank goodness for people like you."

People like me? What's that supposed to mean?

Per usual, Sebastien's confirmation bias pointed him in the direction of suspicious negativity when it came to other people's opinions of him. The fact that he was supposed to be a man of science, who built his foundation of knowledge upon evidence and not conjecture, was an irony of which he was well aware. He was doing a bit better though. At least, he was better able to keep his thoughts to himself rather than jumping to conclusions verbally. This was a big improvement.

"Didn't you tell me we're also going to help a friend out with a case while you were there?" Tiffany asked.

"Oh, yeah. I did. That was kind of interesting too."

"Well, we have another mile and I've heard that the sound of people talking will scare away a mountain lion."

"I hope you're kidding."

"You mean you hope I'm *not* kidding. Now tell me about this case."

"The guy who runs the archaeology department at the university was one of my professors in grad school. One of his students was re-examining an ancient Roman site in Bavaria. The site is called Red Cave. There were five human burials in the cave and all but one of them showed signs of malnutrition in their skeletons. The fifth one, the one that looked well-nourished, was a child of between six and ten years old. It clearly did not fit the pattern of the others and they asked for my opinion on why that might be. There was also a burial of a small dog."

"Well? Did you figure it out?" Tiffany asked as she hopped a shallow puddle that had pooled onto the trail.

"You've heard of Ockham's razor, right?"

"Sure. That's where the simplest explanation is the correct one."

"That's basically it. Specifically, Ockham said, 'entities should not be needlessly multiplied.' In other words, we shouldn't add factors to an explanation without specific reasons to do so. But yes, you could say, 'the simplest explanation is the correct one.'"

"I just did."

"Haha."

"Okay, so?"

Tiffany's questions were bringing out the pedagogue in him. It had been a few years since he last gave a lecture in a classroom. This exchange was reminding him of how much he enjoyed it.

"You tell me, detective. What would be the simplest explanation for the child not fitting the nutritional pattern of the others?"

"I guess the child was eating different things than the individuals were?"

"Now, you see, you've introduced another factor. Another entity. What six-year-old child eats differently from the rest of the group?"

"Still nursing?"

"That's a great suggestion. But the individual was a little old for nursing and, besides, if the mother was malnourished, then the child would also show at least some signs of that."

"Well, maybe the child didn't belong there?"

"Now you're on to something."

"You think the child belonged to a different group?"

"Not quite. I think the child didn't belong to the time. I believe it's a modern child with modern nutritional and health patterns. At least, that's my theory."

"How did you come to that conclusion?"

"Mostly due to the fact that the child's skeleton showed good growth and nutrition and no signs of disease—all things that were present in the other individuals at the site. Of course, there was also the curious incident of the dog, to use a Sherlock Holmes referencce."

"Sebastien . . ."

"Okay, okay. My point is that I don't believe the dog fits either. It's too small. I'm not an expert in dog skeletons, but it appears to me to be a terrier."

"So?"

"Again, no expert, but smaller dog breeds did not make it to Central and Western Europe until the sixteenth or seventeenth centuries. They were first bred in Asia, then brought westward when the trade routes were opened up."

"Ah, the dog was modern and the child was modern, but the other individuals were not."

"Yep. That's just my hunch though. They have some work to do on their end. They promised to keep me in the loop."

"A modern child had been dumped in an archaeological site along with their dog," summarized Tiffany, still keeping a brisk pace down the trail.

"Exactly, although not completely modern. I'm thinking late-nineteenth to early-twentieth century. The site was first discovered in 1923. Oh, and get this . . . the child was murdered."

"Well, do they know who did it?"

"Not a clue."

"Don't tell me. You have a hunch, don't you?"

"Not me, but Ockham does. Who would he say did it?"

Sebastien was so engrossed in his impromptu lecture that

he forgot about his fear of being ambushed by a predator. He was feeling relaxed, in his element, useful.

"Now you're being a show-off."

"Indulge me."

Tiffany looked back over her right shoulder and said, "Ha! You wish."

"Seriously."

"Well, okay. Let me think for a second. Hmmm. I would have to say it was someone who knew the site was there. Someone who knew the child would be attributed to the archaeological site and not a modern homicide."

"We make a great team, Tiffany."

"Let's see how this case works out before coming to that conclusion. Okay, Ockham?"

Tiffany paused on the trail and pulled out a water bottle. As Sebastien waited for his turn to drink, he looked back in the direction they had come, noticing a drastic change in the land-scape, which had wholly eluded him while he was in deep conversation. The canyon was almost lush now with tall grasses, bushes, and needled pines. The road noise from the highway was now gone too, only wind and the screeching of vigilant hawks broke the stillness.

"Just up here, according to the map." Tiffany pointed ahead to where trees began to hug the trail as it bent to the right. "We'll leave the trail at that curve and walk about fifty yards northwest to the base of that cliff."

Soon the pair were standing shoulder to shoulder at the foot of a tall, craggy rock face, studying the scene diagram and photos that had been in the case binder.

"So that's the cave where the bones were found?" asked Sebastien, pointing at the small opening in the granite.

"Really more of a hole than a cave," answered Tiffany. "But yes, that seems to match up with the photos and the diagram. I don't see any others like it, so I think we're in the right spot."

Tiffany pulled off her backpack and approached the dark cavity with her flashlight.

"I'm going to check it out. Wait here." She knelt down and inched carefully forward.

"Hey, be careful! Maybe I should go in."

Tiffany pulled her head back out of the opening and gave Sebastien a toxic stare.

"Oh, sorry. I just meant, you know, snakes or whatever."

Tiffany said nothing as she resumed her crawl into the narrow hole. Her body began to disappear a few inches at a time as she flexed her knees up then pushed them against the bottom of the cave to propel herself forward. It looked to Sebastien like a granite snake swallowing a lithe, lovely rat in a bizarre peristalsis. Soon, only her black boots were visible.

"I don't see anything except some dirt and sticks and a soda can. Definitely no bones," Tiffany called out.

"How big is it in there? Does it get wider?"

"Nope. It's just a narrow shaft. Goes back maybe six, seven feet."

"Is it all rock, or is there soil in there?"

"No, it's all rock."

Tiffany backed out of the hole and looked around the area.

"What do you think? Is this a major search? Do we need to call out search and rescue?"

Sebastien scanned their surroundings, calculating the relative effort required to cover all of the crevices, crags, bushes, trees, warrens, dens, trails . . .

"In order to do it properly, yes. It would be a massive undertaking. Also, bear in mind that anything left in the open thirty years ago would be reduced to fragments, especially with the array of scavengers out here. I mean, you and I can take a look around. But if our hypothesis is that only the head and limbs were dumped here . . ."

"Which it is," Tiffany interrupted while fingering through her hair for any stowaway debris.

"Yes, which it is. Then everything left here, except for the skull, would be highly portable. I would expect the remaining limbs to have been dragged away from the cave. Maybe even to a pretty great distance. Certainly, the fingers and toes would be in woodrats' nests, birds' nests, gopher holes . . . those kinds of places. The more I think about it, it's a miracle anything was found at all."

Tiffany approached, placed her hands on Sebastien's hips, and caught his eyes with her own.

"Don't you believe in miracles, Dr. Grey?"

"I didn't used to."

The kiss was brief, but it was sufficient to both stir and alarm him. Circumstances, largely beyond his control, at least now, were pulling him far away from his native shore, reversing all his efforts to create a carefully constructed predictability. The contemplation of those wide lips with their sharp vermillion borders, the thin philtrum leading up to her small upturned nose, the pale-lilac lids doming the large caramel eyes swept over by chocolate bangs—it was all too powerful. Fear and anxiety took hold where joy and gratitude should have been, and he hated himself for it. Shelby was right: It was, if he recalled correctly, a misuse of imagination.

"Are you okay, Sebastien? You look distracted."

"I've never kissed someone so beautiful."

It was something of a lie, of course. But it was far better than the truth. Wasn't it?

"Well, thank you. You're a sweet man."

Tiffany retrieved her backpack from the ground and fed her arms through the straps.

"You know what I was thinking?" she asked.

"What's that?"

"We don't even know if the rest of the limbs were put out here. They could be anywhere."

"That's a great point."

"So, coming out here was a waste of time," replied Tiffany, slightly dropping her shoulders.

"Actually, quite the opposite. Coming out here has told us a great deal about this crime. It was a great idea."

"You flatter me. What am I missing?"

"There were no projectiles or casings found when the area was searched originally, correct?"

"Correct. I think they even used metal detectors."

"That's right. So, we can be pretty sure the person was not killed here; he was only dumped here—parts of him, anyway. I mean, I don't think you could get an entire body in that hole. Do you?"

"I doubt it. Our guy was five-nine, give or take. I'm five-eight and I can't get all the way in. Plus, it was barely wide enough for me and I'm a bit of a stick."

"No comment. So, in that case, the head and arms would have been brought out here after they were removed. And the distance from the trailhead to here also suggests that it would have been very difficult to transport an entire body to this location."

"That's true. It's not like you can drive a car or truck up here. Whoever it was probably carted the parts up in a duffle bag or something."

"Exactly," replied Sebastien. "So that further suggests that the rest of the body is somewhere else."

"Like Cheyenne."

"Like Cheyenne," Sebastien repeated. "And it also tells me, suggests to me, that whoever dumped the head and limbs here probably knew the area. They probably knew about these holes and caves and rocks. This place was a deliberate choice, not an opportunistic one."

"In other words, whoever did this was probably a local."

"Yes. A local. And that means . . ."

"We don't have the evidence for Cheyenne's case. They have the evidence for our case," broke in Tiffany, nodding her head in understanding.

"Exactly—assuming I'm right about the Cheyenne torso matching our bones."

"I've only known you a few months, but I've yet to see you get something wrong." Tiffany smiled.

Sebastien replied with a tepid grin.

Tiffany closed the distance between them one more time, curling her index fingers through the belt loops at his hips and smiling into his eyes.

"I'm glad you're here. I know I said that already, but I really am," she said before stealing another brief kiss.

"I've been warned about the winters," Sebastien replied drily before rebuking himself for such a silly response.

Tiffany started back through the trees toward the trail.

"Oh, yeah. You're in for it. You know how many Californians I've seen come up here for the cost of living and no taxes only to run for their lives the first time the wind chill goes below zero? I hope you make it."

"That's why I want my building to sell. I don't want an escape plan. I want to make this work. I want it to be all I have."

"That reminds me, have you thought about getting your own place? You can't stay with Hank forever."

"I definitely want to get out of their way as soon as I can. I don't want to overstay my welcome."

Tiffany suddenly stopped on the trail and turned to face Sebastien.

"You know, I'm always honest. I always say what I think," she said.

"Uh oh. What are you thinking?"

"I would invite you to live with me, but I'm not there yet. We're not there yet. I hope you didn't think . . ."

"No, no. Not at all. Really. I wouldn't want to. I mean, I need to have my space. And, if I'm honest, too, I'm not sure you would want to live with me."

Tiffany turned and resumed walking.

"You're probably right. Your brother tells me your taste in music is pretty questionable. I'll tell you what. Let's go house hunting this weekend. I'll show you around. It'll be fun!"

7

The pair found Hank sitting with two others at a picnic table behind the Sheriff's Office building, fogged in by white smoke and the heavy smell of cigars.

"Sgt. LeGris, Sgt. Adams, Lt. Breed, how are you, sirs?" Tiffany asked deferentially as she and Sebasiten approached.

"Well, hello there, Detective Reese. Who is this you have with you? Taking another one to the drunk tank?"

Sebastien could feel his face catch fire with embarrassment.

"Hey, be nice, Rich. That's our forensic consultant, Dr. Sebastien Grey," cut in Hank. "Dr. Grey, this is Rich Adams, our resident wit. And I believe you know Lt. Breed?"

"I was just kidding, man."

Sgt. Adams extended a massive arm across the table, and the men shook hands.

"Dr. Grey, we are very grateful to have you back and working with us. I understand you plan to stay," said the lieutenant.

"Yes, I do. For a while at least."

"Well, we have a lot riding on these cold cases. People think the government sends you money and calls it good. But the fact is we have to show progress. It's not easy for an agency like ours to get one of these grants, but it's pretty damn easy for it to get taken away."

The statement almost felt like a threat to Sebastien. He glanced over at Tiffany and marked her downward eyes. She was clearly as uncomfortable as he was.

"We got this," replied Hank. "Detective Reese and Dr. Grey briefed me earlier and there are several promising cases to pursue. It's going to be a great first year for the grant."

"Good. I'll expect monthly updates in writing. And we already have a reporter wanting to do a story on it. Reese, I'll send you his info. I want you to speak for us on this."

"Not the PIO?" asked Tiffany.

"Are you the public information officer, detective?"

"No, sir."

"Congratulations. Now, Rich let's get going. We don't want to be late for the sheriff. Oh, and Dr. Grey . . ." The lieutenant turned just before pulling open the back door to the building. "If you have any problems or see any issues, I want you to come to me. Let's be clear about this: You report to me, not your brother." With this, the pair disappeared into the building.

"Ho-ly crap," exclaimed Tiffany. "He knows Sebastien is your brother! How did he find out?"

"You know that saying about how it's better to ask for forgiveness than permission?" replied Hank, pulling the cigar out of his mouth.

The detective and anthropologist both nodded as they slid onto the bench opposite Hank.

"Well, it turns out that's a bunch of BS. Somehow, Lt. Breed figured it out. He called me in this morning and asked if there was anything about our consultant that he should know. I came clean."

"Geez, was he mad?" asked Tiffany.

"Should I leave?" added Sebastien.

"No, and no. He's fine. You know me. I can talk the yellow off a fire hydrant. It's good."

"Except for the part about me reporting to him," replied Sebastien with his elbows on the table and hands open in front of his face.

"Actually, that's the best part. This makes you truly independent. And . . ."

Hank turned his head away from the table and launched into a coughing and hacking fit before spitting a massive gob of phlegm into the bushes.

"Sorry. Anyway, as long as you don't screw anything up, it will give Breed the impression I know what I'm doing."

"You mean, make him think all is well?" replied Sebastien.

"That's right, doctor. You keep thinking like that and you'll be ready for management."

Sebastien knew this was meant to dispel the tension and make light of things. But he wasn't buying it. Sebastien wondered what was going through Tiffany's mind.

"What do you think, Tiffany?" he asked.

"I agree with Hank. It makes sense and it puts a little professional distance between us."

"Great minds, you and I, Reese," Hank responded.

"By the way, when did you start smoking cigars, boss?" Tiffany made a disgusted face.

"I just took it up."

"Clearly," grinned Sebastien.

Hank poked the ashen tip of the cigar across the table.

"And don't either of you tell Melissa. Not yet anyway."

Tiffany waved her hand in an effort to disperse the accumulating miasma.

"Why? I mean, why did you start smoking cigars? You don't exactly make it look fun," she asked.

"I'll tell you why. He's always trying to fit in. Always wanting to be one of the cool kids," remarked Sebastien with crossed arms and a sly grin.

Hank jabbed his cigar in his brother's direction. "There's a lot to be said for fitting in, little brother. It's wouldn't hurt you to try it for once."

Sebastien was stung, but knew he'd asked for it, and the truth of Hank's statement could not be ignored.

"So, anyway. Tell me about your day. How did the Bobbsey Twins make out with day one of cold case domination?"

"Don't you remember from the briefing we had earlier?" Tiffany laughed.

"Hey, never mind what I told Breed. And you, my friend, still report to me. So don't get snippy," Hank said, smiling past the fat cigar that was now awkwardly bobbing as he spoke.

"We actually made some progress," said Sebastien. "We have a good candidate for DNA analysis already."

"Yep, and we think we've matched an old case with one that Cheyenne PD has. It goes all the way to the late eighties. We're heading down there tomorrow to meet with the detective and the coroner."

"See? That's great stuff. Turns out I do know what I'm doing."

Tiffany straightened her back and removed her sunglasses.

"Sarge, do you remember the Amber Harrison case? It's from 2013."

Hank stroked his goatee as he considered the question.

"2013? Oh, sure. But I was on patrol at the time, if I recall."

"Did you work it?"

"Respond, you mean? No. I was never on the beat where her car was found. Are you thinking about tackling that one? Have you read the file?"

"Yes, we did," she answered. "And we talked about it. We think we should move that to the top of our list."

Sebastien nodded vigorously in agreement, though his eyes were far away, fixed on the surface of the picnic table.

"That's not really a DNA case, is it?" replied Hank. "I mean, we know the blood in her car belongs to her. But, as I recall, nobody quite agreed on whether it was enough to suggest she was seriously injured. She just disappeared."

"Disappeared but possibly injured, and we can't rule out foul play. But you're right. It's not really a DNA case," Tiffany admitted with a hint of disappointment.

"What do you think, Sebastien? You look like you have something to offer here."

Sebastien was pensively tracing his finger around a knot in the table. The Harrison case bothered him. It seemed like the general opinion of the public held more weight for the Sheriff's Office than the fact that blood was found in the car. Although he was certainly one to follow his hunches, hard science always trumped supposition. But in this case, it didn't. In fact, the scientific avenues were mostly ignored. This wasn't the first time he had run into this problem. Several years ago, he worked a case in which a potential homicide victim's arm bone was found in a creek. He offered to take his students to the recovery scene to see what else could be found, but the investigating agency refused to let him search the area, nor would they bother to search it themselves. They were too busy, they'd said; there were too many murders on their plate. And, moreover, the victim was known to be homeless and there was no proof it was a homicide anyway. *Well, no duh*, he told them. *Proof doesn't just jump into your evidence bag. You have to go search for it*. The idiots remained unmoved, and to this day, the case is unresolved.

"Well, unless I read the file wrong," began Sebastien, "or missed something, the only DNA testing that was done was on the blood in the driver's seat. Nothing in the car was tested. And touch DNA was not collected."

"Like I said, they couldn't agree on foul play. And did they have touch DNA back then?" asked Hank.

"Yes, they should have," answered Sebastien firmly.

Tiffany broke in, tapping a cadence into the surface of the table with the tip of her index finger as she spoke.

"But that's the point. We'd like to go back to square one and see if any items from the car are still in property. Maybe there is some testing that can be done."

"That works for me," said the sergeant. "It's a big enough case. People are still talking about it."

"Exactly. And no one has heard from her still; it's looking less likely that her disappearance was voluntary—especially in light of the blood, which no one outside of law enforcement knows about."

"That's a mistake," said Sebastien. "If the public knew it was possibly a homicide, they may have been more likely to share information, to talk about anything that seemed suspicious. But as long as people think she just went away, anyone who thinks they saw something important might dismiss it rather than report it."

"These are good points," observed Hank.

"So we'll go ahead and look into it." Tiffany's voice was now more eager.

"Wait. Just hang on. You both are right. But this will be one of those retrospective deals, a Monday morning quarterback thing."

"What do you mean?" asked Sebastien.

"He means it's now political," said Tiffany, shaking her head and crossing her arms.

"Now don't panic, detective. You two check out your Cheyenne angle and I'll shake the trees on the Harrison case, see what kind of appetite we have for it. Now, if you'll excuse me, I have to go throw up and brush my teeth."

∾

THE *EX-CATHEDRA* OFFICE of the *Custer County Signal* consisted of a small desk tucked into a basement corner in a small split-level home on 1st Street. The desk itself was superposed by three large computer monitors, an open laptop, a small digital voice recorder, assorted notepads and sticky notes, a digital camera, and a crude ceramic cat head performing the service of a paperweight. The room's walls were covered with various posters reflecting the interests of the *Signal's* own editor-in-chief. In addition to the extra-large *X-Files* "I Want to Believe" poster mounted just above the desk, there was also a signed headshot of Gillian Anderson herself; a wide placard bearing the elemental symbols for nitrogen, erbium, and dysprosium (NErDy); a huge map of the Black Hills and surrounding environs; and a large, framed likeness of a cover from *Real Crime* magazine circa 1947.

It was upon this latter image that Derek Manly fixed his eyes after hanging up the phone. The large-chested, blond woman on the poster held a smoking gun and was naked, save for a blue towel around her torso. She stared down at him with a knowing grin, as if to say, "go get 'em, Derek." Behind her, slumped in an armchair, was a dead man.

And indeed, Derek Manly had every intention of going and getting. After several weeks of covering news of the trivial and tedious varieties (car wrecks, the Buffalo Roundup, the grand opening of a feed store, high-school football matchups), he was due for something juicy. Granted, the *Custer County Signal* was on online-only newspaper, and really more of a blog than a newspaper, but it was also inescapable that the *Signal's* readers had high expectations for both the quality and significance of the publication's output. After all, it was the *Signal* that uncovered the bribery scandal in the school district. It was the *Signal* that was the first media outlet to report on the arrest of that lady who knifed her boyfriend in her Hermosa mobile home. And it was Derek's own dogged investigative journalism that exposed those "bigfoot hunters" who were growing pot in the hills east of Pringle. This was the kind of hard-hitting reportage his readers demanded. Not to mention the triple facts that his mortgage was due, his alimony was behind, and his advertising income was, well, a little sparse lately.

Yes, it was time for something big. He was due. And what a lucky break! He was the only reporter who bothered to show up at the Board of Supervisors meeting last month when the sheriff happened to be giving a budget presentation and, wouldn't you know, the sheriff also happened to mention something about a cold case grant and the formation of a cold case unit. And DNA. And mysteries yet to be solved. And families in despair. Just in time for Halloween. Just in time for the holidays. Some might call it a fortuitous coincidence. But none of those people knew about Manly's carefully groomed source within the Sheriff's Office. This was the kind of hard work and self-sacrifice upon which his readers insisted.

That detective who called him back wasn't super helpful though. She wouldn't give any details about specific cases that are being re-opened as part of the grant, or information on how those cases are going to be approached.

"Are you going to look into the Amber Harrison murder?" he'd asked the detective.

"I'm not aware of that being a homicide, Mr. Manly," she'd said. "Adults are allowed to move out of the area, aren't they?"

"How about that Cleary lady? The one left in the field where the supermarket is now. You know her granddaughter owns an ice cream shop in Keystone?"

"That would certainly be on our list" is all the detective would say.

"Well, what about that guy who killed his wife back in '78? Rumor has it he killed her boyfriend too."

"Like I said, Mr. Manly, we are really just getting started. But, believe me, we will need the help of the public and the media if we are going to bring resolution to these cases and closure to the families of the victims. We will certainly let you know if we develop anything significant in these old investigations."

Ah, yes, Derek. You sly bugger. They don't know who they're dealing with.

"I'm sorry, Detective Reese, but who do you mean by 'we'? How many detectives are working on these cases?"

"Well, we don't have much of a grant, so it's a small team. Really just myself and a forensic anthropologist."

"You mean like on that TV show?"

"Ha! Sure. Something like that."

It was a little weird that she laughed like that. But whatever.

"You must have specific cases in mind if you brought in an anthropologist," he had insisted.

"Yes, there are a number of cases where we will need to get another examination of the victim's remains. But Dr. Grey is also an expert investigator. I'm sure you've heard about the bodies that were recovered in the hills this past summer."

"Oh, it's that guy?"

"Yes. Dr. Grey has graciously agreed to lend his support to our cold case investigations."

"Wasn't he also involved in the case with the lady who . . ."

"Yes, Mr. Manly. As I mentioned, he is a capable investigator and an experienced forensic scientist. We are lucky to have him."

"Hey, do you think your forensic anthropologist would mind doing an interview? And you, too, of course."

"Oh no, you don't need me. But he's all yours. His name is

Dr. Sebastien Grey. That's Sebastien with an 'ien' and Grey with an 'e.'"

How's that for a special Halloween edition, eh? Skeletons, death, murder. Right here in our sleepy little tourist trap. Manly, you did it again.

One more glance up at the *Real Crime* magazine poster got Derek wondering what that Detective Reese looked like. Did she have blond hair? Was she built like the lady in the poster? Had she ever shot anyone and stood over the corpse, blowing the gunpowder smoke from the barrel of a Smith & Wesson Model 27? Did she own a blue towel?

TIFFANY THREW her phone on the bed and got in the shower. She had hoped to get rid of that reporter a little more quickly. Now she would have to hurry to get ready for her dinner with Sebastien. To be honest, the call irritated her somewhat. She did not anticipate such rabid media interest in the cold cases. That was always a bad sign. And that Manly guy seemed a little too eager, too pushy. She hoped he would not cause trouble.

As she tipped her head back to let the warm water rinse the shampoo from her hair, Tiffany's mind turned toward Sebastien. She would have to warn him about Manly. And, of course, downplay her own culpability in roping him into the interview. She wondered how he would take it, wondered if he would be upset with her. It was difficult to imagine, but if she was to be honest with herself, she didn't really know him *that* well. Everything has moved along so fast.

There was one thing she was certain about. Sebastien was not the media-savvy type. He wasn't even much of a people person. How was it that he once explained it? "I'm an acquired taste and best in small doses." All things considered, maybe this interview was a bad move. What if he said something he shouldn't? What if Manly tricked him into talking too much? About what though? There really isn't much to say at this point, is there?

Suddenly aware of her mind wandering against the clock, Tiffany hurriedly finished her shower, wrapped a blue bath towel around her naked torso, and went to search her closet for something to wear.

8

Tiffany picked up Sebastien before daylight and they made their way southward. The duo made their first stop in Edgemont to grab some breakfast.

"By the way, I forgot to mention last night that I talked to that reporter—the one the lieutenant asked me to call," Tiffany said matter-of-factly as she poured ketchup on her hash browns.

"Oh? How'd that go?"

"He's very interested in the whole cold case unit thing. And he's well-acquainted with some of the more high-profile cases."

"You mean like this one? The Hell Canyon remains?"

"Well, no. He didn't mention this one. But he did ask if we were looking into the Amber Harrison murder."

Sebastien looked up from his omelet in an expression of concern.

"You heard that right. He called it a murder."

"Nothing like a little pressure," quipped Sebastien.

"Exactly. Oh, and speaking of the reporter, you might be getting a call from him."

Sebastien dropped his fork on his plate with a *clink* and instinctively crossed his arms.

"What? It's not a big deal, Sebastien. He just wants to learn more about your work. He's very impressed by what you were able to do for us on the biker homicides."

A surge of alarm spread through Sebastien, starting, as it often did, at his upper thighs and working its way into his chest where it twisted into a grip. He sat back in his chair and looked into the pretty oval face across the table, which carried a look of disarming affability—as if this were not a big deal. Now was the time, he realized, to suck it up. *Do not show your pathetic insecurities, Sebastien. Act normal. Make that sacrifice. For her.*

Sebastien forced his voice into an even tone as he asked, "How does this reporter even know about me? How does anyone know about me?"

"This isn't the Bay Area, Sebastien. It's not easy to fly under the radar in this town. People talk. You should know that. After all, you remember why your brother asked you up here in the first place, don't you? It was all the rumors about a man-eating cougar running through town. He needed to get to the truth, to contain it, before real panic set in. Those same wagging tongues have been talking about the brilliant and handsome Dr. Grey who came to save them."

It took Sebastien a second before he fully broke down what Tiffany had just said. His left hand found his smooth chin as he worked through it.

"I didn't realize I had made that kind of an impact or that I had saved anyone. And, by the way, I have never been accused of being handsome. You can't lay that one on me."

Tiffany smiled widely and pointed a fork-impaled hash brown at him. "Oh really? Dr. Grey, if being attractive was a crime, I'd have you in cuffs right now."

Such a response was fully and genuinely unexpected. He forced himself to make a humble reply. "Thank you, Tiffany."

"You're welcome. So, just be aware that this guy is going to call you. He seems pretty shifty to me, so be careful. He may try to trick you."

"Trick me?"

"Well, you know. Trick you into saying something about what we're working on. Obviously, it's too early to discuss this case, or any others."

"For sure. I'll keep it generic. If he calls, that is."

"Thank you, Sebastien."

"Sure. I fully plan on leaving all of the public stuff to you and Hank. It may be hard to stay out of the public eye, but it suits me better."

"No, I mean thank you for being okay with meeting the reporter. I'm glad you aren't upset with me."

"I don't think I could ever be upset with you."

"Oh, you can. And you will. Now, finish up that omelet and let's get rolling. We have to meet the Cheyenne detective at the torso scene at eleven."

TIFFANY MADE a right turn into a subdivision just on the northern edge of Cheyenne. One- and two-story houses of brick and wood siding flanked the streets. Their driveways, if not empty, displayed mid-to-high-end trucks, SUVs, and sedans. The grass in all of the yards was well manicured, though yellowing in preparation for the winter torpor. Mature spruce and pine stood guard throughout the neighborhood, as if to ward off the high-desert landscape that dominated outside of this bucolic enclave.

One block into the neighborhood, Tiffany made another right turn onto Boxwood Avenue. Sebastien tried to square what he was seeing with the image of a smoldering, dismembered human torso. The math was not adding up. This was clearly a nice neighborhood, not a place for villainy and mayhem of any kind, much less the violent varieties.

A man in a green down jacket, jeans, and cowboy boots emerged from his parked Chevy Malibu and walked toward them as Tiffany pulled to the curb in front of number 1487.

"Detective Reese. Hello, I'm Detective Aaron Kelly with the CPD. Thanks for coming all the way down. That's a helluva drive."

Tiffany shook hands with the middle-aged man with a graying beard and longish dark hair.

"Thanks for meeting us. This is Dr. Sebastien Grey. He's our forensic anthropologist."

Sebastien took the man's hand and offered a polite "good to meet you."

His Barbour field jacket would not protect him from the biting wind, Sebastien quickly realized. He cursed himself as he watched Tiffany reach into the back seat for her parka.

"So, this is the place?" Tiffany asked as she poked her right arm through a puffy blue sleeve.

"Yes, it is, although it was very different thirty-three years ago. There wasn't a house here yet, just an empty lot. And everything north of here on both sides was also just lots. The houses hadn't been built yet, but the ones you passed on the street coming up were."

Detective Kelly waved a long arm, like an orchestra conductor, to emphasize his description of the neighborhood.

"Were you with the department then, Detective Kelly?" Tiffany asked, looking dubious.

"Oh, heck no. Not by a long shot. I was just asked to review everything so I could fill you in."

Sebastien thought he detected a tinge of lust in the detective's eyes as he addressed Tiffany. He impulsively checked the man's left hand for a wedding ring before reproving himself.

"That's great, det—"

"Call me Aaron," the detective interrupted.

"Okay. In that case, call me Tiffany. And this is Sebastien. So, Aaron, all we know on our end is that the torso was found down here. It had been set on fire. Our anthropologist at the time checked our remains to see if what we had could match what you had."

"And what did you have?"

Sebastien spoke up. "We have a skull, some vertebrae, and a leg bone."

"Damn. That's one helluva of a coincidence. No wonder you thought you had a match. When was your stuff found?"

Detective Kelly sure likes the word *helluva*, thought Sebastien.

"Eighty-eight," said Tiffany. "About eleven months after your torso was dumped. But, at the time, a connection between the two cases was ruled out. Sebastien thinks that was a mistake, that they're from the same person."

"I think you are on to something," Detective Kelly said, addressing Sebastien.

"Oh? Why's that?" asked Tiffany.

Detective Kelly pointed to the one-story ranch-style house just in front of them.

"When the torso was found, this lot here had nothing on it but a construction trailer and a backhoe parked farther back behind the trailer. On the day in question, a neighbor comes up from down there, the south end of the street. Those houses, some of them anyway, were occupied. That was the first phase of the development. Anyway, the guy comes out of his house to check for the paper and sees the smoke down the street. He runs up to check it out and thinks it's coming from the trailer. But as he gets closer, he sees it's actually coming from outside the trailer."

"Could he tell what was on fire?" asked Tiffany.

"At first it just looked like some branches. But he said it smelled like hell, like gas on a hog."

"Gas?" queried Sebastien.

"Affirmative. The backhoe that was on the lot had been siphoned and used to start the fire. The guy didn't know that, of course. We figured that out later."

"Then burning it was not necessarily the plan? That was a spur of the moment thing," observed Tiffany. "Were there any witnesses?"

"No one was living on this end of the street, like I said. And when we canvassed the occupied houses, no one reported seeing or hearing a car."

"Any fingerprints on the backhoe?'

"Negative. Which, by the way, is itself suspicious."

"Detective Kelly, you said you thought we were on to something. Why is that?"

Sebastien couldn't bring himself to use the detective's first name.

"That's where I was going with this. There was one guy who said he heard kids playing around in the middle of the night, like teenagers running around or something."

"Really?" replied Tiffany.

Sebastien was truly beginning to freeze and hoped this was getting somewhere quickly. He shoved his hands deep into the front pockets of his cotton chinos.

"Yeah, but here's the thing, the guy said he lives down the road, a few houses past that street on the left. But when we canvassed, we found out that the house he said he lived in was actually unoccupied. It had sold, but it hadn't closed yet. No one was living there."

"How'd they get the guy's statement, then?"

"We didn't, technically. But when the fire department was putting out the fire, a small crowd of people came up to watch. They were standing on the other side of the road, over there. The guy I'm taking about was in that crowd. He walks up to the police tape and asks one of the officers about the fire."

"What do you mean asked about the fire?" asked Sebastien. "What specifically did he ask?"

"Well, doctor, he specifically asked what was on fire."

"Interesting," murmured Sebastien.

"Anyway, the officer asked him if he saw or heard anything, and that's when he tells him about the kids he heard in the middle of the night."

"Did he get the guy's name?" Tiffany had pulled out her ratty spiral notebook and was poised to write.

"Bob Jones."

"So that's a no," Tiffany replied, tucking her pen back into the inside pocket of her parka.

"That's a no. But here's where it gets interesting. After the guy disappeared, the original detectives followed up with the neighbors who were standing in the crowd to see if anyone knew who the guy was. No one did, which is not super surprising since the neighborhood was basically new. But one person did say she saw the man get in a blue pickup truck and drive away."

"Really?" Tiffany exclaimed for the second time.

"I don't suppose they got the plate?" asked Sebastien.

"Not the number, but the state. Wanna take a guess?" Detective Kelly gave a smirk as he leaned back on the rear of his car and folded his arms.

"South . . ." began Sebastien

" . . . Dakota," finished Tiffany.

"You guessed it. And there was something else the neighbor saw. There was another person in the truck. A man was in the passenger seat."

Tiffany and Sebastien gave each other a look of muted excitement.

"What did the Cheyenne PD do with that information?" asked Tiffany.

"There was nothing about that in our file," added Sebastien. "When the Custer detective made contact after our remains were found, there was no mention of the man, the truck, or the truck being from South Dakota."

"I'm not surprised. It was quickly assumed that there was some sort of mix-up, either with the house the guy lived in or with what the neighbor saw. At most, it was believed the guy was just a bystander who couldn't be tracked down. I mean, why would the person who dumped and set fire to the victim come back? That lead was buried. And as far as what CPD did with the case? Well, we did the usual. We beat the bushes around town to see if anyone knew of anything. We checked missing persons."

"Any efforts to ID the victim?"

"How?" replied Detective Kelly to Sebastien with a somewhat snarky tone. "No fingers to print. No dental to check against. And DNA was not a thing then. There wasn't a helluva lot we could do."

"But what about subsequently? Since the original investigation, I mean. Have you tried DNA since then?" asked Tiffany.

"The lab thinks it's too burned up to try."

Tiffany looked at Sebastien. "Guess you were right."

"Detective Kelly, you said the torso was on fire outside of the trailer."

"That's right."

"Was the trailer burned at all?"

"Negative."

"Interesting. Do you mind if we get a copy of the report?"

The detective stood up, pulled his car keys from his jacket pocket, and pointed the fob over his shoulder. The trunk clicked free and the detective turned and reached into the darkness.

~

SEBASTIEN SCANNED through the report as Tiffany drove northward, away from the Laramie County Coroner's Office. Detective Kelly had only made copies of the original report, the autopsy report, and most presciently, the supplement describing the encounter with "Bob Jones."

"It says here, late thirties to mid-forties, about five foot ten, dark-brown hair, mustache. He was wearing jeans, a black jacket, and an orange knit cap. The truck was described as a long bed Chevy Silverado, blue with a silver stripe along the side. There was a truck box in the bed. No real description of the passenger. The witness just had the 'impression' it was a male."

"What do you think, Sebastien? CPD has a point. I mean, why would the guy, or guys, come back to the scene after they set the torso on fire?"

"Lots of reasons. Maybe they came back to see if the body was burned all the way. Or maybe it was just a curiosity thing. Arsonists are well known to watch the fires they set. That's the main thrill for them in a lot of cases."

"I suppose so. Seems pretty risky though, especially since there is way more than arson here."

"Is it though?" Sebastien challenged her. "It seems the opposite to me. I mean, with a fire situation, you expect to get crowds of onlookers. And you expect some of those onlookers to ask about the fire. Plus, there's the general chaos of the fire department scrambling around. No, I think the fact that we have a South Dakota connection in the truck is way too compelling to rule out 'Bob Jones.' In fact, I'd be willing to bet he's our guy."

"Too bad we couldn't get DNA to compare with our remains."

"Yeah, that would have been nice, but you just saw for

yourself: when I put our third cervical vertebra against the fourth cervical from the torso in the Coroner's Office, it was a very good match—despite the fire damage. And the tool marks matched up perfectly too. I feel fine about our cases connecting. I think we'll get the final resolution to that at some point."

Tiffany looked over at him and grinned.

"I just love that you keep saying 'our.' Our vertebra, our case, our file."

Sebastien wasn't sure if there was sarcasm in this. The mental gymnastics must have shown on his face.

"You don't have to overthink that, Sebastien. I'm just really glad that you feel like a part of this, that you feel you belong here. Because you do."

"I'm very happy you feel that way."

"You know what I'm not feeling?"

Uh oh. "What?"

"That fancy jacket. You're going to freeze your giblets off and it's not even winter yet."

"Oh, trust me. I've figured that out."

"We'll add that to the weekend plans—house hunting and winter wardrobe—but be warned: I'm not sure we'll find your high-end clothing in our little burg."

"I'm not that snobby."

"Sure you are. But I like that about you. It makes you different."

"Hank says I use snobbery as a social buffer."

"Oh, you totally do. I think it's adorable, although your hoity-toity taste in music is sure to take a beating up here."

The next three and a half hours went by too quickly for Sebastien as the pair made their way back up to Custer. Their conversations spanned topics such as family (hers), international travel (his), and the relative benefits of wildlife crossings over busy highways. Also, Sebastien learned that

Tiffany has not just one brother, but also a brother who is a full-time rodeo clown.

"What is a rodeo clown?" he asked her.

"You know. He's the guy who runs in front of the bull to distract it from stomping on the bull rider. It's not just that though. They have to be funny too. There's this whole schtick they do to get the crowd involved."

"Is there money in being a rodeo clown?"

"There must be. My brother has a $70,000 RV. He travels a lot though. That's the hard part. But he's not married and has no kids, so I guess that's not so bad."

"How do your parents feel about his choice of career?"

"Is this the snob coming out?" she laughed, squeezing his knee. "I'm just kidding, Sebastien. Actually, my dad is probably prouder of him than he is of his two kids in law enforcement. You see, he was a rodeo clown too, until an injury forced him to quit."

AN HOUR OR SO LATER, after switching drivers, Sebastien looked at Tiffany who was fast asleep in the passenger seat. A sliver of pale moonlight fell across her face, causing her lip gloss to sparkle. He wondered if it would wake her if he took her hand in his. He dared himself to try, but before he could reach out, she began to stir. He quickly returned his right hand to the steering wheel only for Tiffany to pull it off and lay his arm around her neck and shoulders. She then leaned against him and closed her eyes.

Sebastien realized he was in a good mood. A very good mood, in fact. His certainty about the Hell Canyon remains and the Cheyenne torso being from the same person was nearing 100 percent. And he had learned today that he was, in fact, handsome. And he did, also in fact, belong. And the woman of a lifetime was nestled comfortably up to his chest, the fruity scent of her shampoo filling his nose. The move from California was starting to look and feel good. He hoped, crossed his fingers even, that things wouldn't change.

Still, there was some small thing bothering him. There was something about this case he could not quite put his finger on. He traced the events of the day in his mind, but the erstwhile cause of concern was utterly eluding him. Maybe he was just too tired. Maybe the lights of the oncoming cars were stultifying him, whizzing by and hypnotizing him into a stupor of thought. This was dangerous, he realized. He'd better focus on the road. Sebastien rolled his window down an inch and stared forward, trying to keep himself alert by naming all of Verdi's operas, in order, along with where and when they premiered. *Snobbery for the win.*

9

"You came in late last night, sunshine."

Sebastien looked up from the file he was reading as Hank took a seat opposite him at the LeGris dining room table.

"Yeah, well . . . it was long trip."

"Remind me again what that case is about," Hank asked, dumping a packet of sugar into his coffee.

"Our end of it goes back to 1988. That September, hikers in Hell Canyon found some human remains. There was as skull, some vertebrae, and a leg bone. When I was going through the file, I saw a reference to a report out of Cheyenne concerning a dismembered torso that was found in '87."

"You think ours and Cheyenne's are connected?"

"I do. At the time, a connection was ruled out based on estimated statures. But I think that was a mistake. Bad science, if you will."

"I will," replied Hank with a wink. "And what did you find out in Cheyenne?"

"There was a witness who saw a truck with South Dakota plates near where the torso was found."

"Hot damn," Hank exclaimed over the sound of his spoon stirring the sugar into his coffee.

Kirby emerged from the kitchen wearing her pink unicorn pajamas. The little blond six-year-old tugged at Hank's sleeve in urgency.

"Daddy! Daddy!"

"What is it, sweetheart?" Hank pulled her in close and kissed her on the crown of her head.

"Purple won't eat his breakfast."

"Purple? Who's Purple, Kirby?"

"I think she means Parsifal," offered Sebastien.

"Oh. Well, Purple's name is really Parsifal. Can you say it with me? Par-si-fall."

"No, that's a dumb name. His name is Purple."

Hank looked over at Sebastien with an unvoiced laugh. Sebastien shrugged ambivalently in return.

"Okay. Why won't Purple eat his breakfast? What *is* Purple's breakfast?"

"Cereal. I'm sharing with him."

"That is very nice of you, honey. But I'm not sure Purple wants cereal for breakfast. What do you think, Uncle Sebastien?"

"I think you are very nice for sharing your breakfast with Par—, er, Purple. But I think he would like his own food better. Come on, let me show you where his food is and how he likes to be fed."

"O-kay. Thank you, Uncle Sebastien."

"Kirby!"

"She's in here, Melissa."

"Oh, there you are," said Melissa. "Kirby, what happened in the kitchen? Why is there cereal on the floor and how did poor Parsifal get milk on his head?"

"I'm sorry, Mommy."

"Kirby and I were just going to take care of that," said

Sebastien as he took the little girl's hand and led her into the kitchen.

"Well, that was nice," said Melissa, sitting down at the table.

Hank let out a laugh. "She's named the dog Purple. That'll teach Sebastien not to name his dog after a stupid opera character. Dweeb."

"Be nice. Isn't it sweet though? He's doing really well with Kirby."

Melissa gazed wistfully toward the sound of dog food being poured into a metal bowl.

"Yeah, he is. He's always been a good guy. It's just the shy thing that makes it hard."

"I think he's doing better, don't you?"

"For sure."

"I wonder why that is though. I mean, it's great. But I wonder what the difference is."

"If you ask me, it helps a lot that he's not locked away in his apartment in Vineyard. That can't be healthy."

"That's true. And he's around family. And Tiffany."

Hank nodded and swallowed a mouthful of coffee. "Now that's probably the biggest thing. Tiffany wouldn't tolerate the withering flower crap. She forces him out of his shell. Plus, he's used to talking to dead people all day—being around them, I mean. You know, just bones and decomposing corpses. No need to be charming in the morgue."

"Speaking of charming, thank you for that visual."

"Sorry, dear."

"Aren't you a little worried though? About them working together and seeing each other?"

"Yes, I am a bit."

Hank stared out the front picture window, working on his coffee while Melissa feigned examination of the file Sebastien had been reading.

"I need to get one of those leaf blowers. Raking is such a hassle," Hank declared.

"Hank, do you think maybe you lured Sebastien up here with Tiffany as bait?"

"Huh? What's that supposed to mean?"

"I don't mean on purpose. But let's face it. He was a huge help this summer and having him here means he can continue helping. Plus, you missed him. You two didn't talk much for years. Now you have your brother back."

"Well, I certainly did not lure him."

"Okay, okay. Lure was the wrong word. I'm sorry, sweetheart. But knowing he's lonely and seeing how they hit it off so well when he was here, I guess it just makes sense to sort of package all of that together as an added benefit to moving here."

"You know, I never told you this, but Sebastien and Tiffany had been talking a lot since he left here in August. Like, every day talking. So no, I had no idea that was part of the package. But I know what you're saying."

"I think Tiffany is lonely too."

"*Was*, you mean?"

"How do we keep this from going sideways? Workwise. Familywise."

"We don't," replied Hank. "They're adults. We'll deal with it however it turns out."

Melissa leaned over and kissed her husband on the lips.

"I'm going to go hop in the shower, my wise old man."

"Right back at ya, old lady."

Melissa gave Hank a smack on the shoulder blade.

"Ow! Kidding, sweetheart. Kidding."

"ABOUT TIME YOU SHOWED UP," declared Tiffany as Sebastien walked into the cramped storage room-turned-office.

"How long have you been here?"

"Long enough to pull a list of all eighties Chevy trucks registered in every county west of the river."

"Which river are we talking about?"

"Really?"

"I'm not from around here. Remember?"

"The Missouri River cuts the state in half, north to south. South Dakotans generally identify as being from either west or east of the river. There's quite the competition between the two, in fact. You've been warned."

"Thanks. So, what are we looking at? A long list?" Sebastien leaned over the desk to get a better look.

"A few hundred. It could be worse, for sure. But either way it's a long shot. For all we know, the Chevy in question is now a three-by-three cube in a scrapyard somewhere. Maybe even in a different state. The truck may not help us at all."

"I agree. The truck is the wrong thread to pull, although the list may very well come in handy later. It's good we have it."

"Okay, then. What thread *do* we pull? The description of the guy in the knit cap is super generic, and if he's still alive, he'll have changed a lot since then."

Sebastien dropped the case files in front of Tiffany and perched himself on the edge of her desk.

"Let's step back a bit and look at the big picture, look at the whole thing."

Tiffany leaned back in her chair, intrigued.

Sebastien continued. "We're approaching this from the assumption that our skull and Cheyenne's torso are from the same victim. And I think that is most likely correct."

"We've established that. But now what?"

"Again, big picture. How far is Cheyenne from Hell Canyon?"

"I don't really know, exactly. But Cheyenne is about 250 miles from Custer. I can plot it out on the map and find out if we need to know exactly."

Tiffany leaned forward and poised her fingers over her laptop keyboard.

"There's no need. The bottom line is that there is a relatively huge distance between the two recoveries—massive compared to other similar types of cases where body parts are in different locations."

"Yeah, I can't imagine why anyone would go that far, especially when there is so much land between here and Cheyenne. There would be millions of places a lot closer to Custer to dump a body. I mean, Hell Canyon is the obvious one. Why not just put the whole thing out there? Cut it up, spread it around. Why go that far?"

"Yes, and why go to that exact location? The construction site, I mean. That neighborhood."

"Hmm," Tiffany thought for a moment. "It's just about the farthest point north in the city of Cheyenne, especially back then. So it would be the closest place in Cheyenne from Custer."

"Sure. But who cares about how close it is when you just drove 250 miles? What's an extra block, or mile, or five miles? Why not the south side of Cheyenne? Or farther west? Or east? East of the river?"

"The Missouri River does not go through Wyoming. It's basically the eastern border of Nebraska. I thought you were educated?"

"You know what I mean."

"Yes, I do. And you have a great point. I don't suppose you have any suggestions?"

"There was something that Cheyenne detective said that nagged at me. But I couldn't put my finger on it until this morning when I re-read the case files he gave us."

Sebastien tapped a finger against the folder on the desk.

Tiffany leaned back again. Sebastien noticed for the first time that her hair had been gently curled and her brown eyes were lightly brushed in peach eye shadow. Her cheeks bore the faintest hint of a matching blush, from the strong jut of her zygomatic arches down to where her zygomaxillary suture would be. *Good grief, what a lovely face,* he thought.

"Well? Are you going to leave me hanging?" she asked.

"Detective Kelly said the backhoe was behind the trailer."

"Did he?"

Sebastien flipped open the Cheyenne file and turned to a drawing about ten pages into the report.

"He did. And the scene diagram in the report shows that it was. See?"

Tiffany tilted her head to get a better look.

Sebastien continued: "Now, gas from the backhoe was used to start the fire. So, we can assume a couple of things. First, the suspect knew that the backhoe, the source of the fuel, was there. It was not visible from the street, or at least not very visible, because it was behind the construction trailer."

"That would mean the fire was not opportunistic. It was part of the original plan."

"Exactly. Which leads to the second thing. It would be different if the rest of the body were local to the torso site. In that case, you could argue that the fire was . . . what do you call that thing in football when the guy who throws the ball changes the play?"

"Are you joking with me right now? It's called an audible and the guy you reference is called the quarterback. You have me worried."

Sebastien ignored the statement.

"An audible. If the suspect were local, we might say setting fire to the torso was an audible. But since the construction site is so far from Hell Canyon, we can suppose that the suspect intentionally went there and that the gas was part of the reason."

"That seems a little shaky to me. I mean, there would be plenty of places to stop and get gas along the way."

"Yes, and that's why I said it was only *part* of the reason."

"What would be the rest of the reason?" Tiffany asked.

"The trailer. I think the torso was meant to be in the trailer when the fire was lit. I believe both the torso and the trailer were supposed to go up in flames. Maybe our suspects thought they could burn down the trailer and the torso would be reduced to the point of being unidentifiable."

"Then why put the rest of the body in Hell Canyon?"

"The hands and the teeth? Insurance against identification."

"They didn't recover the hands, Sebastien."

"They're there. Somewhere."

"But the torso was not in the trailer. If your theory is correct, then why? Why was it left outside?"

"That I don't know."

Tiffany thought for moment, then stood up behind the desk, tapping a knuckle against its surface as she continued thinking.

"If the trailer was the target, that means the construction company is the thread," she finally muttered, almost to herself.

"I think you're right, boss."

"What do mean I'm right? You're the one who fig . . . Where are you going?"

"I have to meet that reporter while you question whomever that trailer belonged to."

"Wait. We don't even know if that construction company is still around."

"Check supplement two, the list of witnesses on the A page. The first guy listed is still alive, although he's in Nebraska now."

"How . . ."

Sebastien made a right turn out of the office toward the back door of the building. Had he passed anyone on his way out, they would have marked the enormous smile on the well-dressed young man.

~

TIFFANY SHOOK her head as she flipped open the folder with the Cheyenne reports. *Why didn't the little jerk just come out and say it from the start instead of leading her to it? Damn show-off. And what did he mean, 'while you question whomever that trailer belonged to'? He's not the boss. I am.*

Dana Redmond, age thirty-two in 1987, was listed as a witness in the original report. Redmond, Tiffany came to learn, was part of a crew from L&J Reinforcing that was working in the neighborhood, three blocks from the trailer site, when the call was made to the fire department. He had not been to the construction trailer, nor was it his habit of doing so before starting his work. Redmond and two others were laying rebar at a home site when the men heard sirens. An officer by the name of Westbrook documented his conversation with the witness:

When asked if he noticed the smoke from the fire, Mr. Redmond said he had not, or, if he did, he may have thought it was from someone's chimney. When asked if he had heard or seen anything suspicious, he again stated he had not. When asked if he knew what was on fire, he said he did not. It should be noted that Mr. Redmond did not ask me (Officer Westbrook, Badge #3217) if I knew what was on fire, or what damage the fire had caused.

I asked Mr. Redmond if he knew of anyone who would start a fire at the trailer site. Mr. Redmond stated he could not think of anyone who would want to do such a thing. But he did state that some of the subcontractors did not get along. He also stated he was aware of drug use at the construction site. I asked him who was involved in said drug use and Mr. Redmond could not say, as these were only rumors.

I advised Mr. Redmond that the Cheyenne Police Department may want to talk to him again, to which he answered, "No problem, man. But I don't know nothing."

During the interview, Mr. Redmond did not appear to be nervous. He was polite and cooperative. A subsequent check of his criminal history (attached hereto) shows only a receiving stolen property conviction out of Weld County, Colorado from 1973.

Clearly, to Tiffany, this Mr. Redmond was an unlikely suspect. But that really wasn't the point, was it? L&J Reinforcing was the point, the thread. And it was time to start pulling at it.

10

Sebastien took a seat at the only table available in the café, which was by the window overlooking the side-walk. There were few passers-by on this cold and drizzly day, which suited him just fine. Window dining made him feel like a fish in a bowl—every move a performance, every bite an invitation to public assessment.

"Well, hello! Welcome back."

"I'm sorry. Um, do I know you?"

Sebastien looked up at the waitress in confusion.

"I'm Daisy. I saw y'all come in with Hank, I mean Sgt. LeGris, a few months ago. You asked for a spinach omelet, but we didn't have that on the menu."

"That's incredible. How in the world can you remember that?" Sebastien asked with genuine curiosity.

"Oh, it's the job. Gotta have a good mind for 'membering things, like orders and stuff."

"Well, that is very impressive. I'm waiting for someone, so if you don't mind, I'll order when he arrives."

"Aren't you the one who found those bodies in the hills a

few months ago? It was those guys from Rapid City? You're like a detective, am I right?"

Sebastien turned quickly in his chair and looked upward to face the waitress again.

"Um . . . well . . . not really. How did you know about that . . . exactly?"

"Everybody was talking about it. Anyway, you just wave me over when your friend comes, okay darlin'?"

Sebastien turned to look out the window at the brick buildings and the occasional pedestrian hurriedly darting from their vehicle to the bakery, souvenir shop, rock shop, bike shop, or chamber of commerce. My, oh my. How did this happen? His life's dream—no, his life's *work*—was to be unnoticed, unrecognized, to fade into the background. But now this. The reporter, the waitress, the "everybody was talking about it." He was beginning to feel like a fish in a bowl indeed. How would Mr. Shelby put it? A real big fish.

"Dr. Grey, good to meet you! I'm Derek Manly, editor-in-chief of the *Custer County Signal*. We spoke on the phone."

The man approached frenetically, gesticulating as he spoke and offering his business card before sitting down opposite Sebastien. He wore jeans and a brown blazer over a t-shirt with AREA 51 across his chest. His hair was nearly shoulder length, light brown and uncombed.

"Oh, uh, hello. How did you know I . . . ?"

"I tell you, those incompetent morons . . . Sorry I'm late. I swear. How long should it take to mail a package?"

Sebastien suddenly felt assaulted, attacked. Derek Manly had not just shattered his personal calm; he drove a tank straight through it, leaving him speechless.

"Oh, sorry about, ya know. I just hate to be late. Hey, Daisy! Couple of coffees? Thanks, babe. So anyway. Dr. Sebastien Grey, with an 'ien' and 'ey,' I'm told. Mind if I record this? It's just a standard thing. I'll just put that right there.

Daisy . . . sweet cakes . . . coffee? Daisy is a good girl. You know. Just a bit of a . . . So how do you like our little town, doctor?"

Sebastien's head began to spin—a vertigo brought on by sudden panic. He rested his head on the tips of the fingers of his left hand and squeezed his right thigh under the table.

"You okay, doc? Geez, you look sick. Daisy! Water! Over here, by the window."

"I'm coming, Derek. Hold your horses," replied the waitress from a few tables away.

The dozen or so customers in the small restaurant were beginning to take notice of the relative ruckus caused by the newly arrived man at the table by the window. Though, to be fair, none looked too surprised by the over-the-top obnoxiousness of Derek Manly. It was as if they knew him, knew what to expect. There were a few smiles and at least one shaking head among the morning habitués.

Manly dipped his head to make eye contact with Sebastien.

"Yes, yes. I'm all right. I think I just ate something bad last night."

Daisy approached with their drinks. Sebastien promptly took a gulp of water and left three ice cubes in his mouth to shock his mind out of the spiral.

"Oh, that's too bad. You want to do this some other time?"

"No, it's fine. I'm fine. Let's do this now," Sebastien replied as he held his water glass against his forehead.

"Get it over with, you mean? Don't blame you, doctor. You want something to eat?"

"Absolutely not. Coffee is fine."

Manly took a huge gulp of his coffee and hit the red button on the digital recorder. The pulsating red light from the mechanism mirrored against the stainless steel napkin dispenser, like a pair of alien eyes scanning Sebastien for his experimental suitability.

"So, forensic anthropologist, eh? Like that lady on TV, right? Or is that stuff not accurate?"

This was an oft asked question and Sebastien somewhat resented it. The Hollywood version of forensics was probably about as accurate as its version of anything else. Things were oversimplified while at the same time made to seem much more dramatic than they really were. He had a few favorite examples to cite in that regard: Work was never done in a darkened lab, DNA analysis never has a quick turnaround, and there's no such contraption that will give a three-dimensional hologram of a complete individual based on their skull. In truth, there were probably more and better examples, but Sebastien couldn't stand to watch fictional forensic shows, so his dataset was small.

"It's somewhat accurate. The goals are the same. Essentially the job of a forensic anthropologist is to help identify deceased individuals from . . . usually from . . . their skeletons."

"What? You mean with the clay on the face? That kind of thing?"

"No, not really. That's more of an art. Sure there is a science behind it, of course. But generally, I bring in a forensic artistic to do that kind of work. Which is very helpful, by the way. You should be talking to one of them, not me."

"Sure, sure. So, how then do you identify dead people?"

Sebastien noticed a middle-aged woman at a table diagonal from theirs. She had stopped cutting into whatever was on her plate and was staring at them in wide-eyed horror while whispering to the man across from her, who then turned his head to look in their direction.

"Well, maybe I should back up a bit," replied Sebastien. Despite the audience, he was noticing a precipitous drop in his anxiety. Evidently, talking forensics had a focusing effect. He needed to remember that. "Yes, we do identify the, um . . .

deceased, if needed, but we also help determine trauma and disease."

"Like cause of death kind of stuff." Manly spoke several decibels above the needful volume. Somewhere, a diner dropped a utensil onto a plate with a loud clank.

"That's right."

"Nice."

Manly's right knee was bouncing like a jackhammer under the table, Sebastien noticed. He wondered what the man's blood pressure was like, what stage of hypertension the journalist was currently experiencing.

"What's the process of identifying someone, Dr. Grey? How do you actually do it?"

"Are you sure you want to hear this?"

"Oh, don't you worry, doctor. I'll make it interesting. That's what I do."

The exaggerated grin that accompanied that affirmation failed to comfort. Sebastien was less concerned about being interesting and more worried about sharing details that others might find disgusting, or even ghoulish. More than once he had obliged with some detail about a case, only to find the interlocuter's face turn green. He would try to keep it relatively sterile for the article.

"Okay, then. We, or rather I, examine the skeletal remains to assess their stage of development or, in the case of adults, the signs of aging. Basically, there are changes in the skeleton due to growth and changes due to aging. So, those changes in the various elements—that is, bones—help me determine the approximate age of the decedent."

"And teeth too, right?"

"Sure, although that would really be the area for a forensic odontologist."

"Oh, man. Thank goodness for the recorder, am I right? I couldn't spell this stuff to save my life."

"But you're writing it up?"

"Spell check. Blammo!"

Sebastien nodded, feeling a bit stupid.

"Right. Now let me ask about what went down this summer. Those guys you found in the hills, did you identify them by those bone changes, or whatever?"

"Mr. Manly, I'm not sure I should be discussing those cases. The trial hasn't started yet."

"Real-ly? I heard there was going to be a plea bargain."

"All the same," replied Sebastien.

"Sure. Sure. I suppose trauma and disease are the same kind of thing. You just look for evidence on the skeleton that might be left by a weapon."

Manly made a dramatic stabbing motion as he spoke.

"Exactly. And disease too. In fact, I just consulted on a case in Germany. It was pretty fascinating, actually."

"I'm all ears, Dr. Grey!"

"And recorder," added Sebastien, pointing at the small black rectangle propped up against the napkin dispenser.

"Always the recorder, Dr. Grey."

For the next fifteen minutes, Sebastien rehashed the case of the Red Cave remains and his part in it. Manly looked to be engrossed as he did so, but it was difficult to know for sure.

"So, you see, that's a pretty good summary of what a forensic anthropologist does—determine adult versus child, identify the stab wounds that caused the child's death, and assess pathology in the skeleton. Of course, I could not give a positive identification of the remains. And it doesn't really matter since the case is too old to be forensic."

"That's fascinating, Dr. Grey. Let's riff off of that and talk about this cold case work you're doing."

"There's not a lot to say at this point. We just got started."

"Detective Reese tells me you've re-opened the Amber Harrison homicide."

Sebastien tried to suppress his grin. *What does this coked-up reporter take me for? An idiot?*

"I'm not aware of that case, Mr. Manly. Perhaps you misheard Detective Reese."

"Maybe, although . . . trusty recorder . . ." Manly tapped the recorder with a coffee stirrer. "Well, what can you tell me, Dr. Grey? My readers would love to hear how they can help. I mean, there must be information out there somewhere that would help you. The public can't help if they don't know what you're working on."

"That's fair enough, Mr. Manly. Let me ask you a question."

"Fire away, amigo."

"Are you aware of any cases from the eighties? I'm talking about missing people or rumors of murder, that kind of thing."

"I was barely weened in the eighties, Dr. Grey."

"That wasn't the question, Mr. Manly."

The reporter gave a canny smile.

"I can tell you this much, doctor. There was a lot of chicanery going on back then. Highway 90 was notorious for missing hitchhikers; biker gangs were a lot more violent then—recent examples notwithstanding, of course. But I can't say I know of any specific missing people."

Sebastien reflected for a moment, wondering how far he should push this, calculating the risks and rewards.

"I will tell you that we are including some unidentified individuals in our cold case work. These are people who were murdered, and their remains were found in the county."

"That seems to happen quite a lot around here."

"It's been my experience that it happens a lot everywhere. People—regular people—just don't know about it; they're not aware," replied Sebastien.

"These missing people, the cases, are they connected?"

"I don't think so. It's an accumulation of things over time. We have forty- or fifty-years' worth of unresolved cases."

Sebastien could see the wheels turning in Manly's rectangular head. The reporter looked thoughtful, measured. He was no longer in a frenzy. It occurred to Sebastien that the whole explosive entry thing could have been an act, an effort to throw him off balance.

"Look, doc, you and I both know this will make for great reading, just in time for the Halloween spooks and goblins. I can write about forensic anthropology. I can talk about how the great Dr. Sebastien Grey is on the case . . ."

"Please don't do that."

"But if we don't give the reader something they can help with, something they can talk about, we—you—are missing an opportunity. It will end up being just a puff piece, filler."

Sebastien knew the reporter was right, but this put him in a sticky situation. Tiffany had warned him about Manly. It was almost as if she expected him to be outsmarted by this guy. He would just have to trust his own judgement.

"Okay, Mr. Manly. Here's what I can tell you. Some human remains were found in Hell Canyon back in '88. I'm sure there was news about it somewhere. Anyway, the remains have not been identified. But, yes, it was murder."

"Male? Female?" asked Manly with a tinge of excitement in his voice.

"Male. Caucasian. Possibly in his thirties or forties but could be younger. He was between five foot six and six feet. Again, I'm sure it was made public at some point. I haven't looked into that yet. So, yes, it would be great if you could include that in your article."

"That's great, Doctor Grey. Now we're talking. Is there anything else at all about the case that I should know? Something else I should include?"

"No, sir. That's all we have. I'm sure it's a long shot, of course. I mean, if the public couldn't help in '88, I doubt they can help now."

"Oh, Dr. Grey, I think we both know the opposite is true. Don't we?"

DEREK MANLY MOVED to the opposite side of the table so he could get a better view of the anthropologist as he walked away from the diner.

Strange kid. Is that a Range Rover he's getting into? What the hell? How much does anthropology pay? Ooh, could there be corruption in this? Perhaps some graft? Misuse of public funds? Hold on, Derek. One thing at a time. Finish what's on your plate.

Once the Rover made a left turn onto Fifth Street and was out of sight, Derek took out his cell phone and punched in the number for Roxanne Bishop at the Sheriff's Office.

"Hey, baby. What's going on?"

"Hey, honey. I'm just making sure the monkeys don't run away from the circus."

"Yeah, I bet you are. You practically run that place, don't you, baby?'

"Someone has to. Whatcha up to?"

"I just met with the forensic guy, the one the sheriff brought in to help with the cold cases."

"Oh yeah? I haven't met him yet. I hear he's cute though."

"I think he's too young for you, Roxie."

"In that case, I guess I'm too young for you."

"Oh baby, don't break my heart."

"What can I do for you, Derek?"

"Dr. Grey is supposed to get me a copy of one of the cold case files; it's for a story I'm doing. The problem is he can't get it until next week. He's on his way out of town or something. Well, I have a deadline. I need that report ASAP. You know what I mean?"

"Derek, I don't think I can do that. Maybe you should just wait to get it from the cold case team."

"No, no. It's not like that at all. It's a clerical deal, ya know? The case is dead cold and I promised to include it in my story. The guy practically begged me. I mean, I don't want to rush the guy to do it himself. He's busy. I just figured you could take care of it. No big deal."

"I don't know . . ."

"Okay, okay. Like I said, no big deal. So anyway, I was thinking maybe you, me . . . and your husband could get together for a few drinks. What do you think about Sunday?"

Derek had been in similar situations before. Many times, in fact. He was well practiced at setting the timer and enjoyed waiting to see whether the bomb would explode. He relished the tension. It was something of a skill to him, like fishing. You don't want to pull your fly off the water too soon. Just wait an extra second.

"I guess it couldn't hurt to just ask him for the file."

"There's my girl. But, like I said, he's outta town. Here's what I'm thinking: Why don't you just pop into his office and make a copy later on tonight? That way he doesn't have to be bothered and the file will be where it's supposed to be when he gets back."

"What exactly am I looking for?"

"I totally forgot to get the case number. But it's from 1988. It's about a John Doe out of Hell Canyon."

"What if I can't find it?"

"Well, then just try again tomorrow night. You have plenty of time to find it. Heck, you can even go in on Saturday—if it's convenient, that is. I think it'll be fine as long as I get the report . . . by Sunday."

"Oh, Derek."

"I love you, baby. I was thinking about Vegas the other day. We should do that again. Real soon. Wouldn't that be great?"

ROXANNE HUNG up the phone and looked around to see if any of her colleagues in the Sheriff's Administration Office had been listening. One woman looked up from the paperwork on her desk and smiled. *Did she hear me? Could she hear Derek?* Roxanne anxiously tried to replay the conversion in her head. *What exactly had she said? Was she vague enough?*

It was not lost on her that Derek, her lover of the past few years and the man who promised his undying devotion, actually threatened her. Threatened her! He threatened to expose the whole thing to her husband. How cruel and desperate that was! Didn't he realize the danger that would put her in?

These favors for Derek had become much too frequent for her liking, and certainly for her safety. A voice from the dark folds of her mind was telling her she was being used. *Derek is taking advantage of you*, the voice said with increasing frequency and volume. *He doesn't really love you.*

She pushed these thoughts away for the hundredth time as she rose from her desk and made her way downstairs. She wasn't sure where the cold case room was, but she was smart enough to know it would be easier to find during the day and with all of the lights on. Now would be a good time to scout it out.

11

"We really need to get you a desk in here," said Tiffany as she stood with her hands on her hips in the middle of the room.

"And put it where? Even if we put all of these binders back on the shelf, there still wouldn't be room. I'm okay though. Really."

"No, it's not okay. It's not going to work. You need to settle in. We have a lot to do. Hopefully we'll be at this for a few years . . . or however long it takes for me to pass the stupid sergeants' test."

"In that case, there's no point in me settling in, as you put it. One more try should do it."

Sebastien was pleased with himself for thinking of that subtle compliment.

"I appreciate your optimism. But I'm going to ask Hank about us getting a larger office, if one is available. Let me text him. Anyway, you were telling me about your interview with Manly."

"I think the guy's on coke. Either that or he was just trying to throw me off balance."

"What do you mean?"

"He just came in all jumpy and aggressive at first. He calmed down a bit once we started talking."

"What did he ask you about?"

"The first question was about the Harrison 'homicide.' To which I told him I'd never heard of the case."

"Ooh, clever dodge. I'm sure that'll throw him off the trail."

Sebastien caught the sarcasm, but let it go.

"We mostly just talked about forensic anthro. I guess he wants to do an article on it, and us, for Halloween."

"Look at you, superstar." Tiffany winked and gave a wry smile before pocketing her cell phone and kneeling down to rearrange some of the binders on the floor.

"No, please *don't* look at me. You should be the face of this whole thing, not me."

"No way, José. I've thought a bit about this Manly business, and I like the fact that it's you and not me. It gives us some wiggle room for plausible deniability."

"You mean, if I screw up, you'll tell him I'm just a contractor who doesn't represent the Sheriff's Office and doesn't know what's what?"

"Don't take it personally."

"Why would I?" replied Sebastien dubiously. "Oh, and on that topic . . ."

"The topic of you screwing up?"

"Never mind."

Tiffany stopped what she was doing and put a hand on his knee.

"Sebastien, I'm kidding. Now, what were you going to say?"

"Manly asked for a case to include in his article. He wants to end the piece with a call to action for the public. You know, 'if you have any information, please contact . . .' That sort of thing."

"And what did you tell him, Sebastien?"

Sebastien marked the concerned look on her face.

"Not much. I told him about the bones found in Hell Canyon. And no, I did not mention anything about Cheyenne." Sebastien shot this last sentence off quickly as he saw Tiffany's mouth begin to open. "I didn't see any harm in it. Maybe someone knows whom the skull belongs to or even who may have killed the man. Plus, I'm sure it's out there anyway. There must have been a public appeal or news release when the remains were first found."

Tiffany stood up and made her way to the chair behind her desk. She sat down slowly with a faraway look on her face. It might have been a full minute before she spoke.

"Okay. Yeah. I guess that's fine. We'll need to tell Hank, and quickly too. And the public information officer and the sheriff. Oh damn. No, no. It's fine. That's fine. This is how we have to work these things. And what's the point of keeping the public in the dark? We need them. Thank you for not telling him about Cheyenne though. I think that was the right thing."

"Of course."

Sebastien wanted to add, "I'm not a total idiot," but he caught himself.

"You know, Sebastien, I am kind of wondering about this whole thing. The whole approach we're taking, is it even necessary? I mean, this is a DNA grant. Let's just have the Hell Canyon DNA analyzed and compared to genealogical databases. We're bound to find a relative. Hell, we can do that with most of these cases. Whether it's victim DNA in the case of the unidentified subjects or potential suspect DNA. I think we may be overworking things here."

Tiffany swept a supinated hand in the direction of the binders that littered the floor as she spoke.

Sebastien played this out in his mind. His head made a light thumping sound as he leaned back against the wall and fixed his eyes on the ceiling.

"True. True. But let's say we submit everything. How long would it take to get the results? How big is your lab? How busy is it? And, just keeping it to the Hell Canyon case, knowing whom the victim may be related to doesn't solve the murder."

"Oh, but it has to help. That's the first step in any homicide case, the victim identity. Everything else comes after that. I just . . . I talked to the guy from L&J Reinforcing while you were out, and it just seems like such a long shot. He told me there were a dozen subcontractors on that development. The list of people who knew the backhoe and trailer were there has to be massive —if we can even put those names together, that is."

Sebastien moved his eyes from the ceiling back to Tiffany.

"Wait. You talked to that Redmond guy? From the Cheyenne report? That was quick."

Just then Tiffany's phone gave off a *ding*.

"Yes, I did. Oh, thanks a lot, Hank," spat Tiffany as she looked at her phone.

"What?"

"He replied with a bunch of laughing emojis. I guess no office for us. I'm going to get him down here though. We need some direction."

Sebastien did not see the need for direction from his brother, but he also realized it was not his place to say that. He had often been accused, throughout his adult life, of being too obstinate, too contradictory, and overly cynical. It was one of the things that made working with others so difficult for him. He could be direct and opinionated. Detective Tiffany Reese was providing ample motivation for him to fight that propensity. Perhaps this was evidence that Mr. Shelby was wrong. Introspection could, in fact, be helpful.

"While we wait for Hank, would you mind telling me what Redmond had to say?"

"Of course. It was actually a good interview. I can just feel it leading to a bunch of boring dead ends. But, anyway, Redmond reiterated that he did not see anything suspicious or know who set the fire."

"But he remembered it?" asked Sebastien.

"Oh, yes. He did. He knew exactly what I was referencing. He said he'll never forget it."

"So, he knows it was a torso that was on fire?"

"Yeah. The local media figured that out pretty quickly. It caused a bunch of commotion down there. Still, Redmond never heard anything about who the victim may have been or who may have started the fire. Once L&J was done with their part of the project, they moved on."

"To where?"

"Not here. Not South Dakota. The company was out of Fort Collins and most of their work was in Colorado."

"Was?" asked Sebastien.

"Was. Same with the general contractor, North Plains Development. They're no longer in business either."

"Redmond gave you the name of the general? That's great!"

"It's been a busy morning, Sebastien. And a boring one. Damn boring."

Sebastien leaned his head on the wall again and looked upward with closed eyes.

"Is that why you got into police work? For the excitement?"

"Like I said, the company is out of business and the owner is long dead."

"Any family?"

"Widow in Denver. How does that help?"

"You never know. She might be a hoarder. We could get lucky."

"I thought with my little brother in the mix, the housekeeping would improve. Are you asleep, bro?"

Hank was standing at the door, shaking his head in feigned disgust.

"No, I'm not asleep!"

"That's why we need a bigger space, boss," replied Tiffany.

"Oh, you want to fetch up a bigger room?"

"Your poor brother has nowhere to work."

"Guess that explains the sleeping."

"I wasn't sleeping!"

Sebastien's face was beginning to turn red.

"I checked with the admin sergeant, Tiff. All of the offices are accounted for."

"Then can we swap with computer crimes? It's just Cooper there now."

"He needs the room for all the hardware. It's like an electronics store threw up in his office. I'm afraid you're just going to have to get creative down here."

Sebastien moved his head between Tiffany and Hank, watching the tennis match from his chair against the wall.

"Well, how's this for creativity? I am formally requesting permission for Sebastien and I to work from home until we can find a better space in the building."

"Work from home? Whose home?"

"My home," replied a defiant Tiffany.

The triangle of space between the detectives and anthropologist quickly turned heavy. Hank's lips pursed notably. Large veins in his forearms bulged as his hands squeezed the door frame.

After what seemed like an eternity, Sebastien opened his mouth to speak. What he would say, he was not sure. But the tension was killing him. Before he could get a mumble out, Tiffany broke in.

"Thank you, sergeant, for not saying what I know you really, really want to say."

"Detective Reese, I don't know what you're talking about. But you have my permission to work remotely, as long as you check in often. Very often."

"Thank you, sir."

"Okay, what else do you need?"

"Sebastien has something to tell you."

If the tension was gone, Sebastien didn't notice. He looked at Tiffany in confusion.

"The interview, Sebastien. Your interview with Derek Manly."

"Oh, yeah. The reporter whom Lt. Breed wanted us to contact . . ."

"Wanted Detective Reese to contact, I think you mean," cut in Hank.

"I did contact him. We had a conversation. Manly asked if he could also interview Sebastien for a piece about forensics."

"O-kay." Hank's eyes narrowed.

"And I did do an interview with him. He also asked if we had any cases he could mention in the article, anything with which the public might be able to help."

"What did you give him?" asked Hank, closing his eyes as if to prepare himself for the worst.

"I just told him about the bones that were found in Hell Canyon. That's all. Maybe someone will remember something. Or maybe a witness who was too scared to come forward back then will be willing to now."

"That's the one with the Cheyenne connection?"

"Yes, it is. But I didn't mention anything about that."

Hank looked to be mulling this over from the doorway. His hands were now down at his sides, his face more relaxed.

"Oh. That's not so bad. In fact, I think the sheriff will like that—except for the part about Sebastien being the one who was interviewed. I tell ya what. Tiff, you get a hold of that reporter and ask him if he will leave out Sebastien as his source. Ask him to just make it generic. He can talk about all the cool forensic stuff and mention the Hell Canyon deal, but I don't want the info to have come from our consultant here."

"I can do that."

"Great. Anything else?"

"No."

Sebastien was caught off guard by Tiffany's curt reply. He was expecting more questions for Hank. In particular, questions about how they were to approach their cases.

"All right, then. Oh, wait. I do have one thing for you, Reese. I need you on a search warrant tomorrow. Be here by six. And text me when we're square with the reporter. See you kids later."

"Why didn't you ask him about the cases?" asked Sebastien once Hank was gone. "I thought you were going to get his direction on whether we should just be submitting DNA instead of tracking down questionable leads."

Tiffany's face began to pucker, and she pursed her lips angrily. Her arms were crossed tightly at her chest.

"Because, Sebastien, we are going to work these cases the hard way. Yes, we'll submit the DNA. But we're going to investigate the living crap out of them too."

Sebastien had never seen Tiffany so mad, or even mad at all. He was afraid to ask. But he did anyway.

"Are you okay? What's the matter? What was that between you and Hank?"

"I'm fine," Tiffany spat through her teeth.

"Are you sure? What did you think he was going to say when you asked about working from your place?"

"Oh, I *know* what he wanted to say. He was going to make a remark about you and I at my place screwing all day."

IT WOULD BE a bit before she calmed down, Tiffany knew. It wasn't the first time Hank pissed her off. And, no, she wasn't jumping to conclusions. She knew with certainty what he was thinking. She knew by looking at his dumb smug face: lips tight, eyes bright with laughter.

Reflecting on the incident as she drove home, Tiffany admitted to herself that she may have asked for it. Maybe she knew he would go there, or at least would *want* to go there. He's a guy after all. Not much better than the rest. Okay, that was not true. Hank *was* better. In fact, he was one of the best. He always treated her with respect and never tried to take advantage. Maybe subconsciously she was daring him. Maybe she was looking to be offended. Maybe there was something at the root of this.

By the time she pulled into her driveway, she thought she understood a little better why she had gotten so angry. She fell into a trap that every working adult knows to avoid at all costs. She mixed her work and her personal life. And it didn't even happen on accident! She ran headlong into it without consideration of the consequences. And what were those? Sexual innuendo, gossip, behind-the-back snickering, accusations of preferential treatment. How stupid! Being a woman and a cop was hard enough. This was her career. This was not going to work.

Tiffany sat in her car, examining the leaf-shaped shadows on her windshield cast by the light above her garage door and wondering what to do next. Finally, she decided to call the one person she felt she could trust with such a sensitive problem.

12

"Thanks for letting me stop by," Tiffany said as Melissa took her coat and hung it in the hall closet.

"Of course, Tiffany. You're always welcome here. I kicked the boys out. Hank is introducing Sebastien to the world of sports bars. I think it's Denver and Kansas City for the Thursday game."

"Ha. Good luck getting Sebastien to enjoy that. Is this his dog?"

Tiffany knelt down and patted the corgi.

"Yep. That's Parsifal. He's a neat little dog actually. Pretty calm. Seems to be tired most of the time."

"You are cute, aren't you?" Tiffany held Parsifal under the chin and stroked his head while the dog's tongue lolled out of his mouth several inches.

"Come on in and have a seat on the couch. I would get us some wine, but I can't drink right now and you don't look like you should drink alone."

"No, you definitely should not drink. With Hank's genes, the baby already has a disadvantage. Don't introduce alcohol."

The two women giggled.

"True story. Now, let's cut to the chase before the menfolk return. What's bothering you?"

"It's this thing with Sebastien. I'm not sure about it."

Tiffany sat on the couch. Parsifal followed and stared up at her from between her feet.

"Oh gosh, already?"

"What do you mean, 'already'?"

Melissa pulled her legs up and crossed them as she settled into the opposite side of the couch.

"I just mean he's only been here a few days. Are you not getting along? I hope you don't feel obligated just because he's Hank's brother."

"Oh, heck no. No. It's nothing like that. We get along great."

"You like him, then?"

"Yeah. You know, I really do. He's sweet. And smart. Very smart. And attractive."

"The LeGris genes, again," laughed Melissa.

"I mean, sure, he's insecure and shy."

"Are you going to try and fix him?" Melissa asked with a smirk.

"No. It's not like that. He's actually been a lot better. I can see him really growing."

"I bet," Melissa winked.

"Oh, shut up."

"I'm sorry. I'm sorry. But that's good, right? Maybe you're just what he needed. Heaven knows, Hank and I haven't been much help in that department."

Tiffany gestured to the dog.

"What does Parsifal want? Why is he looking at me like that?"

"Oh, that's his 'help me' look. We thought he was cross-eyed when he first did it. I think he wants to sit on your lap."

"What a strange little dog."

"He's only strange until you get to know him. He's actually very sweet. And he's very patient with Kirby."

"I see what you did there," replied Tiffany, as she hefted the placid corgi onto her lap.

"You still haven't told me the problem," prompted Melissa.

"It's just the work and dating thing. It's a bad idea. I don't think I can do it. I don't want people talking and laughing behind my back."

Melissa's face showed concern. She placed a hand on Tiffany's thigh.

"Are they?"

"Well ... no. Not really. But today, I could just tell that Hank wanted to make a comment about us. About Sebastien and I being ... physical."

"Are you? Are you and Sebastien ..."

"No. And I don't want that to be a topic, you know what I mean?"

"No one's damn business. Oh, and sorry I asked."

Tiffany laughed at that.

"No, you're fine. I want your advice. I don't mind talking to you."

Melissa took her hand off of Tiffany's leg and put it on Parsifal's head, stroking the dog down his neck.

"I'll tell you what. I'm going to tell Hank to shut his fat mouth," she said.

"Please don't. He didn't actually say anything. I just kind of felt it. But that's exactly what I'm saying. I want work to be work, and my personal life to be personal."

"You're very smart, Tiffany. Very smart. Workplace relationships are nothing but trouble."

"That's the problem. I'm in the middle of one and I don't think I can get out of it."

"You can always get out of it."

"I know. I just don't want to let Sebastien down. I know he loves the work."

"And you."

"I love it too."

"Not what I meant."

"I know."

"Look, if you need to put a stop to this situation, nothing should prevent you. You know that, right?"

Tiffany nodded.

Melissa folded her hands into her lap and straightened her back.

"Does anybody else know about you and Sebastien? Anyone at the office?"

"I don't think so. Just Hank."

"And you're happy with Sebastien and want to continue seeing him?"

"Yes, I do. I really do."

"And you want to continue working with him? You want him to be part of this cold case thingy, whatever it is?"

"I do. He's really helpful. And we work well together."

"Sounds like you just need to set some boundaries."

"Oh, I have. With Sebastien, anyway. He knows at work it's all business, 100 percent. Zero exceptions."

"And he's okay with that?"

"Yes, he seems to be. It took a little reminding though."

"So, if no one knows, and Sebastien is behaving, it sounds like the problem is Hank."

"What do you mean?"

"Well, like I said, if no one in the office knows, then they can't be making you uncomfortable about this thing with Sebastien. And you've set boundaries with Sebastien. The only one who can be the cause of any awkwardness is Hank. Maybe Hank is projecting his inability to act like a dang professional."

"Hank is very professional."

"Is he? Does he talk to you the same way now as he did before Sebastien got here?"

Tiffany thought for a second.

"Now that you mention it, he has referred to us as 'you two kids' a couple of times. And he told us to 'behave' once."

"Well, there you go. As usual, it's my big dumb husband. My sweet, lovable, unthinking hulk of a man."

"I don't want to put this all on Hank, Melissa. He really is a great boss. And a great friend. He's always done right by me."

"Of course he has! Why do you think I married him?"

Parsifal rolled over in Tiffany's lap, exposing his white belly. Tiffany accepted the invitation and gently scratched him.

"What do you suggest?"

"It sounds to me like you've done everything right. I suggest you keep doing what you're doing. Keep those boundaries clear and consistent. I also think it helps that Sebastien is a contractor and not an employee. That takes some pressure off. It's not like you two would be competing for promotions or evaluations. You just need to keep your eyes open. Both of you. And him being a contractor means you can make adjustments. I mean, if there needs to be some distance, you and Sebastien can game plan it and adjust his role accordingly."

"I hadn't thought of that. You know what? I think you're right. Maybe I just got emotional. Maybe I overanalyzed it. Melissa, you are so smart."

"I appreciate that, Tiff, but let's be clear: You did not get emotional or overanalyze anything. You're just trying to figure it out like a normal person. If you'll let me, I would really like to have a talk with Hank."

Tiffany began to shift on the couch, rousing Parsifal, who lifted his head momentarily.

"Now, I won't do it if you don't want me to. But I know how to talk to Hank. And he's humble enough to listen. And he really cares about you. If he realized what he was doing, he would be ashamed of himself."

"I think that's true."

The pieces were beginning to fit together and the weight was beginning to lift.

"It doesn't have to be a big deal, Tiff. He just needs to know. Please trust me."

"I do. I do trust you."

A swell of emotion burst from somewhere deep and Tiffany began to tear up.

"I love you, Melissa. Thank you so much," Tiffany whispered into Melissa's left ear as she leaned forward to hug her friend in gratitude.

"I love you too, Tiffany. *We* love you—me, Hank, and Kirby. And I think Sebastien too."

Parsifal, for his part, went a little cross-eyed as the two women crushed him in the embrace.

HAD anyone been on the upper floor of the Sheriff's Office, they might have heard the *sh-shump, sh-shump, sh-shump* of the copy machine. But there wasn't, so no one heard it. Likewise, had the mailroom of the Sheriff's Office featured windows, people outside might have noticed the single light on in an otherwise dark building. But, again, it didn't, so no one noticed.

Roxanne Bishop, clerk level two in the Sheriff's Administration Office, expected some difficulty in finding the Hell Canyon file. In her mind, she pictured herself spending all night pulling binders off of shelves, opening drawers, shining a flashlight into banker's boxes—real cat-burglar stuff. But, no. The whole mission, as she chose to view it, was ridiculously easy. Right there on the desk, in plain sight for all to see, was the semi-thick binder with the spine that read: 88-301, Hell Canyon Doe.

Couldn't have been easier. But it was an even greater point of pride to the scrupulous clerk that she managed to deduce that the semi-thin file folder, which lay next to the binder, was part of the same case. After all, the report number CPD 87-2360 bore little resemblance to 88-301. But something told her to open it. And yes! Never mind that she hadn't finished her criminal justice degree. Never mind that her awful husband called her a fat dingbat in front of all of her colleagues at the Sheriff's Office Christmas party. No dingbat here. No, sir. No, ma'am.

Returning the binder and file might prove to be a bit more difficult. Graveyard shift roll call was due to begin downstairs in ten minutes in the patrol conference room, just a few feet away from the storage room. She would either have to wait or hurry and go down before anyone got there. Which to do? Probably best to wait a bit, she concluded. No sense rushing. After all, that awful man is home. Life is so much more peaceful when he's gone on one of his long hauls, or at least hooked up to his CPAP and fast asleep. So much calmer. Yep. May as well wait. Most wives would be concerned about arousing suspicion if they were absent too long. Not Roxanne. The man she married did not care one bit. Complete indifference had scarred their relationship these last few years. She could come and go as she pleased. Just don't use the credit cards. Or get the car dirty. Or buy the wrong bread.

It was nearly one o'clock when she at last got the chance to return the binder and file to their rightful home. Okay, she fell asleep a bit while sitting in the darkness at her desk. So maybe she could have done it sooner. But no matter. All's well that ends well. Derek would be happy, in any case. Derek. The man who truly loved her for who she was. The man who promised to marry her once she got up the nerve to leave that awful, awful man.

~

Tiffany woke up at three to relieve herself, habitually checking her phone as she rolled out of bed. There were two unread texts. The first was from her brother, asking for details about their mother's upcoming surprise birthday party. The second was from Hank.

"Okay, detective. I pulled some strings and got you a bigger office. I'll give you the details tomorrow before the briefing. Let's make it 5:45 a.m. sharp. I'm sorry."

Tiffany wondered how Hank had found a new office so quickly and where it might be. Hopefully, she and Sebastien wouldn't be sharing with anyone else, she thought. It was her hope to set up a whiteboard for notes and maybe even put crime scene photos on the wall. As for the apology, Tiffany knew full well that it had nothing to do with the lack of suitable workspace, or the next day's earlier start time.

13

A half-dozen cops with badges prominently Velcroed to their black tactical vests sat on the narrow benches that lined either side of the cargo area of the marked sheriff's van.

"Now remember, this guy is only on probation for burglary, but we're looking for a Glock .45," instructed Hank as the van made a final right turn and came to a smooth stop. "So, we assume he's armed and possibly tweaking. The yard only has a three-foot chain link fence and there is, reportedly, no dog. Reese, Akers, you two take the back. Summermire and Pearson flank the door while Hardy and I do the knock and announce. We good?"

"Yes, sir," came the unanimous reply.

The cadre emerged, and Tiffany and Detective Akers made their way to the left side of the small house where Tiffany gripped the top of the fence and deftly hopped both legs over in one smooth motion. Akers, a bit larger and less fit, stuck the toe of his right boot in between the links and swung his left leg over in a motion that nearly performed the vasectomy his wife had been bugging him to get.

"You okay, Rod?"

"Yes . . . damnit."

Tiffany put a finger to her lips, and the pair walked carefully toward the back, stopping at what appeared to be a kitchen window. She raised her head slowly to the lowest corner of the window and quickly eyeballed the interior.

"Anyone?" whispered Akers.

Tiffany shook her head and they continued past the window to the back corner of the house. Once there, she peered around to the back yard where she saw an open patio and a rectangle of dirt where a lawn should be. There was a large slider on the rear of the house and a single swing door farther down. The house was box shaped, so there were no recesses or ambush points along the back wall.

Akers crouched and walked ahead, looking into the sliding door before turning and holding up one finger. *One person in view.* Tiffany likewise peered in and saw the same figure, standing in the small hall that led from the entry presumably to the bedrooms at the other side of the house. The man inside looked to be shifting on his feet with his back against the wall while Hank and the entry team knocked on the door.

"Custer County Sheriff, Mr. Carson. This is a probation search. Open the door now."

"Just a minute! Give me a minute!"

Tiffany could hear and see the man respond.

"Oh shi—"

Tiffany grabbed her radio mic from her vest.

"This is 1Y3. The subject is in the hall and he has a gun in his hand. The subject is armed."

The man spun to his right, looked directly at Tiffany and Akers, then raised the gun and started firing. Glass from the slider shattered all over with a remarkably concise popping sound. Tiffany folded her body and backed toward the corner of the house as fast as she could. Glass was still being blown out of the window as she fell backward into the dirt.

The next several seconds were a blur. It all happened at once. The sound of the front door being smashed in, the volley of gunfire, the shouting, the smell of gunpowder, the sight of Akers returning fire through the film of blood that began to accumulate in her eyes.

Tiffany quickly got her bearings and scrambled back to the side yard amidst the commotion. She sat under the kitchen window with her back against the wall, expecting to be showered with more glass. It didn't happen. She quickly found a fist-sized rock in the yard and threw it through the window, then rolled to her right, away from the anticipated shots. They did not come. Firing at this point continued but was more sporadic. More measured.

Tiffany wiped the blood from her eyes with the back of her hand before raising her head slowly to peer through the same corner of the window she had looked through just a few minutes ago before chaos broke out. This time she could see the suspect through the kitchen window. A thin vertical wedge down the center of the man was exposed between the kitchen wall on the left and the hallway wall to the right. She could see his shaky hand holding the gun at his midsection. His face was blocked. She didn't think he could see her. She hoped he couldn't, anyway.

Tiffany stood upright and took a shooting stance with her arms extended through the broken window, both hands on the pistol. She aimed as carefully as her adrenaline would allow. Hot shells whizzed past her cheek as she squeezed off round after round.

With Tiffany wrapped up in the search warrant, Sebastien took the opportunity to sleep in a bit, then catch up on some personal business.

First, he had to check in with Shelby and see how the Block was doing. It appeared from checking his email and bank account that all was running as it should. But you never knew. And he wanted to stay close to things anyway. He did not aspire to be an absentee landlord.

Next, he did his laundry and went shopping, trying his best to fill the LeGris refrigerator with things he thought they would like. It was the least he could do, which reminded him that he really needed to find his own place to live. Despite their generosity, he felt underfoot in the LeGris household. Plus, Parsifal was on the verge of being re-christened to Purple. Sebastien loved that little kid, but he was not about to let Kirby change the name of his dog.

"Whatcha up to?" asked Melissa as she entered the dining room.

"Just catching up on housekeeping stuff."

"You really didn't have to buy all that food. But it was very kind of you."

"It's no problem. I just didn't want anyone thinking I was taking advantage."

"We know you're not. No work today? Did Hank wear you out running around last night?"

"Ha, no. I guess they're doing a search warrant this morning."

Melissa took a seat at the opposite end of the dining room table.

"How are you liking it so far? Are you getting to know anyone? Making friends?"

"No," answered Sebastien, expecting a gentle reprimand.

"Well . . . you will. Give it time. I talked to Tiffany last night. She said you're being very helpful. She likes working with you."

"She does? She said that?"

"Why so surprised, Sebastien? You too are great together."

"I really like her," he replied, surprising himself with the candor.

"She really likes you, Sebastien. So, what else is on your housekeeping list?"

"I'm looking for a place of my own."

"Oh?"

"Yeah. I can't stay here forever."

"You don't want to wait until your building sells?"

"No, I don't really need to. By the way, did Hank tell you about that? My plan for the Block, I mean?"

"Are you talking about your offer to split the proceeds with us?"

"I guess he did."

"That's amazingly kind. If you don't mind my asking, why? Why are you doing that? Don't get me wrong. I'm not complaining."

"To be honest, I don't want any bad feelings between us, especially since I'm here now. I don't want any awkwardness."

"I'm not sure you're giving us enough credit, Sebastien."

"It's not only that. I feel like I owe you for getting me up here, for pulling me out of my shell. I didn't realize how isolated I'd made myself."

"Can I ask you about that?"

Melissa picked at the tablecloth nervously.

"About what?"

"Your social anxiety."

Sebastien began to feel his chest tighten and his tongue lock up. The force field was about to engage.

"I'm not judging you, Sebastien," she added, quickly placing her hand on his. "I'm just asking as a family member who cares about you. That's all."

"What do you want to know?" he reluctantly replied,

looking down at their hands stacked on the table. Tactile communication tended to make him extremely uncomfortable —although, as he reflected on this, he noted he had no such problem with Tiffany.

"I guess I'm just wondering, hoping, that being up here, around family, around Tiffany . . . I'm just hoping this is all helpful with that."

Sebastien thought for a moment. He hadn't considered that aspect of things.

"I suppose it might be helping. I'm trying hard. But my therapist back in California says I have a disorder—avoidant personality disorder—and apparently that can't be cured. All I can do is adapt, she says."

"I find that hard to believe. Maybe you should get a second opinion."

"Please don't tell Tiffany what I just told you."

"You have my word, Sebastien. But, you know, Tiffany is a detective. I'm sure she's aware enough to know that you're shyer than most."

"She doesn't know I'm a hopeless case."

"Okay, now you're being stupid."

Melissa heard her phone ringing and went into the bedroom where she'd left it. Once alone, Sebastien began to second-guess his openness. He began to flush with embarrassment.

"What!? Oh no! Are you sure! No!"

Sebastien sprung up from the table and darted toward the master bedroom.

"What? What is it? What happened?" he asked from the doorway.

Melissa was pacing at the foot of the bed, one hand on the phone against her ear, and the other gripping a clump of hair at the top of her head.

"Where? Which hospital? Are you sure? Oh my God!"

The fear and panic shot though Sebastien like a lightning bolt, freezing him in place as he absorbed the horror coming off of Melissa.

"Okay. No, no, no . . . okay . . . No, I can drive myself. Okay. Okay. Thanks."

Melissa lowered the phone from her ear and ended the call.

"What happened?" Sebastien urged.

Melissa ignored him as she punched a number into her phone and put it back up to her ear.

"Mom. Hey . . . no . . . No, Mom, I need you to listen. Can you pick up Kirby from school and bring her back to your house? Hank's been shot."

THE HOUR-LONG DRIVE to Rapid City felt more like two hours. Sebastien insisted on driving since Melissa was in no state to, and it allowed her to call all of the friends and family she could think of while they made their way east.

Sebastien sat in silence as Melissa played bearer of bad news, his own thoughts spanning the depths of every worst-case scenario he could think of. *Just when things were good. Just when the family was in one piece again. Of course. Of course it all goes to hell. Poor Melissa. What will she do? What should he do? What would a normal person do? Oh, wait. Did anything happen to Tiffany? Is she dead? Is she being autopsied right now, her guts pulled out so her organs can be removed, weighed, dissected? Just stop, Sebastien. Just drive. Just drive. You can't do this. Be strong. Focus. Just drive.*

Once they checked in with the nurse's station, Sebastien and Melissa were led to a special waiting area, which Sebastien took to be a bad sign. But he was determined to fight against his negative impulses, so he made no mention of it. His family needed him to hold it together.

"I'm sure it will be fine, Melissa. He's in surgery, so that's a good sign. Right?"

Melissa didn't answer. She sat there next to him, red-eyed, red-nosed, and clutching a bouquet of used tissues.

"You want me to get you something? Coffee? Soda? Something to eat?"

Melissa shook her head.

Sebastien leaned his head back against the wall and stared up at the bright white lights on the ceiling of the waiting room. He was suddenly struck with the irony of finding himself sitting, leaning his head against a wall, and looking upward during a tense situation for the second day in a row. Only here, in the hospital, there was no dust, no yellow covering over the lights.

He began to count the tiles above his head, only making it halfway across the ceiling when he caught movement in the doorway of the waiting area.

"Tiffany! Oh my—what happened to you? Are you okay?"

Tiffany looked like she'd been through a battle. Her forehead was bandaged, the big white square above her left eye covered in blood. There were also bloodstains on the collar of her tan sheriff's polo, and what looked to be dirt all down her right side.

Sebastien stood and rushed to give Tiffany an embrace, which she returned tightly, kissing him on the cheek before breaking away and leaning down to hug Melissa.

"Melissa, are you okay? I'm so sorry about this."

"What happened? Can you tell me what happened?"

"Well, the details aren't important. Let's just say the guy we served the search warrant on had a gun and stared firing when we approached."

"Did you get shot too?" asked Sebastien.

"No. Broken glass hit me. Is Hank going to be okay? Have you talked to the doctors yet?"

Melissa shook her head, then began to cry. Tiffany sat next to her and stroked her back and her thick blond hair, and softly cried herself.

"Mrs. LeGris?"

A man in a white coat entered the room. He had smooth dark skin and a full head of dark hair. He appeared to be no older than twenty-five or so. The man introduced himself as Doctor Jalli.

"I'm Mrs. LeGris."

Sebastien noted the doctor's already severe countenance drop when he saw Melissa was pregnant. Another bad sign?

"I'm sorry about the wait, Mrs. LeGris. Your husband is still in surgery, but I wanted to give you an update as soon as possible and let you know that it looks like he'll be just fine."

Melissa doubled over and burst into sobs of relief.

"Where did he get shot?" asked Tiffany, wiping her nose with a tissue.

"It looks like he was hit in his vest, just under the armpit. The bullet was lodged in his back, between his ribs."

"The back? Is he going to walk again? Is he paralyzed?"

"No, Mrs. LeGris. Your husband is incredibly fortunate. We think the vest altered the course of the bullet, sending it away from vital organs. But there is significant damage to muscle tissue, and he has two broken ribs. Getting all of the fragments out of the bone and soft tissue will take a while. That's where we are now."

Melissa stood up with the help of Tiffany and asked, "When can I see him?"

"We have another hour or so in surgery, then he'll need to recover. You should be able to see him tonight, but it will be morning before he's fully awake and aware."

"Oh, thank God. Oh, thank God."

Melissa collapsed back in the chair. Both Tiffany and Sebastien caught her by an arm to ease her down.

"I agree, Mrs. LeGris. I'm going to go back in there. I'll come talk to you again as soon as we're done."

The doctor disappeared swiftly out the waiting room door.

Melissa turned her head toward Tiffany.

"I hope you got the son of a bitch," she declared through clenched teeth.

"The son of a bitch is dead," replied Tiffany.

14

"You going to the hospital?"

"Yeah, I told Melissa I'd bring her some stuff from the house," Sebastien replied.

They were sitting in their small office, staring into their respective spaces. A thick air of perplexity hung on top of them, as if they were unsure of what steps to take or what to do now. The weekend had been a blur, with multiple trips back and forth to the hospital for Sebastien. Tiffany, too, had visited Hank a few times. But Sebastien hadn't seen or heard much from her himself. It seemed her phone was off most of the weekend.

"You wanna come with?"

"I'd like to, but I have another after-action briefing in an hour. Sebastien, I think it's possible I'll be caught up in this crap for a bit. Internal affairs, the deputy's union . . . there's a lot of sorting out."

"You didn't do anything wrong. That guy came after you. He tried to kill you," insisted Sebastien.

"It's standard. It's just a hassle. A whole thing."

Tiffany looked pale and drawn.

"Are you okay?" Sebastien asked.

"What's the matter? You don't find my bandaged head attractive?"

"Come on, Tiffany. This has got to be heavy stuff. You didn't return my calls on Saturday or Sunday. That's okay, I understand. I'm just worried."

"No, you do not understand," she replied firmly.

"I'm sorry. You're right. I don't understand."

"No. No. I'm sorry. Thank you for being concerned."

"I really am."

"I know."

Sebastien lowered his eyes and traced a seam in his pant leg with his index finger as he considered what, if anything, to say next.

"You know what gets me?"

"What? What, Tiff?"

"I don't think I'll ever get over seeing Melissa like that. Poor woman almost lost her husband. With a six-year-old and another one on the way. Brutal. Just brutal. I've never been that close to it, you know? I've always been a step removed. Emotionally, I mean. I suppose you can relate."

Tiffany's eyes were lost as she spoke —unfocused, fixed on nothingness.

"I don't think so. What do you mean?"

"What was the first forensic case you worked? I mean the first *real* one, not just a deer bone. I mean a real person."

"Hmm, let me think for second. Okay. I guess it was a guy who got shot in the forehead and buried in someone's backyard."

"How bad was it?"

"Pretty bad . . . especially for a first case. The guy was a mass of rotting flesh, except the ends of the arms and legs, which were only bone. Still attached at the sockets though. I actually had to use a scalpel to remove them so I could take measurements. That was the only way I could assess sex. The pathologist wouldn't let me dig out the pubic bone, since they were pretty sure of an ID anyway. But talk of dead bodies can't be helping. Where are you going with this, Tiffany?"

Tiffany did not turn her head to look at Sebastien. She remained entranced by the void of what could have been.

"How did you get through it? Were you grossed out? Did you feel bad for the guy?"

"Not at all. It was very . . . clinical. In fact, I remember feeling a lot of pressure to impress the detectives and coroner so I would keep getting cases. I wanted to come off like an old pro. Dig right in, I guess you could say. Fake it till you make it."

"See?" Tiffany finally jerked her head to look at him. "That's what I'm talking about. A victim you don't know, whom you're not attached to. If you're taking a statement, you can't get all caught up in the fact that someone's loved one just got injured or died. You have to be detached and professional. You have to treat it like a job. I can't do that with Hank or Melissa. I can't detach on this one."

"I don't think you're supposed to, to be honest."

Tiffany's eyes went back to the surface of her desk and she made no reply.

"So what now, boss?"

"Huh?"

"I'm just wondering. If you're going to be busy with the aftermath of the shooting, what do you want me to do? Should we shut it down?"

"Obviously, Hank and Melissa come first. I think it's good you were here when this happened."

"Me too, actually."

Tiffany looked up at Sebastien again. Her lips started to form a reply, but they only managed a weak grin.

"We shut her down, then?"

Tiffany sat up, as if a switch was finally flipped and the light in her eyes returned.

"No, we don't. I'm not paying you to sit on your butt all day."

"I didn't realize it was you who was paying me."

Tiffany reached into the top drawer of her desk and threw a ring of keys to Sebastien.

"Good catch. I didn't expect that."

Sebastien held up the keys.

"What's this?"

"Those are the keys to our new office."

"Really? Where is it? When did you get these?"

"Hank gave them to me Friday morning before . . . before . . . I guess he made some calls. There's an annex above the crime lab. It was used for storage years ago, before the lab space was remodeled. The chief criminalist said we can use it as long as we clean it out first. She'll give us one or two people to help if we need it though."

"Wow, that's really nice of her."

"She's a nice lady. I'll introduce you."

"Where is the lab?"

"It's the building across the parking lot. Once you get it in shape, I'll call general services and have some desks and cabinets put up there."

"Me?"

"Are you serious?"

Tiffany looked at him with a stone face. Sebastien made a quick U-turn.

"You know what? It sounds like you'll be tied up with the shooting stuff. Why don't I get started on the new office and you finish up whatever it is they need you to do?"

"Look, I really appreciate it. I just can't really focus on that right now. And it shouldn't take long at all to get situated."

Sebastien reached over the front of the desk and put his hand in Tiffany's. She squeezed his fingers lightly in response.

"Once that's done, do you think you could track down your hoarder in Denver?"

"The wife of the owner of North Plains Development?"

"Yep."

"I said I *hope* she's a hoarder."

"Just find out whatever you can about the business. Maybe she knows a lot about it. Maybe she worked in the business."

"Sure. I can do that. I'm going to head out. I need to swing by the house on the way to the hospital. I'll give Hank your well wishes."

"Tell him I said he's a lazy bugger and he better get back to work soon."

Sebastien laughed as he got up from the chair and made for the door.

"Oh, hey. Sebastien . . ."

Sebastien turned around just before crossing the threshold into the hall.

"Have you been in here since Friday? Did you come in here and work or something?"

"No. I was way too traumatized to think about work. Besides, I don't have a key to the building. I can't get in after hours without you. Why?"

"Maybe I'm losing my mind. I could have sworn I left the Cheyenne folder on my desk, but it wasn't there when I came in."

"Hmm. Did you put it in the Hell Canyon binder?"

Tiffany opened the binder for 88-301 and leafed through the contents. Close to the middle and obscured behind a sheet of photographs was the Cheyenne folder. She pulled it out and held it up with a look of puzzlement.

Sebastien gave her a sympathetic expression.

"You've gone through a lot in the last seventy-two hours," he said.

"Yeah . . . maybe. But I put the sticky note with Dana

Redmond's phone number on the front of the folder. Now it's gone."

Sebastien walked back to the desk, then took the folder from her and opened it.

"No. No. It's right here, on the A page."

"I am telling you, Sebastien, that is not where I left it."

"I believe you, Tiff. I believe you."

"JUST DRINK IT. I don't care if it tastes like rattlesnake piss."

"Mommy said 'piss'!"

"That's right, Kirby. See, honey. You should watch your language."

"You said it first. And please, have some juice. You look dehydrated."

"Honey, I'm not thirsty. I just had some wa-humph-ter."

"Are you okay? Do you want me to call the nurse?"

"I'm fine, Melissa. It just hurts to breath, or move, or think. Well, hey, there's Cousin Sally."

"Oh good, you're still alive," Sebastien retorted sarcastically as he entered Hank's hospital room. "Here's your stuff. I think I got everything. And these flowers are for you, Melissa."

"Thank you, Sebastien, and thank you for getting Hank's clothes."

Hank opened the small duffle bag and started digging through the contents. "I hope it all matches."

"You must be feeling better," observed Sebastien.

"He's not. He's in a lot of pain. He's just trying to act tough," Melissa explained.

"Uncle Sebastien, don't touch that button."

"Which one, Kirby?"

The little girl pointed to the nurse's call button.

"That one right there. It makes the nerds come in and they poke Daddy."

"Oh, well I certainly won't touch it, Kirby. How are you really doing, Henry?"

"I've been better."

"You're lucky to be alive," added Melissa, scoldingly.

"Any update on getting discharged?" asked Sebastien as he leaned on the rail of Hank's bed.

"They said I could go home tomorrow."

"What about work?"

"I'm trying to get him to retire," said Melissa. "Looks like we'll be able to afford it now. Right, Sebastien?"

"I would say that's a fair statement."

"Not happening," Hank replied in his wife's direction before addressing Sebastien. "Four to six weeks and I'll be back giving you orders."

"Good," Sebastien replied genuinely. "Anything you need? Anything I can do?"

Hank made eye contact with his younger brother and took his hand, squeezing it tightly. A single tear fell from Hank's left eye as he gently shook his head.

Shoot-out at the O.K. friggin' *Corral*, thought Derek Manly, fingers superposed over the keyboard, ready to rain down journalistic brilliance on the bumpkins of Custer County. In instances like this, a special post was called for. Readers would demand it. Advertisers would pay for it. But what tone? In these times of ours, a little police brutality wouldn't hurt the click-through rate, although there was that shot-up cop . . . in stable condition, to be released within the next week, they said. The hero angle might play well with the locals. The deceased, a life-long criminal who ambushed the cops in cold blood.

These things had to be weighed. Most people didn't know that. They didn't realize what a tenuous business journalism can be. You're only as good as your best lead, and leads depended on relationships—and relationships could dry up, just as bridges could be burned. Manly knew he needed the cops more than they needed him. The string-and-tin-cup system was proving to be less reliable these days; word on the street was harder to come by. No, he better not burn the cops. Decision made, brain engaged, nervous system activated, down go the fingers.

FRIDAY'S SHOOT-OUT on the 1400 block of K Street in Custer left one man dead and at least two sheriff's deputies wounded—one seriously. The perpetrator, Jason Carson, 23, of Custer, was previously known to police with several arrests for violent crimes. Law enforcement arrived at Carson's home Friday morning to conduct a probation search. It is unclear what prompted the search of Carson's residence, but evidently, the perpetrator lay in wait as the deputies approached the front of the home before he opened fire without warning.

The quick action of the sheriff's deputies most certainly prevented more deaths. An investigation is ongoing. As for the injured deputies, one was treated and released at the scene, the other was life-flighted to Pennington General, where he is reported to be in stable condition.

Since the unfortunate events of last week, the Signal's *most dogged reporter, Derek J. Manly, has combed through his network of reliable sources, both within law enforcement and among those who may have special insight into the events. One confidential source tells the* Signal *that Carson is noted to be a white supremacist who may have had a cache of automatic weapons at the location. Furthermore, it is also rumored that Carson and the weapons are tied to an infamous drug cartel, the name of which is being kept secret to protect sensitive ongoing investigations. Keep an eye on the* Custer Signal *for all of the latest developments.*

Manly sat back in his chair and re-read the post. *Yep, that should do it. Just the right balance of indisputable fact and untraceable supposition. And thank heavens for confidential sources.*

Turning to other matters, Manly realized the post would play well with his feature on the cold cases. Thus, the mountain of paperwork on his desk—or, to be more accurate, the *box* of paperwork—was his next order of business. Not that Manly was expecting much. It seemed like a pretty straightforward matter, if Dr. Grey was telling him everything. But it wouldn't hurt to look, and Manly resolutely refused to be intimidated by the volume of information smuggled out by that gullible rube. If there was one thing he'd learned from his wife's divorce lawyer, it was the power of the technical truth. "Technically no leads" might reasonably be interpreted as quite the opposite. Same with "technically no ID of the victim." It was true that Dr. Grey hadn't used the word "technically," but he may as well have implied it—technically.

Manly coaxed his Great Dane off the sagging couch and began sorting through things, breaking the information into consumable bits and laying the stacks on the dog-hair-covered cushions. Recovery scene diagrams, a huge report describing the subsequent search for more remains, coroner's reports, interviews with the hikers who found the remains, a few supplemental reports dealing with their potential culpability, and from the bottom of the box, a report with an unfamiliar format circumscribed by a fat pink rubber band. Manly deduced that this must have been separate from the rest. *Good girl, Roxie*, he thought. Squinting at the top margin of the top page of this orphan report, he saw the header: Cheyenne Police Department Report of Crime. This looked interesting.

The irritated dog stood and stared at Manly eye to eye as the editor-in-chief settled into his desk chair to read through the Cheyenne report.

"What? I'm trying to work here, Toby. Now git."

Toby hung his head and turned to wander off in search of an alternate napping spot.

"Oh, and your rent is due, ya lazy mutt. Don't you look at me in that tone of voice . . ."

About three pages in, the dimmer switch on Manly's brain was beginning to rotate to the right. This random report from a city that was hundreds of miles away was beginning to look a bit less random. Well, a good deal less random if his grasp of anatomy was to be believed. And it was. You didn't need to be a Sebastien Grey to know that a head wouldn't do much good without the rest of the body. And it appeared that's just what Cheyenne had found in 1987—the "rest" of someone's body.

Manly pulled the forensic report on the Hell Canyon remains from off of the couch. He didn't understand the medical jargon, but fortunately, that didn't matter. One of the pages consisted of an outline diagram of a body in both frontal and profile planes. The head, the top of the neck, and the upper left leg were filled in with black ink. The torso wasn't.

It now made sense why the CPD report was in the file. But that didn't answer why the case was still cold. If both sets of remains were from the same individual, then Grey would have mentioned it. The linking of the cases was surely the sexiest part of the whole matter. So why not tout it? Maybe the torso was ruled out—just a coincidence, a simple red herring. Hell of a coincidence though.

Manly decided it wouldn't be prudent to drop this lead without a little more research. Obviously, he couldn't ask Dr. Grey or Detective Reese about it. *Hey, I was looking at this report I stole from you, and I have some questions about the Cheyenne lead. Got a minute to discuss?* No. That was the problem with some of his methods. But no matter. There was still a lot of reading to do. Something would come to him. It always did.

15

Sebastien was pleased with himself. Quite pleased, in fact. He had managed, in a relatively short space of time, to identify the crime lab storage room and give it a quick once-over, finding that it really wasn't such a major job. He had even introduced himself to the man at the front desk of the crime lab and asked to be pointed in the direction of some cleaning supplies. The man provided him with a garbage can-slash-cart with everything he could possibly need to transform the upper room into a very reasonable working environment.

There was no doubt, however, that Sebastien was taken off guard by his new friend at the front desk.

"How's Sgt. LeGris doing? Such a great guy. Man, I hope he's okay."

Sebastien quickly and confidently informed the man that Hank was, in fact, going to be fine. He'd probably be out for several weeks. But he would be back. He could count on it.

How the man came to ask him about his brother was puzzling at first, until Sebastien realized the criminalist was probably not asking him as Hank's brother. He surely didn't even have that bit of lesser-known information. Rather, the man no doubt concluded that, as a fellow member of the investigations team, Dr. Grey should, most assuredly, have the latest scuttlebutt on the revered sergeant's condition.

True to her word, Tiffany had arranged for furniture to be delivered, and all was in place by mid-afternoon: two desks, two chairs, a large bookcase, a garbage can, and a file cabinet. No lamps or other light fixtures were provided, but those would not be necessary, as the ceiling lights were just as bright as anywhere else in the lab, and there was a large window facing south that would also provide ample illumination.

Sebastien stood back and surveyed the setup in situ. It was definitely a major improvement over their current arrangement, and as he scanned the space, he made a mental note to pick up a large whiteboard for one of the two walls that remained clear of obstruction. Tiffany would appreciate that, he supposed. She seemed like a whiteboard kind of person. Maybe his new criminalist friend could point him in the direction of an office supply store.

By 4:30 p.m., Sebastien was dialing the last numbers into his phone in anxious expectation of getting some answers from Elizabeth Kinder, wife of Charles Kinder, late owner of North Plains Development.

"Hello? Mrs. Kinder?"

"This is Mrs. Jackson. Kinder is no longer my name."

"Oh. I apologize. My name is Dr. Sebastien Grey. I'm part of the investigations team at the Custer County South Dakota Sheriff's Office."

"You're a detective, you say?"

"No . . . well . . . yes. And I'm looking into an incident that happened at one of your husband's job sites in Cheyenne, Wyoming in 1987."

"The fire, you mean?"

Sebastien was taken off guard by how quick the heart of the matter had been reached.

"Yes. You know about that?"

"Of course. Who could forget it? It was horrible. Almost gave Charles a heart attack, all that chaos it caused."

"What do you mean by 'chaos,' if you don't mind my asking?"

"I'm sorry, what is this about? You said you were from South Dakota, right?

"Yes, ma—"

"Well, what does that have to do with what happened in Cheyenne?"

"I'm not sure if it does, Mrs. Kin—er . . . Jackson. But we have an old case up here from the late eighties that we think could be connected."

"What kind of case?"

"A homicide."

"Oh my. Look, I'm not really in a good place for all this right now. My husband has cancer, and it's just not a great time."

"I'm very sorry to hear that, Mrs. Jackson. I really am. Actually, my question is quite simple. I was just wondering if you had any information about the subcontractors your husband Charles used. I mean on that Cheyenne development, specifically."

"Oh . . . well . . . I didn't really have much to do with the business. I mean I did some office work from time to time. But I don't recall much about the contractors he used."

"Would you happen to have any of the paperwork from the business? Something that might have the names of the companies, or any information about the business during the time of the incident in Cheyenne?"

"No, I don't. I'm sorry, but I don't think I can help much."

"I understand. Last question, Mrs. Jackson, can you think of anyone who might?"

"You could always try his business partner?"

"Business partner? I didn't realize it was a partnership."

"I suppose it was really more of an informal thing. Larry Bonner. Bonner Framing. That was the name of the company. He and Charlie did a lot of developments together. Fed each other work, you could say."

"Great. That's terrific. Do you have his contact information?"

"Well, hang on, let me get out my phone book."

"I really do appreciate this, Mrs. Jackson."

Sebastien tested the swivel motion of his newly delivered office chair while he waited for Mrs. Jackson to come back on the line. He found he could do 360s if he pushed off just hard enough from the side of the desk.

"Detective Grey?"

"Yes, yes. I'm here."

"All right, here's his information. Like I said, his name is Larry Bonner. I'm pretty sure he's still alive. It's been a while since I talked to him, but I went to his granddaughter's wedding a few years ago and he seemed fine. Anyway, his number is six-oh-five . . ."

"I'm sorry, Mrs. Jackson. Can you repeat that number, please? Did you say the area code was six-zero-five?"

Sebastien wrote down the number and thanked Mrs. Jackson once again before hanging up. This was exciting. He couldn't wait to tell Tiffany about the South Dakota connection. But before he did, he had one more hunch to check out. He found the sticky note with Redmond's phone number and dialed it in.

"Hello."

"Mr. Redmond, my name is Sebastien Grey. I believe my partner Detective Reese called you the other day."

"Yeah, she did. And I told her everything I know."

Sebastien found himself swiveling again as he ventured on.

"Yes, you were very helpful, Mr. Redmond. We do appreciate it. I just had one more thing to ask about. It's very basic, really. It's about the construction site in Cheyenne."

"Shoot."

"Do you recall there being any burglaries at the site? You know, any tools being stolen, houses or cars broken into? That kind of thing?"

"Oh, for sure, man. We were getting hit pretty hard, as I recall. In fact, somebody took bolt cutters on our job box and took a bunch of cords . . . let me see . . . yeah, it was cords, a rebar tying gun, and even a rebar bender. After that, we never left tools on that job again."

"But you didn't mention that to the Cheyenne PD at the time. Or to Detective Reese."

"I didn't think of it. That stuff happens all the time on every jobsite just about. Kind of part of the deal, you know what I mean?"

"Sure, sure. I understand. Did anyone else—any other subcontractors—experience tools being taken?"

"I'm pretty sure they all did. I think the framers had some circular saws taken, and nail guns even. And the plumbers moved their job box off-site too. Or maybe it was the electrician. It's hard to remember. That was a long time ago."

"That's fine, sir. I don't need too much detail. It just helps to know there was a problem with that sort of thing at the time.'

"Okay, man. And sorry I missed your call earlier."

"Excuse me? I didn't call you, Mr. Redmond."

"Oh? Somebody up there did."

"My cell phone has a California area code, Mr. Redmond. Are you saying you received another call from the Sheriff's Office? Maybe it was Detective Reese."

There was silence on the line for a moment.

"Oh, yeah. Nine-two-five. I didn't notice that. I guess it could have been Detective Reese."

"Can you check, sir? Can you look at the number she called

you with before and see if it's the same as the missed call you had?"

Another few moments elapsed. Sebastien could hear Redmond shuffling the phone.

"No. Not the same number. Must have been someone else. Another cop, maybe?"

"Could you read that number to me, sir? It probably is one of our people."

Sebastien wrote the number down, which he did not recognize. Not that he would have or should have.

TIFFANY HUNG up her phone as she walked out of her office, nearly colliding with Sebastien, who was walking in.

"Hey, I was just coming to find you."

"You found me," replied Sebastien. "What's up?"

Tiffany reached out and brushed the dust from the front of Sebastien's shirt.

"I thought you would have changed out of your fancy clothes before cleaning the office. What is that? Cashmere?"

"It's wool."

"Right. Follow me."

Tiffany pinched his Peter Millar quarter-zip by the belly and pulled him in the direction of the stairs at the other end of the hall.

"Where are we going?"

"Breed wants to see us."

"Lieutenant Breed?"

"He's the only one we have," she replied snarkily.

Tiffany knocked against the lieutenant's door jamb.

"Here, sir."

"Come in, detective, Dr. Grey."

The pair of cold case investigators took their seats in front of the lieutenant's large desk.

"Detective Reese, how are you holding up?"

"I'm fine, lieutenant. Just fine."

Tiffany hoped the lieutenant was not going to prod for trauma, especially with Sebastien in the room.

"Excellent. You let us know if you need anything. You know how this works. We have support if you need it."

"Thank you. I will."

"You've visited Sgt. LeGris, I take it?"

"Yes, sir. We have. He seems to be doing well, all things considered."

"The sheriff and I were up there on Saturday. He was pretty out of it."

"Dr. Grey was up there today. How'd he look, Dr. Grey?"

"Yes, Dr. Grey, tell us about your brother," asked the lieutenant, grinning.

Tiffany swallowed a laugh as Sebastien gulped nervously.

"He's doing very well. They're letting him out tomorrow."

"And I understand he'll be down for a few weeks?"

"That's what he said," replied Sebastien. "Four to six weeks."

The lieutenant swiveled slightly left and peered out the window.

"Well, thank God he's okay. That could have been a lot worse. We're all very relieved."

The room feel silent as the lieutenant fixated on something in the parking lot.

"I'm sorry, lieutenant, was there . . . was there something you needed?" Tiffany ventured.

"I just want to level set. Make sure our ducks are in a row. We're down one person in investigations now. I'm trying to figure how to patch things together until the sergeant returns."

"You want me to stop working the cold cases, sir?"

Lt. Breed eyed them both, apparently assessing their reaction to such a move.

"To be honest, I really wanted to give you a choice. I can put you back on regular case work or bring in someone from patrol. We have one or two out there who have done a stint in investigations."

"And who will be in charge while Sgt. LeGris is out?"

"Does it matter?"

"No, sir. I'm just curious."

"I'm putting Tomlinson in charge. He was just promoted and will run the unit until Hank returns. After that, he'll move on to the jail."

"Sounds like a good plan."

Breed brushed some dandruff from the shoulder of his dark-blue suit.

"So, what about it, Reese?"

"If it's all the same to you, I'd like to stay on the cold case work. We're on to some really good things, and I would hate to stop now. Plus, if I switched, that would leave Dr. Grey without a partner."

"It goes without saying that in that case, we would pause the cold case thing for a bit."

"I'd rather not do that."

"Fine. That clears things up."

"Thank you for giving me a choice."

"Now, what's this about the Amber Harrison case? Hank tells me you want to work it."

"Yes, we do. I think we should put it next on our list."

"Dr. Grey?"

Tiffany turned to look at her partner, anxious at how he might respond.

"I agree with Detective Reese. I don't think Harrison left town."

"Based on what?"

"Just a hunch."

"That doesn't sound very scientific, Dr. Grey."

"All of my hunches are based on science, in the end."

"Okay, Mr. Science. As of right now, you have a lot of credit in the bank. We'll see how long that lasts. Det. Reese, you can make some inquiries and dig into the Harrison case. But let's not sound the alarm about a homicide. Let's approach from the angle of 'we're just following up to see if anyone has heard from her yet.'"

"Sounds good, sir. Will do."

"Mr. Science? What was that?"

Sebastien looked indignant as he sat in his seat in front of Tiffany's desk in the case room.

"Oh, forget him. Let's call it a day. I'm exhausted."

"Don't you want to hear about my call with the hoarder?"

"Was she a hoarder?"

"Not so much."

"Then it can wait. I'm going to go home and crawl into the bath. I suggest you do the same."

Tiffany expected some sort of questionable response from that, but none was offered. Not even a semi-lewd eyebrow flicker. Whether it was difficult for him or not, he was clearly trying to be professional. Ironically, his consideration and effort made her want to kiss him, in this room, again. But she wasn't about to break her own rule.

16

Gravel crunched under the Miata's tires, prompting Manly to cross his fingers as he drove up the long unpaved driveway to the large house. It was this same driveway that had caused his last flat tire, one of many in the old car's long history.

Manly parked in front of the stairs that ascended to the large wrap-around deck, catching the subtle wave of curtain movement in the front window as he slammed the car door. He was halfway up the stairs when the front door flew open and a very tall, very elderly man appeared in the doorway.

"Derek, what brings you out here? I told you I ain't paying for that tire."

"Oh, I'm not here about the tire, Mr. Bonner. Do you have a few minutes?"

"What's it about?" the old man asked, wrapping his burgundy cardigan tight against the wind. "You looking for Richie? He ain't here."

"No, Mr. Bonner. I'd like a few minutes with you, if you can spare them."

Larry Bonner watched carefully as Manly retrieved his briefcase from the passenger seat.

"Business, then?"

"Yes, sir. I'm working on a story and I figured you may be able to help."

"Well, come on in and let me close the damn door."

Manly surveyed the capacious front room as he took a seat on the couch. Last time he was in Larry Bonner's home was a few years ago, at the wedding reception of the old man's granddaughter. The space seemed so different when it was wasn't filled with people.

"Is that you, Mr. Bonner? In the picture with the lion."

"Hm? Oh, yes. South Africa, '92."

"Very impressive!"

"That was nothing. We accidentally crossed the border from Limpopo to Botswana and got chased by a group of Ngwato with rifles."

Manly only understood "chased" and "rifles," so he hoped his reply would resonate.

"Wow. Close call, eh?"

"What can I do for you, Derek?"

Right to the point, hm? Cranky old man hasn't changed a bit.

"I've got a special feature I'm working on. You know the sheriff got a grant from the Department of Justice? He started a cold case unit with it."

"Cold case unit?"

Bonner played with the end of his mustache as he looked at Manly with suspicion.

"Yeah. You know. They're going to look at old cases that couldn't be solved before and try to solve them now."

"I know what a cold case is, son. I'm not an imbecile."

"Oh. Sorry."

"What does this have to do with me?"

"One of the cases involves some human remains that were found in Hell Canyon back in 1988."

"Okay."

"Do you recall that, Mr. Bonner? You were in Hot Springs at the time, I think. You may have read it in the news."

Manly watched the old man's face, looking for deception.

"No. Never heard about that."

"The detectives are working an angle on the case. They seem to think the remains they found are related to some other human remains that were found in Cheyenne the year before. They were found at a construction site."

"Okay."

"Mr. Bonner, it was your construction site. The Boxwood Estates development. You did the framing on that job, correct?"

"You know how many developments I worked on over the years, Derek? Just about half of everything west of Rapid City was my crew. Not to mention all the houses we built in Northern Colorado and Northwest Nebraska. Commercial buildings too."

Manly wanted to point out that the number of houses in Northwest Nebraska could probably be counted on two hands and, maybe, one foot. Especially if you subtract the homes built before 1950.

"You were not aware of the body that was found at the Boxwood site?"

"No, I was not."

"Well, maybe you recall the fire, then. The body was set on fire."

"That was a long time ago. I don't remember that. I guess I can't help you, Derek. Now, if you don't mind, I have a doctor appointment in town."

Manly was done collecting data from Bonner's facial expressions. The man was a liar.

"Sure, sure. Sorry to bother you. It's just, I talked to Lizzie

Jackson. You know her, I think. She was at your granddaughter's wedding reception a few years ago. That's where I met her, anyway. She's the widow of Charlie Kinder, whom I think you did a lot of business with."

Bonner pursed his lips and gripped the arms of his chair. His fingertips began to turn wine red.

"I hope you said hi for me, Derek," he spat. "Now I really must . . ."

"She remembered the fire. She said it shook up Charlie quite a bit."

Bonner pushed himself to a stand and walked toward the door. Then, pausing with a hand on the doorknob, he asked, "You ever meet Charlie Kinder, Derek?"

"No, sir. Just his widow and her husband."

"He was a crooked son of a bitch. Tried to operate outside of the unions. He made a lot of enemies. Not to mention hiring criminals for cheap labor. If anyone was responsible for that fire, I'd say it was Charlie. He attracted trouble like flies on a road apple. You should really talk to him about this stuff. But then, it's too late for that. Isn't it, Derek?"

Manly dipped his head in goodbye and slid through the front door.

"HOLD UP. Isn't that the reporter David Manly?" Sebastien pointed out the window of Tiffany's cruiser.

"Derek Manly," corrected Tiffany.

"Derek Manly. That's him."

"What's he doing at Bonner's house?"

"No idea."

Tiffany made an aggressive U-turn on Pass Creek Road and followed after the Miata.

"You going to pull him over?" asked Sebastien.

"I can't. No probable cause. Doesn't mean we can't talk to him though."

Tiffany caught up to the convertible and pulled even with it in the opposite lane. Sebastien lowered his window.

"Hello, Mr. Manly," he yelled over the Miata's coughing muffler.

"Dr. Grey. Are you trying to get yourself killed?"

"I'm not really in control. But Detective Reese is wondering if you could spare a moment."

Manly slowed down in the middle of the road.

"Is my brake light out again?"

"No, sir. You haven't done anything wrong. We were just hoping for a word."

Manly drove up to the nearest pullout and parked in a plume of dust. Tiffany followed behind him.

"What did I do, officer?" Manly asked, smiling from the front seat as Tiffany walked up.

"Mr. Manly, I'm Detective Reese. We spoke on the phone."

Manly removed his sunglasses and took a long look at the detective before replacing them.

"Hello there, detective. They got you on traffic duty, have they?"

"No, Mr. Manly. We did not pull you over."

"And yet, here I am, both pulled and over."

"You're perfectly free to leave, Mr. Manly. We didn't stop you. I was just wondering if you could tell us why you were at Larry Bonner's place. You did just come out of his drive, did you not?"

"That illegal?"

"How do you know Larry Bonner, Mr. Manly?"

"I don't. Not really. His son and I are pretty good friends though. I thought he might be there, but no luck."

"Who is he, sir?"

"His son."

"Mr. Manly, *who* is Mr. Bonner's son?"

"Richie Bonner. Really tall. Ugly as sin. Good looking wife though. Reminds me of you actually."

"So, you're saying that was a social call?"

"Sure. What else would it be?"

"It could be that you were working on a story."

"No, ma'am. Taking the day off. What about you? You, uh, working on one of your cold cases?"

"Thank you, Mr. Manly. I'm sorry to have bothered you."

Sebastien sidled up to Tiffany as she stood on the shoulder of the road and watched Manly drive away.

"You believe him?" he asked.

"No. No I do not."

"Larry Bonner? Hello, sir. My name is Detective Reese and my colleague is Dr. Grey. We're with the Sheriff's Office. We were wondering if you had a moment."

Bonner pushed his nose through the barely opened door and replied, "What's this about?"

"May we come in?"

Bonner opened the door all the way and motioned them in.

"Have a seat," he said, pointing to the sofa in the living room.

"Do you know Derek Manly?" Tiffany asked, jerking her head in the direction of the road.

"Only a little. He runs around with one of my boys."

Tiffany nodded.

Sebastien examined Mr. Bonner scrupulously. The man looked to be in his eighties, though he retained most of his white hair, and he had a carefully groomed French-style mustache, the thin ends curled upwards. His skin was heavily blotched with age spots and his forehead was scarred and scabbed from what looked to be years of sun damage. Despite the inside of the large home being warm, he was dressed in a thick cardigan over a turtleneck sweater. His blue slacks barely obscured light-blue, whale-patterned socks. On his feet were a pair of suede driving moccasins. At least, that's what Sebastien would call them.

"What can I help you with, detective? I haven't done anything wrong, have I? Are the neighbors complaining about my cows again?"

"No, nothing like that. You aren't in any trouble. We just wanted to ask you about something that happened a long time ago at one of your company's construction sites. You have a framing business, correct?"

"I *had* a framing business. Been retired almost twenty years."

"Of course," replied Tiffany. "But back in 1987 you were in business, correct?'

"That's right."

Sebastien marked the man's blue-gray eyes narrow a millimeter.

"Well, there was an incident at one of your construction sites down in Cheyenne. You may remember it. A fire broke out at one of the lots, near your construction trailer."

"Wasn't my construction trailer, detective. I believe you want to talk to Charles Kinder. That trailer was his."

"We will do that, Mr. Bonner. Thank you."

Sebastien wanted to interrupt and remind Tiffany that Kinder was long dead. But he let it go.

"Excellent. Say hello to old Charlie for me. Been quite a while."

Bonner stirred in his armchair, as if he was preparing to stand.

"We sure will, Mr. Bonner. In the meantime, if you could just answer a few questions for us, that'd be very helpful."

Bonner gave off a faint smile. It looked utterly forced from where Sebastien sat.

"Of course," the old man said.

"Terrific," replied Tiffany. "Do you remember the fire? I believe your crew was working there at the time."

"My crew, detective, but not me. If I recall, I never made it down there. I was busy up here. We were in the middle of an apartment complex in Rapid City. That job was a bear. As I remember it, we were very shorthanded that season. I had to bring in guys from all over just to meet the deadline, and even then, I think we took a late penalty."

"So, you didn't hear about the fire? None of your workers mentioned it?"

"I'm afraid not. May I ask what this is about? Why is the Custer County Sheriff's Office concerned with a fire from over thirty years ago in Cheyenne, Wyoming?"

Sebastien broke in before Tiffany could answer.

"Mr. Bonner, you mentioned having to bring in workers from all over. What exactly does that mean?"

"It means we were shorthanded. I had to get more guys on the job."

"Sure, sure. But where did you find those workers?"

"Is this about illegals? Look, I only hired skilled American labor. Real carpenters. Top-quality craftsmen. Look around you, detective. This is the biggest and most beautiful house west of the river. You think a man achieves this by cutting corners? My reputation is gold. Always has been."

"Mr. Bonner, I'm certain you can find very skilled craftsmen from anywhere, including south of the border. But no, that is not what I mean. I'm asking you where these extra workers came from in the US. How did you recruit them? Did you put ads somewhere? Do you have connections that could provide more men?"

Sebastien glanced at Tiffany, who, thankfully, gave him a

nod of understanding. She evidently knew where he was going with this.

"Oh. I see. Um . . . I did run ads in some of the trade papers and some regular newspapers. And, of course, the union referred some to me."

Tiffany took up the line of questioning.

"Mr. Bonner, the men you did end up using, do you know where they came from? Geographically, I mean?"

"Oh hell . . . let me think. Well, we got a few from Denver, Omaha, Des Moines maybe, Kansas City, and I think a few from up in Minnesota."

Tiffany jotted the locations down in her notebook before looking up to ask, "Thank you, Mr. Bonner. So, to be clear, you never heard about the fire?"

"Young lady, I have already told you twice now. The answer is no."

Sebastien braced himself for a contentious reply from his partner. But she didn't take the bait.

"What about missing people? Do you recall hearing about anyone going missing around that time? Did any of your people go missing?" she asked.

Sebastien stared into Bonner's face, looking for the smallest sign of concern. He could not detect any.

"No, ma'am. I wasn't missing anyone. Look, can you please tell me what this is about?"

Sebastien again glanced at Tiffany, wondering how she would answer.

"Mr. Bonner, the fire in Cheyenne was an attempt to burn a body. That body has never been identified."

"Oh my! That's terrible. I never knew . . . So, what does that have to do with you all?"

"We think that body is connected to another case from around the same time, a case here in Custer County," she replied.

Bonner's face remained unchanged, and he offered no comment.

"Mr. Bonner, can you think of anyone who would want to cause trouble at the Boxwood Estates site? Would there be any reason, in your opinion, for someone to be murdered? Or for someone to attempt to burn down the construction trailer?" Sebastien asked.

Tiffany flashed him a confused look.

"Not really. But I can tell you this, Charlie was in deep with the mob."

"The mob, sir?" Tiffany asked.

"Well, okay. Not the mob so much. But he definitely attracted criminals. I think half his crew was on drugs. Plus, the unions had it out for him; he was always trying to get away with using non-union labor, paying them under the table. I think there would be plenty of reason for someone in Charlie's circle to get murdered. You should really talk to him. Like I said."

"Mr. Bonner, how many children do you have?"

Bonner looked to be taken off guard by Sebastien's question.

"Three. I have three kids. What does that have to do with anything?"

"And who are they? Their names, I mean. And their ages."

Tiffany readied her pen at this.

"Well, there's Greg. He's my oldest. He's sixty-four. Richie is in the middle. He's, um, let me see, 1957 . . . '58 . . . that would make him . . . sixty-two. He's sixty-two. And the youngest, Pammie, she was born in '63 . . ."

"So, she's fifty-seven," Sebastien offered.

"That sounds right. She'll be fifty-eight in January."

"Excellent, Mr. Bonner. Thank you so much."

"Why? Why are you asking about my kids?"

"Just wondering how old they were when all this happened. We'll have to ask them what they remember of it."

"What makes you think they will remember, Detective Grey?"

"Pardon me, Mr. Bonner, it's Dr. Grey. I'm not a detective. And I assume your boys worked for you?"

"Should you be assuming?"

"Did they work for your company, Mr. Bonner?"

"Yes, they did."

"Do you recall which site they were working in '87?" Tiffany asked.

"Both. They were my supervisors."

"So, they worked together?"

"No, Richie was helping out down south. Greg was on the apartment job up here."

Tiffany stood, prompting Sebastien to do the same. They thanked Larry Bonner for taking the time to answer their questions, then excused themselves.

It began to rain while Sebastien and Tiffany were in the house. Shallow puddles had collected in the long gravel driveway, sending splashes of water into the soggy grass that lined the road as they drove past.

"You need to get the windshield wipers changed," said Sebastien, referring to the residual streaks that accumulated across the glass at every swipe of the blades.

Tiffany, looking sternly ahead, did not answer.

"That went pretty well, I think," Sebastien offered, without getting a reply. "What's wrong, Tiffany?"

"I can't believe you did that," she said, shaking her head and looking straight ahead through the windshield.

Sebastien felt a sudden twist in his gut.

"Did what? What are you talking about?"

"I can't believe you told Manly about Cheyenne. And Dana Redmond. And Elizabeth Kinder."

"I did not! I told you I only mentioned the remains from Hell Canyon. I wouldn't do that."

"Then how did he know? What the hell was Manly doing here on the very day we figured out Bonner's connection? Why, Sebastien? Can you tell me that?"

Sebastien could not believe what he was hearing. Here it was—finally. The crashing down of the house of cards that was his happiness. He should have known. He hated himself for letting his guard down, for not seeing it coming.

"I'm telling you. I did not tell Manly anything about Cheyenne, or Redmond, or Kinder, or Bonner. You heard the old man. Manly is a friend of his son. It was just a coincidence."

"You and I both know that's BS. I swear Sebastien, this is not a joke. You can't just go rogue to make yourself look good. This is my career. You don't have a career. You're rich. You don't need this. I can't even pass a damn test for promotion. I cannot afford this, Sebastien. This could really screw me. You really screwed me."

Sebastien felt his face lose color and his mouth fill with saliva—the precursor to being sick. It was all he could do to keep himself from vomiting during the long and awkward drive back to the station. A drive during which no further words were spoken.

17

Sebastien got tangled up in a length of white ribbon hanging from a Mylar balloon as he entered the house, which looked like a flower shop. There were bouquets of varying species and colors on nearly every flat surface—the table in the entry, the dining room table, the coffee table, even the fireplace hearth and mantle. Hank was lying on the couch, looking through get well cards.

"Hey, bro. How's it going?" he asked.

"It's going fine. How are you holding up?"

Sebastien decided not to mention that Hank's favorite detective now hated him and the whole cold case thing had crashed like the Hindenburg.

"Pretty good. I'm sore and it hurts to breathe. On the bright side, there's a box of candy as big as my head on the table there. Help yourself."

"Where's Melissa?" Sebastien asked.

"She and Kirby went to the store. Don't ask me where your dog is. Not my turn."

"Speaking of that. Do you think Melissa would mind if I left Parsifal here with you for a few days?"

Hank lowered the card he had been reading.

"Where are you going?"

"I need to run back home. There's some business at the Block I have to handle."

"All the way to California? I thought this was your home now?"

"I'm still trying to figure that out."

Hank moved the stack of cards from his lap to the coffee table and gave Sebastien a troubled look.

"Are you okay, Sebastien?"

"Oh yeah, yeah. Fine. It's all good. I just need to run back."

"Are you going to fly?"

"No. I need to bring a few things back with me."

"What's going on, little brother? Everything okay at work?"

"Sure. We've made great progress. I actually think we're just about halfway there with the Cheyenne thing."

"O-kay. That's good. Good job, bro."

"Yeah, thanks." Sebastien pointed down the hall and said, "So, I'm just going to grab some stuff and head out. Thanks for watching Parsifal."

"You don't want to wait for Melissa?"

"I want to get going before it gets dark."

"It is dark," replied Hank, now totally confused.

"Well . . . yeah. Anyway, thanks."

Sebastien started down the hall to the guest bedroom.

"Sebastien?"

"Yeah?"

"How are things with Tiffany?"

"She's good. I think the first few days after the shooting were hard. But she seems to be getting back into the swing of things."

"That's not what I asked, Sebastien."

Sebastien ignored his brother and resumed his way to the guest bedroom.

I<small>T WAS</small> easy to find the offices of the *Custer County Signal* and even easier to find Manly's home address. They were one and the same, although finding the house that matched the address was trickier in the dark of the early evening and through the continuous sheets of rain.

Whether it was that selfsame rain that kept him from leaving his car, or some inward trepidation about confronting the reporter, Sebastien could not discern. On the one hand, he really wanted to give Mr. Manly the business, maybe even offer him a good throat punch. Sebastien was by nature timorous and not a violent man, but at this stage, he was quite willing to learn. On the other hand, confronting Manly would only, *could* only, make things worse.

Sebastien killed the running lights in the Rover and surveilled the split-level home as he pondered his next move. Oh, he would be leaving town—he had been truthful about that. But where to, he did not know. He would be going away though. Yes, away. Away from his epic failure that was South Dakota. Would he come back? Who knows? He was good at running and an excellent avoider. If anyone could put the "avoidant" in avoidant personality disorder, it was Sebastien Grey. Cowardly? Perhaps. But what was left to prove? Who cared anyway?

D<small>EREK</small> M<small>ANLY</small> <small>WATCHED</small> through the darkened basement window as the Range Rover pulled away and asked himself what that was all about. What had Old Man Bonner told them? And did they have any clue whatsoever that he had the inside skinny on the case? Or did they believe him when he said it was just a social call? Based on the look that cop gave him, there on the side of Pass Creek Road, they did not. And what a smoking-hot detective she was! Tallish. Nice body. Big gun. *Derek, you old player, you have the wrong insider at the Sheriff's Office. Maybe it's time to upgrade from that wing nut Roxie to the lovely Detective Reese.*

Still, this could not be good. They were clearly on to him. Why else would that weirdo anthropologist be watching his house? Was she in there too? *Probably should have invited them in, Derek. Where have your manners gone?*

Speaking of manners. Larry Bonner was still the same jerk he's always been. Same arrogant, condescending . . . Now that man was clearly lying. He knew full well that Charlie Kinder was dead. Lizzie Kinder-Jackson was talking all about it at Larry's granddaughter's wedding reception. Wouldn't shut up about it, in fact. "Poor Charles, he was in so much pain at the end." Unless the old man had forgotten. But no. Bonner had not forgotten. The old man's memory was just fine. He probably remembered everything.

TIFFANY WAS TOO WORKED up to go home. Blind rage, that's what it was. She decided to take a look at the new office space and maybe even start moving some of the case binders, if the rain would let up a bit.

She had to admit that Sebastien had done a good job on the new office. The whiteboard was a nice touch and would be put to good use. But then again, would it? Where did this leave them? Tiffany knew that if she couldn't trust Sebastien, then the whole thing would not work. *Let's just call if off right now.* Or, if the cold case work was to continue, she'd need a new partner. Hank would just have to understand. And Breed. This wasn't some sort of academic exercise, like looking at old German dog bones. No, this was real life. They had gotten so far on this case, and Tiffany was reasonably sure Bonner knew more than he was saying. If nothing else, several very promising new avenues had opened up.

Thinking through things from the new chair behind her new desk, Tiffany realized it was more complicated than just starting over with a new partner. Breed, for example, would have questions. She imagined the conversation.

"What happened, Reese? Why can't you trust Dr. Grey?"

"Well, sir, he told the reporter about the Cheyenne connection to the Hell Canyon remains."

"What do you mean, 'he told the reporter'? Why was Dr. Grey talking to the reporter, detective? Didn't I expressly instruct *you* to speak with the reporter?"

No, that would not do. Maybe she would just need to tell Sebastien privately he had to go. This was not going to work. Just go away. Say you changed your mind. Something like that. If you love me, you'll do that.

If you love me. Oh Lord.

HANK HAD DONE A PRETTY good job of resisting the pain meds. But by ten o'clock, he felt like his whole right side was being crushed by a sledgehammer while being simultaneously run through with hot knives. He finally acquiesced and agreed to let Melissa bring him one of the large white pills she had picked up from the pharmacy earlier that day.

"You'll feel better. Give it about thirty minutes. Need anything else, sweetheart?"

"No, hon. Thanks. I love you."

Hank leaned back on the pillow and closed his eyes. The charm on Melissa's necklace tapped his hairy chin as she bent over and kissed him on the forehead before retreating, he supposed, into the bedroom. Left alone, Hank's mind began to replay the shooting . . . the noise, the flying wood and glass, Carson's maniacal eyes, bloodshot and dilated, staring at him as he pointed the .45 straight at Hank and pulled the trigger. The faces, the underside of the covered porch, the porch light with the broken cover—all staring down at him as he lie there in hot pain. In his mind, he could hear the yelling that turned into screaming.

Hank had never been one to consider the weightier matters of life or death. Mortality to him was an act of being ever present. Unlike Sebastien Grey, Hank LeGris didn't dwell too much on the past or worry too much about the future, but then his past and future nearly cancelled each other out right there on K Street. He was too close to losing everything. No watching Kirby grow up and get married. No welcoming the new baby— Jake, he would call him, if the baby was a him. No promotions. No retirement party. No twentieth anniversary with the love of his life. It was all too much. Maybe this was what his brother felt like all the time. Dwelling on what-ifs and imagined losses. But this was real. Too real.

And he wondered what was going on with Sebastien. Something was up. It was a long drive to California. It must be a real emergency back at the Block. Maybe he should have offered to go with his brother. No, wait. That was stupid! Don't be stupid, Hank. You can't go anywhere in your condition. He'll be fine. The little nerd will be fine. One thing was certain: He would definitely be back, if for no other reason than to get his ridiculous dog.

A sense of warmth began to wrap around Hank's mind, a euphoria that both numbed and reassured him. It must be the pill, he thought. Did his broken ribs and lacerated flesh hurt any less now? He couldn't tell. All he could feel was a kind of joy. A lack of concern. An inability to count his troubles, a void where the distress used to be.

After several minutes, Hank began to drift off. He began to

dream. He was a teenager again, at his grandfather's cabin in Tahoe. He had that big hammock all to himself, the one that spanned to great Douglas firs in the back. He was swinging softly, gently, smiling up at the bars of sunlight that broke through the branches above. Suddenly, hearing sticks break on the ground behind him, he sat up, put his feet down, and turned. There in the dirt, staring up at him, was a goofy little dog—black with a white belly, triangle ears pointed up like arrows, and an absurdly long tongue hanging out over black gums and corn-colored teeth.

18

The farther south Sebastien drove, the better he felt. It was like a weight lifted; his burdens couldn't keep up with the pace set by his flight into a comfortable isolation. The only trouble was that his mind was too fogged up to make that right turn at Cheyenne, a turn he would have made, perforce, to point him toward California. Not that it mattered. Despite what he told his brother, Sebastien had no business to handle back home, nothing pressing anyway. And as for bringing things back? It was all a lie to facilitate his escape, although there were one or two CDs he wished he had brought with him.

Between the ebbs of self-pity and the flows of self-recrimination, Sebastien thought about the Hell Canyon-slash-Cheyenne case. He was reasonably convinced Larry Bonner knew more than he was saying. He was likewise convinced Bonner was dishing out total garbage when it came to his now-dead business partner Charles Kinder of North Plains Development. After all, if Kinder operated in the demimonde of the construction business—dodging unions, hiring thugs, pissing people off—why would Bonner have been involved with him in the first place? And, furthermore, why would Kinder's widow have been invited to the Bonner grandchild's wedding if there was bad blood there?

It's just too bad that all this drama happened when it did. Sebastien was feeling very confident that the edges of the puzzle were well in place. And he was almost as confident that the pieces in the middle had been nearly identified and collected. Now they just needed to be turned and positioned to see where they fit. When he and Tiffany left Bonner's place, Sebastien was eager to compare notes with her. Did she pick up what he picked up? Would the next steps have been as obvious to her as they were to him? At this point, would he ever know?

By one o'clock in the morning, he found himself on the outskirts of Denver, approaching the 470 loop. Sebastien noted the sign for the airport and considered heading that way. Maybe he should fly home? It couldn't hurt. Maybe a surprise visit to see how Shelby was running things, just to make sure the Block was still standing, make certain it wasn't on fire. But there was that voice, the growing murmur in the back of his brain telling him not to go too far, telling him he enjoyed being the victim way too much and was throwing a temper tantrum. Tiffany has obviously been under a lot of stress since the shooting, and he should not have blamed her for coming to a conclusion that, while utterly false, was not altogether unreasonable. He made this much worse than it should have been. *You sniveling child. Don't go too far. You know you'll be turning right around soon. No. No I won't. They don't need me. They don't want me.*

After exiting the highway, a series of peregrinations found him on narrow streets, squeezed by towering buildings. By the look of it, he had entered downtown Denver. Despite the late hour, the sidewalks were nearly filled with well-dressed people heading southward, en masse. There must have been a theater or play or something that just let out. A police officer was directing traffic at the next intersection and instructed Sebastien to make a left turn, which was fortuitous. He saw a parking garage up ahead, the entrance of which was super-posed by a sign that read Curtis Hotel Parking. He pulled the Rover in, took a ticket, and parked.

For whatever reason, rooms at the Curtis were plentiful, and he was checked in within ten minutes. Within another ten, he was fast asleep. The long drive and spun-up emotions had exhausted him.

THE RAIN HAD CLEARED up by morning and Tiffany decided to start the day by finishing the office move. As she stood at the door of the storage room, she surveyed the mess and made a mental game plan. There wasn't much in the way of office supplies to be moved, and the empty box she brought should hold everything both in and on the desk. The case binders on the shelves could obviously stay. The only ones that needed to go to the new office were the cases they were actively investigat-ing: Hell Canyon, Amber Harrison, and maybe the shoulder girdle from out by Fairburn, at least as a reminder that she still needed to submit a request for DNA analysis on the bones. She would consult Sebastien on any others.

Yes, she would consult Sebastien. After a sleepless night in which she replayed in her mind her reaction to Manly's inter-ference, Tiffany concluded that maybe she had been a little harsh. Or maybe a lot harsh. There was definitely something shady going on, but she probably shouldn't have assumed Sebastien spilled the beans, so to speak. Manly is pretty aggres-sive . . . Sebastien said so himself. Maybe he was able to trick him into unknowingly revealing an important detail. That was her big concern anyway, wasn't it?

And there was something else that occurred to her during the small hours of the morning as she lie in bed listening to the rain tap against her roof. If Manly was at Bonner's house to interview him about Cheyenne, that would mean he knew about the connection between Bonner and Elizabeth Jackson, and from Jackson to Dana Redmond. But Sebastien didn't know what Redmond had to say until *after* Manly interviewed him for the story. In fact, Tiffany spoke to Redmond *while* Sebastien was with Manly. And Sebastien only talked to Jackson the afternoon *before* they went to Bonner's place.

Tiffany thought hard about the timeline and finally concluded that, unless Sebastien was in direct contact with Manly after his interview for the article, it wasn't possible for Manly to end up at Bonner's as a result of something Sebastien may have said during the interview. But would Sebastien be feeding Manly information? There was no reason for him to do that. Was there? If not, that left just two possibilities. Manly either got his information from somewhere else, or his visit to Bonner was in fact purely a social call. But where would Manly get that information if not from Sebastien? Literally no one else knew. Sure, Hank had a general idea of the Cheyenne connection to Hell Creek. But he had no details. Not yet anyway.

Tiffany was never good at math, as evidenced by her need to change her major from forensics to criminal justice. But even she could see how these variables were adding up—or, rather, *not* adding up. She might owe Sebastien a very large and very awkward apology. The poor man looked crushed last night as he meekly and silently got out of her cruiser, head and shoulders slumped. She was too mad to care at the time. But, looking back, she knew he was deeply hurt. But why had she gotten so mad? Why hadn't the timeline occurred to her earlier—right away, even? Why did she explode? Maybe it was witnessing one of her colleagues and best friends get shot. Maybe that affected her even more than she realized. She hoped Sebastien would understand, if he actually had nothing to do with this.

And *if* she could get a hold of him. He hadn't responded to any of her texts, nor answered her phone calls. This was shaping up to be a real crappy day. Hopefully Sebastien would cool down. In the meantime, the office transfer would keep her occupied.

"Hey, Reese! How's the head?" asked Patrol Sergeant Shepherd, as Tiffany entered the copy room in search of a cart to haul the binders.

"Hello, Sarge. It's much better, thanks. I'm just down to this small bandage now," she replied, pointing to her forehead.

"I hear Hank is doing okay."

"Yeah, Sarge, he's doing really well. He's home now."

"Do we know who got 'em yet?"

"Who got whom?"

"Carson. Was it you who shot him? You know, I must have hauled his skinny white butt to detention half a dozen times in the last year. A real winner. I'm not surprised he acted a fool."

"No, they haven't said yet. But I'd be willing to bet it was a group effort. I think Sergeant LeGris got off a few rounds before he was hit."

"You're good though, right?"

"Yes, sir. I am. Thank you."

"Nice. Do you need the copier? I'll be awhile, so you can cut in if you want."

"Oh, no. But thanks. I'm just looking for the rolling cart thingy."

"Hmm," the sergeant looked around the small room. "There it is, under the recycling bag."

Tiffany lifted the long narrow bag off of the plastic cart and set it against the wall. As she did so, the overstuffed sack spilled onto the floor, throwing balled-up papers and various scraps onto the vinyl in front of the work counter.

"Let me help you with that," offered the sergeant, bending over to collect the trash.

As they were scooping up handfuls of scrap, Tiffany caught sight of something in the pile. It was one of those moments in which a familiar image was found in an unfamiliar place, or maybe vice versa. Among the torn-up papers was a sheet that looked to have been extracted from the bowels of a copy machine—presumably the result of a misfeed or paper jamb. It bore the telltale black linear smudges of a half-printed page that had been forcefully pulled from the copier drums, or fusers, or whatever they were called. About the only recognizable printing on the paper was a partial report header—one she had recently encountered for the very first time. It read, "Ch . . . . lice Repor . . . . . . ime." To the left of the letters was a blurry and creased image that looked an awful lot like the shield of the Cheyenne Police Department.

"Whatcha got there, Reese?"

"Oh, nothing. This just looks like something that should have been shredded. I'll handle it. I'm going to empty this recycling bag, too, while I'm at it."

"Good idea," he replied. "I'll tell Margie you said hi. She's been pretty worried. She wanted to call you and see how you were, but she didn't want to bother."

"That's very sweet. I'll give her a call. Maybe we can have lunch."

"That would be great, Reese. She'd really like that."

Without answering further, Tiffany scrambled out of the copy room with a fistful of crumpled paper in one hand and the end of the recycling bag in the other. After heading down the stairs, she shot straight past the cold case storage room and out into the chilly daylight of the back lot. It was only two or three more minutes until the entire contents of the recycling bag were emptied onto the floor in the center of her new office above the lab.

Tiffany wondered if this was how Sebastien felt as he sorted through bones and put them in—what did he call it?—anatomical position. Could her frantic effort to separate, categorize, and reconstruct the torn and twisted papers be likened in any way to putting them in anatomical position? Probably not quite, she supposed. But in her mind the task was no less important—maybe even more important! The whole thing reminded her of that first day going through the cold case binders and separating them into stacks of potential.

Some of the contents of the bag would not qualify as paper or perhaps even be recyclable. But that was a concern for someone else. She conveyed four plastic cups, two of which contained the dregs of tobacco spit; several pieces of chewed gum folded into otherwise perfectly good paper; and a potato chip packet to the heretofore unused garbage can next to her desk. The rest would have to be sorted through much more carefully.

Most of the bag's contents amounted to nothing more than inkless paper-jamb debris. It was also apparent that someone had emptied the contents of old binders into the bag; there was a SWAT training manual, a radio code guide, and standards and practices for DUI checkpoints. Beyond that were numerous aborted copies rescued from the mechanical guts of the copier. And, of these, a half dozen bore the likeness of the Cheyenne report, including the A page from supplement two. She flattened out another crumpled sheet to discover the skeletal diagram from the original analysis of the Hell Canyon remains. On the top of that page was the typed case number 88-301.

Tiffany took all of the pages that bore any likeness to the Cheyenne and Hell Canyon reports and flattened them out as best as she could on the floor. She then took out her phone and got pictures of everything, including the innocuous paper jambs, discarded manuals, and the trash in the can. The last picture she took was of the entire collection as it was laid out on the floor, including the empty recycling bag.

Tiffany attempted to sit and think, but her mind was spinning too fast for lucidity. She paced the room, beating a circular path around the mess on the floor, fingers meshed together on the back of her head. This was bad. Right? There was no explanation for this. Right? Could Sebastien have made the copies? No. Sebastien didn't even know where the copy room was and, if he did, he definitely didn't have the code to activate the copier. Somebody made copies of the Cheyenne and Hell Canyon reports and that person likely fed the information to Manly. That would be Ockham's explanation, right? *Oh Lord. Ockham. Sebastien. Oh, Sebastien. What have you done, Tiffany Reese? Look what you've done!*

Tiffany's hands were shaking as she pulled her cell phone from her back pocket.

"Hank, you hungry? How about I bring you and Melissa lunch?"

"What's the matter, Tiff? Your hair on fire? Or is it just my drugs?"

"I just need to run something by you. No biggie. I figured you wouldn't mind being fed in the process."

"You know me too well. Melissa's out at her mom's place. Pick me up one of them steak and cheese numbers from the deli at the market."

"I will. And Hank, have you heard from Sebastien? I can't reach him."

"What do you mean? He's not picking up?"

"No. And he's not answering my texts."

"Oh, dang. I hope he didn't get in a crash last night."

"A crash? What do you mean?"

"He didn't tell you he was heading back to California for a few days?"

Hank tossed the sandwich wrapper on the coffee table, leaned the recliner back, and repositioned the pillow behind his back with a stifled grunt.

"Well? What should we do?" Tiffany asked from the couch.

"First of all, who's 'we'? And second, are you talking about your neurotic boyfriend, or the fact that someone took files from your office, copied them, and probably gave the copies to your reporter?"

"He's not my reporter."

"You know what I mean."

"Should we be worried about Sebastien?"

Hank thought for a moment, recalling Melissa's concern about this romance going sideways and his response about dealing with it when the time came. Looks like the time was already here. Was it all worth it? It was too early to tell.

"I don't think so. I have his dog as a ransom. He'll be back."

"It's a long way to California and back."

"I doubt he'll make it that far."

"What do you mean? Where else would he go?"

"I don't honestly know. But I know him well enough to know he's madly in love with you. I haven't seen him this happy since he dated that opera singer in college. Did he tell you about that?"

Tiffany shook her head slowly, elbows on her knees, fingertips tapping fingertips.

"They were in college together. That's how he got his taste for that stupid music. He went to all of her rehearsals and shows. He worshipped her."

"What happened?" asked Tiffany.

"She dumped him. Couldn't handle his social phobia. Poor kid wouldn't talk to strangers, wouldn't go to her afterparties, wouldn't meet her friends, family."

Tiffany bent over, her head in her hands, fingers through her hair.

"Ah geez, Hank. Why did you tell me that?"

"You know what I've noticed?"

"What's that?" she replied looking up to face him, her fingers pulling her bottom lip gently downward.

"He's not that bad anymore. I mean, sure, he's got a ways to go. But the fact that he's up here and not squirreled away in his cave shows he's becoming a different person."

"He's not exactly up here though, Hank. Not now, anyway."

"Like I said, he'll be back. And you know what the difference is?"

"Please don't say me."

"It's you. Sorry, Tiff. That's the fact. Like I said, I've known the twerp his whole life. You make him better. No pressure, of course. I'm just stating the facts. I'm still a detective, even though I'm on couch duty."

"I do like him, Hank. A lot. I don't know why I freaked."

"You've been under a lot of stress lately."

"That's what Sebastien said."

"Well, never mind that for now. Who is our infiltrator? Any idea why someone would care to make copies of those reports?"

"No clue. I'm not even sure the copies ended up with Manly."

"Of course they did. There's no other explanation. Do you have any idea when those files would have been taken?"

"Let's see . . . I last saw them on Thursday. It was on Friday afternoon that I noticed them out of place. I was getting ready to write up my report on the search warrant and the Cheyenne report was not where it should have been."

Hank closed his eyes and thought hard, squeezing his

temples between the middle finger and thumb of his left hand. He tried to imagine himself in the headquarters building in the middle of the night. Who would typically be there? Who would be out of place? Could it be one of the patrol deputies? The patrol line-up room was just down the hall from the cold case room, after all. But why? Maybe Manly found himself a source among one of the beat cops. A detective? No—although a detective entering the cold case storage would not arouse any suspicion whatsoever. It occurred to him that there would be an easier way of going about this.

"Let me put a call into the admin sergeant and see if anyone used their entry card on the main office door after hours."

"That would be great, Hank. You aren't going to tell him . . ."

" . . . tell him that someone entered your office and made unauthorized copies of those reports, then fed them to the media? Hell yes, I'm going to tell him. Not yet though. First we need to figure out who it is."

"It could be the admin sergeant, you mean?"

"We got a real Agatha Christie deal going on here. Everyone is a suspect. But no, Sergeant Egan is too ambitious . . . and lazy."

"In the meantime, do I just go on as planned and act like nothing happened?"

Hank knew from his own years of experience that the last thing a detective wants to do is nothing at all. Waiting impotently for information or further developments was arguably the worst part of the job. The very act of doing something, anything, preserved the sense of hope. Hank was glad to give Tiffany that, at least.

"Not yet. See if you can tail that reporter for a few days. Try to figure out what's going on there."

Tiffany exhaled and stood up.

"Sounds good. Thanks, Hank. I really appreciate your help with this."

Parsifal emerged from behind the couch and flopped in front of her, offering his belly for a rub. Tiffany kneeled down to stroke him.

"Of course. That was a good sandwich. Oh, and keep trying my brother. I want him back here. We need him. That ridiculous mutt needs him. And he needs us."

19

A fter a long shower, followed by breakfast in the hotel restaurant, Sebastien considered his next move. He had awoken to several more texts and a few missed calls from Tiffany. Hank, too, had been trying to reach him for the last thirty-six hours. This was probably not fair to them, but he was not ready yet. After two nights holed up in the Curtis, mindlessly watching TV and browsing the internet in his darkened hotel room, the pity party still had some life left.

Sebastien was weighing a handful of options. Would he proceed to California, thus maintaining the appearance of busy obligation that he had portrayed to his brother? Would he go elsewhere? Maybe take a little trip to cool off and reset? Or would he, *should* he, just go back up to Custer and face his insecurities? Surely, running away from an uncomfortable situation was not going to score him points with Tiffany, although that no longer mattered. Right?

Waiting for his laptop to boot up, Sebastien stared out the window and down to the street below. It was a very bright and sunny day, though obviously quite cold outside. Warm exhalations from the few brave pedestrians turned white in the frigid air, which reminded him that he needed to pick up a decent jacket.

Sebastien's eye caught hold of the building on the opposite side of the street. He hadn't noticed it before, as this was the first time he'd opened the curtains in his hotel room since checking in. The two huge stone structures bisected, or connected, by a long glass dome looked to be some sort of theater. That would explain the gowned and suited crowds he saw the night he drove in. He pulled up Google Earth on his laptop and navigated to his current location. Indeed, it *was* a theater, he learned. The Ellie Caulkins Opera House. Hmmm. A few more clicks on his computer and he found the website for Opera Colorado. It was *Die Fledermaus* tonight. Interesting. Sebastien was not a Strauss person or a comic opera person either. But it could be just the excuse he needed to continue his self-quarantine. He could always book a third night at the Curtis.

Returning to the map and zooming out, Sebastien searched alternative destinations. Where might he go if not home? In which cardinal direction? North was out; he just came from that direction, after all. West, over the mountains? Could be tricky this time of year. South, like a snowbird? Maybe. East? East of the river?

Sebastien's grasp of geography was perhaps his largest weakness. What was this business about the river, he asked himself, zooming and panning the map back toward South Dakota. Ah, yes. There it was, the Missouri River, splitting South Dakota down the middle, just like Tiffany had told him. But one wouldn't use the phrase "East of the river" while perched three stories up in a hotel room in downtown Denver. Would they?

Denver. South Dakota. East. West. North. South. Sebastien's mind clicked over to the case that had, until so recently, occupied his attention. There was something Larry Bonner said during the interview that he meant to check out. It was a response to one of Sebastien's own questions. The emotional melee with Tiffany made him forget. But now, with the map open, he remembered it—not verbatim, of course, but in a vague rendering, he thought it went something like this:

"Mr. Bonner, where did you find the extra workers for your Rapid City project?"

"Denver, Omaha, Des Moines, Kansas City, and up in Minnesota."

How interesting, he thought, to find himself in one of the very cities listed by Mr. Bonner—although, in reality, it wasn't the cities Mr. Bonner told them about that were the most interesting. It was the one he quite obviously neglected to mention.

Sebastien zoomed and panned further until those five geographies were visible on the laptop screen. Geographical place names were not his forte, so he had to explore a little to find what he was looking for. But he did find it. At least, he was reasonably confident he did. Sure enough, anyway, to forgo both *Die Fledermaus* and a third night at the Curtis.

"Good morning. I'm fine. I'll be back this afternoon. In the meantime, I suggest you put in a call to the Sioux Falls Police Department and get a list of anyone who went missing in 1987."

Sebastien made sure his text to Tiffany was curt and to the point. He was surprised to receive an immediate reply.

"Can I call you now?"

TIFFANY PICKED up Manly coming out of his street and turning left on Mt. Rushmore. From there, she tailed him about a mile down the road to where he pulled into the back parking lot of a coffee shop. She continued past, searching for a spot in the neighboring lot behind a real estate office. The view was relatively unobscured from this vantage point, and she used binoculars to watch him enter the coffee shop through the back door. Her cell phone pinged just as she reclined the driver's seat for a comfortable stakeout.

The morning sun washed out the screen on her phone. She had to cup her hand around the display to see who had texted her. It was Sebastien. She didn't expect him to reach out so soon or really at all at this point. She hadn't rehearsed her apology yet. She nervously typed in her response and waited. Another text message came in a few moments. This one also from Sebastien. It was a simple "Sure."

"Hey, Sebastien. Where are you?"

"I'm in Denver."

"Denver? What are you doing in Denver?"

"Well, you were right about not finding my kind of clothes up there, and I needed a new jacket, like you said. So I just popped down for a few days of shopping."

"Hank said you went back to California."

"Did he? He must have misunderstood me."

Tiffany didn't buy it, of course. But she felt bad enough. Sebastien was allowed this . . . whatever it was.

"Look, Sebastien, I'm really sorry. I really am. I don't know why I went off like that. I know you didn't tell Manly about the Boxwood Torso."

"The Boxwood Torso? Is that what we're calling it now?"

"I'm serious."

"You were serious the day before yesterday too."

Tiffany closed her eyes and swept her fingertips across her forehead.

"Sebastien, do you really want to do this? I screwed up. I admit it. I'm sorry. Are you going to forgive me or not?"

The phone went silent, except for what sounded like some muted shuffling. This was it, she thought. After a few moments, Tiffany lowered the phone from her ear and put her thumb over the End button.

Just before she lowered her thumb to end the call, she heard him say, "I'm sorry too." A swell of relief came over her as she lifted the phone against her ear once more.

"You don't need to apologize, Sebastien. I'm . . ."

"No, I do. I shouldn't have run away. I was just pissed off. I'm sorry."

Tiffany decided not to pick at it. Just move on.

"It's okay, Sebastien. Really. I don't blame you one bit. Look, I found out how Manly ended up at Bonner's place. At least, I think I did."

"Really? How?"

Here was another pivotal intersection in both their working and personal relationship. She now had to admit that the real reason Manly showed up at Larry Bonner's was a lot more obvious and made way more sense than Sebastien playing the mole.

"Before I tell you, I just want you to know, again, that I know I messed up on this one. When I tell you, you're going to be even angrier that you got blamed. Please promise me you'll let it go."

"I promise, Tiffany. Believe me."

He sounded sincere, so she continued.

"Okay, then. Do you remember when I mentioned how the Cheyenne and Hell Creek reports were out of place?"

"I'm not sure . . . I . . ."

"It was Friday afternoon. I was in the office getting ready to write up my report on the warrant and I asked you about it as you were walking out."

"Oh. Okay. Yeah, I do remember that. Are you saying someone *did* mess with those files?"

"Yes. They absolutely did. I found some copied pages from both reports in the recycling bag in the copy room. You didn't copy the reports, did you?"

"Here we go again."

"No, I mean, I know you didn't. You couldn't have. Unless you somehow got the code to the copier. I didn't give it to you."

"Nope. That never came up."

"Exactly. Somebody copied those reports and gave them to Manly."

"Then you were right about the reports being in the wrong places. You suspected they were tampered with and I told you it was just stress. But you were right all along. You were right, but I didn't believe you."

This bit of exculpatory testimony had not occurred to her. How kind of Sebastien to frame it this way, she thought. Though she wasn't too eager to celebrate this little win. The ultimate result was the same.

"I still don't know who, exactly, copied the reports. But I think I'm getting close. And Hank is going to pull the entry logs to the sheriff's building. This was a nighttime job."

"Okay. Well, good. I mean, I'm glad we cleared that up."

"So am I, partner."

Tiffany waited and listened carefully for a response. She got none. She began to doubt that the olive branch was fully accepted.

"Sebastien? You there?"

"Oh my . . ."

"What is it?"

"I just remembered something. After I talked to Elizabeth Jackson, Kinder's widow, I called Dana Redmond."

"Why?" asked Tiffany.

"I wanted to ask him if the Boxwood construction site was experiencing any burglaries or thefts."

"Why would that matter?"

"I think the torso was meant to go inside the construction trailer. I think whoever dumped the body did so because they couldn't get inside. They were hoping to burn it all down, but they had to settle for setting the torso on fire in the lot."

"That sounds reasonable, but what does that have to do with burglaries?"

"Well, we may never know for sure. But Redmond told me there was a lot of theft on that site. Like, it was a huge problem. So I believe the locks on the trailer door were changed. Or the door was otherwise reinforced somehow, in the wake of all the burglaries. Whoever dumped the body didn't expect that."

This was exactly the kind of thinking the sheriff's department lacked but needed, thought Tiffany. What was it called, non-linear thinking?

"That's actually brilliant."

"Thanks. But anyway, when I spoke to Redmond, he told me someone else from up here had called him. He got a missed call from the six-zero-five area code that same day. I think that may have been Manly."

"Wow. I'm going to rip that jerk's larynx out. Did you get the number?" she asked hopefully.

"Of course. It's on my desk."

Tiffany caught two figures exit the door of the coffee shop. She fished her binoculars from the glove box.

"So, what's this about Sioux Falls?" she asked while looking through the lenses.

"It's a bit of a hunch."

"You know how I feel about your hunches."

"I was looking at a map this morning and I recalled what Larry Bonner said about his extra workers."

"About where they came from, you mean?"

"Exactly."

"Just a sec . . ."

Tiffany quickly confirmed it was not Manly who exited the shop. She put down the binoculars and searched her bag; finding her notebook, she flipped a few pages.

"Here's the list of cities Bonner gave us: Denver, Omaha,

Des Moines, Kansas City, and someplace in Minnesota, he thought."

"That's right. But he didn't mention Sioux Falls," offered Sebastien.

Tiffany squinted down at her bad writing and wondered where this was going.

"So?"

"Like I said, it's just a hunch and it's probably stupid. But if you plot those locations on a map—without Denver, that is—you basically the major cities just east of South Dakota."

"That's true," replied Tiffany, "although Bonner didn't name any cities in Minnesota."

"There aren't many major ones," said Sebastien.

"Also true. So, what does this have to do with Sioux Falls?"

"Why would Bonner neglect to mention the one major city in South Dakota that is nearest those other cities? Especially considering it's in the same state as his Rapid City development. I'm no expert, but wouldn't workers from the same state as the project be more convenient? You know, licensing, unions, and networks. That sort of thing."

As Tiffany stared down at her notebook, she searched her mind for any indication that this angle would have come to her own mind. No, she realized, it would not have. Not in a million years. This was another indication that her partner's brain worked very differently from hers—and Hanks, for that matter. She and her sergeant tended toward running headlong down the cleared and open path, whereas Sebastien was busy wondering what, if anything, was lurking in the bush.

Her silence must have prompted Sebastien.

"I know. It's a reach. It just seems odd to me."

"No. No. You're right. It does seem like a major miss, now that you mention it."

"It could be nothing. But I just think we should add Sioux Falls to our list of cities to check for missing males from 1987."

"Makes sense to me."

"Great. Hey, I have to check out of my hotel now. How about I call you from the road in a few hours? I'm dying to know who the spy is."

"Um, where are you headed, doctor?"

"Where do you want me, detective?"

Tiffany put her head down and closed her eyes, again running her fingertips over her ivory forehead, just above her manicured eyebrows.

"Sebastien, I've had some time to think about that . . ."

"So, California it is."

"Do you know why I jumped all over you the other day?"

"You thought I was a traitor."

"Well, I suppose. But deep down, I think I knew you didn't tip off Manly."

"Then why?"

"I think I was just afraid."

"Because of the shooting, you mean?"

"Well, sure. But not really."

"Okay, Tiff. I'm confused."

Tiffany once again raised the binoculars and pointed them back toward the parking lot of the coffee shop. She could see Manly and a woman leaning against the red Miata. Manly's lady friend looked familiar to Tiffany. She had medium-length blond hair styled into wavy layers. She was rather short and stout, certainly not petite. Zooming in to the woman's face, Tiffany saw it was round and fleshy, with a button nose. Her mouth was covered in sky-pink lipstick. Manly had his hand on her left cheek as he gazed soulfully into her heavily mascaraed eyes and went in for a kiss.

"I think I just reacted out of fear for my feelings about you, about us," Tiffany explained after lowering the binoculars.

"So, like I said, California, then?"

Surely Sebastien could not be this dense when it came to personal feelings. Of course he wasn't.

"I'm in love with you, you idiot. Now get back up here. We have work to do."

As Tiffany raised the binoculars to her puffy, sleep-deprived eyes, she wondered if she shouldn't have told Sebastien her true feelings. But it was too late now. And there was no point in denying it. Why she felt the way she did was not clear to her . . . Sebastien's shyness and insecurity were frustrating. But these things were more than counterbalanced by his good looks, intelligence, and genuine sweetness, so maybe it all made sense. He was so different from the alpha males she'd dated, especially that one Neanderthal who dumped her two months before the wedding.

Tiffany did not have to zoom in too far to get a good look at the female with Manly, the female whose right hand was now cupping the reporter's left buttock as the pair ogled each other lewdly.

"Hey, Hank."

"What's up, my homie?"

"'What's up, my homie?' Is that how you talk now? Are you still taking those painkillers?"

"Don't you worry about that. How's it going with the reporter?"

"I've been watching him all morning."

"And?"

"What's the name of that lady who works up front at HQ? She's the subpoena clerk, I think."

"You mean Roxanne? Roxanne Bishop?"

"Yep. That's the one."

"Why? Do you think she's the one who tipped off your reporter?"

"Well, judging by the sight of her hand on his ass, I would say that's a fair bet."

"Aww, damn it. Okay, let's keep this on the down low until I can get those entry logs back. If she came into the building in the middle of the night last Thursday, then we'll know who our leak is."

"Works for me. Hey, Hank, Manly is getting in his car. I'm going to stay with him."

"Ten-four. Is she getting in his car too?"

"Negative."

As Manly headed toward and through Hill City, Tiffany worried that she may have committed herself to following this jerk all the way to Rapid City or maybe even farther. But no. The dilapidated Miata exited at Rockerville and went south.

Tiffany kept a good distance, trying not to be noticed. She wasn't in her cruiser, of course; she checked out a white Malibu from the investigations carpool. But still, the road was empty except for the tandem Miata and Malibu, and most of it was straight with only occasional bends. It wouldn't be too difficult for Manly to notice her following and even ID her if she got too close.

About two miles south of the highway, Manly made a left turn on Quarter Horse Road. Unfortunately, the intersection was smack in the middle of hayfields on all sides. Rolled-up bales, covered in tarps, dotted the terrain. She would need to let Manly continue a good quarter mile or so before making the left turn herself. Otherwise, she might be too conspicuous. Tiffany drove straight past the intersection and made a U-turn a few hundred yards farther down the road.

Shoot, thought Tiffany, once she made the turn onto Quarter Horse herself. There was no sign of the Miata. She must have gone too far before the U-turn and given Manly too big of a lead.

She scanned the landscape on either side of the road. It was all farmhouses at the end of long dirt drives, all of which were behind electric gates. Up ahead and to the left she thought she spotted a flash of light far up on a knoll. She quickly stopped and trained her binoculars in that direction. It was the Miata, winding its way toward what looked to be a large estate. Tiffany drove up to where the drive intersected with Quarter Horse and got the address off of the mailbox just outside of the gate.

"1Y3 to dispatch."

"Go, 1Y3."

"Can you run an address for me?"

"Affirm, 1Y3. Go ahead."

"4-8-2-3 Quarter Horse Road, Pennington County."

"Copy, 1Y3. That location comes back to a Richard and Evelyn Bonner."

Tiffany racked the mic on the dash and stared in the direction of the big white farmhouse on the top of the hill. After thinking for a moment, she posed a question aloud.

"Is this another social call, Derek? Or are you one step ahead of us?"

20

"You want a beer?" Richie Bonner asked as he leaned behind the large oak bar and opened the refrigerator.

Derek Manly approached the bar and surveyed the massive floor-to-ceiling windows that looked out over the miles of billowing pine-covered landscape behind the house.

"Yeah, sure. That'd be great. So how are things going?"

"Just peachy. Evelyn got a job. Did I tell you that?"

Bonner popped the cap off a bottle and handed it to Manly before taking a seat at the bar next to the reporter. Both men nursed their respective beers and gazed out the window. A herd of whitetail deer darted between the trees about a half mile away.

"No, I don't think so. Where?"

"Some art gallery in Rapid. I think the owner is a coke dealer, but I can't prove it."

"And that doesn't worry you?"

"Nah. She says she's bored. Ever since the daughter got married, she's been pacing the house. And drinking a tad too much. But don't tell her I told you that."

"Ha! I won't." Manly raised the bottle as if to toast the irony. "Business good?"

"Better than ever. All the coastal money coming in is making the custom home business boom. And who's the best custom home builder in all of South Dakota?"

Bonner turned and jabbed his right index finger twice into Manly's chest, near his left nipple.

"You are?" Manly answered, clutching his breast in pain.

"Damn skippy, kid. You know, you should really do an article on me. 'Local man brings jobs to the Hills, winning industry awards in the process.' What do ya think?"

"Sure, Richie. That's easily done."

"Well, that's great. You know, I could use some positive press."

"I heard about that DUI, Richie. That sucks, man."

"Hm? Oh, DUI? No, man. That's small carrots. You didn't hear about the fraud thing? Total BS, of course. It was my accountant who screwed up, which is why I punched him. I go to court next month for that one. Hey! You ain't gonna write about this, are you? I swear, Derek."

Bonner gave him another poke in the chest, and this one hit his sternum.

"No way, man. I couldn't care less. I got something else I'm working on. And please. Stop doing that."

"You're getting fat, Derek."

"Thanks for noticing, Richie." Manly rubbed his chest to dissipate the stinging.

"Is that what you wanted to ask me about? You doing an article or something?"

"Yeah, I am. I was hoping you could help me with it."

"Well, fire away! I'm always happy to help out someone who owes me money. Keeps 'em close, if you know what I mean."

Manly gave a nervous half-chuckle, expecting another shot to his body.

"You hear the sheriff started a cold case unit?"

"Oh really? About time that lazy SOB did something with the money I've donated. Is that why you're here? You wanna talk to the money man? Ooh, good timing, *mi amigo*. I like the way you pay your debts."

"Um, actually, no. It's Custer County SO, not Pennington."

Bonner swiveled fully in his chair. He was now facing Manly square on.

"Custer is doing a cold case thing? Hmm. Cool. I guess. What's that got to do with me?"

"Probably nothing. I'm sure it's nothing. But one of the cases they're working is connected to your dad's old business, Bonner Framing."

"What do you mean by 'connected'?" Richie asked, betraying no concern.

"Back in '88, some bones were found in Hell Canyon. The cops think those bones are connected to a body that was found on one of your dad's developments the year before."

"I don't recall any of that. Which one?"

"It was a neighborhood development down in Cheyenne. Boxwood Estates."

"Huh. I'll be damned."

"So does that ring a bell?"

"Not even a little one."

Bonner turned to once again face the window and raised his bottle to his lips.

"You didn't know about the body that was found next to the trailer down there?" Manly prodded.

Richie finished the long drag on his beer.

"Nope."

"That's kind of what I figured, ya know? I just wanted to check."

Bonner nodded.

"Do you have any idea who might have left a body at that site? I mean, was there anything crazy going on down there?"

"Aside from bodies being torched, you mean?"

An electric shock ran down Manly's spine and the hair on the back of his head stood up. He couldn't tell if Richie noticed. He raised the bottle to his lips to buy time.

"Yeah. Was there any other criminal activity down there?"

"That depends. Does a bunch of crank-heads pouring concrete rise to the level of criminal in your book? Hell, kid. That place was a nightmare. Tools stolen. Portable toilets vandalized and turned over. Place was a nightmare."

"I guess so. Do you, uh . . . do you think Greg might know about the body they found?"

"No, I do not. He was working up here that summer, as I recall. You know that big apartment complex downtown? The one off of Columbus?"

"No. Sorry. I don't."

"Well, anyway, that was one of Pop's jobs. Greg was looking over that for him. He wouldn't know anything about Boxwood."

"How is your brother? He holding up okay?"

"No clue. Haven't talked to him in, what, seven years."

"What about your dad's partner, Charlie What's-his-name?"

"Kinder? Charlie Kinder?"

"Yeah. Would he know anything?"

"Probably. In fact, I'm sure he would. I bet he was at the center of the whole thing. Dude was shady, now that you mention him. Of course, you'd have to hold one of them seances to find out. Guy's been dead for a while, I think."

"True. I met his old lady at Jackie's reception."

"Well, there you go. I would talk to her, if I were you."

Manly nodded and pulled at the last dregs of his beer before pushing himself to his feet.

"Thanks for the beer, Richie."

"So, this case . . . I guess I should expect a visit from the cops, then?"

Manly stopped halfway to the entry hall and turned.

"I think so. They've already talked to your dad."

Bonner stood up and caught up to Manly, putting his face within a few inches of the reporter's.

"They talked to Pops? When? When did they talk to him?"

Manly thought back to when that pretty detective nearly ran him off the road.

"A couple of days ago."

Richie Bonner tilted his head, squinting in suspicion and tracing his snow-white Fu Manchu mustache with his thumb and forefinger.

"Tell me, Derek, how do you know all this? You working with the cops or something?"

Manly was taken aback by Richie's accusatory tone, the sudden seriousness in his eyes.

"Ha! No, Richie. I'm just doing a story on the cold case stuff. You know, a Halloween sort of thing."

"You seem to know an awful lot about it, what they found and who they're talking to."

"What can I say, Richie? I have great journalistic skills."

Richie stabbed his beer bottle in Manly's direction.

"You certainly do, Derek. You certainly do. Let's hope they don't get you in trouble someday."

The Miata threw rocks onto the front porch as Manly sped away from the house. A check of the rearview mirror did not reveal any sign of Richie watching him drive off, but that didn't stop the feeling of danger, of suddenly being on the wrong side of something. Richie Bonner had a reputation for making things happen to people who got in his way. This was the first time Manly felt that himself. He offered a silent prayer that the gate at the end of the drive would open, then exhaled in relief as it did.

With some distance between himself and Richie, Manly was better able to process the import of what he had just heard for himself. In short, he had caught Richie—absolutely—red-handed. That arrogant hump had made the classic mistake of giving back information that had not been given in the first place. *Bodies being torched*. Ha! Both guilty and stupid, that was Richie. It was an empowering feeling, having a card up one's sleeve. But when to play it? And how?

By the time he reached Hill City, the outer edges of an idea were beginning to form in his mind. It would be bold. But that never stopped him before. Dog eat dog—that's what the world is. Kill or be killed. Live or die. Go big or go home.

TRAFFIC OUT of Denver was horrific and reminded Sebastien of the Bay Area. He had been in the sticks for less than two weeks and he was already used to the absence of traffic jams, high-speed chases, and road rage incidents. He gripped the steering wheel hard and willed the cars in front of him to move, move, move. He had places to go, someone to see.

The shock of hearing the "I love you" from Tiffany had not worn off. Half of him wanted to pull the car over so he could jump up and down; the other half of him, of course, was drowning in shame for not giving her more credit and for running away. But this was good, he realized. This was the first major bump in the road, and they had survived. Maybe it was meant to be after all. The relief had lightened him considerably and he liked the feeling. He needed to work harder to foster that, to look for it in his daily life.

He saw a sign for an outlet mall as he approached Thornton and recalled the shopping he told Tiffany he had to do. It was doubtful she believed him, especially since Hank told her he was headed home to California. But he may as well complete the fabrication, play the whole lie out. He needed to use the bathroom anyway, so he pulled off.

It was an hour or so later when he got back on the road, richer by one down jacket and a cashmere overcoat. The latter he doubted he would ever wear in his new country life. But he bookmarked Opera Colorado on his laptop's browser. You never know.

Passing through Cheyenne, Sebastien couldn't resist the urge to visit Boxwood Estates again. He may as well, he reasoned; he would literally be driving right by the entrance on his way north.

Once on Boxwood Avenue, he tried to imagine where the blue truck might have been parked and which neighbor it was who saw it. It probably didn't matter much anymore, since it was highly unlikely the same neighbor would still be living there. Even if they were, they surely would not remember any details after such a long time.

Sebastien parked across the street from the house that now stood where the torso once smoldered. The Rover's wipers did their best against the rain that began to fall hard, but there was little hope of getting a long, cold look at the neighborhood. Any visual cues he hoped would prompt a clearer understanding of the Boxwood Torso case, as Tiffany had christened it, were not likely to come. Not that he expected much.

For Sebastien, it was a steadfast rule that events only seemed random because we, the observers, either lacked information or possessed too much information; that is, we included causal factors that did not belong. In the case of the dismembered and charred torso, the problem was probably the former. Because I *think* the torso and Hell Canyon skull are connected, I *assume* that any South Dakota association will be the key to the matter. But, at present, there were just two such associations: the blue truck with the South Dakota plates and the Bonner family. Surely there could be much more than that. Was he being narrow-minded? Myopic?

And yet . . . there was no denying the fact that Larry Bonner was lying, or at least holding something back. *Don't forget to add that to the dataset, Sebastien.* No, it was too early to leave the Bonner path. Like Tiffany had said, there was work to do. The answer was not here in the suburbs of Cheyenne. Sure, this place may have formed the backdrop of act two in their little opera. But the final act, like the overture, would surely be set in the Black Hills, 250 miles north. It was time to dim the house lights.

The sudden shriek of his phone through the car speakers shook him from his reverie.

"What's up, Hank?"

"Denver? Denver, you little prick?"

As usual, Hank did not sound too serious or particularly bothered.

"What's it to you?" Sebastien spat back.

"Your dog crapped on my carpet."

"No, he didn't," Sebastien replied defiantly.

"No, he didn't. But he could have. What's the deal with Denver, bro?"

Sebastien considered going through the whole story of Tiffany blaming him for the leak to Manly and his gross overreaction, but he was feeling too happy to regress through that. It's all good now. That was all that mattered.

"I just needed some time. That's all."

"Are you and Detective Reese okay?"

"Yes, we are. We really are."

"And I take it you're heading back?"

"Yes. I'll be there later this afternoon."

"Good. Did you hear about our rogue clerk?"

"You mean the person who leaked the reports?"

"Yep. Tiffany saw her talking to that reporter this morning."

"What are you going to do about her?"

"I'll leave that up to her sergeant. It's the reporter I'm more concerned about. Tiffany followed him to an address associated with Richie Bonner earlier."

"That's the son of Larry Bonner. He was a partner on that Cheyenne development."

"That's what Tiffany said. She also said that Richie Bonner was next on your interview list."

"Probably so."

"This one is getting squirrely. You two be careful. Tiffany ran out the Bonners, and that Richie has not been a good boy. Oh, and his brother, what's his name . . ."

"Greg Bonner," offered Sebastien.

"That's it. Greg Bonner. He's doing fifteen in the state pen for manslaughter."

"WHAT DO you want me to say?" asked Roxanne.

"I told you. Just read the paper. Word for word." Derek tapped on the paper in Roxanne's hand from his desk chair. Roxanne stood next to him, looking dubious about Derek's next mission.

"Well, what if he asks me something?"

"Ignore it. Look, are you gonna do this or do I gotta find someone else?"

"No. No, I'll do it. I want to get this right. Or would you rather I screw it up?"

"Don't screw it up! Now, here. Here's the number. We gotta do this before it's too late."

The clerk's fingers shook as she punched in the number on the burner phone.

"No! Damnit! That's a two, you idiot. Here, give me the dang thing." Derek ripped the phone from her and typed in the number. "There, it's ringing," he said, handing the phone back to her.

"Hello, Mr. Bonner? Is this Larry Bonner?"

"Who is this?" came a deep and suspicious voice from the phone's speaker.

"Never you mind that."

Roxanne began to read from the piece of notebook paper, which was now shuddering almost audibly in her hand.

"Five hundred thousand dollars, Mr. Bonner. Five hundred thousand or the cops get the full story. You have twenty-four hours. And no going to the police. If you do, we will know about it and you will be sorry."

"Who the hell is this? Why, you little bitch. Do you have any idea who you're screwing with? I will find you and I will . . ."

"What the hell, Roxie! Why did you hang up?"

"I don't know, Derek. I was scared. Did you hear him? I don't think this is a good idea."

"Ah, for cryin' out loud. Here, I'm going to dial it again. You just say that last part and hang up." Manly pointed to a handwritten line on the paper.

"Look, you little . . ."

"Mr. Bonner, you have twenty-four hours to get the five hundred thousand in cash. We will call you back in twenty-four hours. If you do not comply, we go to the cops and tell them everything. There's no statute of limitations on murder, Mr. Bonner."

Roxanne ended the call and smiled with pride. Manly shook his head in return.

"You made that a lot harder than it needed to be, you nitwit."

21

Tiffany and Sebastien were at their respective desks in the new space. Tiffany was leaning back in her chair with her fingers knitted at her chest, looking upward and slowly swiveling her chair. Sebastien pretended to read through the list of missing persons from Sioux Falls as he fixed his eyes on her thoughtful profile.

"So, what do you think?" she asked. "There's not much there."

Sebastien skimmed quickly.

"One or two look promising."

"There is a thirty-eight-year-old in there. Rodney something-or-other," Tiffany offered, pointing to the sheets of paper in Sebastien's hand.

Sebastien flipped to the next page. "Nope. Black male. Definitely not a match. But what about this guy? James Dunn, white male, thirty-one, five foot eight? And it says here there's dental. Should be an easy thing to check against our skull."

"I'll send that over to Gerry at the Coroner's Office."

Sebastien continued to browse the two stapled sheets.

"Most of these guys were reported missing well before the torso was discovered, which was in October of '87," he said.

"Does that matter?"

"No. I guess not. Here, what about this guy, Martin Alexander, white male, twenty-eight, five foot eleven? It says here he was reported missing in early December by his mother."

"The original anthropology report for our skull had the victim at thirty-five to forty-five years old though," replied Tiffany.

"That range is way too narrow. Once a person reaches adulthood, age is far more difficult to assess. The ranges usually span twenty or more years."

Tiffany turned her chair to face Sebastien and sat up.

"What? What's the matter, Tiff?"

"See this stack?" Tiffany ran her thumb up the side of a two-inch stack of paper on her deck, making the sheets sound almost like a deck of cards being shuffled. "These are the missing persons from 1986 through 1988 for all of the places Bonner mentioned."

"Eighty-eight?"

"I know. I just don't want to rule anything out. You know ... ranges."

"Fair point."

"The other thing is that just because Bonner claimed not to use migrant labor does not mean he didn't. If the Hell Canyon Doe is from Mexico or somewhere else down south, it will be virtually impossible to ID him."

"He's not. I'm telling you, that guy is straight-up Caucasian. The more I think about that skull, the more it fits the Northern European typology, which is perfect for the Upper Midwest."

"Okay. We still have a big stack to go through right here."

"Let's do this," he replied. "I suggest we let the coroner work on the dental for the one guy . . ." Sebastien checked the list one more time. "Dunn. In the meantime, let's put a call in to

Sioux Falls and see if they can track down a relative of Alexander. Maybe we can get a DNA sample."

"We won't need to call. Our plane leaves in two hours."

"Wait. What?"

"We're hitching a ride on the state plane. I figured we should speak to Greg Bonner."

Sebastien grinned and shook his head.

Tiffany smirked in return. "Oh, I'm sorry. Does this little trip interrupt some important business, doctor? Did you have a date or something?"

THE FRONT of the state penitentiary resembled a grand old manor with a covered porch, steep hip-and-gable roofing, red stone exterior, and whitewashed block trim. The structure would pass for a mansion if not for the massive wings extending on either side of the entry, with their high and narrow institutional windows. There was a sort of beauty in the facade, considered Sebastien, which was quickly and thoroughly dismantled once they made their way inside.

Like the prison itself, Greg Bonner was not what Sebastien expected. The sixty-four-year-old had a full head of dark hair, cut just long enough to allow a part. His eyebrows were also dark and heavy. Faint lines circumscribed his thin lips, giving an indication that the man had probably been a smoker for a good portion of his life but gave it up at some point. Sebastien marked the man's hands clasped on the table in front of him and was alarmed to see that Bonner wasn't cuffed.

"Mr. Bonner, thank you for meeting with us."

Greg Bonner scanned Tiffany from her face downward, like a piece of meat.

"I haven't seen a cop like you before," he laughed.

"I'm sorry. Like what, exactly?" replied Tiffany pleasantly.

The man smiled but gave no response.

"Mr. Bonner . . ."

"Call me Greg."

"Okay, Greg. My name is Detective Reese and this is Sebastien Grey. We're with the Custer County Sheriff's Office."

"You must be lost," the inmate observed.

"No, sir . . . Greg. I don't think we are. You see, we'd like to ask you a few questions about your father's business."

"Which one?"

"We're referring to Bonner Framing. I didn't realize your father had more than one business."

"Pops had his finger in a lot of pies," he replied while licking his lips salaciously. Sebastien instantly hated the man.

"Greg, do you recall the Boxwood Estate development? It's in Cheyenne, Wyoming."

Bonner's eyebrows lifted.

"Hmm. Well. Let me think now. I know Pops did a fair amount of work in Wyoming, and Colorado, for that matter. I'm not sure I specifically remember that one though."

"But you worked for your father," Sebastien cut in.

Bonner looked at Sebastien with contempt, as if to say, *Who said you could talk?*

"Did I?"

"According to your father, you did," replied Tiffany.

Bonner crossed his right leg over his left knee and sat back in his chair. His attempt at laissez-faire indifference did not quite land.

"Well, then I guess I did. Been a long time since I worked for Pops."

Sebastien stopped himself from saying "*seven years.*"

"Mr. Bon . . . Greg. You were working for your father in 1987. Is that correct?"

The man twisted his lip, rolled his eyes to the ceiling, and bounced his head laterally.

"Maybe. Possibly. Hard to say. That was a long time ago."

"We can find out pretty easily. Tax records and all that."

Bonner lifted his hands. "Oh, sweetheart, I didn't pay taxes in the eighties."

"Mr. Bonner, your father told us you worked on his Cheyenne development in 1987."

Sebastien brushed Tiffany's hand under the table, hoping she would receive the signal and not interrupt his line of questioning with any facts.

"My father has dementia, detective."

"When was the last time you spoke to your father?"

"Talk to him all the time."

"Really?" replied Sebastien. "That's a pretty easy one to check."

Bonner uncrossed his legs and crossed his arms.

"Look, why don't you two tell me what the hell you want?"

Tiffany bit.

"We want you to tell us how a dismembered body ended up at Boxwood Estates in October of 1987. Who put it there and whose body was it?"

"You're out of your friggin' mind. I don't know anything about a body. And I didn't work that site and Pops damn well knows it. That was Richie's deal down there. He was helping Pop with that job."

"Your brother Richard?" asked Tiffany.

Bonner gave a nod before Sebastien cut in.

"Job? Are you referring to the housing development or the body, Mr. Bonner?"

Bonner shot out of his chair and pointed his finger at Sebastien.

"Hey, screw you, man!"

The door suddenly opened and a guard stepped in.

"That's okay. We're okay," Tiffany told the guard. "We just need a few more minutes with the inmate and we'll be done."

The inmate. *Nice touch*, thought Sebastien.

Bonner sat down and the guard nodded and left the room.

"I apologize for Dr. Grey, Greg. He's a smart ass."

Sebastien nearly shot her a look but caught himself.

"Doctor? You're not a cop?" Bonner looked Sebastien up and down.

The doctor of philosophy smiled and shook his head.

"Look, I already had the psych screenings. I don't need any more doctors poking around my head."

Neither of the non-prisoners bothered to correct the inmate.

"Greg, I'm sorry we barged in like this. Let's start over, okay?" Tiffany said in a contrite voice. "Can you just tell us if you heard about the body at the site—back then, I mean? Did anyone tell you about the body that was found? It had to be a big deal. It's not every day that kind of thing happens."

"I'm sorry. Like I said, I had no idea."

"Fair enough. Can you think of anyone who *might* know? Any guesses? Anyone we should ask?" she replied.

"No, I don't. Like I said, I was working in Rapid City that summer."

"Mr. Bonner, you father told us you were short-handed on the Rapid City apartment complex. He said you had to bring in extra labor."

"Probably. That sounds about right. I remember we were rushing to get it done in the end."

"Well, do you recall any trouble with anyone on that job? Did anyone get hurt or even go missing?"

Sebastien watched closely as Bonner answered.

"No," Bonner quickly replied.

"You're sure?" Sebastien asked.

"Positive."

"Okay, well, that's all fine, Mr. Bonner. We may come back if we have more questions."

"You can come back anytime, sweetheart. Not so much you, Doctor Smartass."

Sebastien didn't react, but he did offer an entirely different line of questioning.

"Mr. Bonner, what are you in here for?"

"I killed a guy."

Sebastien forced himself to remain unflinching as Bonner grinned and spat his response directly at him.

"What guy? And why?"

"My psychiatrist. He asked too many questions."

"WELL, what did you make of that?" asked Tiffany from across the roof of the rental car.

"Did you see the look on that guy's face when I asked if anyone went missing?"

"I know, right?" replied Tiffany before removing her sunglasses and dusting the lenses on her shirt. "He definitely knows way more than he's saying. Maybe we should have pressed him more."

"He's not going anywhere," replied Sebastien, gazing up at the massive prison walls. "You know the most suspicious part of that conversation?"

Tiffany replaced her glasses and looked across the roof.

"What's that?"

"Greg Bonner just told us the same thing his father did— that he wasn't in charge of the Cheyenne site, but his brother, Richie, was."

"Nice try on that one, Doctor Grey," Tiffany snickered. "So, what's suspicious about that?"

Sebastien thought for a second. "Well, when we asked him whom we should talk to, someone who might know about the body, why didn't he say his brother?"

"Maybe he assumed we talked to him already," observed Tiffany.

"Or maybe he doesn't want us to talk to his brother."

Tiffany tossed the key fob over the car to Sebastien, who caught it precariously between his forearm and stomach.

"What's this? My turn to drive?"

"Yep. I'll navigate."

"Okay, boss, where to?"

Ten minutes and several stop signs and turns later, the pair pulled into the small parking lot of Duck's Auto Repair. A man about their age greeted them from behind the counter, then escorted them through a door and into the garage.

"Duck. Visitors."

A man rolled out from under an SUV.

"Whassat? Oh."

"Are you Jerry Alexander?" asked Tiffany.

"Only to my fourth-grade teacher. Call me Duck."

The man stood up with a series of grunts and flashed his grease-covered palms to preempt any handshakes.

"Okay, Duck. I'm Detective Reese, and this is Dr. Grey. We're with the Custer County Sheriff's Office."

"Westies, eh? What can I do ya for?"

"Why do they call you Duck, sir? If I may ask."

The man turned to Sebastien and smiled proudly, showing an incomplete set of teeth.

"Won the county waterfowl hunting competition when I was a youngster. It's been Duck ever since."

Sebastien nodded and tried to feign appreciation for the accomplishment.

"That's amazing, Mr. Alexander. I competed as a kid too, although I never won anything. My dad always said I rushed my shots," said Tiffany.

Sebastien couldn't tell if she was being sincere or just trying to get in the man's good graces. He made a mental note to ask her later.

"Don't be bothered, honey. A lot of kids do that. Or they just shoot at the whole damn flight. Me? I had a knack."

"You don't hunt anymore, Mr. Alexander?"

"No, ma'am. Arthritis in my hip."

"That must make it really hard to work on cars," observed Sebastien.

"It took me twenty-five years to become the busiest repair shop in town. Lots of people count on me. They'll have to carry me out in a box."

Despite the unfortunate segue, Sebastien pushed the conversation to the point of the matter.

"Mr. Alexander, we're here to ask you about your brother, Martin."

Duck's face turned somber.

"Come on, then. Let's have a seat in my office."

All three took seats in the tiny office adjacent to the counter up front. Tiffany and Sebastien took the two metal folding chairs in front of the desk, which was completely covered in invoices, notepads, and other business debris.

"So, what's this about Marty? Don't tell me he's shown up after all these years."

"Well, no. We're just following up on some of these missing people—you know, taking a fresh look—and we wanted to check in to see if you'd heard from your brother or might know where he is. Is he even still missing?"

"He ain't missing. He's dead. And why would you be following up on Marty's case? You're from Custer, you say?"

"Yes, we are," replied Tiffany. "What makes you think Martin is dead, Mr. Alexander?" she added quickly.

Duck pulled open the top drawer of his desk and pulled out a can of tobacco. He pinched a wad and shook the loose pieces free over the can, then paused, looked up, and smiled.

"I tell you what, detective. You tell me why *you* think he's dead, then I'll tell you why *I* think he's dead."

Tiffany shifted in her chair, which made a metallic cracking sound in response. Sebastien caught her quick glance and replied with a slight nod.

"We found some remains in our county—actually, they were found in 1988. We have no specific reason to believe the remains belong to your brother. But they fit his description generally."

"Interesting," replied Duck as he tucked the chew into his cheek.

"So if we could just get a DNA swab from you, that would be really helpful," said Tiffany. "Do you both have the same mother and father?"

The mechanic looked irritated by the question.

"I'm sorry, Mr. Alexander. I just have to ask so we know if the DNA will be useful."

"Sure. Sure."

Sebastien contemplated just how disgusting that task of swabbing would be in light of the massive hunk of tobacco in the man's mouth.

"Why do *you* think your brother is dead, Mr. Alexander?" he asked.

"Marty wasn't a great guy. He was impulsive. Had a lot of enemies."

"What do you mean by 'impulsive'?"

"Let's just say he liked what the ladies had to offer, but he didn't like to ask for it."

"He was a rapist," said Tiffany.

"Marty did time in jail for sexual assault. He attacked some lady in the restroom of a bar. Her old man found out and reported him—after beating what little sense Marty had out of him, of course. That's why he left town. He was afraid the guy would come back for more."

"Was that the only time he'd done something like that?"

"No, ma'am. It was the first time he got reported. Probably about the fifth time he got pounded though. Like I said, he had lots of enemies."

"And you reported him missing?" asked Tiffany.

"No. Mom did. Poor woman. She never got over it. She was waiting for him to come back until the day she died."

"You said he left town. Where did he go exactly?" asked Sebastien.

"That I don't know. But he said his buddy hooked him up with a job."

The pair of investigators looked at each other furtively.

"What did your brother do for a living, Mr. Alexander?"

"Well, ma'am, he did lots of things. He worked on a road crew for a bit. He did a stint with the power company, working in one of their plants. I think he was learning to do finish work about the time he left."

"Finish work," echoed Sebastien. "You mean, as in construction? Like houses?"

"Yeah. They're the guys who come in and do the molding and painting and whatnot. As a matter of fact, that's what his buddy was going to help him with. Apparently, the guy had a connection in that line of work."

Tiffany fished out her notebook and pen.

"Do you know who this buddy is, or was?"

"Oh heck. I told the cops when they came round to take the report. I think it was Clyde, or Carl. Maybe Chris. Pretty sure it started with a 'C.'"

Tiffany looked up from her notebook and asked, "And where, Mr. Alexander? Where was Martin going to get this finishing job?"

"Somewhere west." Duck's eyes suddenly lit up and he wagged a filthy finger in the air. "Hey! That would make sense, wouldn't it? You guys coming here from the west."

Sebastien and Tiffany looked at each other again and smiled, without the slightest effort to conceal their enthusiasm from the equally enthusiastic junior waterfowl hunting champion.

"So, how does this DNA thing work? Do y'all need me to piss in a cup?"

"SON OF A GUN," exclaimed Tiffany, beaming once the pair was inside the car.

"We'll need to check a few things. The name of the 'buddy,' for example," Sebastien replied.

"I'm way ahead of you."

Tiffany was reading off of a sheet in her notepad and dialing into her phone as she spoke.

"Hello? Yes, this is Detective Reese with Custer County. We spoke earlier about the missing persons from back in the eighties. Yes. Oh good, you do remember. Hey, I was wondering if my partner and I could swing by and get a copy of one of the reports. Yeah, we're in town on another matter. That's perfect. Thanks. The name is Martin Alexander."

Sebastien watched her from the driver's seat as she made the call. He noticed, for the first time, a small freckle on her neck about two inches up from her left clavicle, almost hiding behind a drape of her hair and the top edge of her shirt collar. The small bronze spot moved up and down ever so slightly as she spoke, drawing him into a trance.

TIFFANY LAY BACK on the bed in her hotel room and closed her eyes. On her abdomen was a stack of papers, a copy of the missing person's report on Martin Alexander, which rose and fell with her breathing. The lights were out; the television was off. Reading through the scant report made her tired, or maybe it was just the long day.

The report didn't offer much in the way of novel information. Duck Alexander's version of events was essentially echoed in its pages. The name of Martin's supposed new employer was in there—Carl—so that was a helpful clarification. Aside from that, the original Sioux Falls investigators followed up on all of the logical leads, including the possibility that Martin was killed by someone who didn't appreciate his treatment of women. Nothing came of it. It seemed as though Martin really did leave town.

Reading through this case and the others she'd read recently gave her an appreciation for how different investigations were now compared to twenty or thirty years ago. There were no cell phone records to look through back then. And the expectations that a person would or could communicate were decreased considerably. Inter-agency communication and collaboration were also less efficient, certainly less automated. And although credit cards were a thing, they were not as frequently used as they were now. That was especially true for individuals on the lower end of the income spectrum, as Martin was. The digital world was much smaller and the footprints left in that world were very shallow and far apart.

The Carl angle would be interesting. But as she felt herself sinking deeper into the mattress, Tiffany wondered how to connect Martin to an otherwise unknown Carl. She thought of Sebastien and what he might suggest. He would probably give her a lecture about pulling the thread that sticks out the most. She imagined him, for some reason, in front of the newly installed whiteboard in the newly acquired office space.

"Okay, here we will write Carl. And over here, we will list our threads. Do you remember what they were?"

"They were a blue Chevy and South Dakota," she imagined herself replying.

"Yes. And the construction site. Let's not forget that."

"What about North Plains Development and Bonner Framing?"

"No. As of right now, we can't be sure. But we *can* be sure someone saw the truck with South Dakota plates and the torso was in the construction site. We only *think* the Bonners may be involved. But we are not currently aware of any Carls being connected to them."

While she imagined Sebastien scrawling on the board, she realized she didn't even know what his writing looked like. All the same, she thought of him making lines from Carl to each of the other factors. *Does Ockham's Razor apply to this?* she mused. No. That was something different. What did she currently know and what could she currently find out?

In her mind's eye, she watched Sebastien walk toward her holding out the marker. He then sat down and beckoned her to step up to the board. She did so, staring for a moment at Sebastien's neat writing—surely it had to be neat. After a moment, she took the cap off of the pen and in black ink circled the words "blue Chevy."

Tiffany got up from the bed and wrote a reminder to herself to check out the list of Chevy Silverados she put together last week. She then changed and went into the bathroom to brush her teeth. Looking at herself in the mirror with a bandaged forehead in her ratty, old Cody Night Rodeo t-shirt and purple, bleach-stained sweatpants, a crest of appreciation overtook her. It was a relief to know she did not have to do herself up for a night with Sebastien. He seemed to understand, and it only made her love him more.

22

Roxanne Bishop was blubbering uncontrollably into a wad of tissues, and indeed had been doing so ever since she entered the office of Sgt. Egan, administrative sergeant for the Sheriff's Office. Egan had staged the scene for maximum effect—shock and awe, one could say. Not that he should have felt the need to instill so much terror in a woman so timid. It was just easier to get it all over with quickly. That was ultimately the best way. It would be unproductive to draw things out with a bunch of pointless denials. A desk covered in rejected copies of the two reports, an eight-by-ten photo of Roxanne and the mystery man talking in the coffee shop parking lot, and a printout of the front door entry-key logs seemed to do the trick.

"Why, Roxanne? Why on earth would you steal these reports and give them to the media?" Egan emphasized the word *steal*.

"I didn't steal them. I just copied them. Derek told me he had permission."

"And who is Derek?" the sergeant asked.

"The reporter. Derek Manly."

The sergeant held up the photo.

"This guy?"

"Um huh."

"You are clearly on more than just a first-name basis with this reporter," observed the sergeant.

Roxanne lowered her head and resumed her convulsive crying. The clerical supervisor, who was sitting next to her in front of Egan's desk, handed her a fresh box of tissues.

"Roxanne, if you thought you had a legitimate reason to copy those reports, why did you do it in the middle of the night? See here," Egan lifted up a sheet from the entry log and pointed at one of the printed lines. "This says your card was used to enter the building at 11:08 p.m. Why?"

"Well . . . I . . . uh . . . I just . . . I didn't want to tie up the copier. You know? During the day."

"Bullcrap," growled the sergeant.

"Roxanne, just tell the sergeant everything. Come on, dear. It will be a lot easier if you do," said the supervisor with a pat on her clerk's knee.

"Okay. Okay. Look. Derek—Mr. Manly—he told me the detectives gave him permission to have the reports. They just didn't have time to make the copies."

"And you honestly believed that?"

"Well . . ."

"No, you did not believe that. Otherwise, you would have checked with Detective Reese to make sure it was okay. And you wouldn't have come in the middle of the night. So why? Why did you do it? Are you and this reporter involved?"

Roxanne gave a nod into her tissue. The woman next to her uttered an "oh Lord," and raised her right hand to her right cheek.

"Here's the deal, Roxanne. I am suspending you, pending an investigation and a determination on whether or not we file criminal charges."

"Criminal! But . . . but . . ."

"Please turn your entry key over to Heather," the sergeant instructed, pointing to the woman sitting next to Roxanne, "as well as all of your other office keys. Heather and I, and the captain, will discuss how to move forward. I highly suggest you stay away from Mr. Manly. He will be part of our investigation. And do not speak to him. Do you understand me? It will be obstruction if you do."

"I won't. I promise."

"Good. Heather here will be in touch. Now please leave the premises."

Roxanne couldn't bring herself to turn the ignition key. She wouldn't have been able to drive away anyway. Her eyes were too swollen with tears, her mind spinning too fast, her head too light. It was all hopeless now. It had all come down on top of her. The weight of every consequence poised to crush her dead. The only question now was what her husband would be angriest about: losing her job or the affair? Probably losing her job, she concluded. Maybe it's for the best. Maybe this was the excuse she needed. Now she and Derek really could be together. Who cares what the world thinks? Maybe they could run off to Vegas again. This time permanently.

After wiping her eyes with a clean tissue from the glove box, she checked her phone. Still nothing from Derek. *That bastard!* Didn't he know what she was going through? Couldn't he sense it? *Oh, come on, come on, Derek*, she thought. *I don't care about what that horrible Sergeant Egan said. Call me. Let's run away now! Oh, I need you, Derek.*

It was the following Saturday morning when Detective Jarvis looked back to the driveway as Detective Penny knocked on the front door. *That's it,* Jarvis thought. *That's his red Miata. The guy has got to be here.*

"Sheriff's Office, Mr. Manly. We have a search warrant."

"I don't hear anything," Detective Penny declared. "Let's take a look around back."

The men unholstered their weapons and made their way to the side of the house. A wooden gate separated the front and back portions of the side yard. It was unlocked.

At the back of the house was an elevated deck, which connected to the main level, possibly the kitchen. The windows below the deck looked into the basement.

Jarvis, both hands on his weapon, motioned to the deck with his head, and the detectives ascended the stairs cautiously. There was a large sliding glass window that did lead into the kitchen. Inside, on the floor looking out the sliding door, lie a massive Great Dane.

"Oh, watch it," cried out Penny. "There's a big-ass dog."

"He doesn't look dangerous. Look at him. He's just lying there looking up at us."

Penny knocked on the sliding glass door and called out, "Mr. Manly. Sheriff's Office. We have a search warrant. Open up immediately."

The dog appeared to be indifferent to the two men.

"Maybe he's deaf," suggested Penny.

"Manly or the dog?" replied Jarvis.

The men found the slider locked, so they descended the stairs.

There were no doors on the lower level, just a few windows. Penny tried each, and all were likewise locked.

Jarvis put his face up to one of the windows. The walkout basement was dark, except for some beams of light that came in through the windows at the front of the house. As his eyes adjusted to the pale luminescence, he could make out a desk under one of the basement windows at the front. Squinting more, he thought he could see someone sitting in the chair in front of the desk, facing the opposite direction from them. The computer screens, which were on top of the desk, did not appear to be on.

"He's in there. The guy is in there. Mr. Manly, we know you are in there. Sheriff's Office. Open up. We have a warrant."

The silhouette did not move, nor did the chair.

"Man. I think he's asleep," said Jarvis.

"Let me look," replied Penny, putting his face up to the window. "Something isn't right. Let's hit the front."

The men ran back to the front door. With a few well-placed and forceful kicks, Penny was able to break it free of the jamb. The men stepped into the house and onto the entry landing. Jarvis led the way down the short staircase to the walkout basement level.

"Mr. Manly! Derek Manly! Custer County Sheriff!"

There was no answer. Detective Penny looked up to the kitchen from his position on the stairs and saw the large dog, still lying on the kitchen floor but looking back in their direction.

"Smells like blood and gunpowder," whispered Jarvis.

Once at the bottom of the stairwell, the detectives surveyed the layout. To their left was a large living room with a door on the opposite side. It looked to be the interior garage door. Across from them to the left was a small bathroom, and to the right of that was a bedroom. The window of that bedroom was the same window they had been looking through from the back yard. Which meant that just to the right of them was the dark room with the silhouette of a man sitting at a desk.

"Manly! We know you're there! Acknowledge yourself!"

Still no answer. Jarvis gave Penny the signal and they

quickly turned the corner into the hall, pointing their weapons into the blackened room.

"Get down! Get down!"

The figure of the man sitting in the office chair, facing the desk and monitors, remained unmoving at Jarvis' loud command. Penny lowered his firearm and ran up to the figure, laying two fingers on the bent neck in search of a pulsating carotid.

"Dead. He's dead," said Detective Penny.

"You're kidding? When? No, we just landed. Yes, we can be there."

"Who was that?" asked Sebastien as they walked through the terminal with their overnight bags.

"Lt. Breed. Derek Manly is dead."

"Wait. What? Who's dead?" Sebastien pulled at Tiffany's elbow, forcing her to stop mid-stride.

"Derek Manly, of the *Custer Signal*. Somebody murdered him."

"Are you serious?"

"Very. We're headed to the scene now."

"Where? Where's the scene?"

"His place. A couple of our guys went to serve a search warrant and found him in his basement."

"Are we taking this case too?"

"Negative. But we're witnesses, Sebastien. The purpose of the search warrant was to find the reports that Manly and our clerk stole from us. So, we're wrapped up."

"You mean we're suspects?"

"Oh, Sebastien. And you said cops take things too literally."

"Did they? Did they find the reports?"

"Great question. The lieutenant didn't say. But we'll find out soon enough."

BY THE TIME Tiffany and Sebastien pulled up to Manly's house, it had started to rain again, a freezing rain that chilled Sebastien's West Coast constitution to the marrow. He zipped his new jacket up to his manubrium as they made their way under the crime scene tape and up the front walk.

"Hey, Reese. Who's this?"

"Hey, Jarvis. This is Dr Grey, our forensic anthropologist. He's working the cold cases with me."

"Oh. Hello."

Sebastien was almost sure the detective gave him a look of suspicion. But he forced himself to let it go. "Hello," he returned.

Tiffany inspected the man in the desk chair and asked, "Well, Dr. Grey, is that our reporter?"

Sebastien nodded and mentally appreciated Tiffany's formality.

"Yep. That's the guy with whom I met."

Jarvis let out a condescending snicker, presumably at Sebastien's prepositional placement.

Sebastien clasped his hands behind his back and surveyed the scene. Manly's pale corpse sat somewhat erect in a chair behind his desk, though his head lolled to the left. His forehead bore a large, round exit wound. Blood ran into his eyes, which were open, fixed into eternity. Blood and brain matter were splattered all over the desk, computer monitors, and the wall. There was a headshot of a woman with red hair in a frame on the desk, but her face was obscured under a splash of deep red. The room smelled of metal.

"CSI been here?" Tiffany asked.

Jarvis turned from speaking with another detective.

"Not yet. On their way. So don't touch anything. Coroner's coming too, obviously."

"You check for a pulse?"

"Very funny, Reese."

Sebastien looked around the room. It was a long but shallow rectangle, maybe ten feet deep at most. At one end, roughly behind the chair and desk, was a hall leading to the basement landing. At the other end of the rectangle was a door that led to, perhaps, another bedroom. Along the other long side of the rectangle were low windows situated near the ceiling and overlooking the front yard and driveway. Underneath the windows was an old brown couch. It was covered in dog hair and sagged desperately. Between the couch and the desk was a two-drawer metal filing cabinet. On the desk were three computer screens, a laptop, and various office knickknacks.

Sebastien's cursory survey of the space provided no signs of the two photocopied reports; it did reveal a few potential clues, which Sebastien decided to keep to himself. *They know what they're doing*, he reasoned.

"So, Reese, Dr. Grace, you wanna tell me what you know about this guy?"

"Grey. It's Doctor Grey with an 'e.'"

"Whatever. What's the deal here? I mean, besides the fact that Roxanne Bishop was screwing this guy and giving him reports without authorization."

"They *were* lovers," noted Tiffany.

"Affirmative, although I can't even imagine."

"Very nice, Jarvis. Super classy," she responded.

"Oh, don't get high and mighty on me, Reese. So, what's the deal?"

"All we know is that Manly wanted to do an article on the cold case work. Lt. Breed asked me to reach out to him, so I did.

We ended up giving him an overview of the grant and some general info on one of the cases, but nothing specific. We also filled him in on Dr. Grey's role as an anthropologist since he had shown some interest there."

Sebastien tried to make eye contact with Tiffany and give her a subtle signal of approbation for her liberal use of ambiguity. He couldn't tell if she got it.

"Did Roxanne know about the cold case work?" asked Jarvis.

"Not that I am aware of. I never talked to her about it. Hell, I don't think I've ever really talked to her about anything, except for when she was routing me a subpoena."

"Let's go outside. I need a smoke," demanded Jarvis.

On the back deck, Jarvis lit up a cigarette and inhaled deeply before blowing the smoke into a question.

"Any idea who would want to off this guy? I mean, do you think this has something to do with the reports he stole?"

Tiffany shook her head. "I don't know, Jarvis. This guy ran a local blog that reported on all kinds of things. I guess he could have a lot of enemies. Or maybe he uncovered something compromising on a totally different matter. I think it's best to keep an open mind on this one."

"Thanks for the advice," Jarvis replied sarcastically. "I talked to Sgt. LeGris."

"Oh yeah?"

"Yeah. He tells me you tailed this guy for a few days."

"Yes, I did. I was trying to find out who was leaking the information on our case. Manly had contacted one of our witnesses. That's how I knew he was getting information. Plus, someone came into my office the Thursday night before last and rearranged the two reports on my desk."

"But that was the same night Bishop came in to make the copies. Why did you have to follow Manly to figure out it was her?"

"Because we didn't have the entry logs yet. Sgt. Egan can verify that. Look, what are you getting at?"

"Nothing, Reese. Don't get your panties in a twist. I'm just trying to figure out if your cold case and this murder are connected."

"Hey, you watch it, jackass."

Sebastien was impressed. Tiffany didn't take any crap.

"Once forensics is done, we'll know if the copied reports are here. If they're not, then it's a pretty good bet they're connected," Sebastien offered in a conciliatory tone.

Jarvis looked him up and down with obvious contempt but made no reply.

"Dr. Grey is right. Let's let the crime scene techs do their thing, then go from there."

"Oh, well. If you say so, Reese."

Jarvis tossed his cigarette butt over the deck rail and onto the grass, then started for the door to the kitchen.

"Hey, Jarvis!"

"Wassat, Reese?"

"Where was Roxanne Bishop when this guy's brains were blown all over the basement?"

"Leave it alone, Reese. It's big boy time now."

"Can he do that?" asked Sebastien with a look of shock once Jarvis was out of earshot.

"What? Be a dick? He does it all the time."

"No, I mean throw his cigarette butt into a crime scene."

"He's a jerk."

"Don't you think you should have told him you followed Manly to Richie Bonner's house? Bonner could be the last person who saw him."

"Oh, yeah. I forgot about that. Must have slipped my mind. Guess we'll have to ask Richie Bonner about that ourselves." Tiffany's statement was contradicted by her devious smirk.

Sebastien followed Tiffany into the house and out the front

door. A young African American woman carrying a large yellow case brushed by them on the front porch.

"Hey, Tiffany," the woman said.

"Hey, Trish. How's it going?"

"Oh, you know. Another day, another nickel. I hear it's pretty bad."

The woman, who was wearing a Sheriff's Office uniform, indicated the interior of the house with a tilt of her head.

"It is. I admire your strength. Oh, hey, when is the next girls' night out? I could use it." Tiffany laid her hand on the woman's arm to stop her.

"There's a new country band coming to Deadwood. Supposed to be pretty good. I'll send you the info and see if we can get some interest from the others."

"Sounds like a plan. Good luck with this mess."

"Excuse me, ma'am."

Sebastien addressed the woman with the case, who turned and looked surprised by the stranger.

"Could you take close-up photos of everything on the desk? Then send them to Detective Reese as soon as possible?"

"And you are . . . ?"

"Sorry, Trish. This is Dr. Grey, our forensic anthropologist. He's not great at small talk."

"Oh. Okay. Sure thing, doc. Everything on the desk."

THE CAR RIDE from Manly's to the Sheriff's Office had been a quiet one, but as Tiffany pulled up alongside Sebastien's car in the parking lot, she broke the awkward silence.

"Are you mad at me for the small talk crack? I was just kidding."

"No, not at all," Sebastien lied. He was, in fact, a little

offended. But he had been too deep in thought to let it sink in. "What's on the bill for tomorrow?"

"I wasn't kidding about visiting Richie Bonner."

Sebastien got out and retrieved his bag from behind the passenger seat.

"He could be a murderer. Are we just going to ring the doorbell?" he asked through the open door.

"I'm going to do a probation check on him. I think we can get some guys together and do it that way."

"Another shoot-out, you mean?"

"Too soon, Sebastien," she smiled wanly. "But I also want to check our list of South Dakota blue Chevys to see if any were registered to a Carl."

"South Dakota? I'm sorry, you must have misheard me. I meant Colorado."

Sebastien slammed the car door and hit the Range Rover's fob, sending a beep over the nearly empty lot. Behind him, Tiffany rolled down her passenger window.

"Sebastien. Seriously? Can we not do this? Come on. What do you mean Colorado?"

"Just call me when you get those crime scene photos. I'll explain then."

Small talk. I'll give you small talk, he thought to himself, grinning and backing out of the parking spot.

23

Parsifal closed his eyes and lifted his head as Sebastien stroked both sides of the dog's snout with the backs of his fingers.

"He misses you when you're gone. Yesterday he was wandering around the house looking for you," said Melissa.

"Looking for me or hiding from Kirby?" Sebastien smiled.

"That's probably true too," replied Melissa.

"Where'd Hank go?" Sebastien looked toward the kitchen then down the hall from his spot on the couch.

"He went to bed. He's been in a lot of pain. Poor guy can't get comfortable. He took a sleep aid and some ibuprofen."

"Is he any better though?"

"He's getting there. We have an appointment on Monday to get his stitches checked and do some follow-up x-rays or something."

"I'm really sorry this happened, Melissa. But I'm glad it's not any worse."

"Thanks, Sebastien. I am too. And I'm glad you're here. We are very fortunate to have the family in one place, I think."

Melissa got up from her chair and approached Sebastien,

kissing him on the forehead, which caught him completely off guard.

"I'm headed to bed myself. Thanks for cleaning up the dishes."

"It was no problem. Good night."

Sebastien picked up Parsifal and carried him out to the backyard, placing him on the dormant grass by the chicken coop. As the dog took care of his bedtime business, Sebastien looked up at the sky. One or two stars peered out between the cloud cover, and the moon managed a faint glow, transforming the bare trees into the silhouettes of eerie skeletons, their arms terminating in grotesque claws.

For whatever reason—the somber mise en scène or perhaps his own fatigue—the events of the last few weeks and months began to overtake him. It was truly amazing, Sebastien mused, that one's circumstances could swing so drastically on the hinges of small decisions. Had he not agreed to come help his brother this past August, and in the process mend their relationship, he would not now be here, in this place, in this chill wind. Neither would he have met Tiffany. He would have continued on in his self-punishing isolation, completely unaware such a woman even walked the earth. Someone who likes him for who he is. Someone so patient, so kind.

And now here he was, getting kisses on the forehead from a sister-in-law he barely knew six months ago, feeling needed, feeling a part of something for maybe the first time in his life. How strange. He couldn't help but wonder how long it would last. Maybe he should call Tina, his therapist back in California. He needed help. He needed not to screw this up. He was beginning to feel wrapped in a gossamer of faint happiness, the threads of which he knew were very fragile.

Parsifal's scratching at the sliding door caught his attention and Sebastien grabbed the dog, heading inside and to the spare bedroom. After installing the dog on the end of the bed, he stripped down to his underwear, turned out the light, and got under the covers. The glow of his phone screen lit up his face as he scrolled for a playlist that suited his mood. Finally, he found one—"Tenebrous"—and hit play. Lying there on his back in the dark, with the phone on his chest, the warm cellos and haunting voices recalled to his mind one of his favorite quotes from Shakespeare:

"But it is a melancholy of mine own, compounded of many simples, extracted from many objects, and indeed the sundry contemplation of my travels, which, by often rumination, wraps me in the most humorous sadness."

Sebastien tried hard to focus on the individual instruments, their unique tones and vibrations. The trick seemed to work; he was nearly asleep when his sternum vibrated. It was a text from Tiffany telling him to check his email for a link to the crime scene pictures.

"Thanks for sending those pictures," he spoke into the phone a few minutes later.

"No problem," she replied. "I hope I didn't wake you."

"Not at all."

"What, besides all the blood and brains, am I supposed to be looking at here?" Tiffany asked.

"Scroll through to image eleven," he instructed her.

"Okay. I'm looking at it."

"You need to zoom in. Do you see that sticky note on the desk?" asked Sebastien.

"Wait, just a sec. Okay, yeah."

"Can you see the writing? The first word is obscured by the blood, but the first letter looks like a 'C.'"

"Could be an 'O' too," countered Tiffany.

"Possibly. But now look at the rest of the writing on the top there. There's blood blocking some of it, but it looks to me like 'kson.'"

"I agree with you there."

"Now, most of the writing on the bottom of the note is pretty clear."

"'NPD Civ . . . . . . V-87-100327,'" recited Tiffany.

"Exactly."

"I'm glad we agree. But what does it mean? And how does this relate to Colorado?"

"The string at the bottom there looks like a court docket number."

"I guess NPD could be a police department. You might be right."

"I was actually thinking more like North Plains Development. The 'Civ' could mean 'Civil,' and the 'V' before the '87' could be part of CV, also referring to civil. Maybe forensics can recover the rest of it. But '87' is pretty clearly a year."

"That all makes a ton of sense. It's worth checking out—although what does it mean to us?"

"First of all, it means Derek Manly was way better at his job than we gave him credit for."

"In addition to being a thieving prick."

"Right. But more interesting to me is the writing at the top, 'C . . . kson.'"

"Or 'O . . . kson.'"

"Don't be a buzzkill, detective."

"Sorry. Proceed, doctor."

"What if 'C' stood for Carl? And the rest would obviously fit with Jackson."

"You think this could be the Carl who hired Martin Alexander?"

"Sure. Why not?"

"Fine. But . . . Colorado?"

"I don't remember if I told you, but when I called Charles Kinder's widow in Colorado, I found out she is remarried. She doesn't go by Elizabeth Kinder anymore."

"And you're about to tell me her last name is now Jackson, aren't you?"

"Should be easy to find out her husband's first name."

"Hang tight. We don't know what Elizabeth looks like, do we?"

"No. I just spoke to her on the phone. Why?"

"I'm checking Facebook now."

"I didn't think of that."

"You mean you aren't a social media person? I'm shocked."

No. No, I'm not, thought Sebastien. The thought of even putting up a profile made his stomach turn, much less stocking it with personal photos and anecdotes about his life. It made his skin crawl to think about people scrutinizing his life like that. His therapist assured him this was just more of his avoidance behavior. She challenged him to dip his toes in the social media waters. He resolutely declined. Fortunately, he had a ready excuse. As a forensic scientist, he didn't want any of the defendants he had to testify against to track him down. Most people had no problem buying his logic.

"No I'm not," he replied.

"There are a lot of Elizabeth Jacksons in Colorado, too many to go through by hand," reported Tiffany after a few minutes. "We'll have to check the official databases tomorrow."

"Sounds good."

"What is your theory here?" she asked him.

"I don't have one. Honestly. It just seemed like a potential Carl for us."

"A Carl who happens to be connected to the developer of Boxwood Estates."

"It's worth a shot."

Tiffany changed the subject.

"How's Hank doing?"

"He's okay. He's been out cold since dinner. Melissa says he still has a lot of pain."

"Poor guy. If you see him in the morning, tell him I'm thinking about him."

"I sure will, Tiffany."

"Thanks, Sebastien. This is really good stuff. It feels like we're making progress."

"I think we are."

"A-ha! Then you do have a theory."

"I have a few ideas," he replied. "But they're just guesses at this point. We need more information. There's still a lot to do."

"Then let's get some rest. Goodnight, my dear."

"WHAT ARE YOU DOING?"

"Never you mind what I'm doing."

"I told you it's in great shape. I hardly ever fired it."

"Look, I ain't dropping five bills on a gun without a little due diligence. You got a problem with that? And calm down. You look like you're going to wet yourself."

"I just need the money, that's all. Just fire it. Why don't you just fire it? You'll see it works. You don't need to take the whole damn thing apart."

The man sat back, the gun still in his left hand, and stared into the eyes of his counterparty without saying a word.

"Okay. Fine. Fine! Do whatever you gotta do," the hopeful seller said.

The man removed the grips from the pistol as well as the magazine. He then reached into his coat pocket and took out a small spray bottle, the kind they use for nasal spray.

"Hit the lights, Mikey," he commanded.

A large bald man in the corner of the room flicked a switch, causing the florescent bar in the ceiling to go out. A *spish spish spish* sound indicated something was being sprayed from the small bottle. Flecks of bluish white glowed dimly on the table's surface.

"Lights! Mikey, check his pockets."

"Why? What? I didn't know! I swear I didn't know! Augh! Let go of me!"

"Nothin' on him, boss."

"Fine, Mikey. Listen to me, you sonofabitch. You trying to frame me? I oughta smoke you right here, right now. Now here's your bloody gun. I'm keeping the bullets. You so much as look back on your way out and Mikey here will unload. You got me?"

Mikey put his .44 back in its holster when he heard the sound of tires screeching.

24

The day after Hank's check-up he woke feeling optimistic. The x-rays had found only a few miniscule bullet fragments remaining. These, he was told, were too close to the spine to extract safely, yet far enough away not to cause too much trouble. It was best to leave well enough alone, they said. The stitches, too, were coming along, although he was warned against scratching them—surely they would begin to itch in the coming days. As for the pain, physical therapy would help his lower back muscles heal once the stitches were out. Sleep, plenty of water, and anti-inflammatories were the key, along with endurance. Unless, of course, he wanted to hit the stronger pain meds. Which he did not. He would endure.

"What's the word on the Manly homicide? Do we think it's connected to the Hell Canyon deal?" he asked before stuffing a Danish into his mouth.

Tiffany and Sebastien were sitting opposite him at the dining room table. Each had been sipping at Hank's muddy coffee as the patient regaled them with his various medical prognoses.

"We're not sure," replied Tiffany. "The crime scene techs found both copied reports in a file cabinet at Manly's. Whoever shot him wasn't there to get the reports, or at least they didn't find them."

"There wasn't really any sign of a burglary though," added Sebastien. "It doesn't appear that whoever killed him was looking for something."

Tiffany nodded.

"There was evidence on the desk that Manly was looking into the Hell Canyon case and the Cheyenne connection," she said.

"Fine," said Hank, sweeping Danish crumbs from his sweatshirt onto the table. "Don't let Jarvis keep you out of the loop on that one. Make sure you get updates. Tell me if that's not happening. And how is your case going? What have you two been up to?"

"It's going really well," replied Sebastien. "We just about have it wrapped up."

Tiffany gave Sebastien a sideways glance. Neither of the men noticed.

"Oh really? Easy peasy, eh? Well, next time let's give you a harder case," replied Hank. "So, what are the particulars?"

"We're still waiting on the nuclear DNA comparison of the Hell Canyon remains and the brother of the missing guy out of Sioux Falls," replied Sebastien.

"Remind me who that is?"

"Martin Alexander. He was reported missing in December of '87, about a month and a half after the torso was found in Cheyenne," Tiffany answered.

Sebastien continued, "The lab was able to get a mitochondrial profile and it does match the brother, Jerry Alexander."

Hank hated the technical talk. It made him feel dumb. And his brother rarely helped him feel smarter. "Microcondrial?"

"MITO-chondrial," corrected Sebastien. "The mitochondria are located in the cytoplasm. There are dozens of them and they regulate energy production for the cell. They have their own DNA, which gets passed down the maternal line. The paternal line doesn't pass it down because . . ."

"The point! Please."

"What Sebastien is trying to say is that Martin Alexander and Jerry Alexander have the same mother."

"Probably have the same mother," said Sebastien.

"So, you've likely identified the Hell Canyon remains as Martin Alexander out of Sioux Falls?"

"Yes," replied Sebastien and Tiffany in unison.

"Well, that's excellent. Great job!"

"It was all Sebastien. It was his idea to focus on Sioux Falls as opposed to all of the other possible locations."

"Let's not make his head any bigger."

Hank saw the look in his brother's eyes and realized he may have gone too far.

"Seriously though, Sebastien. This is amazing. Great job. So it's nearly wrapped up? Does that mean you know what happened? And you have officially connected Alexander to the Cheyenne torso?"

"I'm going to let Sebastien answer that one," said Tiffany, sitting back in the chair. "I personally wasn't aware we were that close to solving the case."

"Going rogue again, eh, little brother? Well, lay it on me."

"It's possible I am getting a little ahead of things. But we found out a lot yesterday, and I think we're prepared to formulate a few hypotheses."

"I can't wait to hear them," Hank replied.

Tiffany folded her arms and turned toward Sebastien "Neither can I," she said.

"Martin Alexander was brought out to work on the Rapid City development by a friend of his named Carl. We think that

Carl is Carl Jackson, who is married to Charlie Kinder's widow."

"Charlie Kinder?"

"His company built the Cheyenne neighborhood where the torso was found. And, at the time, Carl Jackson ran a company in Hot Springs called Jackson Lumber Supply. He provided all of the wood trusses for the development."

"Interesting. So the dude's widow married one of the suppliers. When did he die?"

"Charles Kinder died in 1988. Heart attack."

"And Jackson swooped in? What a player."

"But that's not even the interesting part. Charles Kinder filed a lawsuit against Jackson in '87. He claimed Jackson was double charging him for materials. The suit was dropped by his widow after his death."

"Then that same widow married the guy who was evidently ripping them off," observed Hank.

Sebastien nodded. "Yep. And that same widow did some office work for the business."

"You think they were in cahoots?"

"We think so."

"What does our dead guy have to do with all of this?"

"I'm not exactly sure how it fits. But I've always felt that the torso was meant to be in the trailer, and the fire was meant to destroy the whole thing. I now think the motive for that was to destroy evidence of the accounting fraud."

"By using a random guy's body as kindling? That doesn't make much sense, does it?"

"No," cut in Tiffany. "This is where I think Sebastien is over-reaching. No offense, Sebastien."

"None taken. But I would also point out that Carl Jackson lived in South Dakota in the eighties and had a Chevy truck registered to him as well."

Hank scanned the faces opposite him very carefully, trying

to determine if there was any animus between his two cold case investigators. Thankfully, he could not detect any.

"So, what do you think, Tiff?"

"Both Sebastien and I agree that Alexander was killed up here. He was shot in the head. His torso was then transported down south so that it would be far away from where the head and limbs were left."

"Hell Canyon," said Hank.

"Yep," Tiffany continued. "That was to make sure the body parts would not be connected, and thus not identified. But, to me, the thing that connects the two locations is the Bonners. Bonner Framing. They had the Rapid City job and the Cheyenne job. And we know they're violent, at least we know Greg Bonner is."

"But why would the Bonners try to burn down the trailer? If indeed that was the original intent."

"Maybe the trailer was just extra fuel for the fire. Maybe they thought that when all was said and done, the whole mess would make it harder to ID the body."

"But the body was not inside the trailer, correct?" asked Hank.

"True."

"That's where I have a problem," said Sebastien. "The trailer belonged to North Plains Development. The Bonners wouldn't have a key to it; therefore, they wouldn't have an expectation they could get the body into the trailer. But Elizabeth Jackson—I mean, Kinder at the time—would have had a key."

"The body wasn't inside of the trailer though." Hank felt like he was repeating himself.

"Like I said, I think it was *meant* to be in the trailer. I think the locks were changed in response to all of the burglaries and thefts the site was experiencing."

"What's the motive, Tiffany? In your scenario, I mean. Why

would the Bonners kill Martin? He was working on their Rapid City site, and didn't you say they were short-handed on that one? Why get rid of one of their guys?"

"That, I don't know."

Hank spotted something out the front window. Sebastien and Tiffany turned to see what had grabbed his attention.

"Melissa! We got deer in the witch hazel again! I swear, I keep telling her we need to take that out."

"It's pretty though," offered Tiffany.

"Well, tell me this," continued Hank, returning to the case, "is there a connection between this Jackson guy and the Bonners? I mean, why does it have to be one or the other? If Jackson brought our victim out here, and the victim worked on the Bonner's project, then Jackson must know the Bonners. Plus, a lumber guy would certainly know a framing company and vice versa."

Tiffany smiled and looked at Sebastien, who dropped his eyes and bit his lip.

"Ah ha! See? The old man still has it. Neither of you thought of that, did you?"

"We only just learned about Carl Jackson," explained Sebastien. "We were getting there."

"Sure, sure."

"So, what do you suggest, boss?"

Hank drained his coffee and looked back out at the yard.

"Damn deer. Melissa! Come look at this. I told you! Now, you see that? Those deer are opportunists. Do you know why they travel in groups like that?"

"Sure. It's safety in numbers. More eyes and ears to spot predators," answered Sebastien.

Hank marked the look of assuredness on his know-it-all brother's face.

"Maybe so, little brother. But it's been my experience that the deer spend less time looking for predators and more time looking to see what juicy limbs their fellow herd mates are chewing on. In fact, that's how the herds get so big. They tend to come together when one herd spots an opportunity. The added protection is just a bonus."

"There's a word for that: mutualism," announced Sebastien. "Some New World monkeys do that, like saddleback and emperor tamarins. They follow each other around when searching for food so they don't waste time on flowers that have already been drained of nectar."

Tiffany looked confused. "Wait a minute. Hank, are you talking about the case now?"

Hank got up from the table with a grunt.

"Let's just say, detective, as our egg-headed anthropologist puts it, don't rule out the possibility that our saddlebacks and emperors may be giving each other a hand."

"HE HAS A POINT," said Tiffany from behind the wheel of her cruiser. "Especially since we now know that Jackson lived up here at the time and had a Chevy."

"He could still have it," replied Sebastien.

"Exactly."

"Like I said, we would have gotten there."

Sebastien tried to resist the urge to make a big deal out of things. But he felt embarrassed. It was so obvious, the Bonners and Jackson being mixed up together, but he just didn't see it. He was supposed to see things like that, wasn't he? Or was his newly earned reputation as a savant going to wear away like a sandcastle in a stiff wind? He wondered what Tiffany thought. Did she think less of him? *Oh, stop it, Sebastien. Get a grip.*

"You're probably right," replied Tiffany. "But I think it does help to approach things from that angle. Tell you what, let's drop in on Richie Bonner and do a full-court press on his relationship with Jackson and everything else. It's about time we talked to him."

"What's a full-court press?"

"Oh my, Sebastien. It's a good thing you're handsome."

THE GATE at the end of the drive lifted slowly, like an axe being readied for the drop. Tiffany put her phone down and went under it as quickly as she could.

"He didn't sound surprised at all. I think he was expecting us."

"I bet Manly tipped him off," suggested Sebastien.

"Probably so."

"You never did tell them, did you?"

"Tell whom what?"

"You never told the other detectives about Manly coming here shortly before he was murdered."

"Not yet. But I will. I want to feel it out a bit first. I don't want Jarvis to muck up our investigation unless he needs to."

The road to the house was long and crooked. As the car ascended the hill, Sebastien got a better view of the fields below. All was yellow, except for the circular rolls of hay that were covered in brown plastic tarps. He tried to imagine living out here in the country. What would he do with all this land? Maybe he could become a gentleman farmer or rancher. He spotted some horses in a corral across the highway and wondered how much work went into keeping livestock. Probably much more than he realized or was willing to do. In any case, someday he would have to get serious about weighing his options. He didn't want to live with his brother any longer than he needed to. The lack of solitude was starting to take its toll.

Richie Bonner had silver hair down to his shoulders and a gray, horseshoe-shaped mustache. His jeans were clean and dark and looked expensive. He wore a salmon-colored golf shirt and Polo deck shoes. Clearly the youngest Bonner son was not out mending fences.

"Wow, what a beautiful view you have!" exclaimed Tiffany as Richie led them through to the living room. "Is all that your land?"

"Just ten acres. Basically, my land ends where that wood fence runs between the trees there."

Tiffany followed his outstretched hand. "Yeah. Is that the property line?"

"It is. I asked the guy on the other side if he would sell. But he won't. Not that I blame him. Can I get either of you something to drink? A beer? I have wine too."

"None for me," answered Sebastien.

"We're on duty, Mr. Bonner. But I'll take a water if you have it."

"Coming right up."

Richie disappeared behind the bar that backed up to the huge window and re-emerged with two bottles of water.

"Here you go. So, duty you said. What is it I can help you with? Have a seat. There, on the couch."

"Thank you, Mr. Bonner. Like I said on the phone, I'm Detective Tiffany Reese and my colleague is Dr. Sebastien Grey. We're working on some old cases and we think you might be able to help with one of them."

"Ah, yes. Derek Manly told me you might be coming by."

"You know Mr. Manly? I mean, you knew him?" asked Tiffany.

"Yeah, I read about that. Poor guy. Did they catch whoever did it?"

"No, but we are very close," she replied.

Sebastien watched Richie's face closely. He failed to detect any alarm.

"When did Mr. Manly tell you about us wanting to talk to you?" asked Sebastien.

"Let me see. A few days ago. He came by and said he was working on a story about a cold case thing the sheriff in Custer was doing."

"Did he mention a specific cold case?"

"Well, ma'am, he said you were looking into a homicide from back in the eighties. He asked if I'd heard about some bones that were found in West Custer County."

"And had you?"

"No, ma'am. I hadn't. I didn't really pay much attention to the news back then. Too busy chasing chicks and drinking, I guess."

Tiffany removed her heavy coat, then continued, "Where were you back in '87, Mr. Bonner? Were you living in Custer County? Were you working there?"

"Eighty-seven, eighty-seven. Hmmm. Let me think. Hmmm. No . . . no, I believe I was in Rapid City that year. We were working on an apartment complex—it was a bear, if I recall."

Sebastien was already losing patience.

"Mr. Bonner, we have it from both your brother Greg and your father that you were supervising a neighborhood development down in Cheyenne, Wyoming that year. Are you saying you remember things differently?"

Richie faced Sebastien. He appeared unmoved by Sebastien's veiled accusation of dishonesty.

"Well, I mean, sure, Pops had a job down there, and I may have spent a little time on it. Not much though. I think Greggie and Pops may have memory issues."

Richie began to trace his mustache between his thumb and forefinger.

"What about Carl Jackson, Mr. Bonner? Would he have memory issues too?"

Tiffany's question surprised and impressed Sebastien. He was starting to get a better idea of a full-court press.

"I'm sorry. Carl who?"

"Mr. Bonner, Carl Jackson supplied the roof trusses for both developments, the one in Rapid City and the one in Cheyenne."

"Did he?"

"Yes, he did. In fact, he told Dr. Grey here quite a lot. Didn't he, doctor?"

Richie jumped in before Sebastien could answer. Sebastien was grateful for a few extra seconds.

"Okay, I don't know what kind of doctor you are. But I don't know Carl Jackson and I don't remember who supplied us on either of those jobs. You'll have to ask Pops about that. It was his company."

"Like I said, sir, your father told us you supervised the Cheyenne project. He also said Carl Jackson supplied the trusses and you were the one who worked with Jackson on making sure they were the right ones. And Carl Jackson corroborated all of that."

Richie's mustache appeared to grow whiter as his face turned red.

"Okay, this is bullcrap. What are you guys getting at, anyway? Who cares what job I worked and who I knew thirty years ago? What's your point?"

Tiffany flipped a few of her notebook pages and pretended to remind herself of some detail.

"The point, Mr. Bonner, is Martin Alexander. The body found in West Custer County in '88 has been ID'd as Martin Alexander of Sioux Falls. He was recruited to work on your Rapid City project by Carl Jackson."

"Hold up. A minute ago, you were saying I handled the Cheyenne job, and now you're saying the Rapid City job was mine! Which is it?"

"You tell us, sir." Tiffany sounded calm and even. "Did you work the location our homicide victim disappeared from or the location where half of his body was found on fire? Have your pick."

Richie fell into deep thought, his eyes shifting laterally, his fingers tracing his mustache at a greater speed. At one point he almost spoke, but then caught himself and looked upward to the extra-large brass fan high up in the center of the ceiling. Sebastien was happy to let him stew for as long as it took. Tiffany seemed to feel the same.

"Look. It was a long time ago. Those jobs—both of 'em—were a family deal. You know what I'm saying. We all worked 'em all."

A sudden realization came to Sebastien. There was another hole yet to be filled, another road yet to be traveled. He kicked himself mentally.

"Fair enough, Mr. Bonner," he said. "Speaking of the family, what was your sister doing during all this? Did she work in the business?"

"Pammie? Hah. That's a laugh. Pammie didn't do nothin' for the business, except for showing her little butt off as she strutted for the guys on the job."

Sebastien noticed Richie's language slipping perceptibly as he dug himself deeper.

"Interesting. We'll be sure to ask her about her strutting," replied Tiffany.

"Good luck finding her," Richie replied with a laugh.

"You mean you don't know where she is?"

"Nope."

Tiffany took out her pen and flipped a page in her notebook.

"And when did she move away?"

"Hell. Been over thirty years."

"But she did come to the Rapid City project, right? Is that where she was showing herself off for the workers?" asked Sebastien.

"Oh, yeah. Why the hell do think the thing took so long?"

Tiffany looked up from her pad.

"Are you saying she left during the apartment project?"

Richie didn't answer.

"Why did she leave, Mr. Bonner? Was this a planned thing? Was she taking a job somewhere? Did she leave for a man?" Tiffany sounded insistent. She waved her pen for emphasis as she spoke.

"I tell you what, I don't know. If you can find her, you can ask her. Look, I really gotta go. We're gonna have to pick this up another time."

"Sure. No problem," replied Tiffany. "Just one last question: Have you ever been to Derek Manly's house?"

"No."

"Then there would be no reason for your fingerprints to be found inside his residence?"

"That's two questions, not one. Now have a safe trip down the hill. The gate opens automatically."

25

Just as he did with that idiot Manly, Richie Bonner watched the detective drive off down the road with her little boy toy, Doctor Grey. Oh, he could tell. He could tell from the way they sat so close together on the couch—his couch!—practically leg to leg. The way he looked at her with half-melted eyes whenever she asked a question. Her all dolled up. The smell of her perfume. Was it all even legit? Maybe he should put in a call. He had a buddy down at the SO, two if you count that girl Manly was fooling around with. Well, maybe it'd be best to leave it alone, Richie concluded.

Richie poured himself a drink and poked a number into his cell phone. A number he knew by heart. Didn't even have to look in his phone book. Just knew it by heart. He put the phone on speaker and laid it on the bar top.

"Hey, it's me."

"Hey," a woman's voice replied.

"Is that all you got for your favorite brother?"

"I'm working, Rich. We open in a few minutes. Big rush with the cruise ship crowd."

"Yeah, well, I guess I'll let ya go."

"Sorry. Maybe we can talk later. I'll give you a call."

Richie took a sip from the tumbler and nodded to himself.

"Yeah, that would be great. Maybe then I can tell you about the two detectives who just left my house."

"What? Detectives?"

"Talk to ya later, sis. Give me a call when you have more time."

Richie abruptly killed the call and whispered into his scotch, "Ungrateful bitch."

"WHAT A LOAD OF CRAP," declared Tiffany from behind the wheel as they made their way back to HQ. "How do you not know where your sister is? And for thirty years!"

"Yeah, that guy was lying the whole time."

"I'm going to give Larry Bonner a call. Maybe he will tell us where his daughter is."

"I doubt that. He wasn't very forthcoming either. But isn't it interesting that Richie Bonner lied about knowing where his sister went? You know what that means."

"I do," replied Tiffany. "It means she's at the center of all of this."

"That or she has key information."

"We're going to have to figure out where she went. Can't be that hard."

"Unless she changed her name."

"Way to be optimistic, Sebastien."

"Hey, that's how I roll. You know that."

Tiffany smiled widely and replied, "I know."

"Can we get a search warrant for Larry's or Richie's phone? Or both?"

"Nope. Not enough probable cause for that. Not even close."

"Dang. Well, I don't think the Bonners are going to offer anything up. We'll have to come at this more obliquely."

"Translation, please."

Sebastien fixed his eyes forward in thought as they ascended into Hill City.

"What do you think the chances are of finding one of Pamela Bonner's old friends, from back in the eighties, I mean?"

"You mean she might still be in touch with someone besides her family?"

"That or an old friend might know where she went and, more importantly, why she left."

"You think her leaving is tied to Alexander's murder?"

"Has to be. It's too coincidental. Especially since her family does not want us to know where she is."

"Okay. Okay. Let me think about that. You know what? I'm freaking starving."

"CONFERENCE ROOM. NOW," read the text from Lt. Breed. He must have seen them pull into the parking lot.

"Uh, oh. The lieutenant wants to see us."

"Why is that bad?"

"I can tell from the tone of his text. He sounds pissed," replied Tiffany.

Tiffany and Sebastien walked through the door of the investigations conference room and found Lt. Breed sitting at the end of the long table, with Jarvis and Penny perpendicular to him on the far side. No one looked happy.

"What's going on? What's all this?" she asked.

"Have a seat. Both of you."

As Tiffany pulled her chair out from under the table, she

felt an ambush coming. The air was thick with tension. She quickly scanned her brain to determine the potential cause.

Lt. Breed put on his reading glasses and glanced down at a piece of paper on the table in front of him before looking directly at Tiffany.

"Detective Reese, last Thursday you asked Comms to run an address in Pennington County: 4823 Quarter Horse Road."

"Sounds about right."

Ah. So that's what this is about. Tiffany tried not to sound as nervous as she felt. It was difficult with Jarvis and Penny staring straight at her with stone faces.

"Why were you out that way?"

"I was tailing Manly to figure out who our insider was."

"Oh, yes. I heard about that cock-up," replied the lieutenant, removing his glasses and sneering.

"Cock-up? That wasn't my fault."

"Did you not tell the reporter about the Hell Canyon case?"

Tiffany could almost feel her brain shift from forward to reverse.

"I did," interrupted Sebastien, raising his hand. "He asked to interview me about how forensics play into cold cases. I used the Hell Canyon case as an example. I didn't give him any details, nor could I—or Detective Reese—have known you have a rotten member of staff."

Tiffany braced herself, resisting the urge to put her head in her hand and stare into the table.

"You should just mind your own damn business," barked Detective Penny. "You don't even work here."

"That's enough, Penny," said the lieutenant. "So, Reese, are you saying Derek Manly visited 4823 Quarter Horse on Thursday?"

"Yes. I followed him there."

"And whose address did that turn out to be?"

Jarvis crossed his arms and gave a malicious grin at the lieutenant's question.

"Richard Bonner's. Look, I know where you're going here. I was going to tell these guys about Manly's visit to Bonner. I just needed to verify a few things first."

"It's an active homicide, Reese. Not one of your stupid cold case goose chases. You have no idea what you're doing. And we don't have time for playing games."

Detective Jarvis pounded his fist on the table as he spoke.

"That's enough!"

Lt. Breed's neck was beginning to turn red.

"Reese, at what point were you going to let these boys in on Bonner's involvement with Manly?"

"As soon as I had a chance to question him on our case."

"Is that what you were doing there this morning?" asked Detective Penny.

"Are you following me?" Tiffany pointed across the table.

"Damn right we're following you!" Penny thrust a finger back at her. "You're screwing up our investigation. You're sitting on a prime suspect without sharing information. You shouldn't even be involved. If I had my way . . ."

Sebastien abruptly rose to his feet and pointed his own accusatorial finger at the two detectives.

"Why don't you just shut up? Both of you!"

All four of the others at the table looked at Sebastien in complete shock. Even Breed was speechless. The meek scientist stared them all down defiantly as he continued.

"First of all, if anyone is screwing up the investigation, it's you by throwing your cigarette butt into the crime scene. And second, Richie Bonner is not your prime freaking suspect. There was no forced entry, the cold case reports were not taken, and, oh, by the way, did you bother to notice the angle of the bullet? It went into the wall just a few inches below the level of Manly's head. Richie Bonner has to be at least six-three. If he fired the shot, the bullet would have entered the wall farther down. Not to mention the blood blowback against the wall behind the desk chair. There's a nice void in it about the shape of a person. A rather short person. Did you so-called detectives notice any of that?!"

Jarvis and Penny sat stupefied by the brazen and abrupt lecture. Sebastien sat down, visibly shaking.

"Well," said the lieutenant calmly, "it seems our anthropologist has one or two helpful points. Reese, anything to add?"

"Are you just going to let him . . ."

"Stop, Jarvis. You deserved it. Detective Reese?"

Tiffany tried to read the lieutenant. Was he being sarcastic? Was he egging her on to dig the hole even deeper?

"Sir, I don't know if Richie Bonner should be a suspect. And I do apologize to Jarvis and Penny. I'm sorry, guys. I should have told you sooner. I wasn't trying to screw up your case; I was thinking about mine. But I should have let you know."

"Very generous of you, Reese. I'm sure the guys here will let bygones be bygones. Right?"

The men across the table nodded unconvincingly.

"But back to my question, Reese. Is there anything else you know that might help in the Manly murder?"

"No, sir. We didn't question Richie Bonner at all about the murder or where he was when it may have happened, although the subject did come up and I used the opportunity to ask Bonner if he had ever been in Manly's house. He said he hadn't."

"In that case, Reese, it appears as though you owe these fellas a supplemental report documenting that conversation. I would like that done immediately. Do you understand?"

"Yes, sir. I do."

"Excellent. And stop by my office in the morning. You and I need to discuss a formal reprimand. I'm documenting this meeting, and when your regular sergeant gets back from injury leave, he and I will decide the consequence. It's a serious matter. You know that, right?"

"Yes, sir. I do," Tiffany repeated.

"Good. You are all dismissed—except you, Dr. Grey. I'd like a word."

Tiffany threw a look of horror toward Sebastien. She truly appreciated him defending her; it meant a lot. But this was trouble.

"Reese!"

Tiffany turned halfway down the hallway to see Jarvis and Penny running to catch up.

"Yeah. Hey, sorry about that, guys. . . . I'll talk . . ."

Jarvis stuck his finger in her face.

"You keep your friggin' lap dog away from us. If Tinkerbell tries to throw me under the bus again, I'll send him back to California in a body bag. You got me?"

Tiffany slapped the detective's hand away with a resounding *whack*.

"No, Jarvis. I do not *got you*. You know what your problem is?"

"I don't like little girls messing with my cases?"

"I'm going to ignore that, and you're welcome. Your problem is that Tinkerbell is making you look like a day one recruit."

Jarvis's face turned beet red. He opened his mouth to speak but Tiffany was already twenty feet down the hall.

"Well, you got some cajones, son."

"Sorry about that. I just didn't think it was fair and I don't think those guys should be worried about Detective Reese. She's too smart to screw up their case."

Breed examined Sebastien carefully, tapping the end of a pen into his left palm as he did so.

"Do you want me to go? I don't have to help. I don't have to work here at all, in fact. If I'm causing trouble, I'll just go."

The lieutenant took a deep breath. The pen continued to pound against his palm, making a sequence of dull thumping sounds.

"Sgt. LeGris tells me you have our Hell Canyon victim identified."

"Martin Alexander. He's a construction worker out of Sioux Falls."

"And he's likely connected to human remains that were found at a construction site in Wyoming in '87?"

"Correct," Sebastien replied.

"And Larry Bonner and his sons worked on that site?"

"That's also correct."

"You think the Bonners killed this Martin Alexander?"

"I think it's a bit more complicated than that. But we do think they are involved."

Breed's face fell as he went into semi-deep thought again.

"You've worked around cops quite a bit, haven't you, son?"

"I guess you could say that."

"You know, cops—especially cops like Jarvis and Penny—they don't like to be called out or challenged."

"Anyone who thinks they have all of the answers is asking for a challenge, in my experience anyway. But like I said, I can go away. Detective Reese is more than capable of working the cold cases without me."

Lieutenant Breed stood up and walked to the window that overlooked the parking lot. His hands were behind his back now; the pen continued drumming.

Sebastien was still shaking from his outburst. *This might be it, after all.*

After a few moments, the lieutenant turned to face Sebastien. His countenance had softened slightly.

"Dr. Grey, I don't know what, if anything, is going on

with you and Detective Reese. And you may be surprised to learn I don't give a hot damn either way. But there are two things I do know. First, I want you here. I want your skills on these cold cases. What you've done already is remarkable. Just identifying our Hell Canyon victim is a major win for us."

"It's been a team effort, sir."

"Oh, I know. Reese is one of our best. Which leads me to the second thing, and I don't want you to take this the wrong way. You're not exactly the life of the party. And you're drawing fire in Reese's direction. I'm not willing to compromise on that, but I also don't want you to compromise on how you do whatever the hell it is that you do."

"It's seems we're at an impasse."

"No, we are not. I want you to continue working with Det. Reese. But maybe don't come around HQ so much. I can't have this contention in my shop and I very much doubt that you are the kind of person to adjust."

Sebastien thought on this for a moment. His initial urge, as it often was, was to be offended, just like those buffoon detectives offended him by yelling at Tiffany. But as he let the idea percolate, it actually seemed like a good thing. Splendid isolation, once again.

"What about our space over at the crime lab?"

"That's fine. You can be one with the propellor heads over there. Just keep a low profile around the other detectives."

"Fine with me. Low profile is my sweet spot."

Breed gave out a chuckle in response.

"No, I'm serious. That works out fine for me. But I need you to do me a favor in return."

"It's a good thing you don't work here officially; otherwise, I'd be laughing even harder right now," replied the lieutenant. "But go on."

"Don't let those detectives give Tiff—er . . . Detective Reese trouble, and don't hold it against her that I'm not the life of the party."

"Don't underestimate our Detective Reese, Dr. Grey. You don't need to worry about her. Both of those asses will be fetching her coffee in a few years."

"Banished?"

"Oh, don't make me laugh! It hurts too much! Sebastien finally showed some balls and he got kicked out! Oh geez. Priceless."

"I don't see how this is funny, Hank."

Sebastien watched as, once again, his partner and his brother sparred, this time from Hank's dining room table.

"I don't see how that's funny either, to be honest," added Melissa.

Sebastien put down his forkful of steak and offered a correction.

"Well, maybe banished is too strong of a word. Breed just wants me to stay away from the detectives. 'Keep a low profile,' he said."

"I just think it's rude."

"Thank you, Melissa. So do I," replied Tiffany. "How is this so funny, Hank? It ruins the whole thing."

"Now, wait a minute. Hang on," Hank said, trying to bottle his laughter. "Sebastien said he's still working with you. Breed just doesn't want him around the detectives. I personally think it's a great thing. Plays right into our hand, if you think about it."

"How so?" asked Tiffany.

"I kind of agree, actually," said Sebastien. "Breed thinks my presence is going to make things harder for you. He thinks you're a great detective and doesn't want me creating problems for you with the other detectives—which I fully intend to if they keep treating you like crap."

"I can take care of myself, Sebastien."

"I know that. I just have a difficult time keeping my mouth shut around stupid people. It's better for you if I don't get tempted."

"There, you see, Tiff?" said Hank. "It's the best of both worlds. You get to keep your partner, and Sebastien doesn't have to deal with the office drama. Not to mention the fact that I have to go back there in a few weeks. I can take care of Jarvis and the others. But it'd be nice to have things cool off a bit."

"Speaking of office drama. Did the lieutenant give you the impression he knows you and Tiffany are . . . um . . . involved?" asked Melissa.

"Now that is a great question. What about it, little brother?"

"No. He did not," lied Sebastien. "I don't think anyone knows anything."

"See, Tiffany? It's all good. It's just a matter of time until someone notices how hard our forensic consultant is crushing on you. Best to keep him away."

"Daddy, what's 'crushing'?" asked Kirby.

"Ask Mommy." Hank smiled before jamming a forkful of potatoes into his mouth.

Tiffany smiled too and turned a little red.

"Well, sweetheart. I think what your dad means is that your uncle Sebastien is in love with Tiffany."

"Ew!"

Tiffany leaned over and whispered something into the little girl's ear, which made her laugh.

Sebastien wasn't sure what to make of this homey tableau, but it felt good. The fact that he'd been outed, so to speak, didn't bother him in the least. And, best of all, it didn't seem to bother Tiffany.

"Now, Kirby, what do we say about keeping secrets?" admonished Melissa.

Kirby looked up at Tiffany, who smiled widely and nodded.

"Tiffany crushed Uncle Sebastien," exclaimed the little girl before launching into more giggles.

26

"I'm sorry to keep you waiting. It's back-to-back meetings today. Well, every day, actually."

"No problem at all, ma'am. We were just enjoying the view."

The law offices of Pedretti, Meyer, and Kohn were situated on the fifth floor of one of the few modern buildings in downtown Rapid City. The brick and glass structure towered over its neighbors, except for the Rushmore Hotel two blocks north. It was said by some that on a clear day, you could see all the way to the billowing moonscape of the Badlands from the firm's shiny waiting area, with its reproduction Eames chairs and *Golf Digest*-covered coffee table. And fortunately for PM&K's visitors, it was a very clear day.

Lisa Pedretti greeted them with a weak and cursory handshake, the silver bangles on her wrist clanging each time she reached out. She was wearing an ivory silk blouse under a charcoal-gray pantsuit, both of which appeared to Sebastien to be expensive. Her hair was a stunning uniform silver, her features trim and athletic. Sebastien would have liked to examine her skull, to have dragged a finger along the inferior edges of her zygomas, the flare of her ascending rami. He found himself mentally calculating her nasal index as she spoke.

"It is a lovely view, isn't it? We're very lucky. We only moved in six years ago, you know. I hope we never leave. Now, if you'll follow me back please, you can tell me how I can help the Custer County Sheriff's Office."

Pedretti's huge office occupied an entire corner of the building. Post-Impressionist paintings hung on the wall.

"Toulouse-Lautrec?" ventured Sebastien.

"Ah, yes. You know your art, um . . . I'm sorry. I don't believe I got your name."

"Sebastien Grey."

"Well, if you can spot a Toulouse-Lautrec, I wouldn't be surprised if your name was spelled with an 'e.'"

"Yes. Both of them."

The woman's large white teeth beamed approval from behind her glass desk.

"That's a beautiful coat, Detective Grey. Jaeger?"

"Ted Baker," he replied, deciding to forgo correcting her on his title. "My partner here thinks it makes me look like a stockbroker."

"There's nothing wrong with that," she smiled. "And you must be Detective Reese."

"Yes, ma'am. Thank you for seeing us on such short notice."

"It's no problem at all. I'm from Custer County, you know. Originally, that is. Although we don't handle criminal matters in this firm, I'm curious to know what I can do for you."

"We were actually hoping you might be able to help us find someone," said Tiffany. "She's an old friend of yours."

"Oh?"

"Yes. Pamela Bonner."

Pederetti's eyes lit up.

"Now that is a name I have not heard in quite a long time. And how did you know we knew each other?"

"This."

Tiffany handed a large book across the desk and opened it at her business card, which was stuck inside as a bookmark.

"Oh my word! Where did you get this? I haven't seen it in years. I think my husband threw out all of my high-school yearbooks. He denies it, of course."

Tiffany ignored the question.

"That's you, then, correct? In the picture next to Pam?"

"Oh yes, that's Pammie and me. And the caption says it all, doesn't it? 'Pam Bonner and Lisa Pedretti enjoying the sun at the senior picnic.' Oh my goodness, look at that."

"You kept your maiden name," observed Sebastien.

"Absolutely. Adam and I got married several years after I started practicing law, and I wasn't going to rebrand, if you know what I mean. Plus, Pedretti is lot more elegant than Farmer. Don't you think?"

Tiffany reached into her bag to find her notebook.

"It's a lovely name," she replied. "So, can you tell us when you last spoke with Pamela?"

"Hmm. Let me think back . . . We kicked around for a few years after high school. Then, when I went off to law school, we would talk on the phone occasionally. And I came home during the summer, so I saw her a few times when I was back. Why are you trying to track her down anyway? Is she in trouble?"

Sebastien looked at Tiffany, who responded.

"No, it's nothing like that. We're just going back over some old cases and her name came up as a potential witness. We'd like to talk to her. When was it that you last saw her? When you came home from law school, I mean. Do you remember what year that was?"

"Oh, that would have been about . . . I graduated in '87 and came home for good. She was out of the area by then . . . so . . . the last time would have been the summer before. Maybe the summer of '86."

"Did you ever talk to her after you graduated law school, or did you lose track of each other?"

"No, we lost track. She just disappeared. Haven't heard from her since." Pedretti lifted and lowered her arms to emphasize her bewilderment.

"What about the summer of 1986? You said you saw her then," asked Tiffany. "Do you recall anything from that summer, like was she working, who was she hanging out with, was there any trouble in her life?"

Pedretti drummed her fingers against the desk blotter and tilted her head in thought. Sebastien noticed, for the first time, a kite-shaped amethyst hanging from a silver chain around her neck. It was lodged in her cleavage—like a mountain climber emerging from a crevasse. He quickly diverted his eyes when she began her answer.

"I vaguely remember some trouble with a man. But that was Pammie. Her love life was always pretty chaotic, even going back to high school. She had a talent for finding men who were abusive, as I recall. Poor girl. And she may have been working for her father. I don't know."

"This man trouble, did she mention anyone specifically?"

"No, Detective Reese, she didn't. Maybe a friend of one of her brothers. She was into older guys back then, I think."

"What about now?" asked Sebastien.

Pedretti grinned and wagged a slender finger in his direction.

"Very clever, Mr. Grey. But, as I said, I really haven't had any contact with Pam since back in the day."

"And what was your relationship like—back in the day, I mean?" asked Sebastien. "Were you close?"

"Yes. I would say we were quite close. We certainly got into a lot of trouble together, as teenagers do."

"You spent a lot of time together, then?" he replied.

"Inseparable, I would say."

"But not so much after high school?"

"Well, no. But that's natural, isn't it?"

"What law school did you attend, Mrs. Pedretti?"

"Hmm. I'm not sure why that is important, detective . . ."

"Doctor."

"I'm sorry?"

"It's not detective; it's doctor. I'm a forensic scientist."

"How impressive. Smart and attractive."

Sebastien glanced at Tiffany to see if she picked up on the compliment. Her snickers told him she had.

"The law school, ma'am?"

"USD, in Vermillion."

Sebastien turned toward Tiffany with a confused look.

"Other side of the state," she said.

"And when, Mrs. Pedretti, when did you come back? Specifically? Law school graduation was in the spring, I assume."

"Yes. It was May."

"Did you come back to Custer right after, or did you stay in Vermillion for a bit before coming back?"

"Oh, goodness. Now you are testing my memory, Dr. Grey."

Tiffany broke in with, "So, you are saying it could have been later that year?"

"Yes. In fact, I do recall being out there for a bit. I was working as an intern at a firm in Sioux City. It was a tiny little operation. One-person show, really. I do recall staying there to help out until a new intern could arrive."

"A student, you mean?" Sebastien tried to get clarification. "Someone who would be there for the fall semester?"

Pedretti's once pleasant face was beginning to look tired, even exasperated. She offered a non-committal shrug.

"This is very helpful, Mrs. Pedretti. It really is," began Tiffany. "One last question, can you think of where Pamela might have gone? Did she mention anything about traveling or places she wanted to visit? Or maybe a job somewhere?"

"No, she never did. Not to me anyway. But here, you take my card and if you think of any other questions, please call me."

Pedretti took a card from the silver holder on her desk and scrawled a few lines on the back. She handed it to Sebastien as they all rose from their chairs.

~

SEBASTIEN AND TIFFANY spent their lunch time at Main Street Square eating Chinese food from Styrofoam boxes. The weather was just nice enough to entice a few of the proletariat out of the salt mines and into the out of doors. But the wind had picked up a bit and finding an open table was not difficult.

"Ah, you just spilled on that beautiful new coat."

Sebastien looked to his chest in alarm.

"Ha ha. Very droll," he replied, after realizing it was a joke.

Tiffany shook her head as she poked chopsticks into her noodles.

"Droll? You are an odd one, Dr. Grey."

"And yet, according to my niece, you have a crush on me."

"I know. I can't figure it out either."

"Are you trying to hurt my feelings?" Sebastien grinned.

Tiffany looked up and caught his eyes with hers, then went back to stabbing her lunch.

"What do you make of Pedretti?" he asked.

"I would kill to be that beautiful when I'm her age," replied Tiffany.

"You're off to a great start. And I hope I'm around to find out."

"Very droll, Sebastien. I like it."

"Thank you. But seriously. Do you think she knows more than she's saying?"

"It doesn't seem like it, does it? That woman is just so . . .

classy. It's like she's totally disconnected from the likes of the Bonners."

"Elegant is the word she would choose, I think," replied Sebastien.

"Ha ha. True. But no, I don't think she's hiding anything. She's far from that world and she seemed genuinely surprised to hear Pam Bonner's name. But what do you think? You were leaning in pretty hard on her law school."

Sebastien checked his cashmere coat one more time, scraping a stray grain of rice to the ground.

"I think it's important though. Don't you?"

"You mean, if she came home in May and Pam was gone, then Pam probably didn't have anything to do with Alexander's murder. But if she came home later in the fall, then Pam could have."

"She appeared to be having issues with men, according to Pedretti."

"*Abusive* men. That's how she put it, since we're being specific," corrected Tiffany.

"Always. And Martin Alexander certainly fits that description."

Sebastien looked up from his food to see Tiffany staring blankly over his shoulder.

"What is it, Tiff?"

"Well . . . I know we already know this. But it just really hit me. We've interviewed Larry Bonner, Greg Bonner, and Rich Bonner, and none of them seemed at all worried about their missing daughter-slash-sister. It's just really glaring, you know? She's been gone over thirty years. I mean, obviously they know where she is, or that she's okay, or whatever. Otherwise, each of them would have been pounding the table at us to find her. Don't you think?"

"One hundred percent. If there is anything about this case we've already proven, it's that, whether or not the Bonners are involved in Alexander's death, they're definitely circling the wagons for some reason. Of course, we need to put Mrs. Bonner, Larry's wife, on our list of interviews."

"How is it you know Old West metaphors but not sports metaphors?"

"What do you mean?"

"Oh, never mind. Anyway, I'm starting to wonder if we have enough for a search warrant now."

"On the Bonners' houses?"

"No, their phones."

"I would think so. But not for Greg, of course. He doesn't have a phone."

All of a sudden, Tiffany froze in place, her mouth opened and her hand relaxed, causing the chopsticks she was holding to release the noodles that had been destined for her mouth only a few seconds earlier.

"Ah, damn it! I am such an idiot," she snapped as she pushed her food to the middle of the table. She lowered her head into her hands. Her brown hair hung down like a curtain.

"What? What, Tiffany?" Sebastien reached across the table and grabbed her elbow.

"Maybe Jarvis and Penny are right about me. Maybe I'm not cut out for this."

"Tiffany, stop it! What are you talking about?"

Tiffany sat up again and shook her head in disbelief.

"You're right. We don't need a damn warrant for Greg's phone 'cause he doesn't have one. 'Cause he's in prison!"

"Okay? So?"

"So, all of his calls are recorded! Man, I'm such an idiot."

"An idiot? You're brilliant! That's a great idea."

"No. It would have been a great idea if I'd thought of it sooner. I can't believe . . ."

"Tiffany, stop. Look at me."

Sebastien's voice was calm, yet stern. He stared directly into her disappointed face.

"Do not let me rub off on you, Tiffany. You're better than that. The reason you didn't think of it earlier is because it didn't matter earlier. Right? We didn't know about Pam leaving the area until we talked to Richie Bonner, and we only recently decided that we needed to track her down, that she may know more about Alexander's death. Am I right?"

"Yeah . . . I guess. I mean . . ."

"Detective! Am I right?"

Tiffany's face softened. Her lips untwisted and parted slightly. Sebastien thought he detected a sparkle of moisture in the corners of her right eye.

"Thank you, Sebastien. I don't know why I second-guessed myself like that. I think I'm just feeling insecure from all this crap with Jarvis and Penny. I'm letting them get to me. I should know better."

"Can I tell you something that might help?"

"Please do, before I go nuts."

Tiffany pulled her food closer and resumed picking through her lunch.

"When Lieutenant Breed was telling me to stay away . . ."

"Bastard . . ."

"When he was telling me to stay away, he really did say you are a great detective. And he also said, and I quote, 'both of those asses will be fetching her coffee in a few years.'"

"He did not."

"He absolutely did. I'm completely serious. And I believe he believes it. I believe it, too, by the way."

Tiffany's oval face transformed: Her eyes brightened again, the corners of her mouth pulled up toward her cheeks, and her dark eyebrows lifted.

"Thank you for that, Sebastien. I really appreciate that you care so much."

"I'm glad I can help. You've already done so much for me. I can't even tell you. Ever since I met you . . . you just have a way of making me feel good, helping me feel better about myself. I don't think you even realize it."

"Well, good. Now, what's next? Prison calls?"

"Prison calls and I think we should interview Carl Jackson. His wife says he's sick with cancer. But now I wonder if that was just to keep us away."

"Hank is going to kill me when he gets the travel expenses."

"We can try to get Jackson on the phone."

"Nope. That's not the way to do things, not with a potential murder suspect anyway. Let's get back. I'll put in a request for Greg Bonner's calls, then we can arrange for Denver. And no, we're not going to do this the Sebastien-Grey-road-trip way. We'll fly like normal people."

"Thanks a lot."

"You're welcome, partner. Anytime."

"What's that? On your coat."

"Ah, dang it! I must have spilled something on it at lunch."

"I might be able to get it out," replied Melissa.

"That's all right. I'll take it to the cleaner. Thank you though."

Sebastien looked at the stain using the mirror on the wall of the guest bedroom. It wasn't so bad. A small sweep of dark sauce found its way onto the bottom of one of the lapels. He removed the coat and fished through the pockets for any loose items, finding the business card Lisa Pedretti had given him. It fell face down when he tossed it onto the bureau. The dark-blue ink of Pedretti's neat handwriting caught his attention.

"Sebastien, I'm glad you like my necklace. Please do give me a call sometime. I'll buy you a drink. -Lisa."

27

The Jacksons lived at the end of a cul-de-sac in East Pleasant View, Colorado. Tiffany and Sebastien sat in their rental car across the street and examined the clean, well-cared-for home, with its fastidiously manicured yard. The rosebushes under the front window were covered, signaling the anticipation of an oncoming deadly freeze. Of particular interest to the pair was the vehicle parked on a concrete pad along one side of the house. It was mostly covered by a gray tarp, but the unmistakable Chevy symbol was peeping out furtively where the tarp had buckled and lifted.

"You gotta be kidding me," declared Tiffany.

"Is it blue? I think I see some blue under the tarp."

"I think so. Let's get a better look."

Tiffany opened the driver's side door, then quickly closed it when a white cargo van pulled into the street and made a quick U-turn right next to them. The van backed into the Jackson's driveway and two men emerged. One of the men walked up to the front door while the other opened the rear doors of the van.

"What the . . ."

"Hang back a sec," instructed Tiffany, extending her arm

over Sebastien's lap.

The couple watched as an elderly woman opened the front door and disappeared into the house with the man who knocked. A few moments later, that man reappeared and joined his partner. They pulled a gurney from the back of the van and dropped its wheels onto the driveway.

"What the . . ." echoed Tiffany.

"This doesn't look good," countered Sebastien.

After several minutes of tense anticipation, Tiffany and Sebastien observed what each had inwardly been expecting. The two men re-emerged, lifting the gurney over the threshold and out onto the front walk of the house. A plum-colored blanket covered the stretcher's burden, which, from the shape of it, was obviously a human body.

After the men loaded their cargo into the van and closed the doors, the woman, wearing a light-green bathrobe and matching slippers, joined them and handed one of the men a clipboard and a pen. Sebastien turned to watch the van drive back down the street, noticing a few neighbors gathering on the sidewalk as it turned and disappeared.

"I guess she wasn't lying about the cancer."

"Oh crap. She saw us," cried Tiffany.

The old woman walked into the street and approached the car. Tiffany rolled down the driver's side window.

"Good morning, Mrs. Jackson. We are . . ."

"You may as well come in," Mrs. Jackson interrupted before immediately turning around and shuffling back to the house.

Sebastien and Tiffany took their proffered places on an old wood-frame sofa. The room smelled of stale smoke; the walls and ceiling bore a yellow tinge that likewise testified to years of a tobacco-dominated atmosphere. Sebastien looked to his left and saw a lower-level living room with an empty hospital bed. The irony was almost painful.

Elizabeth Jackson's seventy-plus years appeared to have left their mark and then some. Her leathery cheeks drooped like pouches. Her red and swollen eyes were adorned by only the faintest hint of eyebrows.

"Can I get you anything? Coffee? Tea?"

"No, ma'am," replied Tiffany. "We are so sorry for your loss. I'm sure this is a very bad time. We can come back. It's really no problem."

Sebastien was touched by the sincerity and concern in Tiffany's voice, which added to the gravitas of the moment.

"That's okay. I knew you would be coming, sooner or later."

"Mrs. Jackson, I'm Sebastien Grey. We spoke on the phone."

"Yes, we did," Jackson replied with a tone of surrender.

"Why did you think we would be coming, ma'am?"

"I just knew. It was time. Old Carl was dying as much from the guilt as the cancer."

Jackson tilted her head toward the family room as she spoke. Her arthritic fingers ripped at a soggy tissue.

"Guilt for what, exactly?" asked Tiffany.

Jackson looked down at the shag carpet.

"I'm too old for this. Too tired. Would you mind just telling me what you know, or what you think you know? I have nothing to hide at this point. I'd rather you start. If you don't mind."

Sebastien scooted up to the edge of the sofa. He put his elbows on his knees and clasped his hands together as he spoke.

"Mrs. Jackson, we know that your husband Carl—before he was your husband, I mean—was suspected of defrauding North Plains Development; he was double-billing for materials."

Jackson nodded.

"And we know that your first husband, Charles Kinder, was in the process of suing Carl because of it. Is that all correct?"

Another nod from Jackson.

"But the lawsuit was dropped. Do you know why that was?"

"Charles's lawyer talked him out of it. He said he couldn't prove it."

"If he couldn't prove it, why did he file the lawsuit?" asked Tiffany, her pen ready to record the answer.

"Did he not have the evidence?" asked Sebastien.

Jackson didn't reply to either question.

"He did have evidence, didn't he, Mrs. Jackson?" began Sebastien. "It was in the trailer. That's why the trailer was burned. I mean, it was meant to be burned, but Carl couldn't get in, could he?"

"No," Jackson replied softly. "My key wouldn't work."

Tiffany looked over at Sebastien and mouthed the word "*wow*" before asking, "Then what happened to the evidence?"

"I . . . I don't know."

Sebastien leaned forward a little farther.

"Now, Mrs. Jackson, you *are* hiding something. But you don't need to hide anything anymore. You took the documents that proved Carl's fraud, didn't you? After the fire. You handled a lot of the office work for North Plains Development. You knew exactly where it was. In fact, you probably were the one who doctored the documents in the first place. Did you use your husband's key to go back in the trailer after the fire and remove the paperwork? The paperwork that could prove your husband's case against Carl?"

Sebastien waited for an answer. When it was clear it wasn't coming, he continued.

"Did Charles know you were having an affair with the man who was stealing from him? Did he know you were complicit in the fraud?"

Jackson sat up straight, almost with a hint of boldness.

"No, he did not. He never suspected anything. The man went to his grave without a clue. I'm very proud of that, Dr. Grey."

"You remembered," muttered Sebastien.

"Oh, yes. Like I said, I knew you'd come."

"How did your husband Charles die, Mrs. Jackson?" asked Tiffany.

"Heart attack. There was a family history. What? Do you think we killed him? Carl is not a killer, detective. And neither am I."

"But what about the body that was found burning in Boxwood?"

"Carl swore to me—he absolutely swore—he had nothing to do with that. And I believed him. I still believe him. He said whoever helped him start the fire insisted they put a body in the trailer. It was to make it look as though the person who started the fire died in the process. But it ate him up." Mrs. Jackson paused to blow her nose, then resumed her defense of her second dead husband. "That's how I know he would never have killed Charles. He felt horrible that that poor man died. But he wasn't there when it happened—when he was killed, I mean. He promised me that."

"Do you know who that was, whose body they dumped and set on fire?" asked Tiffany.

"No."

"But Carl knew, didn't he, Mrs. Jackson?"

"I do believe he did, Dr. Grey. I don't know for sure, but he felt some responsibility. Now, you must believe me. I'm very sorry for all of this. It has been a horrible burden after all these years. But Carl is dead now, and . . ."

Jackson began weeping. Tiffany scrambled to pull a few fresh tissues from the box on the coffee table and rushed to the woman's side.

"I'm so sorry, Mrs. Jackson. Here. Take these. We're going to leave you be. If we have any questions, we'll be back in touch. Now, do you have anyone who can be with you? You shouldn't be alone. Is there someone we can call?"

"You're such a sweet young lady. No, my sister and niece are on their way. But please, I do want to be helpful. I just don't know any more than that."

"I wouldn't worry about that, Mrs. Jackson," said Sebastien. "You've been very helpful. You led us right to the murderers."

～

"Wow, that was heavy," exclaimed Tiffany from the driver's seat of the rental car.

Sebastien looked animated as he buckled his seatbelt. His eyes were alive. It was as if they didn't just see a woman put her dead husband's body in a van.

"You know what would be fascinating?"

"What?" Tiffany asked.

"I wonder what the odds are of all this. I mean, seriously. It's like tossing a coin and getting both heads and tails. On the one side, you have the need to conceal a fraud, and on the other, there's an effort to get rid of a body. But the two aren't explicitly related."

"You know what this means though? This means your brother was right. You thought it was Jackson and I said it was the Bonners. Hank predicted it would be both."

"Do we have to tell him?" asked Sebastien.

"Ha. Of course! We beat up on the poor guy enough. Let him have his day. Plus, I think being out of the game is wearing on him. He'll be glad to know we need him."

"Mrs. Jackson was right. You are a sweet young lady."

"Yes, I am. Aren't I?"

Sebastien threw a nod in the direction of Jackson's house.

"What about her? You made it kind of sound like she was off the hook."

"Isn't she? There's not a prosecutor in the county who'll charge her with Martin Alexander's murder, or conspiracy after the fact. There is zero evidence of her involvement in that. And the statute of limitations on fraud is well passed, same with burglary or arson."

As they headed east on Interstate 70, Sebastien admired Tiffany's well-manicured fingernails and gracile hands, which were dutifully positioned at ten-and-two on the steering wheel. In the distance, he could see the massive skyline of downtown Denver. The contrast to Rapid City struck him. As did something else. Was Colorado Opera dark tonight? If not, might there still be some tickets for *Die Fledermaus*? This led him to speculate further about the occupancy status of the Curtis Hotel. Could there be a room available? Maybe one of their nicer suites? Maybe for a few days? Or maybe just one night?

"What are you daydreaming about over there?" Tiffany asked, smiling.

"Oh, nothing. Just admiring the view."

"It will be even better from the plane. I'm anxious to get back and see if Greg Bonner's prison phone calls are pulled yet. I think I have a plan. If we get lucky, that is."

Sebastien grabbed the handle above his window and looked forward down the highway.

"You have that dumb look on your face again," Tiffany remarked.

"Do I?"

DETECTIVE PENNY PUSHED with his feet to roll his chair down the row of cubicles, stopping at the desk of Detective Jarvis.

"Hey, look what came in. Autopsy results on Manly."

"About friggin' time."

Jarvis took the sheets from his partner and scanned to the findings section.

"Not much here. Thirty-eight caliber to the back of the

head. Let's see . . . time of death between eight to ten hours before he was found. We got there at, what, nine-ish? So that puts the murder at between eleven o'clock p.m. Friday and one o'clock a.m. Saturday."

"Yeah, but check this out. This is even better."

Penny pulled another sheet of paper out of a leather folio and placed it on Jarvis's desk.

"I was talking to the girl down in property. You know, the cute one? She wears those crop tops in the gym. She's got that belly button . . ."

"Elaine, you perv. Her name is Elaine. Probably the same age as your daughter."

"Hey, don't act like you don't know what I'm talking about. Anyway, Elaine said Forestry booked a gun on Sunday morning. A .38. Apparently, the officer rolled up on someone at about two in the morning over at Bismarck Lake. The subject claimed to be taking a leak, but the officer heard something splash, like something heavy was thrown into the water. They did a field interview and got the info but let 'em go because they couldn't see what, if anything, had been thrown in the lake. But the officer had a hunch it was more than just a rock. So he went back there with a net or something when it was light. He pulled the gun right out."

"Well, thank heavens those guys got nothin' better to do," replied Jarvis. "Who was it at the lake?"

"Well, that I don't know yet. I was just going to give 'em a call."

"Nice work, Penny. With any luck, it'll be Richie Bonner. Maybe we can get that bitch Reese thrown back to patrol. Kill two birds with one stone."

"I don't know, man. She's not so bad to look at. You know this one time, at the department 10K, she wore these shorts . . ."

"You need help, Penny. I'm serious. Get yourself some help. After you call Forestry."

28

"To what do I owe this honor? It's not like you to call me."

"Hey, I'm your sister. I care."

"No, you don't."

"Screw you, Greg."

"Now that's more like it. What can I do for you?"

"Richie said the cops came by his place."

"Oh? That's fascinating. Is that all you got? 'Cause if I make it to my laundry shift early, I'll get an extra fifty cents this week."

"Greg, I'm serious."

"Oh, I know you are. It was probably the same two cops who came to see me."

"They came to see you too?"

"Yep. Some psychiatrist and a good-looking detective broad."

"Doesn't that concern you?"

"Not particularly. You may have forgotten this little detail, but I didn't do anything. Not to mention the fact that I'm already in the hole. What are they going to do to me?"

"Did they say what they wanted?"

"Probably the same thing they wanted from Richie."

"Well, I don't know what that is. The little jerk won't answer my calls."

"Shame. How's the weather where you are?"

"Oh, come on. Just tell me. Were they asking about . . . you know?"

"The guy you popp—?"

"Shh! You know what I'm talking about. You don't need to say it."

"Yes. They were asking about that—in a way."

"In a way? What is that supposed to mean?"

"They found the guy's . . ."

"Shh! Geez, would you . . ."

"Nice talking to ya, Pammie."

"Wait! Look. Just tell me. Do they know what happened?"

"In a way."

"Gregory Bonner, stop that!"

"Okay, Mom."

"Come on, Greg. I'm freaking out up here. Please. Please tell me what's going on down there. Don't you care?"

"Care? Did you just ask me if I care? Are you for real? All these years me and Richie been sitting around, waiting for the bomb to explode right underneath us while you run around up there acting like nothin' ever happened. We cleaned up your mess and never got so much as a thank you. Don't lecture me about caring."

"I'm sorry. Really, I am."

"I'm sure."

"Please tell me."

"All right, all right. They know about the, uh . . . dude. And they know about the, uh . . . thing down at the place."

"What place?"

"Did Richie never tell you what they, uh . . . how they . . ."

"No."

"Well, don't worry about it anyway. You never came up."

"Oh, thank goodness."

"Not with me anyway. Who knows what Richie told 'em. I hear

he's been getting into some trouble. You might want to send him some crab legs in case he gets any ideas. A good bribe never hurts—that's what my cellmate tells me anyway."

Tiffany pressed a key on her laptop, which was in the middle of Larry Bonner's dining room table.

"Now, I'd love to get your take on that, Mr. Bonner. Seems like your kids know something about what happened to Martin Alexander in 1987."

"Martin Alexander?" Bonner repeated. "I don't know who that is."

"We suspect you do," replied Sebastien. "You may not remember his name, but we're pretty sure you know he ended up in two places at once—head, arms, and legs in Hell Canyon, and the rest on fire at your job site in Cheyenne, Boxwood Estates. We also strongly suspect you know how he got to be like that."

"I have no idea what you're talking about."

Sebastien looked at Tiffany, who offered a look of recognition in return.

"Here, Mr. Bonner. Maybe this will help."

Tiffany stroked the trackpad on her laptop and pressed a few more keys.

"Hey, Pops. How's it going?"

"Gregory."

"Your ticker okay? You taking your medicine?"

"Your mother nags me about that every damn day. Did you call to nag me about my medicine too?"

"I just got off the phone with Pam. She's worried about the cops poking around."

"So am I."

"She's trying to get a hold of Richie. Can you tell Richie to call her, Pop? She shouldn't be calling me. It's too risky. You never know when . . ."

"How are they treating you, son?"

"Oh, don't worry about me. I'm fine. First parole hearing is in a few years. I'm behaving."

"I wish you wouldn't have done that, Gregory. Your mom is a wreck. You shouldn't have handled it like that."

"Dad, I know this. Can you just tell Richie to call Pam? In fact, you might want to reach out, too, if you haven't already. I don't know what Richie told 'em."

"He wouldn't tell them anything. Don't you worry about your brother."

"I hear he's attracting attention."

"He always has."

"Okay, Pops. I'm just trying to help. You know? I don't have a dog in this fight. Not like the other two anyway."

"I know you are, son. Hang on, let me get your mother. She'd kill me if she knew you called without her getting to say hi."

Tiffany closed her laptop and Sebastien watched Larry Bonner carefully. His countenance changed; his face grew angry and his eyes fixed upon Tiffany with a venomous hatred.

"Is that even legal?"

"It is, Mr. Bonner. I assure you it is," replied Tiffany. "You know, at the beginning of any call with an inmate, there's a message that tells you it's being recorded. The problem is, if you hear it too many times, you tend to tune it out."

"Mr. Bonner, we'd like to tell you what we know, then perhaps you can fill in the blanks for us. Would that be okay?"

Sebastien was careful to use a calm and even voice. At this stage, neither he nor Tiffany felt Larry Bonner had much, if anything, to do with the murder of Martin Alexander. But whether he played a part in the dismemberment was another matter.

"No, that would not be okay. I'd like you two to leave my home immediately. I'll be calling my lawyer as soon as your butts clear my porch."

Tiffany immediately folded up her laptop and stuffed it

back into her bag. The pair rose to their feet and started for the front door.

"Oh, before we go, Mr. Bonner, we should inform you that it won't do any good to warn your daughter. The Alaska State Patrol has already picked her up. And we have a search warrant for her phone," said Tiffany.

Sebastien held the door open for Tiffany and the two had just barely breathed in fresh air before Bonner conspicuously cleared his throat.

"I'm sorry, Mr. Bonner. Did you have something to say before we go?" asked Tiffany, turning around.

"Maybe he wants to talk before one of his kids tries to throw him under the bus," suggested Sebastien.

"Oh, I don't know, Dr. Grey. They don't seem like the kind to blame their father for something they did. I mean, sure, it might be tempting. After all, they have long lives ahead of them."

"Fair point, Detective Reese. They seem way too ethical for that."

"All right, come back, damn it."

Bonner motioned them back into the house, then into the living room.

"I'm going to need a whiskey. Join me?"

"No, thank you, Mr. Bonner."

Sebastien and Tiffany each took spots on the living room sofa while Bonner made his way over to a sideboard that was covered in bottles of liquor. They exchanged nervous looks while Bonner poured a dark liquid into a tumbler then added water to it.

"Call me Larry, by the way," Bonner insisted as he turned around and took a leather armchair opposite the sofa.

"Okay, Larry," began Tiffany, "why don't you tell us what you know about Martin Alexander? Who killed him and why?"

"See here, detective. I'm no fool. Despite what I say, I can't imagine you'll be able to prove anything." The glass in Bonner's hand jerked angrily as he spoke. Some of the liquid spilled onto the knee of his corduroy slacks. "So you have little choice but to believe me. And what I'm going to tell you is the truth."

"I think you may underestimate our evidence," declared Sebastien.

"No, sir. I don't think so."

Tiffany gestured with open hands toward the old man.

"We'll believe you, Larry. I doubt that you have much to lose at this point, in any case."

Bonner drained his tumbler and wiped his mouth with the sleeve of his sweater.

"First thing is this: I didn't kill anybody and I didn't dump any bodies anywhere."

"Okay," replied Tiffany. "And . . . ?"

"And this whole blasted thing was self-defense. By the book self-defense. That guy—Martin what's-his-name—he attacked my Pamela."

"Oh? Tell us more about that, Larry," said Sebastien.

"They went to a bar after work. The crew did, that is. Pamela and a friend met them there . . ."

Tiffany looked up from her notebook.

"Who is this friend?"

"Hell if I know. Anyway, after the bar closed, Pamela and this other girl brought some of the guys home."

"Whose home?" asked Sebastien.

"Pamela's. She has a little house in Custer. I mean, *had* a little house."

Tiffany looked confused. "There's no record of her owning property, Mr. Bonner," she said.

"I owned it. I bought it for her."

Both investigators nodded.

"Anyway, from what I understand, after they partied a bit, they kicked the guys out. But Martin came back. He knocked on the door and asked her if he could use the phone. Pamela— stupid girl—Pamela let him in. And, of course, the guy went after her."

"By that you mean . . . ?"

"What I mean, Detective Reese, is that the guy pushed her down on the floor and pulled her pants off. Do you want me to be more specific than that?"

"That's okay, Larry. I think we get it. So, you said it was self-defense? Do you mean Pamela killed him while she was being attacked?"

"I got her a gun, thank goodness. For her fourteenth birth-day. Taught her to shoot. Fortunately, she was able to get away and get a hold of it. Plugged that sonofabitch right between the eyes, she said."

"Nearly," corrected Sebastien.

"I'm sorry?" Bonner said.

"She nearly got him between the eyes. The entry wound was just above the right eye, in the frontal bone."

Larry Bonner and Tiffany both stared at Sebastien incredulously.

"What? Just stating the facts. By the way, what kind of gun? Do you remember?"

"A .22 pistol. Nice and light. Well . . . anyway, like I said, it was self-defense. Poor girl nearly got raped and who knows what else. A medal, that's what she deserves. And you better believe she'll get it. I'm going to hire the best lawyer in the country. No jury will convict her. That's why I'm telling you all this. She doesn't need to hide anymore. We will face this as a family."

"Why did she run off to Alaska, then, Larry? If it was self-defense," asked Tiffany.

"Probably to avoid this nonsense." Bonner extended his arms outward for effect.

"Larry," began Sebastien, "we know Martin Alexander was dismembered. Did Pam do that?"

"My little girl? No way. I raised her better than that."

Sebastien began to make a comment but stopped himself.

"Did you raise Greg and Richard better than that?" asked Tiffany.

"I taught them to help out their little sister. 'Always look out for little Pammie,' I told them."

"They took care of Martin's body for her? They chopped him up . . ."

"Sawed him up, more likely," interrupted Sebastien.

Tiffany looked directly at Sebastien. "Thank you, Dr. Grey, for the critical clarification." She then turned back to Bonner and said, "So, Greg and Richard sawed up Mr. Alexander, then dumped his body parts."

It was a statement, not a question, and Larry Bonner treated it as such by remaining silent.

"Larry, can you tell us about Carl Jackson?"

Bonner's face puckered at Sebastien's question.

"You knew him, correct?" added Tiffany.

"He's a lumber guy. Retired now, I think. He had a yard down in Hot Springs. We got a lot of our framing material and such from him. Pretty good prices, as I recall."

"But that's not the whole story, is it, Larry? Jackson married Charlie Kinder's widow, which you knew. He is also the one who dumped Alexander's body down in Boxwood Estates—along with your son Richard. Which you also knew. And, last but not least, he was stealing from Kinder—with the help of Kinder's wife and, probably, you too. Isn't that right?"

Bonner looked at Sebastien dead in the eye, but once again, didn't answer.

Sebastien took the silence as an opportunity to press harder.

"I don't pretend to know much about construction, Larry.

296

But I would imagine it would be a lot easier to double-bill for lumber and trusses, and that kind of thing, if the framing company was complicit. Am I correct in that? I mean, if Kinder came to you and said, 'Hey, is this invoice right? Did we really need this much material?' You could just say, 'Sure,' then take your cut of whatever Jackson was benefitting. This is why Jackson and your son Richard were hoping to burn down the construction trailer along with Alexander's body. It was to get rid of the paper trail once Kinder caught on to the scheme. Which he did. He was going to sue Jackson. Was he in the process of suing you as well?"

"Wild speculation, Mr. Grey."

"It's Dr. Grey."

"Fine, Doctor Grey. Now, if you'll excuse me, I must make what I anticipate being a very long call to my lawyer. I assume I'm not under arrest. Correct?"

"No, sir. Not at this stage. But we have many more interviews to conduct." Tiffany said after standing up to go for the second time in an hour.

"Oh, and detectives, while you are out chasing fairy tales about me and my children, perhaps you could look into a little matter of blackmail. In fact, I'd like to make a report. I'll come by tomorrow."

"THINK FAST."

Tiffany threw the key fob over to Sebastien, who missed the catch.

"Real nice, detective. Right into the dirt."

"I would say you catch like a girl, but I'm a girl and I catch way better than you—and more consistently, I would add."

"I take it I'm driving?"

"Yes, if you don't mind. I have to make an urgent phone call."

"To whom?"

"Alaska Stake Patrol. We need them to pick up Pam and her phone as soon as possible."

Sebastien clicked the seatbelt in place and adjusted the rearview mirror.

"You're a very impressive liar. Has anyone ever told you that?" he asked.

29

Tiffany and Sebastien entered the crime analysis room unnoticed. There were three workstations in the large office and only one was occupied. The sole analyst on duty—a very slim, almost skeletal, woman in her mid-twenties with dark, flat, pixie-cut hair and round glasses—was busily working at her computer, creating some sort of map. Her earbuds prevented her from noticing the interlopers. Tiffany gave her a tap on the shoulder.

"Hi, Tiffany. Hello, Dr. Grey."

"I told you, you don't need to call him doctor, Erin."

The crime analyst looked at Sebastien sheepishly, as if unsure if the man would confirm that. But he didn't either way.

"So, what did you find out?" Tiffany asked.

"I looked at field interview cards from 1986 and 1987. I had to do it by hand because the computer system only has them going back to 1990."

"Oh, I'm so sorry, Erin. We owe you lunch," replied Tiffany.

"Yes, you do."

"Did you find anything?"

Erin shuffled through some papers on her desktop and

retrieved three small white cards, which she handed to Tiffany. "I did actually. I couldn't believe it, but here you go."

Tiffany took the cards from the woman and squinted as she tried to make out the writing.

"Is this an 'n'?" she asked.

Erin pushed her glasses up her long nose and looked over Tiffany's shoulder.

"Yes. I think that says 'near'—'near 2230.'"

"What's 2230?" asked Sebastien. "An address?"

"Robbery," answered the two women in unison. "It's the code for robbery," added Erin.

Sebastien motioned for a turn to look at the cards and Tiffany handed them over.

"This is amazing," she exclaimed. "Great job, Erin. Really. Whatever they're paying you, double it."

"Yippee," the analyst joked. "Finally up to the poverty line."

Sebastien handed the cards back to Erin.

"So, in July of 1986, both Pamela Bonner and Lisa Pedretti were stopped near the location of a robbery. Who is that on the third card? It looked like a John Stickler?"

"John Strickler," replied the analyst. "I ran him out in the system. He has a ton of arrests. Back then, it was mostly burglary, theft, and one or two domestic batteries. In 1990, he was arrested for robbery. In the mid-nineties, he finally went to prison for it."

"I'd like to read that report," said Tiffany. "The one from 1990."

"I knew you would."

The analyst slowly, and with some difficulty, walked across the room with the aid of an arm crutch. After pulling some sheets from a filing cabinet, she returned and handed them over to Tiffany.

"Ataxic?" asked Sebastien, referring to the young woman's cerebral palsy.

"Yes. It doesn't bother me too much. Just don't ask me to write anything by hand or tie your shoes."

"Sebastien! That's a little rude," protested Tiffany.

"Oh, I don't mind," said Erin. "I'd rather people ask than point and talk behind my back."

"Please do not tell me anyone around here does that," said Tiffany.

"No. The people here are super nice. Except this one detective who makes me sort through thirty-year-old field interview cards for hours at a time."

"I am sooo sorry, Erin. It didn't even occur to me."

"That's fine! I'm kidding! I'm happy to help and very happy I found what you were looking for."

"Well, you did. You are a superstar. Lunch tomorrow? Sebastien is buying. Maybe he'll drive. Have you seen his fancy car?"

"No, but I've heard plenty of people talking about it," the woman winked.

"I'M PROBABLY BORING you to death. But what about you? A forensic scientist? That sounds fascinating. What *exactly* do you do, Dr. Grey?"

Sebastien tried hard to concentrate, but Lisa Pedretti was a study in distraction. Her wraparound dress plunged all the way down to her xiphoid process and its vertical lines of heat stones threw blinding reflections into his eyes whenever she moved. Her perfume, the smell of orchids and hot caramel, sent frantic olfactory signals from his forebrain to his amygdala, almost short-circuiting his ability to form words.

The lawyer and anthropologist were seated in the Hehaka Lounge inside the Monument Hotel, just a few blocks east of Pedretti's law offices. Happy hour patrons were coming and going like the tide as the two talked pleasantly in a far corner booth of the spacious dining room. Cheesy piano standards and the din of conversation made it difficult to hear. At least, that's what Lisa had said when she moved from the opposite side of the table to sit thigh to thigh with Sebastien.

"My specialty is forensic anthropology. I examine deceased individuals to find out who they were and how they died."

"Oh, that *is* fascinating! You know, I only took one anthropology class in college. It was a pre-req, I think. Anyway, I hated it. It was as boring as watching grass grow. But the professor was a hippie and he got the best pot. Oh, I'm sorry. I didn't mean to . . ."

"No, that's fine," replied Sebastien. "I really don't care one way or the other. I'm used to it. When I was in college, people would ask me what my major was, and when I told them, they would reply with 'but why?'"

Pedretti let out a laugh, showing her perfect teeth. Her breath smelled of mint and alcohol.

"I got that, too, but it came from my parents. 'Why law school?' they asked. 'Why don't you stay on the ranch with us? What, we're not good enough for you?' What a nightmare. They were so stubborn that I had to pay my own way through both undergrad and law school. Maybe they should have had a boy."

Sebastien took a sip of his drink, not knowing how to respond.

"What about your parents?" Pedretti asked. "Did they care that you wanted to play with dead people for a living?"

"'*Play with*' is a little strong. Anyway, my dad wasn't around and my mom was mentally ill. So, no. My brother and I didn't get too much involvement from the parental side of things. Which I guess is a positive."

"That's awful. Mentally ill? What illness did she have? If you don't mind me asking."

Yes, I very much do mind you asking, thought Sebastien.

"No, not at all. She had borderline personality disorder, which was exacerbated by a long-term problem with alcohol and drugs."

Pedretti looked down groggily at her half-empty glass of wine before setting it on the table.

"But never mind all that," said Sebastien. "What about your childhood? I remember you saying something about you and Pam Bonner getting into trouble. Anything super serious? Did your parents come down on you for any of that?"

"Dr. Grey, are we back on the Pam Bonner thing? I'm here to enjoy myself."

Pedretti leaned her head on Sebastien's shoulder and whispered into his ear.

"I got us a room."

Sebastien felt her wet lips on his earlobe and mastoid process, just behind his ear. He broke away quickly and scanned the crowded room for anyone who might be watching.

"What's the matter, Dr. Grey? You're not married, are you?"

"Well . . . no, but you are."

"So? It's the twenty-first century, my dear."

My dear. She said my dear. Just like Tiffany.

"Oh, I know. I get it. I'm just . . . can we just get to know each other a bit?"

"You're an interesting man, Dr. Grey. But fine. We have the room all night. What would you like to know?"

"You're a little hell-raiser, aren't you?" smiled Sebastien, trying to reclaim some manhood.

"I'm certainly trying. But you're making things very difficult."

Pedretti picked up her glass and drained it.

"I'm sorry if I'm a buzzkill. I'm just sort of intrigued by the whole parent-child dynamic. I didn't have that really. I find it interesting."

"No need to apologize, Dr. Grey. I'm sorry. You probably think I'm a horny old lady."

"I'm not here to judge."

"Pam and me, I guess we just got bored a lot. We were rebellious. Screw the world—that kind of thing. And we ran around with some pretty bad boys."

"Bad in what way? Law-breaking bad? Or chasing kittens up trees bad?"

"Let's just say I could've gotten kicked out of law school for some of the crap I got up to."

"Wow. I guess it's a good thing you never got caught."

"Oh, we got caught. Fortunately, my father knew the sheriff. Pam's too. We batted our eyes and that was usually enough to get us out of trouble."

"That was nice of them to keep it from the law school. It would be pretty devastating to have a few mistakes prevent you from living the rest of your life. You're a highly successful attorney now. Things could've been much different."

"I would love to give those old farts credit, but the truth of it is that they wanted me out of town. If I got kicked out of law school, I'd have never left. I'd be stuck on my daddy's ranch, probably still causing them trouble. Or strung out. Or both."

"But you did come back," reminded Sebastien.

"Sure, I came back to Rapid City. But I've pretty much stayed out of the hills."

"That's kind of strange though, isn't it? You don't normally associate law students with criminal behavior—at least, not until they graduate."

Pedretti let out a loud snort of laughter.

"Oh hell, I'm going to pee myself. Just a minute. I'll be right back."

Sebastien turned ninety degrees in his seat and watched her walk away toward the restrooms. Her dress shimmered in the dim table lights as she staggered past the diners and drinkers.

"Well," he prompted out loud, still turned.

"What a freaking lush. Was she licking you? I swear I heard licking."

Tiffany slid out of the booth behind Sebastien and sidled in next to him.

"All right, that's enough."

"Were you enjoying it? It seemed to me like you were enjoying it," she teased, pulling at his earlobe.

"Tiffany. Okay. Please," he replied firmly.

"I'm sorry, I'm sorry. I'm just having fun with you."

"But did you hear all that?"

"Yes, I did. Very interesting. You think she could be the girl-friend who was with Pam and Martin just before he was shot?"

"I think it's very possible. And I'm not sure about Larry Bonner's version. Who's to say Pam's girlfriend wasn't there when the murder occurred?"

"Are you just biased because she's an adulteress?"

"I find that vices tend to combine. One bad behavior is often a good indicator that more are out there. But I'm really referring to the fact that she just admitted to having a criminal past."

Sebastien reached his hand under the table to find Tiffany's. He gave it a gentle squeeze before putting his lips near her left ear and saying, "I am sorry though."

"What do you mean you're sorry? What for?"

"You know . . . for . . . this."

He waved his free hand over the table to indicate the ridicu-lous circumstance.

"Oh, for crying out loud. You are so adorably innocent. I would lick your ear right now if it didn't have cougar spit all over it."

"Very . . ."

"Don't say droll. Wait, she's coming back."

"So, how about it, doctor? Are you ready to take me . . . Detective Reese? What the hell are you doing here?"

"Hello, councilor! I was just walking by and I saw my partner here, so I thought I would stop and say hello."

Pedretti tried to stand defiantly at the table, but she was too shocked and full of alcohol to pull it off without steadying herself.

Tiffany feigned a quick survey of the room. "And what are *you* doing here?" she asked. "Is your husband here too? You should invite him to join us. Plenty of room. Right, Dr. Grey?"

"I guess this is goodnight. It was nice to bump into you again, Dr. Grey. Detective Reese, perhaps we will see each other again one day."

Pedretti turned to leave but was stopped by Tiffany's reply.

"I think we will, Mrs. Pedretti. In fact, I'm going to make an appointment with your secretary. Tomorrow, perhaps?"

"As you know, detective, I am a very busy woman. I'm not sure tomorrow will work. What is it you need? I believe I've told you all I know about Pam."

"Yes, you've been super helpful and we appreciate it. I actually just wanted to ask you about someone else."

"Oh?"

"Yeah. His name is John Stickler . . ."

"Strickler," corrected Sebastien.

Pedretti shot a look of betrayal in Sebastien's direction.

"Thank you, doc. Strickler. That was it. Heck, if you have a few minutes, we can get this out of the way now."

Pedretti appeared reluctant as she slid in across from Tiffany and Sebastien. She continued to throw poison at the anthropologist with her beautiful blue eyes.

"Quickly, detective. My husband is expecting me."

"Oh, is he up in the room?" asked Tiffany.

"You're not a very polite woman," Pedretti retorted.

"I apologize."

"And I think it's clear that my private conversation with Dr. Grey was not so private. Is that correct, Dr. Grey?"

Sebastien shifted uncomfortably in his seat. Tiffany saved him.

"So, John Strickler. You know him?" she asked.

"Knew him," Pedretti replied coldly.

"You and he and Pam used to run around quite a bit. Would that be accurate?"

"No, it would not. He was just an older boy who hung around us younger girls. We did our best to avoid him. He was trouble."

"What about in July of 1986?"

Tiffany laid the three field interview cards on the table and lined them up carefully, as if she was preparing to read tarot.

"These are field interview cards. An officer fills these out when they encounter someone who is doing something suspicious or could possibly be involved in criminal activity. See this number in the top corner? The hand-written number?"

Tiffany indicated the number on each card with her finger, then placed her forearms parallel to her chest on the table, with one hand over the other, as she waited for a reply. Pedretti merely gave a silent nod.

"You see, it's the same number. That means the three individuals whose names are on these cards were stopped together. Same time. Same place. Together."

Tiffany tapped one of the cards with her forefinger.

"This one, you can see, has your name. Lisa Pedretti. And that is your driver's license number, correct?"

Pedretti rolled her eyes and turned her head to the wall of the booth.

"It's rather convenient that you kept your maiden name, by the way. Our crime analyst wanted me to thank you for that."

"My pleasure," Pedretti replied before folding her arms tightly in front of her nearly bare chest.

"And this one here is for Pamela Bonner. And this last one, well, here . . . you can read it for yourself."

Tiffany slid the card across the table, but Pedretti made no effort to pick it up or read it. But she did look over at Sebastien as if she wanted to say something.

"So, long story short, Mrs. Pedretti. You did hang around with John Strickler. And, as you pointed out, he wasn't that great of a guy. He's been in and out of prison his entire adult life. And he's pretty sick of it, too, by the way. We talked to him. He'd really like some help with his current sentence."

"You're a real bastard, Dr. Grey. No wonder your mother went crazy. I would go crazy too. Sick creep."

"You're not a very polite woman," replied Sebastien, his own stoicism surprising him. Ordinarily, a barb like that would have stuck deep.

"Mothers aside, Mrs. Pedretti," Tiffany continued, "what we found most interesting was Strickler's first big-boy arrest in 1990. It was for robbery. In Custer County too. Evidently, a couple of Strickler's female friends lured a man back to their house with the promise of sex. But when they got there, Strickler sprang from the closet and stuck a shotgun in the guy's chest while the two women emptied his pockets and took his wedding ring."

"If you are accusing me of that, Detective Reese, you can forget it."

"No, ma'am, we are not. The two women were arrested and convicted. But the crime does remind us of the case we're investigating right now. Our victim is a Martin Alexander, twenty-eight years old. He came out here from Sioux Falls in 1987 to work on one of the Bonner jobs and ended up shot in the head and sawed into pieces. Now, we know Pam Bonner shot him. And we know there was another woman with her—a girlfriend of hers, according to one person we spoke with—either before, or, more likely, during the murder. We also feel pretty confident Mr. Strickler was in on it too. But we'll ask him about that. He seems eager to help."

"I have nothing to do with any of this stuff. I was in law school. And when I was not in law school, I was working hard to become one of the most successful attorneys in the state. And I know my rights, Reese. Do you think you're talking to an idiot here? I'm not some drug-addled jerk off the streets. I am an educated woman. A professional woman. Do you know I have been asked to run for public office? You have no clue. I chew up people like you on a daily damn basis. You're looking at the biggest lawsuit you'll ever face."

Sebastien finally spoke up.

"Actually, Mrs. Pedretti, I believe you just told me your law school didn't keep you from committing crimes with Pam Bonner. You also told us, when we were at your office, that you may have stayed in Vermillion until the fall of '87. Which means that when Martin Alexander was killed—by two females, one being Pam Bonner—you had yet to embark on your journey to legal fame and fortune."

"I bet the student loans were a bitch too," added Tiffany. "I think I heard somewhere that your parents didn't pay for your college."

"That was beyond awkward," said Sebastien as he and Tiffany belted themselves into the Range Rover.

Tiffany leaned over and gave him a brief kiss on the lips. "You did really great," she said. "I'm very proud of you. I think I'll talk to Hank about loaning you to Rapid City. I heard they could use some help on their prostitution stings."

"You are hilarious."

"I try."

"By the way, wow! You are really great at talking to people like that."

"It's your brother. He's the master. I just take good notes."

"That is a talent that has no genetic correlation, I assure you."

"I agree."

"Thank you."

"Welcome."

30

Hank pulled back the curtains in the front window just enough to see on to the porch. It was Lt. Breed, wearing jeans and a white hoodie with US Navy written across the front. This was the first time Hank had ever seen his boss dressed in anything other than a uniform or a suit.

"Who is it?" asked Tiffany from her seat in the family room.

"Breed," mouthed a panic-stricken Hank.

"Took you forever to get the door," the lieutenant barked on his way past Hank.

"Oh good, you know where I live. Please come in."

"What's that?"

"Great to see you, sir. What brings you by?"

"Just checking on my investigations sergeant. We're looking forward to getting you back. What's the prognosis? Still on track?"

"Yes, sir. I'm champing at the bit. Can I get you some coffee or something?"

"That would be great. I'm freezing my dinner rolls off. Oh!

Hello there, Reese, Dr. Grey. I didn't know we were having an office party."

"Hello, sir," replied Tiffany. "We're just briefing Sergeant LeGris on our progress."

"And I live here," said Sebastien.

"Ye-es. You would, wouldn't you? So. Making progress, then?"

"I would say so," answered Hank as he hurried back from the kitchen with a mug for the lieutenant.

"Thank you, sergeant."

Lt. Breed tested the temperature of his coffee as the three others looked on. No one dared to speak or had any clue what to say. To be visited by the lieutenant like this was just too unprecedented.

"What the hell are you all staring at?"

"Oh, uh . . . sorry, sir. I think we're all just surprised to see you like this. I mean, here . . . in my house . . . and not in uniform."

"It's a Saturday, LeGris. I'm allowed to dress down on the weekends, aren't I?"

"Of course . . . sorry."

"Now tell me, honestly, how are you holding up, Hank?"

Hank was taken aback by the softness in Breed's tone, the genuine concern that came through his hard exterior.

"I'm good. Really good, sir. Thanks for asking. The incision is healing well. It's still difficult for me to flex or twist. The doctor says it's something about nicked intercoastals or something."

"Intercostals."

"Thank you, Dr. Grey," replied Hank.

"Are you in pain, son?"

Son? Hank scolded himself for not giving his boss enough credit.

"It's a lot better, sir. I'm down to a handful of ibuprofen a day."

"I'm glad, sergeant. We all are. This stuff is tough. Part of the deal though, isn't it?"

"Yes, sir."

"Well . . . good. So, Reese? You may as well loop me in on your case since I'm here."

"Of course, sir. I think we pretty much have it in the bag. Pamela Bonner has been picked up in Alaska, where she's been living under an alias all these years. And I have an appointment with the district attorney on Monday. We should get some charges filed. I'm crossing my fingers, anyway."

"What about Richie Bonner?"

"We'll have to see on that one, sir. It won't be easy to prove Richie Bonner dismembered Martin Alexander. The only person who we know for sure witnessed the dismemberment— and likely participated in it—is now dead."

"The guy from Denver?"

"That's right. Carl Jackson. But we know Pamela Bonner shot Alexander in the act of robbing him. And we have an accomplice who will testify against her and a third suspect. John Strickler arranged for Martin to be robbed and he used Pam Bonner and a woman named Lisa Pedretti to lure him in."

"Pedretti? Name sounds familiar."

Tiffany pointed to her left and said, "Family owns a ranch near Sanator."

"Ah. Right."

"But here is where it gets knotted up," continued Tiffany. "Strickler swears he never followed through with the robbery plan. He didn't specifically say why. But he thinks Bonner and Pedretti went ahead with it anyway."

"And," interjected Sebastien, "the bullet wound in Alexander was a small caliber and we know Larry Bonner bought Pamela a .22 several years before the robbery."

"Pretty circumstantial," replied Lt. Breed.

"True. But we think it's important. Strickler was arrested for essentially the same type of crime a few years after our homicide. The weapon he used in that crime was a shotgun, not a .22 pistol."

The lieutenant drummed his fingers against his coffee mug. "Why in the hell would these two women pull off robberies like that? The Bonners had a successful construction company, and the Pedrettis are big-time ranchers."

"Pamela Bonner had a pretty bad drug problem and a history of rebellion against just about everything," answered Tiffany.

"And Pedretti?"

"Well, that one is a little less clear. But we think she was supplementing her income to get through college and law school."

"Law school? That's a bit out of the norm, wouldn't you say, detective?"

"Is motive necessary?" Sebastien interjected.

"It never hurts, doctor," quipped the lieutenant.

Hank watched the discussion with a combination of amusement and pride. Tiffany had come a long way as an investigator. And Sebastien seemed to be making wonderful progress in his confidence and assertiveness.

"Dr. Grey, why don't you tell the lieutenant how you connected the skull to the torso?" suggested Hank.

"Easy, the C3 on top of the C4. What? It's a joke!"

"It's not a joke if you're the only one who gets it, Sebastien."

"I got it," beamed Tiffany. "But, er, yes, Dr. Grey. Tell the lieutenant how you figured it out."

"When I went through the Hell Canyon case file, I saw a note in there about a torso that was found the year before in Cheyenne. At the time, the estimated heights for the torso and the Hell Canyon remains were off by a few inches. As a result, they were ruled out as being connected."

"But Seba—Dr. Grey knew better," interrupted Tiffany.

"Yes, I kind of did. It's just that the vertebrae at each dump site—the number of them, I mean—match perfectly for one person. Plus, the Cheyenne remains were dismembered, and I noticed saw marks on our Hell Canyon bones."

"Which the original anthropologist missed."

"Dr. Grey, you seem to have a big fan in our Detective Reese."

"I'm a big fan of her as well."

Hank yelled out an expletive in his head and jumped in before Breed could put two and two together.

"And as for identifying the remains, I believe that was a matter of searching missing persons reports in the Upper Midwest. Why don't you tell the lieutenant about that, Tiffany?"

A ding from Tiffany's phone caught her attention and she pulled it out of her bag to check it.

"What is it, Tiffany? Is something wrong?" asked Sebastien.

"Lieutenant, Jarvis just texted me. He wants me to meet him at HQ as soon as possible. Do you happen to know what that's about, sir?"

"Yes, detective. In fact, I do," the lieutenant replied before draining his coffee.

"Okay . . . um . . . well."

"Well, you'd better get going, Reese."

Tiffany picked up her things and began to excuse herself.

"Do you want me to come along, Tiffany?" asked Sebastien.

"No," howled the lieutenant and sergeant in unison.

Hank waited for the front door to click shut, then asked, "What's all that about, sir? Is everything okay?"

"Everything is perfect. I get my sergeant back in a few weeks, the cold cases are off to a great start, and within the hour, we should have Derek Manly's killer in custody. Say, I don't suppose you have something a little more . . . coffee is great, but it's the weekend, after all."

"How about a beer?"

"Keep going, sergeant, you're almost there."

"Just a sec, sir, I think we can make that coffee a little Irish."

"Great idea, sergeant. Great idea."

"WHAT IS IT, JARVIS?" Tiffany asked as she looked into her colleague's cubicle.

"There you are. Took you long enough," replied Jarvis, turning toward her in his chair.

"I didn't come all the way in for your attitude. What do you need?"

"Relax, I'm just joking with you. Let me text Penny and tell him you're here. Have a seat."

Tiffany took a chair in the cubicle across from Jarvis. She folded her arms defensively and watched him type into his phone. She could feel her chest tighten with anxiety. Her hackles were up in expectation of another confrontation with the pair of nitwits. Her face was getting warm. The muscles in her back were beginning to stiffen.

Jarvis put his phone down on his desk.

"Okay, here's the deal. I'm sorry. I'm sorry for treating you like crap. You're a good detective. Your little friend is a freakin' weirdo, but that's your problem. Anyway, I hope you can forgive me. Penny too. I won't speak for him, but we both didn't give you enough credit."

Tiffany thought carefully. *This could be a joke*, she told her herself. *Don't say anything. Just wait and see if the jerk starts laughing.*

"Okay, then. I expected a little more of a response. But, hey, at least I said it," Jarvis turned back to face his desk.

"You're serious?"

"Sure. Do I look like I'm kidding?"

"No, I guess not. Thanks, Jarvis. I appreciate that."

Tiffany felt a massive mental exhale, like her thorax was suddenly depressurized.

"Not a problem."

"And hey, look, I probably haven't been that civil to you and Penny either, you know? I'm sorry too."

"Apology accepted. How about we start over?"

Jarvis held out his hand and Tiffany shook it.

An abrupt thought invaded Tiffany's newly found sense of peace. What if Jarvis is only apologizing because Breed put him up to it? After all, Breed obviously knew what Jarvis wanted her for.

"Can I ask . . . why did I need to come all the way in for this? You could have just called me. Or talked to me on Monday."

"Oh, I didn't ask you in here to talk. We've got work to do. We gotta go arrest Derek Manly's killer, and I thought it would be only fitting if you put the cuffs on. I'm swell like that."

"What? Who? Wait . . . what?"

TIFFANY'S EMOTIONS were surprisingly mixed as she sat across the interview room table from Roxanne Bishop. On the one hand, here was the woman who not only shot a defenseless man in the back of the head, but she also caused a measure of chaos and pain by giving copies of the cold case files to her victim. It could be reasonably concluded that a few precious days of the investigation had been lost because of that traitorous act.

On the other hand, the woman was clearly pathetic, at the end of her rope, her last nerve exposed like a jumper cable. She sat there, shoulders slumped, face pallid, utterly resigned to whatever Tiffany was ready to unleash. But Tiffany's planned fury had transformed into heart-softening pity.

"Tell us, Roxie. Why did you kill Derek Manly? You were having an affair with him, right?"

Roxanne offered no answer to Jarvis's brusque question. Tiffany decided to take control and spare the poor woman at least some humiliation.

"Roxanne, I'm sure you have an explanation. Why don't you take us through it? You'll feel better if you do," she said softly.

"I'm sorry, Detective Reese. I'm sorry I took your reports and gave them to that awful man."

"I'm sure you are, Roxanne. I forgive you for that, but you need to tell us the whole story. Take us through everything. If there is anything that can help your case, let's get it out now. Okay? When did you start seeing Derek Manly?"

Tiffany noted Jarvis shifting anxiously in his chair as she spoke.

"It's been a couple of years."

"And what was your relationship like?"

"We would see each other once a week or so. Mostly have dinner, then go back to his place."

"For sex?"

Tiffany wanted to slap Jarvis for asking such a stupid and inflammatory question. But she was mindful that the peace between them was still fresh and vulnerable, so she let it go.

"Yes. But it was more than that. At least, I thought it was. He wanted me to leave Trevor."

"Derek asked you to make him copies of those reports. Was that the first time you gave him sheriff's confidential information?" Tiffany asked.

"No."

"I'm sorry to say this, Roxanne. But it sounds like Derek was, maybe, using you."

"I know. I figured it out. Finally."

"Is that why you killed him?" Jarvis asked.

"I told him. I told him I lost my job and that I might be going to jail. You know what he did?"

"We're listening," replied Jarvis doubtfully.

"He denied it. He denied everything. He said I shouldn't have done something so stupid. He said he never asked me for the reports."

"He was distancing himself from it?"

"Yes, ma'am. I said, 'Look, I've lost my job, Trevor knows about us—let's just go away together.' I told him I would get a divorce and we could make it official, make it right."

Tiffany gently put her hand over Roxanne's.

"And what did he say?"

"He said I was crazy. And stupid. He said now that I'm a criminal, he needed to keep his distance from me."

"What an a-hole," exclaimed Jarvis.

Jarvis's response was welcome, yet unexpected. Tiffany leveraged it.

"I agree with Detective Jarvis. That was a cruel thing to do."

"He's an awful, awful man. Not like Trevor. Trevor loves me. I just . . . I didn't see it, I guess."

"So that's when you shot Manly? After he rejected you like that?"

"Yes, sir. He told me to leave. He told me to stay away or the cops would start harassing him."

Tiffany squeezed the woman's hand.

"When you started to leave, Derek turned his back to you. And that's when you shot him?"

Roxanne looked down at the table and nodded.

Jarvis, who had been sitting upright in his chair, leaned forward and forced eye contact with Roxanne.

"Roxanne, that gun is registered to your husband. You brought it with you. You were planning on killing him. Isn't that right?"

The sheriff's clerk level two, assigned to the subpoena desk in the Administration Office, straightened her back and wiped her eyes with a tissue. She ran her thick hand through her wheat-colored hair in an effort to bring it back to some semblance of order. Then, with a stoic's resolve, she calmly and flatly declared, "I think I'm done talking now."

"Hey, boss. Is Sebastien still around?"

"He lives here, Tiff. What's going on? What's the deal with Jarvis?"

"Just get your brother and put the phone on speaker."

Tiffany was sitting on the top of the table, alone in the interview room, feeling utterly spent and emotionally exhausted. Roxanne Bishop was on her way to jail, courtesy of Jarvis and Penny.

"Okay. We're here."

"Tiffany. Are you okay?" Sebastien practically yelled into the phone.

"We were right, Sebastien. It wasn't Richie Bonner who killed Manly."

"Really? Who was it?"

"Late last Wednesday, the Department of Forestry police stopped a guy at Bismarck Lake. They didn't know it at the time, but he was getting rid of a gun, a .38. That's the caliber of round the crime scene techs pulled out of Manly's wall."

"Come on, Reese. Who was it?" barked Hank.

"Trevor Bishop."

"Any relation to our subpoena clerk?"

"It's her husband."

"Jealous husband, eh?"

"Well, no. It was actually Roxanne Bishop herself. Her husband was just trying to get rid of the gun for her."

"Roxanne Bishop killed Manly?" exclaimed Sebastien.

"Yep. At least, that's what her husband says. And the ballistics on the gun confirmed it was the murder weapon that he was trying to dump."

"Did you tell Jarvis to stick it where the sun don't shine for blaming your investigation?" asked Hank with a hint of glee in his voice.

"No. Believe it or not, Jarvis apologized for everything."

"I'll be damned," Hank returned.

"Are you sure? What makes you believe it was Roxanne? Her husband would have had plenty of motive to shoot Manly. The guy was having an affair with his wife after all." Sebastien was still thinking it through.

"It's not what; it's *who*. And the who is my damn boyfriend, Dr. Grey."

"Oh, crap. Here we go," breathed out Hank.

"Sebastien, you were right on about the blood at the crime scene. Jarvis had the techs go back to Manly's and measure the blood spray on the wall behind his chair. They even mapped it with a computer program. Sure enough, there's a gap in the blood pattern where the shooter would have been. And that gap does not match Trevor Bishop. He's about six foot one. Now, Roxanne, she's like five-three, which matches up. Plus, she had a key to Manly's, and there was no forced entry. Manly let her in, but she simply used her key to lock the deadbolt on the way out."

"Roxanne's husband was trying to save his wife by getting rid of the gun for her?"

"Yeah, but when Jarvis brought him in to be interviewed, he did a 360 real quick. I guess he thought a little harder about taking the hit for a woman who was screwing around on him."

"That's amazing, detective. Why don't you come on back here and we'll celebrate? You can fill us in on the details. And don't worry, Breed is gone."

"I don't think so, Hank. I'm exhausted. I need a bath and a glass of wine."

"You want me to send your anthropologist over?" Hank's voice contained an implied giggle.

Tiffany lowered the phone onto her shoulder and exhaled toward the ceiling. After a moment, she took a deep breath and lifted the phone to her lips.

"Yes. Tell him to give me an hour."

EPILOGUE

A line of important-looking and garishly uniformed personages flanked the wooden podium in the sheriff's large conference room. Near the podium were two easels, one bearing an enlarged photo of Martin Alexander, the other displaying the photos of Pamela Bonner, Lisa Pedretti, Richard Bonner, and Carl Jackson.

"The place is packed," Tiffany whispered. "It didn't occur to me what a big deal this would be."

"You should be up there," observed Sebastien.

"You too."

"Nah. I don't work here. I shouldn't even be in the building."

"Oh, I doubt that's even a thing now. All of the press, all of this attention—it's all you."

"Not without you, it isn't. Teamwork makes the dream work."

"Dr. Grey, did you just drop a sports reference?"

"Did I? I don't think so."

"Ladies and gentlemen, thank you for coming. We will go ahead and get started."

Sebastien hadn't met the sheriff yet—he didn't even know

what the man looked like until this moment. Unsurprisingly, he was tall and good looking with a large mustache and confident mien. His voice boomed through the room without the aid of a microphone or any other amplification. The shiny stars on his starched Class A uniform reminded Sebastien of a gelada monkey, for some reason. Probably because the alpha males have the brightest patches of red on their chests and the largest canine teeth, and everyone else in the troop fears them.

"Hey, check it out. Look who's here."

Tiffany pointed a few rows up and to the left. It was Duck Alexander, sitting next to a woman.

"I bet that's his wife," remarked Sebastien.

"First of all," continued the sheriff, "I would like to thank Sheriff Davis of Laramie County, Wyoming for being here. And we appreciate the members of the media for helping us make this exciting announcement. As you may know, the Custer County Sheriff's Office, with the assistance of the Department of Justice, began a cold case investigation program just a few short weeks ago. We are happy to report that our program, with the assistance of Laramie County, has already borne fruit. The man pictured to my right is Martin Alexander. Mr. Alexander was murdered and dismembered in our county in 1987. His torso was found near Cheyenne, Wyoming shortly after his murder. His skull and one of his leg bones were recovered in West Custer County in 1988. At the time, we did not know about the recovery in Wyoming—technology and information sharing were not as efficient back then . . ."

"Oh, they knew. They just screwed up," muttered Sebastien.

Tiffany punched him subtly on the side of his leg.

A hand shot up from among the reporters.

"Sheriff! Sheriff! Can you tell us how you connected the remains in our county with those in Wyoming?"

"Yes. Thank you for the question, Pete. We were able to

connect the sets of remains using DNA technology. We're grateful for the federal assistance that allowed that to happen."

"Wait? Are you kidding me?"

"Calm down, Sebastien. It was a DNA grant, remember? The sheriff just has to pour it on a bit," Tiffany reassured him.

"I know, but if we hadn't . . ."

"This is part of the job. Suck it up, doctor. Once this is over, I want to say hello to Alexander's brother. And then I have something to show you."

"What is it?

"Sshh. Breed's looking at us."

"Once the DNA match was made, our investigators worked tirelessly with Laramie detectives to trace Mr. Alexander's last movements."

"Don't even start." Tiffany punched his knee again.

"Where am I going?"

"I told you I have something to show you. Turn here."

Tiffany pointed to the right and Sebastien steered the Range Rover onto Mt. Rushmore Road.

It was an ambivalent day in the Black Hills. The weather could not decide what it wanted to be. The morning started off well—the sky was clear and bright—but by the time the press conference let out, gray clouds, like an inverted kettle, stalled the sun's hopeful ascent. A chilly wind chased pedestrians back into the buildings downtown.

"This is it," Tiffany declared. "Park right here."

"This is what?" asked Sebastien, looking around in confusion.

Tiffany stood on the sidewalk and surveyed the facade of a two-story brick building. In the center of the bottom floor was a covered entryway, superposed by a halfmoon-shaped window with "Black Elk Apartments" stenciled on it in a decorative, Western-style font. The second floor featured an end-to-end balcony, painted white with a pair of French doors in the center.

"Well, what do you think?"

Sebastien looked at Tiffany in bewilderment.

"What do I think about what?"

"A place to live!" she responded, pointing to the building.

"This place? An apartment? I don't know, Tiffany. I was thinking something a little bigger, you know?"

"No, the building. The whole building. It's for sale. The entire upper level is a huge loft."

Sebastien took a few steps back into the street and gave the structure a better look.

"It's a pretty old building . . ." he replied, unconvinced.

"Total interior renovation."

"How did you find out about it?"

"A friend of the family. She's a real estate agent. She said it's going on the market in a few weeks."

Sebastien tucked his hands into his jacket pockets, surveyed the street in both directions, then gave Tiffany a skeptical look.

"I appreciate this, Tiff. I'm just not sure if I want to go into the landlord business again. Why a building downtown? What made you think of this?"

"I don't know. I just can't picture you out in the country or up in the hills with vengeful mountain lions on the prowl."

Sebastien didn't answer but looked up at the balcony.

"You want to go in? I have the key."

Tiffany held out her hand, which Sebastien took. She led him down the side of the building and to the back, where they ascended a staircase to the rear entry of the upper level.

"Look how nice this is. New hardwood floors, new paint. The electrical and plumbing are all updated. And look . . . come over here."

She pulled him toward the kitchen

"Look at this. It's professional, all restaurant-quality appliances, and look at these countertops."

Tiffany pointed to the various fixtures and ran a lithe hand over the dark granite. Sebastien's hand trailed hers along the cold surface of the island.

"I don't cook," he said.

"I do," she replied with a smile and a wink that nearly melted him.

Sebastien started to wander, debating with himself. He tried to imagine his furniture, books, CDs, paintings, his collection of vintage opera posters and playbills, etc. in the large space. There was a fireplace and a chandelier in what would surely be the dining area. He would need more built-ins, including a wardrobe. But it could work.

"What about parking? Is that garage we saw out back part of the deal?" he asked her.

"Yes. And spaces for the two tenants."

"Who are they?"

"Don't know. But think of it this way. If you reinvest your money from the Block into this building, won't that save you money on taxes?"

Sebastien opened the door to the balcony at the front of the loft and stepped into the frigid grayness. He approached the rail and looked down before raising his view into the hills to the northwest. He felt Tiffany's arms grip him around the middle and her warm breath on the nape of his neck.

"Thank you," he whispered after a few minutes.

"You're welcome. I just had a feeling it would be better, that it would make the transition a little easier."

"I love you," he said, turning around.

She replied with a kiss.

"I'm going to do it. Let's do it."

She kissed him gently again and said, "I'll make a call."

Tiffany took his hand and tugged him back through the loft, down the stairwell, and back to the car.

"You know, there's something I need to tell you," said Sebastien as they got in the Rover.

"Oh?"

He was gazing up at the building from the driver's seat as he spoke.

"You reminded me. This place reminded me. I need to go back for a few days. Back to California. The coroner out there asked for my help on a case."

"Sebastien, you can't go running back out there every time they need you."

"Oh, I know that," he replied. "It's just that I have a few other things to do as well."

"Real things this time? I'm sorry . . ."

"No, you're fine. I deserved that. But yes. I have an offer on the building and they need to do the inspection."

"Sebastien, that's wonderful!"

"Thank you. It's a little under the asking price, but it's plenty. I don't care if I get undercut a bit if it means I can be up here with you sooner. I love you, Tiffany."

Tiffany smiled and put her hand on his thigh.

"I love you too."

"Anyway, I'd rather be there in person than have my tenant represent me. He's a bit of a day drinker. You understand, right?"

"Understand being a day drinker?"

"No, no. I mean . . ."

"I know what you mean," she replied, laughing. "And of course. And it doesn't even matter if I understand. It's not my business."

Sebastien backed out and headed east on Mt. Rushmore.

"And there's one other thing, if I'm perfectly honest," he said.

Tiffany feigned an expression of shock.

"What's her name?"

"Luisa Miller."

"I'm sorry? Excuse me?"

Tiffany removed her hand from his thigh. Her face fell and her eyes narrowed.

"It's an opera. I've been invited to the premier gala, and since it may be the last time, I'd like to go. Plus, I promised my therapist I would. It's been sort of a challenge—you know, bringing myself to do these things."

"I'm proud of you. When do we leave?" She smiled and replaced her hand on his leg, giving him a playful squeeze.

"Are you kidding?"

"You don't want me to come?"

"Are you kidding?"

"Stop saying that," she said, slapping him on the shoulder.

"Yes, I want you to come. Are you sure? Oh my . . . that would be amazing."

"One condition, though."

"And that is?"

"I don't know if you've heard, but there's a new country band coming to Deadwood. They're supposed to be pretty good."

"Sounds like we're shopping for an evening gown and cowboy boots tomorrow," Sebastien retorted, feeling proud of his wit.

"I don't think you should wear cowboy boots with an evening gown. But you do you, doctor."

Sebastien laughed out loud and raised her hand to his lips.

"And when we get back," Tiffany continued, "we need to get going on the Amber Harrison case. Maybe solving the Hell Canyon-slash-Boxwood Torso deal will give us some goodwill with the press and the public. Someone might come forward with information. I also want to re-interview her roommates and her friends at the rock climbing school."

"Rock climbing school? I thought the file said she was a full-time student. And she worked at a gym during the summers?"

"It did. The gym had one of those huge rock climbing walls. And they sponsored guided trips into the hills. She was one of their climbing pros. Pretty good at it, too, evidently. This area is a destination for that sort of thing. Ooh. We should go! I've done it a few times. Once you realize you can't fall to your death, it's actually quite fu—what? What is it, Sebastien? Why are we pulling over? Is something wrong with the car?"

Sebastien jerked the Rover onto the shoulder of the road and put it in park.

"When was the last time anyone saw Amber Harrison?" he turned to her and asked.

"Oh, heck, let me think. I believe her mom reported her missing in mid-January of 2013. Why?"

"But her mom was in Washington, right?"

"Oregon, actually. I thought you were better at details than that."

"The point is, she lived out of the area. And they were only in contact via phone in the months before she went missing."

"Correct. The mom moved out West during Amber's first year in college, I think. She said they exchanged texts on New Year's Eve, according to the report. Or maybe it was Christmas Eve. One of those anyway. I guess I'm not so great at details either."

"We can check the details when we get into the office. But assuming you are correct, let me ask the question again: When was the last time anyone saw her? I'm talking about actually laid their eyes on her."

"That would have been her roommates. They said she took off with her boyfriend in early January."

"I don't recall seeing the name of the boyfriend in the report."

"Neither do I. Neither her friends nor roommates knew his name."

"We need to track down those roommates. It's very possible they know exactly where the rest of her is."

"The rest of her? What are you talking about? We don't even know if she's dead."

"I hope for her sake she *is* dead," replied Sebastien. "Her shoulder girdle is sitting in a box in the coroner's freezer."

THE END

ABOUT THE AUTHOR

Ryburn Dobbs taught biological anthropology and forensic anthropology at several colleges throughout the San Francisco Bay Area and spent ten years as a forensic anthropologist, working dozens of death investigations. In addition to his anthropological pursuits, Ryburn also worked as an investigative analyst specializing in homicides and unsolved cases.

The Boxwood Torso is the second in the Sebastien Grey series of novels. The first, The Comfort of Distance, is available in paperback and ebook.

For more information about Ryburn, his blog, and updates on new books please visit www.ryburndobbs.com.

CPSIA information can be obtained
at www.ICGtesting.com
Printed in the USA
LVHW020631020622
720196LV00016B/1467